About Time

Niamh Shaw

little
black
dress

First published in 2010
by LITTLE BLACK DRESS
An imprint of HEADLINE PUBLISHING GROUP

A LITTLE BLACK DRESS paperback

1

Cataloguing in Publication Data is available from the British Library

ISBN 978 0 7553 4857 2

Typeset in Transit511BT by Avon DataSet Ltd,
Bidford-on-Avon, Warwickshire

Printed and bound in Great Britain by
Clays Ltd, St Ives plc

Headline's policy is to use papers that are natural, renewable and
recyclable products and made from wood grown in sustainable forests.
The logging and manufacturing processes are expected to conform to the
environmental regulations of the country of origin.

HEADLINE PUBLISHING GROUP
An Hachette UK Company
338 Euston Road
London NW1 3BH

www.littleblackdressbooks.com
www.headline.co.uk
www.hachette.co.uk

For Andrew

Thanks a million to:

Róisín for inspiring the stealing boyfriend plot by stealing my boyfriend twenty-five years ago. Also, I forgive you.

Chantal for relocating my books to the bestseller shelf in major bookstores.

Helen/Antipodeese for introducing me to the glorious expression 'baby cheeses'. How poor my life would be without that and 'crotchfruit'.

My friends, both online and in the real world, most of whom are better writers than I will ever be. They inspire me daily: MarkJ for his honesty, remarkable resilience to verbal abuse and entertainingly appalling taste in movies; Di Mackey for the beautiful way she interprets life; Mike/Vet for his intelligence and perspective; and Cian for stalking me with such time, effort and consideration.

Many thanks to the following cafés around New Zealand and Ireland which did not evict me as I huddled over a laptop for hours with my headphones on, occasionally shouting random swear words and – even worse – singing aloud: The Roost, the most cracking café in Oamaru/Flax Café on Henderson Valley Road, Auckland/Prego in Kenmare, Ireland.

The Outlaws who continually inspire me with their décor, and host me even when Husband does not accompany me.

I would like to retrospectively thank myself for

keeping a diary when I was a teenager. While I'm at it, I would like to tell my sixteen-year-old self to lighten up and not worry so much, that teenage years are *not* the best years of your life, and that 'be yourself' is actually a sound piece of advice.

My wonderful agent, Peter Buckman, for the advice, encouragement and fashion tips.

The team at Little Black Dress, in particular my inhumanly patient editor, Leah Woodburn. I hope one day our relationship will embrace a wide range of psychedelic swear words.

My parents, whose bulk purchase of *Smart/Casual* ensured I was Little Black Dress' bestselling Author in 2009. Oh, that wasn't me? Darn. Never mind, you tried hard.

My beloved Andrew, who was ever encouraging, supportive and relentlessly sexy on a motorbike. He could only be improved if he was chocolate-flavoured. Also if he brought me breakfast in bed, did gerbil impressions, and put DVDs back in their cases; but even if he did any of these things, I would still love him thoroughly. Thank you.

Prologue
Limerick to New York:
4973 KM

My life fits into twelve boxes.

I can't begin to tell you how depressing it is, looking at them standing meagrely in the centre of Leonard's ransacked living room. Surely there should be more to show for thirty-five years of existence? A brushed cappumochaccino suede sofa set, for example, or a surround sound stereo system with tweeters and a subwoofer.

Those belong to Leonard.

We're quite clear about it. If we were ever to break up, Leonard would get the properties and investment portfolios, the Natuzzi furniture, the handwoven Egyptian cotton bed sheets, and the set of Arne Jacobsen chairs (I've always slid off them anyway). Everything, in fact, except my clothes and shoes, the espresso machine, and a lifetime supply of books according to a rate of consumption of one per week. We might squabble over the crystal wine glasses from Prague, but I would probably capitulate – as long as I were dumping *him*.

But what am I on about? Leonard and I are not about to split up – far from it. At least, I hope not since in two days' time, I'm moving halfway round the world to live with the man. Well, a third of the way round the world. Limerick to New York is a fair distance, still.

It's just that . . . when Leonard suggested moving to New York last year, it seemed like a jolly screwball adventure; but now – the day before the shippers arrive – I am twitchy with doubt. You know how a cross-dressing Tupperware party seems like a fabulous idea three weeks in advance, but then it comes around and you can't find a PVC thong and the glue-on stubble gets stuck in your teeth and it all seems like too much effort?

Well, it's a bit like that.

It's probably just stress. Isn't moving house supposed to be one of the three things most likely to give you 3-D Technicolor nightmares? Along with bereavement and . . . I'm not sure what the other one is. In my case, being attacked by a stuffed animal.

It doesn't help that I had to give away my cat, Fishy, and haven't seen my lover for over two months. Leonard left for New York in March to find accommodation and start his new job.

Looking on the bright side, at least I don't have to go to the trouble of bursting into tears, since I've been crying on a pretty much permanent basis for the last month. I'm not sure why, because I'm thrilled. What am I talking about? I'm *euphoric*. Don't be misled by the projectile tears, because I am really; I really am. After all, I'm moving to an exciting new country to be with the man I love.

And at least I don't have to give up my job. All a freelance writer needs is an Internet connection, a laptop equipped with a cast-iron spellchecker, and a steady supply of caffeine. The salary tends to be a bit erratic, but it's a portable career.

And – and! – I have done this before, you know. There was the time I went to Dublin to study how to be a student. Then, at the age of twenty-six, I landed in Dubai so green about the gills, people thought I was afflicted with mould. The world was my oyster.

Part of my apprehension is that I know how much effort it takes to digest the aforementioned oyster. There is a world (not to mention nine years) of difference between hiking to another country with a backpack containing the sum total of your worldly possessions, a bucketful of wide-eyed wonder and a bottle of SPF 370 – and this.

I try to heave a heartfelt sigh but, like an aborted yawn, it falls short of a full-glottal tongue-curling lung-filler. Lately, I've been having problems breathing. A bit concerning, considering it's a fundamental skill. I haven't suffocated yet, however, so I suppose I'll survive a bit longer.

I cram another gingersnap into my mouth and turn Bruce Springsteen up a couple of notches. After today, it doesn't matter whether I get on with the neighbours. Anyway, for three years they have kept me awake with inconsiderate shagging at four a.m. in the morning. I don't know why they can't consummate during *Emmerdale Farm* like everybody else.

Eyeing my pathetic stash, which is holding off an army of advancing dust bunnies on the floor, I consider spreading my belongings into another packing crate. That would result in thirteen boxes however, which is unlucky. I'm not about to flick a finger at fate two days before moving country (especially when tempting fate is five times riskier for Leos). I'm wondering how much bubble wrap is required to round it up to fourteen boxes, when the doorbell rings.

Utter crapness! Who the hell is this? I'm not expecting anyone and don't have time for visitors; there are hours of cleaning left. If it's the neighbours complaining about 'Dancing in the Dark', I don't have the energy for spirited, innuendo-laden insults. If it's the Jehovah's Witnesses, I will have to strip to get rid of them, and I am *so* not in the mood.

Wait – maybe this is a *sign*. Not that I believe in that sort of stuff any more (so far, destiny has been entirely uncooperative), but I like to keep my options open, you know?

Let me see: if it is a Martian with a packed lunch and a mind-ray gun, I will *not* move to America.

The portents have all been good so far.

Plotting a course through the scraps of cardboard and packing tape stuck to the floor, I successfully ignore a pending panic attack; I've had plenty of practice over the last few weeks. Instead, I run a hand through my hair, resisting the urge to grip it and pull. As it turns out, I don't have to, since I rip out a clump of hair with the rubber gloves I forget I am wearing.

I unlock the door and swing it open. It is my mother.

I'd have preferred the Jehovah's Witnesses – or a Martian with a mind-ray gun, for that matter.

'Wanky wanky shit bollocks,' I say.

Internally.

Although since I thought it at full volume, there's a fair chance she heard part of it – or at least got the gist.

'Hi, Mother,' I say externally.

Look, I've got to warn you: my mother makes me revert to behaving like a teenager. She winds me up faster and more comprehensively than anyone else on the planet. I always meet her fortified with the best of intentions, but they never last; I can actually *feel* the layers of maturity slough off in her presence. My record to date is twenty-two seconds without wanting to put my thumbs in my ears and wiggle my fingers and blow a great raspberry.

It's not that she's a bad person, oh no; everyone loves her.

Of course, I do too. I would push her out of the way of a speeding bus (assuming I didn't push her under it in the first place).

Admittedly, the impetus would be the guilt.

It's an awkward, bitter kind of love that takes casualties on both sides. Something broke years ago, and neither of us has ever figured out how to fix it – or even patch it up to operational.

Being a family-size bumper pack of Issues, at least our relationship provides plenty of material for my job. Particularly my latest commission: a daily agony aunt column for the *Irish Mail*. I am effectively immunised against anaemia with the irony of *that* one.

'Hello, darling.' Mother kisses the space next to my left cheek. She registered a patent on air-kissing years ago. 'May I come in?'

'Of course.' As I step aside, I notice she clutches what looks like a psychedelic shoebox. The glitter butterfly on the lid looks vaguely familiar, like something I once dreamed. Mum walks into the living room, stepping daintily over a charging dust bunny. I follow her, snapping the fingers of my rubber gloves.

My mother places the shoebox on a packing crate that contains 'kitchen wares #2'. She turns towards me and tucks a strand of hair behind my ear. Overlooking her pressing my doorbell, that's eight seconds before she irritated the crap out of me.

Not bad.

'MOTHER!' I snarl, slapping her hand away.

'God, sorry!' She worries the strand of pearls at her throat in an effort to stop molesting me.

I sigh theatrically and turn away. 'There's nowhere to sit,' I say. My lower back broadcasts a dull throb of pain just thinking about it.

'Is your back sore?' she says as I wince and dig my fingers into it.

'Yeah,' I mumble.

'I'm not surprised. You are lucky to be alive.' I roll my eyes so vigorously I nearly sprain an eyeball. Seven years ago I had a near-fatal accident and I don't know why Mother likes to remind me how fortunate I am for my ongoing thrival and survival. Does she think it will make me more careful? She makes it sound as if I intentionally plunged sixty feet through the air to vandalise a prefab shed with my velocity. 'Goodness, what a mess!' she says, eyeing the pile of shredded newspaper in the corner with distaste.

'Sorry I didn't tidy the place for you, Mother! But you know, what with cleaning the flat, and the shippers arriving tomorrow, and the tenants the day after that—'

'I didn't mean—'

'—and flying in two days' time, it kind of slipped my mind. Probably not surprising, given that I haven't seen my boyfriend in months and am leaving the only home I've ever known—'

'Oh Lara, please! You lived away from Ireland for most of your adult life—'

'And my mother is leeching my drama, which is all I have left in the world—'

My mother giggles. So do I, even though I'm very

reluctant and am sure that, deep down, I don't want to.

My mother rarely looks at ease, but she is completely out of place in the chaos of Leonard's apartment. As ever, her presentation is flawless: hair ruthlessly coiffed, cowering eyebrows plucked into submission, lipliner dictating where her lips should be.

She always makes me feel scruffy, but more so today. It is virtually impossible to project fabulousness in a vintage Spiderman T-shirt with no evidence of elasticity, and tracksuit bottoms featuring Leonard-sized handprints in Taupe Frappe from when we got swept away by the erotic charge of painting. I don't want to think about what my hair looks like – it is inadvertently conditioned with Jif cream cleaner.

After a pause, I say: 'Would you like a gingersnap? There're – oh, there're only two left. I ate the rest to celebrate how well my diet is going.'

'Never mind, darling,' says my mother. 'You're under a lot of pressure.'

'Um, would you like some coffee? There's some instant. Except I've packed the cups. And the kettle.'

'I should have picked up some at Bugley's on the way. I wasn't thinking—'

'Oh wait, I know.'

Squatting offensively on the kitchen bench is a spectacularly ugly flowerpot – a legacy from one of Leonard's ex-girlfriends. I don't know why the bitch couldn't have forgotten some Chanel perfume or a lime zester. Anyway, I intend to throw it out and claim one of the packing men stole it – no, Leonard might press charges – I'll say it got lost in transit. For now, the pot can be useful for the first time in its miserable existence.

I fill it with water and set it on a gas ring. I hope the

heat doesn't crack it; or even detonate a deadly explosion of airborne ceramic projectiles. Death by flowerpot. Depressingly pedestrian, as grand exits go.

'What's with the box?' I ask, nodding at it as I rinse out a yoghurt carton and a discarded Peanut Butter jar. I tip coffee into the makeshift cups.

'I found it in the bottom drawer of your old dressing table. I thought you might like to go through it.'

'Oh, sure. Thanks.'

Mother removes her hat and places it carefully beside the shoebox. She likes hats because they flatter her. Most things do. She is still a beautiful woman. It is how she defines herself, which is a shame, because there is so much more to my mother: the duplicity, the cunning, the encyclopaedic knowledge of my buttons and her unerring ability to press each one.

I am the limited edition beta model of my mother. I feature more curves in a smaller package, but the package itself is directly inherited from Dorothy Callaghan: the indigo-blue eyes which random poetic or more often drunk strangers often describe as 'mesmerising'; the straight, glossy black hair which I always hated because it wasn't curly; the bone structure which I hated because it was my mother's.

I don't thank her for the flat feet either. At the age of fifty-eight, my mother still stuffs hers into six-inch-heeled, pointy-toed stilettos, but I've never been able to operate heels higher than two inches.

At least I inherited my father's charm. Thinking of which, I ask, 'How's Dad?' fiddling with the gas knob. I regret saying it before the words are even out of my mouth, but can't seem to help myself.

'I don't know, darling,' says my mother in a voice

chilled several degrees. 'Haven't you heard from him?'

OUCH! We'll call that love-fifteen; or a switchblade slipped between ribs three and four – choose your metaphor. The fact that I asked for it doesn't make it much better.

'Not for a couple of weeks,' I mumble.

Apologies aren't big in our family; the word 'sorry' is only applied to minor offences: dropping a fork, melting the head off your sister's Malibu Barbie, getting pregnant out of wedlock, stuff like that.

Which is why my mother says, brightly: 'Rosemary says she's meeting you for dinner tomorrow.' She is referring to my older sister, The Favourite One. Me, I am The Other One.

'Yeah.'

'That's nice. All excited about moving?'

'If I were any more thrilled, I would be moved to express my joy via the medium of dance. What the fuck do you think, Mum?'

'Language, Lara.'

'I can offer Pidgin German, or a wide range of Arabic swear words.'

'Why do you always have to be so sarcastic? It's not big and it's not clever.'

'Ah now, come on. It's a bit clever, admit it. I wish you wouldn't pick on my size, but. There's not much I can do about my dodgy genes.'

'I wish you wouldn't speak to me like that, Lara.'

'You mean in sequences of nouns, verbs and other assorted words?'

My mother's lips have almost disappeared. If she's not careful she'll smudge her lipstick. It could be catastrophic if someone saw her.

'Oh,' I say. 'I forgot. There's no milk or sugar.'

'I have some sugar sachets in my bag.'

'You don't have a litre of semi-skimmed in there, do you?'

Another temporary ceasefire.

I loathe conflict and generally go out of my way to avoid it, but this course of inaction has never been open with my mother. Our conversations exhaust me, leave me feeling stretched thin; wrung out.

After today, I'm not sure when I will see my mother again. I expect this thought to be comforting, but for some reason the effect is the opposite. I experience a dangerous emotion malfunction. Blink, blink.

As I place the Peanut Butter jar full of coffee in front of her, my mother massages her knuckles. I have always thought of her as timeless, eternal, largely vampiric; but now I am struck by her age. Her fingers tremble slightly when she picks up the jar – although that could be the strain of trying not to throttle me. The fragile veins in her hands stand out, her shoulders are slightly stooped, and her hair is a brittle grey at the roots.

'Mum.' Impulsively, I reach across the kitchen bar and take her hand. All the things I want to say surge forward and jostle against the barrier that is my mouth. I end up saying, 'Utter crapness. I'm leaking again.'

Actually, I'm not crying *again* so much as simply revving up the bawling to full-throttle wobbler.

My mother gives my fingers a painful squeeze. She's not one for physical contact beyond the mandatory social requirements. She pats my hand awkwardly, or pushes it away. Hard to tell.

'Lara,' she says, in a voice that signals the end of the ceasefire. 'Are you sure you are doing the right thing?'

'What?' I remove a rubber glove to wipe my eyes with the heel of my hand.

'You know.' She gestures vaguely.

'Coffee in a Peanut Butter jar? Yes, well, sorry about the lack of ceremony.'

'Don't prevaricate. You know what I mean.'

I do, but – 'No,' I say. 'Why don't you tell me?'

'This.' She waves her arm around the room. 'Moving.'

'Mum, it's a bit late to be asking that *now*,' I say through gritted teeth and a conflagration of irritation. 'Where did I put the tissues?'

'It's not too late. It's never—'

'Mother, you're talking like I don't want to go – but I do! Of course I do. This is not some reckless, whimsical notion that popped into my head after eleven shots of tequila, you know. It is a considered, measured decision – where the fuck are the tissues?'

'There's no need for that sort of language, love.' I have always found it bizarre how the more angry my mother, the more concentrated the endearments. In this instance, the word 'love' spat out like a poisoned dart.

She reaches into her handbag and hands me a miniature pack of Kleenex, mint condition.

'All I mean is – and please don't get angry—'

'Too late,' I mutter, blowing my nose.

'It's just that – darling, are you sure you're not running away?'

'I hardly think so. In fact, you could say I'm doing the exact opposite, since I'm running *towards* Leonard.'

'Are you sure Leonard's right for you, but?'

The most sensible response would be to bang my head on the table. Instead I say, 'Mother, I thought you *liked* Leonard?'

'I do! Well, he's – he's very pleasant—'

'He is! And he's – he's nice and handsome and clever and er, dynamic and – and caring and he has a great stereo system – and lots of other stuff. He's perfect—'

'But not for you.'

'What's *that* supposed to mean?'

'Darling, it doesn't matter how perfect he is if he's not perfect for *you*.'

'Baby cheeses, Mother! You're hardly qualified to judge—'

'Is that right? Do you not think a failed marriage is sufficient qualification?'

Her use of the expression 'failed marriage' throws me. Although it is fact, Mother rarely refers to it; and if she does, it is more alluded to in terms such as 'a previous relationship' and 'your father'. Certainly not so baldly.

'Has he asked you to marry him?' asks my mother.

'Who, Leonard? Is that what this is all about? How do you know he hasn't?'

She looks at me.

'Mother, I don't *want* to marry Leonard. For a start, I'd be Lara O'Hara—'

'Do you love him?' she asks.

I hesitate, fingering the tiny silver ladybird charm on my bracelet. My mother gives me The Look, which implies she knows exactly what's going on in my head, which is patently ridiculous since most of the time *I* have no idea what's going on in my head.

'Yes!' I'm even angrier because she made me question it. 'OK, look. I don't – it's not like I – it's different. With Leonard. There's no – no churning palms and sweaty stomach and feeling like I'll die if I don't spend every moment of every second of every day with him.'

I don't know why I tell her this. Mother pulls them out of me, these confidences, even though I regret it later – especially when she uses them as ammunition.

'It's been a long time since I've felt that for anyone,' I rush on. That's not entirely true, but I store the thought carefully in the back of my mind under a dusty heap of neurons. 'That sort of intensity, it's exhausting – and destructive. What I have with Leonard is – is – it's comfortable.'

'My darling, you're settling for second best. You deserve so much more—'

'Just on the off chance you are trying to help: you're not.'

I do not understand my mother. She seems to consider it a personal affront that I am not firing out grandchildren at the rate of two per year. For years, she has been trying to marry me off to anyone even vaguely heterosexual – and, when I finally meet Mr Perfect, she doesn't like him. That's pretty much how our relationship works – or doesn't work, to be more accurate.

I have not enjoyed overwhelming success with the fouler sex. Not that there has been any shortage of fouler sex. However, my dating front has tended towards overcast and stormy with a low barometric pressure zone.

My first serious relationship was with Mr Right. I was ecstatically, giddily, wildly in love. The world shimmered in a haze of sparkly pink stardust.

He might have been Mr Right, but unfortunately it turned out I was Miss Not Quite. After three years together, he methodically dissected my heart. I never quite managed to reconstruct it (although I successfully reinforced the external perimeter). His casual cruelty was not intentional. It was more wanton carelessness, which was almost worse.

It's been all downhill from there, a dictionary of disaster:

Erik Kvist n. Norwegian whaler, whose one true love being himself did not stop him sleeping with my hairdresser.

Gavin Henderson n. prone to physical violence when drunk, which did not stop my colleague sleeping with him.

Niall Stanford n. hairy midget whose time-consuming addiction to porn did not stop him sleeping with my flatmate.

Bunch of cocks n. collective term describing the remainder of my lying, cheating, emotionally mutant ex-boyfriends.

After I returned from Dubai, there was a deviation in my applications processing department, and Mr Very Nearly Almost Perfect made the cut: Mark and I moved in together and acquired a cat. We had sex three times a week and twice on Saturday.

I should have known it was doomed: the first time I met his parents, everyone sat around the living room pretending the family pet – a heinous terrier–stoat mix – was not humping my leg.

Mark was sweet, quirky, funny, and obviously adored me – not my type at *all*. Even so, when he asked me to marry him, I accepted. Belatedly, I tried to ignore a sneaking suspicion that I was settling for less. When that failed, I sought to wrestle it into submission. I frantically furnished, I framed photos, I bought kitchen appliances (although the desperate nesting didn't extend to actually *using* them). In short, I pretended everything was simply spiffy.

When the sneaking suspicion metastasised into full-blown qualm – with regrettable timing, three days before the wedding – I called it off. I knew that if I married Mark, I would have to live with the knowledge that I had settled for second best. He deserved better than that. So did I.

My mother was delighted with herself, and spent the next year coming up with creative ways to say 'I told you so'. Mark's mother *still* sends me hate mail.

'Lara.' Mother leans towards me with a wide-eyed innocent expression – a look I can reproduce perfectly, so I'm not fooled. 'I just want you to be happy.'

'Is that so?'

'Oh, for heaven's sake!' says my mother, throwing up her hands. 'You are my daughter. Why would I want you to be unhappy?'

'Beats me, but it appears you've devoted your life to the cause.'

'Oh, please. It may come as a surprise to you that I have better things to do with my time.'

'Sure. Whatever.' I shrug.

'Since your mind appears to be made up—'

'Not that the sealed boxes are a big, fat, cardboardy clue—'

'I just hope everything works out as you hope, love,' she says in a tone that fully conveys how unlikely she considers that outcome to be.

This is what my mother is all about: she casts serious doubt all over my relationship, then wishes me well. I'm too exhausted to point that out, but. We stand on either side of 'kitchen wares #2', waiting for the tension to dissipate.

'Well. What can I do?' says Mum.

'What?'

'The cleaning.'

'Really? It's such a crappy job—'

'Well, it will be half a crappy job if we both do it.'

'OK.' I smile at her. 'Here. Take my gloves.'

'Thank you. Where do I start?'

While we scrub, we sing along to Bruce Springsteen. Really, my mother and I get on great when we don't talk. In fact, we would have the ideal relationship if our lives were a musical.

I have a much better relationship with my father. He's not around much, but we can chat like normal people, about all sorts of stuff: work, his latest girlfriend, the economy, the weather – everything and anything, really. The point is: he accepts me as I am. He's not always trying to *improve* me.

My parents are like chalk and cheese, oil and water, fish burgers and traffic cones. That's probably why they're not together any more.

Late in the evening, Mum makes a mercy dash to the 7-Eleven to fetch a bottle of Sauvignon Blanc. We drink it from the yoghurt carton and peanut butter jar over the box in the kitchen.

'You know the words to "Thunder Road",' I say with new-found respect.

'Lara, I can recite the lyrics of any pre-1990 Springsteen song,' says my mother. 'You played him at high volume, non-stop, twenty-four hours a day for seven *long* years.'

I laugh. 'Sorry about that.'

'It could have been worse. Thank heavens it wasn't The Cure or Rick Astley. Anyway, Bruce is sexy.'

'Mum!'

'What? He has a lovely bottom.'

'*Mu-um!*'

This is a novel experience: being with my mother and not feeling compelled to maim her. It is the best time I've had with her for years – possibly decades. I am grateful to have snatched this memory with her before I leave.

As my mother shrugs on her coat, she asks: 'Are you sure you don't want to stay with Bill and I until you go?'

I hope my feelings for my stepfather do not reflect on my face. 'Yes, ah – thanks, Mum, but that's OK. Leo booked me into a hotel near the airport and it's already booked and er . . .' I shrug and leave it at the white lie.

'OK.' She hesitates on the doorstep. 'I – if you –' She worries the strap of her handbag and swallows. Her chin quivers. 'Take care, love.'

I want to tell her I love her, that I'll miss her, but my throat seizes. In the end, I just say, 'You too. See you.'

When we embrace, the brim of her hat stabs me in the eye, and I accidentally headbutt her.

Memory Lane: Do Not Attempt This On Foot

It is only after Mother leaves that I remember the shoebox still balanced atop 'kitchen wares #2'.

I pour myself another yoghurt carton of wine and set it down next to the box. I run my fingers lightly over the lid. Dust and glitter sticks to the pads of my fingers. A scuffed label says: 'Lara's stuff. Do not open. Trespassers will be persecuted. KEEP OUT!'.

Pictures are glued on to the surface. They are from a time when I thought thirty-five was ancient and I would never go out with someone called *Leonard*. (Apart from rare exceptions, that is still a sound rule by which to live your life.)

My God, was I ever that *young*?

Memories prick my subconscious. These roses here were carefully cut from a valentine card my father gave me. I must have been thirteen? Fourteen? This quote is W.B. Yeats, from the English Intercert syllabus – I can't remember the poem, but I thought it was the most beautiful thing I'd ever read; it used to make me cry. Oh, what do you know? It still does.

There is a Live Aid logo pasted to the box, along with several pictures of George Michael. (The lipgloss slipped my attention at the age of fifteen).

I carefully unpick the knot securing a turquoise ribbon and remove the lid.

I excavate a small bundle of letters from one corner. They are still in their envelopes, all addressed to me in a script that has so many squiggles it is difficult to read the letters. Anne Wilson? Of course, Anne. She was my pen pal.

Beneath the letters is – oh my God! My Jellyfish Swatch! I lift it out and shake it gently. I wonder would it work if I replace the battery?

Putting it aside, I riffle through some papers and find a ticket stub from a U2 concert in 1987 at Croke Park. It should have been one of the defining moments of my young life: getting drunk for the first time and losing my virginity to 'Pride (In The Name of Love)'. Instead, I spent three hours stalking Noel O'Sullivan around the muddy field. Although I still cite the event as one of my all-time great concert experiences, truth is I had never heard of U2 and thought they were largely crap. Noel O'Sullivan snogged Clodagh Wartey behind a bush.

There are three Bruce Springsteen singles and a compilation tape. An admission ticket to 'Champers Nite Club'. A Rubik's cube, the edges of the stickers scabby where I peeled them off. Lipsticks – the colours of which defy nature – worn down to stubs and covered in bits of cornflake and fluff.

I touch the yellowing lid of an ancient pot of Ponds Cold Cream, trying to recall when I had last done so with hard, young fingers.

The diary is exactly where I knew it would be. On the

battered purple cover, Smurfette poses coyly with a flower. The diary is secured with a heart-shaped lock. If memory serves me . . . I unscrew the Ponds Cold Cream and find the key sellotaped to the underside of the lid.

I unlock the diary and thumb gently through the pages. Names leap out at me, people I have not thought of in years, others I had forgotten existed. Scents rise from the paper like ghosts: Anais Anais and cheap deodorant – 'Impulse', as I recall. Fabergé's adverts made a big impression on me. In real life, nobody was ever so inspired by my smell that they hurdled a park bench to give me flowers, no matter how much Always Alluring I sprayed on.

I turn to the cover page.

1988.

I was fourteen years old, and had more on my mind than in it. As I recall, being a teenager was tremendously traumatic: struggling with the weighty responsibilities of what to do after leaving school, determining whom I had a crush on and having to clean my room once a week.

I was just starting to grasp how little I knew about anything – although there was one thing I knew for certain. One thing I was absolutely sure about.

His name was Conn.

You might call him 'The One That Got Away'. Personally, I refer to him variously as 'The One I Never Really Had', 'The Love Of My Life' and 'That Prick'.

Even if I hadn't remembered the date, the diary fell open at the page.

Friday 1 April 1988

Spots: 5

Arguments with Mum: 24½

Dear Diary,

How come other girls have boyfriends, but I haven't even been kissed except for that time Slack-Jawed Spa licked my cheek and that was only for a dare which doesn't even COUNT? Is there something wrong with me? I am nearly 16 (14½) and already collecting dust on the SHELF. At this rate, I will end up some 90-year-old supervirgin. I wish Prince Charming would get a move on. I would even settle for a handsome frog.

Love,

Lara

Saturday 2 April 1988

Dear Diary,

OH MY GOD OH MY GOD OH MY GOD!!!!! It is OFFICIAL: I am IN LOVE!!!!! I have finally been KISSED!!!!! And before my sixteenth birthday – deadly!!!!!
    (ROSEMARY, IF YOU ARE READING THIS, FUCK OFF.)

    Before yesterday, I knew NOTHING about love. I know I've said that before, but this time it's REAL!!! Last week when Richard Elliott didn't sit beside me in double geography I thought I would DIE, but I'm still here so I suppose that tells you something (i.e. I didn't).

This is SO EXCITING – I don't know where to start!!! OK, it was at Champers last night. I wasn't sure whether I'd go because Maeve and I still weren't talking after our fight, except when she asked if she could borrow a pencil in English on Thursday. Then she talked to me – obviously to ask if she could borrow a pencil – but I didn't answer her, even though I loaned her one.

So yesterday Sinéad rang and I was kind of cold because she had sort of sided with Maeve even though Maeve was mega wrong. Sinéad asked if I was going to the disco and at first I said no. Well, I said maybe, but then I said yes, because I really wanted to but not on my own.

After trying on everything in Rosemary's wardrobe as well as mine, I finally wore my stonewashed jeans and my new legwarmers with Rosemary's off-the-shoulder top (I LEFT IT BACK, FATFACE). My hair looked all right after half an hour of backcombing. I can't wait to get a permanent wave – it would save a lot of time (and hairspray) and would look TOTALLY DEADLY. Dad said I could, but Mum said I had to wait until I was eighteen, probably because she wanted to get at Dad. They had a big argument, which started out being about my hair and ended up being about Theresa Mannion, who plays tennis at their club. (I'm not sure how Theresa Mannion came into it. I don't think she has a permanent wave.)

Sinéad's dad arrived and as I came downstairs I heard Mum tell him I had to be home by ten o'clock and I was so EMBARRASSED I nearly BARFED. I very reasonably pointed out that Rosemary is allowed to stay out until midnight, so why can't I? Mum recycled the same lame argument about Rosemary being four years older than me and when I'm that age I can stay out late too, blah blah blah YAWN. She wouldn't have bothered if Mr Conway hadn't been there and she's got to make like she cares. Typical.

Sometimes Mum is such a gargamel. She asked if I was wearing 'that top'. See? GARGAMEL. And I said, No, I'm wearing something else, then she said Less of the sarcasm, so I said if she liked I could be rude instead. Dad came out of his study and he laughed because it was quite funny, really.

Then Mum asked whether I had done my homework, and Dad said to let me go and have some fun, but Mum repeated herself which she does, like, ALL THE TIME. I calmly and maturely pointed out that Mr Conway was waiting, but Mum said, Well?, so I said, Tomorrow. Mum was blocking the door so I squirmed under her arm.

Be back by 11! she shouted at, you know, the WHOLE NEIGHBOURHOOD. If I'm lucky there might have been a couple of deaf geriatrics in Dublin who didn't hear her.

I was nice to Sinéad because her dad had collected me and she said Maeve was mega crummy sitting beside Growler Fitzgerald at Assembly when she totally knows how much I like him.

When we went into the disco, Growler was standing near the bogs and he looked way cool in a lovely shiny jacket with the sleeves rolled up. I walked past him twice and the second time I flirted with him by saying 'Hi' and kind of smiling.

Sinéad ditched me to hang out with Maeve but the music was wicked so I went on the dance floor with a group from my class. I had to keep pulling up my top because it didn't fall off just the one shoulder. After a while the DJ started the slow set so all the girls stampeded for the bogs.

Hanging around would have meant I was desperate which I mega wasn't but when I got off the dance floor, by a total flukey coincidence, Growler just happened to be standing NEARLY RIGHT NEXT TO ME!!!!! I stuck around because I seriously hoped he'd ask me to dance. I didn't want to ask him because Sarah asked Jughead O'Carroll to dance at the Old Crescent Disco and everyone called her a slag for days afterwards.

I once asked Rosemary how you let a guy know you're interested and she said, 'Be yourself', which has to be the stupidest piece of advice EVER. I mean, how can I be somebody else? And who? But I had no better ideas, so I tried mega hard to REALLY be myself.

Then Growler pushed off the wall and I nearly had a COW, but right at that very moment the worst thing EVER happened: my crummy headband fell into my eyes. I scrabbled around for HOURS like a major DORK and finally I got it back in place and I looked up with a big smile expecting Growler to be in front of me, but it was just Stuart Roche licking out the inside of a beer glass.

It was hard to make out anything because the DJ was doing some mad flashing thing with the lights and smoke stung my eyes. I finally saw Growler with Maeve at the side of the dance floor and he leaned down and said something in her ear. Growler took Maeve's hand and pulled her on to the dance floor. I wanted to look away but I couldn't, like when Miss Duggan pulls her knickers out of her arse at the top of class which is SERIOUSLY gross but you can't help but watch.

Maeve had her arms round Growler's neck and they swayed around and he felt her shoulder a bit. He bent over and I couldn't tell if he was maybe just resting his head because he was tired but then I realised he was getting off with her.

My heart shattered into a trillion thousand pieces and my chest was all tight. I felt mega sad, like Meryl Streep in Out of Africa when she gets upset about having to talk in a lame accent for a whole film. I couldn't bear to stay there another SECOND, so I ran towards the exit, kind of in slow motion. The shortest way was across the dance floor and I accidentally pulled Maeve's hair really hard as I passed.

(Hang on a sec.)

(Sorry, Rosemary just came into my room. She said she wanted to tell me dinner's ready, but I know she wants to snoop around. I asked if she'd recorded MacGyver and she said she forgot but I know it was just to spite me.)

Outside in the car park, there was a low wall a few yards away from the door. I sat on it and looked tragic and gorgeous. The bitter acid of my pain gnawed my ravaged, broken soul like a starving rat with mega sharp teeth and scratchy claws that totally doesn't care how much damage it's doing.

I bitterly mourned my young, wasted life. I couldn't understand why Growler asked Maeve to dance instead of me. Even though I'm a bit spotty and have braces, I'm definitely better-looking than her. Maeve has teeth like a chipmunk and the same stupid hair she's had since, like, for ever. She is so uncool, too. She wore baggy jeans to Champers last week, DUH.

Maybe Maeve is more herself than me — although I don't see how that helps since she's obviously a two-faced cow, pretending to be my friend when all the time she was secretly plotting to steal my boyfriend. I suppose technically Growler wasn't my boyfriend, but he would have been, if Maeve hadn't got her claws into him.

I heard George Michael's 'Careless Whisper' start up, which is a song about this guy who doesn't want to pretend he's dancing with a fool even though deep down he knows he is, which was mega appropriate when you think about it. You can tell George Michael really knows about this sort of stuff and he's mega dishy.

The bitter acid of my pain stopped gnawing and swept over the barren, shrivelled wasteland of my soul instead, like a major wave, possibly a tsunami (I just looked that up in Dad's thesaurus).

(Hang on another sec.)

(Mum's screeching up the stairs at me about my dinner getting cold, as if I could actually, like, CARE about eating when I am fatally afflicted with love.)

So anyway, I met this guy from school and we talked for a while and then we kissed and now I'm mad about him.

Love,

Lara

I don't even have to close my eyes to recall every detail of that night. The empty car park outside Champers, the abandoned beer can beside my foot, the hum from the streetlight over the nightclub door, sitting on the wall with the cold seeping through my stonewashed jeans.

Suddenly, the dark beside me moved. Obviously I screamed, since I thought it might be a hostile alien life form.

A low voice said, 'Hey, what's wrong?'

Then I relaxed, because I knew an alien life form would be suckered on to my face, implanting an embryo, instead of just asking what was wrong.

'I didn't know anyone else was here,' I said, gasping.

I thought the stranger was probably tall, dark and handsome, although it was hard to tell because he was hunched over; and I couldn't see him very well because it was dark; but I liked his voice which was sort of slow and quiet, not like the rest of the boys in school who shouted all the time.

'Are you crying?' he asked.

'No!' I said.

'It sounds like you are.'

'Well, I'm not.'

'Oh,' he said. Then, after a while, 'Are you sure you're not crying?'

'What's wrong with your voice?' I asked, because I wanted to change the subject, but also because there was something wrong with his voice.

'I have a stutter,' he said.

'Don't worry about it. You hardly even notice,' I said to reassure him. He didn't answer. 'What's your name, anyway?' I said.

'Conn,' he said.

'Short for Connor?'

'No.'

'Conroy?'

'No.'

'Constantine?'

'No.'

'What, then?'

'Connell.'

'Stupid name.'

'It's OK. At least people know what to call me.'

I remember thinking that was mega profound. Also, I liked how he didn't talk right away but really thought about what he was going to say.

'I'm Lara,' I said, tucking my hands under my bottom to warm them.

'I know,' he said. 'You're in my maths class.'

'Really?' I couldn't remember him. 'Where do you sit?'

'Wherever there's a free seat.'

I thought that was mega profound, too.

'Oh hey, hang on!' I said. 'Are you Brainman?'

'Yeah. That's me.'

'It's a really cool nickname,' I said. 'Well, better than Slack-Jawed Spa, anyway.'

'I suppose so.' His voice was smiling, which was

unusual. Conn didn't smile much in school. He didn't talk much either, except when Brundleslug asked him questions. He always got them right. Conn was the only one in class who understood differential calculus.

'I hate maths,' I said.

'It's my favourite subject.'

'You're joking. We are talking about MATHS here?'

'Yes,' said Conn. 'There are no grey areas in mathematics. The answer is either right or wrong. You don't have to write a ten-page essay on the motive of revenge in calculating an answer.'

'Nah,' I said. 'Maths seriously sucks. I mean, what's the point?'

'The point? Maths is a universal language. Almost everything in the universe can be modelled and described by mathematics. It is the only way to understand the world.'

'Did you read that in some stupid book?'

'No. It was on *Tomorrow's World*. But it's true. Suppose you want to build a bridge. The only way to know how much material to use and make a bridge strong enough is with mathematics. Otherwise, you are just taking chances.'

'Well, I suppose that might be useful, but I don't want to build bridges.'

'It's not only construction. If you ever study law or economics—'

'Oh puh-LEASE!' I said.

'—or psychology, or science, or technology, or engineering, or computing—'

'I'm going to be an actress,' I explained, picking at the ends of my sleeves. 'I suppose if that doesn't work out, I will be a pop star. I would have been a figure skater except there are no ice rinks in Limerick. So I don't need maths, which is just as well, because I suck, especially at trigonometry.'

'No, you don't,' said Conn. 'You just have never been interested enough to bother understanding it.'

'Suppose. So is that what you want to be? A builder?'

'Not a builder—'

'How about being an astronaut? That'd be WAY cool. Or even a doctor. You could go to Africa or Dublin and save all the sick babies.'

'I'm going to study mathematics in UCCD.'

'What if you don't get in?'

'I will.'

'Don't you need lots of points?'

'For a scholarship?' he asked. 'Yes. But I'll get them.'

I remember thinking it must be nice to be so sure about something – or even anything at all. 'Why UCCD?' I asked.

'It's the best university in the country.'

'Oh. Right.'

Then Conn talked more about maths. I didn't listen much because it wasn't that interesting. But when he finished, I wished he would talk more because I was afraid he would go inside and I really wanted him to stay.

'Don't you think it's way gross the way Brundleslug picks his nose with the stem of his glasses?' I asked.

'Does he?' asked Conn.

'Yeah,' I said. 'Haven't you seen him? He flicks the goobers at the blackboard.'

'Is that why you sit at the back of class?' he asked.

'No, that's because I'm trying to be cool,' I explained.

'Why do you want to be cool?'

'Because people look up to you and don't think you're a dork.'

'Oh. I like you the way you are.'

That made me feel – sorry, there's no other way of putting this – totally smurfy. Of course, I didn't say so, because that would have been way uncool. Instead, I asked, 'Did you see *Moonlighting* on telly the other night?'

'No.'

'It was DEADLY!'

'We don't have a television,' said Conn.

'What? No telly?' I said in disbelief. 'Have you seen *The A-Team* or *MacGyver*? How about *The Fall Guy*? *Alf*? *Dallas*?'

'I saw *Dallas* once.'

'That's seriously warped! It's, like, one of the most tragic things I've ever heard! I suppose you don't have a VCR either, since there's nothing to record.' Conn shrugged. 'What do you do?'

'Sometimes I go to Mark's house—'

'Who?'

'My friend, Mark Kinsella—'

'That plonker,' I sniffed.

'No, he's not,' said Conn.

'Really?' I said doubtfully. Even though I didn't know Mark Kinsella, everyone in school knew he was a plonker.

'No. He's OK. He lives down the road. Sometimes I go to his house to watch *Tomorrow's World* and *Star Trek: Next Generation*. His mam makes us Bovril and banana splits.'

'Cool,' I said.

For a while we said nothing. I was worried Conn might get bored and leave, but I couldn't think of anything to say. Eventually, I asked him whether he had been at Champers before.

'No,' he said.

'How come?' I asked.

He ignored the question and I wasn't sure whether he hadn't heard or he just didn't want to answer. I didn't want to pressurise him into saying something he might regret, so I said, 'I come most weeks with Sinéad and Maeve, although I nearly didn't this time because Maeve and me are having this mega argument.'

'OK,' he said. I was disappointed he didn't ask what the argument was about.

'Are you cold?' I asked.

'No. Are you?'

'No,' I said, rubbing goosebumps off my arms. Then I felt bad about lying to him. 'Well, yeah. A bit. I suppose.'

'You can share my jacket, if you want to.'

'Oh,' I said. 'Yeah. OK. Thanks.'

Conn sat next to me. He was much better-looking than I had remembered in school. 'You have bizarro eyes,' I said, gazing into them. They were light blue, like a Fox's Glacier Mint. 'They make you look kind of warped – in a good way. They're the same colour as one of David Bowie's – the light-blue one – he was stabbed in that eye with a compass and his other eye is brown. Were you stabbed in both eyes with a compass?'

'Er, no.'

The light shone on him and his dark hair was lit up. Inspired, I said, 'You're like Sir Lancelot with his head on fire. Except you're sitting on a wall instead of a horse. And of course your head's not on fire or you would be running around screaming, I suppose.'

Conn's proximity made me feel excited and nervous,

although at the time I thought of it as 'sort of squirmy'. I wasn't sure how we would share his jacket, but I was seriously smurfed because it seemed like the type of thing one of the heroes in a Mills and Boon romance would do before brutally crushing me to his chest.

Conn was wearing a snorkel anorak. He unzipped it and wriggled his arm out of the left sleeve, then draped part of the jacket around me.

'Put your arm in the sleeve. No, your left arm.'

'Oh, OK.' The sleeve was still warm and Conn was too. I thought it was all terrifically romantic, except that whenever I touched Conn – which was impossible not to – he jumped and moved away.

'Deadly jacket,' I said.

'Is it?'

He sounded surprised, so I said, 'OK, no, not really.'

'It was my cousin's,' said Conn. 'Used to belong to his brother.'

'Why don't you buy another one?'

He shrugged.

I felt something tickle my hand and looked down. It was a ladybird. 'Oh, see!' I said.

'A coccinellid,' he said, holding up my hand. His hand was much bigger than mine, which made me feel dainty and fragile and sort of swoony. 'Do you know why they're that colour? It's because potential predators interpret certain prey phenotypes as poisonous or tasting bad. Being red stops predators eating them.'

'Oh. That's really very, very interesting.' Conn let go of my hand. 'Maybe it would be – maybe you should put your arm around me,' I said. I was trying to sound cool, but I think it came out a bit squeaky. Although I wasn't cold any more, I was trembling.

'OK,' he said.

He put his arm around me really slowly. I was amazed how he managed to do it without touching me.

'Why are you out here?' Conn asked. 'I mean, instead of inside.'

'I – well, I'm totally mad about Growler Fitzgerald and he's been – I thought he was going to ask me out, and he – he's inside getting off with Maeve McGuinness.'

'Yeah,' said Conn. 'He's a plonker.'

'He is not! He's gorgeous and quite good-looking.'

'He's an idiot. He's so dense, light bends around him. Hahaha. Do you get it? Light bends around him?'

I said icily, 'Growler's very intelligent.'

'Well . . . he chose Maeve McGuinness over you.'

'I suppose.' I started crying with the tragedy of it all.

'I'm sorry,' said Conn. 'Please don't cry. You're nice.'

'I'm not,' I cried, beautifully. 'My life sucks! Nobody likes me. Except for John Henchy and he's a mutant.'

'I like you,' he said. 'You're nice. You have nice shoulders. They're very round.'

'Really?' I said. All of a sudden it was hard to breathe. After a while, I said, 'Would you like to go out with me?'

'Who, me?'

'Yeah.' I picked up his hand and linked my fingers through his, like I'd seen Pam do with Bobby in *Dallas*.

I knew you had to kiss someone if you were going out with them. Of course, I'd seen people kissing on telly and practised on my arm, but I still hadn't figured out how it all worked. I was particularly concerned about my lips sliding off his and accidentally sticking my tongue up his nose.

I kept waiting for Conn to kiss me, but he didn't.

'Would you like to kiss me?' I said. I hoped he would

do it before I passed out from the pounding of my heart.

'All right,' said Conn.

I closed my eyes so I could be transported into rapture. My stomach curled up into my chest when his lips met mine. It was warm and squelchy. I remember thinking it must be like how a walrus would kiss a mermaid. It certainly wasn't anything like snogging my arm. For a while it felt a bit like Conn was trying to *inflate* me.

Although I recall being pleased he kissed me, I was glad it didn't last too long.

Afterwards, we sat for a while and then we kissed a bit more and then Conn said he had to go. I stood up as well and I hoped Conn didn't notice that my belt fell down around my ankles.

Everyone at school was talking about the movie *Cocktail*, which had just been released. I hoped maybe Conn would ask me to see it with him, but he didn't say anything, even though I dropped a few hints.

Conn said he would memorise my phone number. I wrote it on his Champers ticket with my sparkly green eyeliner pencil just in case he forgot, and drew a little love heart around it as well so he would know I was mad about him.

I turn to the next page of the diary.

Sunday 3 April 1988

Spots: 8

Arguments with Mum: 1, but it's lasted all day so it probably counts as, like, a hundred. Since I am officially sulking, at least I don't have to speak to her.

Dear Diary,

Conn hasn't called yet, but he might even call TONIGHT!!!!! I haven't told a single soul except for Róisín, Michelle, Katie, Sinéad, Maeve, Valerie, Áine, Carol, Jane, Hazel, Sarah, the other Sarah, and Hilary.

He is so deadly mysterious; I can't believe I thought he was just sulky. I haven't washed my hand since he held it on Friday, which is totally not as gross as it sounds because it's my left hand so it's not like I use it much. I hope I haven't caught AIDS from kissing him, but I think it's seriously unlikely because Kieren Wylie says it takes a litre of spit and, anyway, I don't think Conn has AIDS because he doesn't have facial boils.

I can't WAIT to see him in school tomorrow!!!!! I know we are destined to be together for ever (unless Johnny Depp wants to go out with me, which is mega unlikely since he's going out with Winona Ryder, which totally sucks).

Love,

Lara

Bruce must have finished long ago. I can't recall hearing the last few tracks of 'The River'. The silence in Leonard's apartment is oppressive.

A tear squelches on to the page. The word 'sucks' expands and blurs. Why couldn't I have aimed for the word 'heart'? I can't even get irony right.

Although, I suppose, as metaphors go, it's pretty appropriate.

S he says, 'Conn?'
  I do not understand the female of the species'
requirement for post-coital discussion. If you don't get
the small talk out of the way *before* going to bed, surely
it's a bit late after sex?

However, I want to do the right thing.

I say, 'Put your clothes on. I'll call you a taxi.'

My companion laughs. People often laugh at things I
say, even when I'm serious. She says, 'Are you kicking me
out?' Waves her bare leg at me. She is still smiling, so
evidently she's happy about leaving.

I say, 'No. I would just prefer you leave, if that's OK.'

She sits up straight, says, 'I can't believe this. Is that it?'

I say, 'I – I don't understand.' I am genuinely confused. I'm in Amman on a business trip and met her for
the first time at a client meeting today. Correction: for the
last two hours, this has technically been 'yesterday'. She
was my client's marketing manager. Probably still is,
unless she has been sacked in the interim. 'Are you
expecting something else?'

I don't normally approach women. Evidence to date
suggests that my chat-up technique and/or terrifies the
opposite sex. This may apply to chat-up techniques in
general, since I find women's chat-up techniques
alarming and/or terrifying.

My client's marketing manager asked if I wanted to have sex with her. Before she came to my hotel room, I told her of my return to London the following day. She said she understood, but sometimes women say one thing when they think/feel another. Because now, when asked to vacate the premises, her lower lip quivers.

I think she is upset.

She says, 'What did I *expect*? How about some fucking respect?'

Now I am almost certain she's upset.

I say, 'I'm s-s-sorry. I did not m-m-mean – you can stay. If you like. I have to work.'

I get out of the bed, walk to the bathroom. My feet adhere slightly to the floor. Hotel carpets feature a vaguely tacky quality in inverse proportion to their star rating (note: this is a general observation rather than a true representative random sample).

I unhitch the bathrobe from the bathroom door. It is stiff, scratchy, smells of bleach.

When I return, my client's marketing manager is circling the room snatching up random pieces of clothing.

She says, 'Can I at least have a shower?'

'Of-of course.'

She holds her clothes to her front, backs towards the bathroom. She says, 'Do you even remember my name?'

I say, 'Yes.' I don't hear enough of her response to approximately extrapolate her meaning, so I say, 'Excuse me?'

'My name. What is it?'

'Janine.' I shrug. 'I have an eidetic memory.' I never forget anything (note: unless it is essentially trivial). Sometimes I fear I might run out of memory. 'A photographic memory,' I explain, when Janine shakes her head. 'I remember all sorts of stuff. Lyrics from seventies folk songs, Kurdistan customs requirements, average gestation periods of the garden snail and various land-based mammals—'

She says, 'You know, it's right. What they say about you.'

'Who?'

'Your employees. They say you're a chilly bastard. Know what your staff call you? Emotional Wanker. And Bollox O'Neill.'

I am aware of this. It still hurts, even though a) I have no control over what others think and b) it is relatively accurate as far as descriptive categorisation is concerned. But it would be nice if my employees called me something like Niceguy O'Neill.

I say, 'Better than Slack-Jawed Spa.' This reminds me of something & I laugh. The sound surprises me. I can't recall precisely when last I did, but it has been in the order of months.

She says, 'You bastard.'

I don't wish to waste time arguing. Especially when, from several perspectives (particularly her own), she is accurate and/or correct.

She says, 'Fuck you.'

Before I can say anything else (note: I cannot think of anything anyway), Janine closes the bathroom door in my face.

When she returns, she has clothes on. I say, 'The taxi is downstairs.' I am concerned that a) she might have no change and b) it is unfair she should have to pay for the taxi, so I say, 'Would you like some dinars for the fare?'

She snatches the money, throws it on the bed.

She says, 'I don't need your money. Put it towards your personality fund.'

'Personality fund? Oh. That's quite funny.'

She slams the door on her way out.

I consider the hours left to daybreak. Time seems to slow down and/or stretch. According to formal definitions of time in physics, linear geometry & quantum mechanics, this is impossible. It must be a psychological-related phenomena.

I don't often have sex with another human being, but often enough to wonder what the point is. I presume the contact will make me feel less isolated. The effect is always precisely the opposite. Physical intimacy highlights/contrasts what is missing & what I had, once.

In most other circumstances, my learning curve is steeper.

I have work to do: I have to revise the proposal for Janine's employer and compile a technical specification for another client.

Instead, I open my wallet, remove two passport photos. They are worn along the crease. This is unsurprising. They have been in my wallet for fifteen years & I randomly, but frequently, review them.

Ignoring my own image, I touch her face, as I always do (note: I have to be careful, because her nose is nearly rubbed away). I wonder what she looks like now. Whether her eyes are still the deep blue of an oil slick, her cheek still as soft as urethane-based synthetic rubber. I understand she lives in Ireland now. I wonder what she's doing. Most of all, I wonder whether she's happy. I hope so.

I replace the photos behind my driver's licence. I

open the minibar, pour a measure from an impractically small bottle, drop in three ice cubes.

As I walk to the window, I finger the scar down my cheek. Seven years later it is still raised & ragged. I stare through my reflection. My features are arranged in standard formation, all present & correct (note: apart from the scar). Women tell me I am handsome.

Lights shimmer & blink in the dark. It could be any big city anywhere, but specifically it is Amman.

I swirl my drink, ice clinks against the glass. Whisky. It is what men who fly business class drink. Men who live in hotel rooms & kick women out of them.

Men like me.

I do not like whisky.

I drain my glass.

I am considering going for a run, when my laptop beeps from the writing desk. I walk over, reactivate the screen. Two hundred and sixty-one emails, three quarters of them spam. The rest are from clients – all urgent, according to the sender – to delete or forward.

I click on my instant messenger. I hope OwnWorstEnemy is online. There is a high probability of this. She stays up late.

She is.

A:42:	Hello.
OwnWorstEnemy:	Hey there, gorgeous1
A:42:	How do you know I am gorgeous? ☺
OwnWorstEnemy:	Vivid imagination ☺
A:42:	You're up late again.
OwnWorstEnemy:	Gosh, is that the time? How are u?
A:42:	OK. Think I upset someone.

OwnWorstEnemy: Did ur social censor malfunction again?

A:42: Think need to recalibrate censor.

OwnWorstEnemy: LOL. Want to tell me about it?

A:42: No.

OwnWorstEnemy: Definitely broken.

A:42: Sorry ☹

OwnWorstEnemy: That's okay u'll have 2 try harder 2 offend me ☺ How come ur still awake? Can't sleep again?

A:42: No. I don't sleep much anyway. 3 hours maybe 4.

OwnWorstEnemy: I know. Have u seen doctor yet?

A:42: Yes. He said it was stress. Advised drinking camomile tea & meditating.

OwnWorstEnemy: At the same time? ☺

A:42: No, I don't think so. I told him I didn't have time to drink camomile tea. He said I was 'prime heart attack material'. So I sacked him.

OwnWorstEnemy: Model patient LOL. What r u doing now?

A:42: Chatting to you.

OwnWorstEnemy: ☺ I think it's my turn.

A:42: OK.

OwnWorstEnemy: First girlfriend.

A:42: How much detail do you require?

OwnWorstEnemy: All of it. The blood, the gore the clashing of teeth.

A:42: Will take long time.

OwnWorstEnemy: So type faster.

A:42:	OK, I will try. Maybe I can use more fingers.
OwnWorstEnemy:	That was a joke, clownface.
A:42:	Oh, right! I see ☺
OwnWorstEnemy:	What was her name?
OwnWorstEnemy:	Hellooo!
A:42:	Lara. We went to school together.
OwnWorstEnemy:	Aw, teenage sweethearts.
A:42:	Not exactly. We didn't talk much at school. She was one of the cool crowd. I was a hard-core geek.
OwnWorstEnemy:	No, I don't believe it ☹
A:42:	Yes. I was polite to teachers, sat at the front of class. My trousers had creases that could shave hairs off a gooseberry, as my nan would have said. I carried four different colour biros in my shirt pocket, always had ink stains in the corner.
OwnWorstEnemy:	Aggressively nerdy!
A:42:	We engineers need a variety of pens.
OwnWorstEnemy:	I'm sure ☺
A:42:	The only time Lara and I spoke in school was when Dom Carmody threw my bag down the corridor once. She stopped, helped me pick up my books. Everyone else climbed over us. One night, my friend Mark talked me into going to a disco. I believe he employed a

technique called 'emotional blackmail'. I was unprepared. At the time, brushing my teeth was a fashion statement.

OwnWorstEnemy: Ew. What about now?

A:42: Now I put on aftershave too.

Own WorstEnemy: ☺

A:42: Mark had a girlfriend. It was a passionate, long-term relationship. It had lasted a week already, looked set to prevail for at least another.

OwnWorstEnemy: LOL

A:42: He needed backup, but he tried to present it as a social service. Said if I didn't go, I would miss an integral part of my teenage development. It was a direct result of 'Project Riker Strike' that I was sitting outside the disco, formulating escape strategy. Then Lara came out the fire exit. She was the most unusual person I'd ever seen. Her hair was stiff and all standing on end. She had black streaks down her face, and puffy eyes. Her top was falling down and she had on a pair of those leg-scarves. Lime-green and orange. She was lovely.

OwnWorstEnemy: Aw!

A:42: Women were one of the few things I knew nothing about. I had no cultural references, either. We didn't have a television. I used to go to Mark's place to watch his. My mam only let me watch four hours a week, so I had to choose carefully. *Tomorrow's World* was my favourite programme, but you didn't learn much about women there. But I liked women. My mam was one. That helped. Lara was snorting and making squeaky noises. I asked her if she was crying.

OwnWorstEnemy: Smooth.

A:42: She said, she wasn't, but I think she was lying (I'm not sure why).

OwnWorstEnemy: Sometimes people don't want others to know how they really feel.

A:42: I have never understood that. Why?

OwnWorstEnemy: Another time, carry on.

A:42: OK. I had to talk to her, to make her stay outside. I didn't know what to say, so I talked about common applications of mathematics, specifically the construction industry. It turned out Lara was really interested in that, which was great.

OwnWorstEnemy: This is one of many occasions where a rolling eye smiley would come in handy.

A:42:

I was happy just being with her, but Lara evidently liked talking and I was running out of conversation. It was not something I had much practice with. I mean, I often talked to my mam. At least, she asked me questions and I answered them. I sometimes talked to Mark about superpowers.

OwnWorstEnemy: SUPERPOWERS?

A:42:

Yes. E.g., what you would do if you had X-ray vision, or could fly. Or whether having the ability to e.g. teleport walnuts, or reach supersonic speeds when immersed in boiling water would have any practical application in reality. That sort of stuff.

OwnWorstEnemy: Right.

A:42:

Lara asked me to kiss her. I wanted to, but didn't know what the format was. I'd seen a programme at Mark's about a cowboy called JR.

OwnWorstEnemy: *Dallas!*

A:42:

Yes, I believe so. I had seen JR and a woman arguing, then JR grabbed her by the hair and mashed his mouth against hers. The woman slapped JR across the face, but then he did it again and she seemed to like it. So I tried that. I also stuck my tongue right

	in, because Mark told me girls love that.
OwnWorstEnemy:	NOOO!
A:42:	Lara didn't slap me across the face. But she didn't moan and groan like the woman did, either. I think she liked it. I still remember how she tasted. Like minty strawberries.
OwnWorstEnemy:	Aw!
A:42:	I'd said I would phone Lara, but I wanted to wait until I had something interesting to say to her. Once I rang her phone but hung up after 1.5 rings.
A:42:	Then she started going out with Growler Fitzgerald.
A:42:	After that we didn't talk again until I met her in college four years later.
OwnWorstEnemy:	Carry on.
OwnWorstEnemy:	Hello?
OwnWorstEnemy:	U still there?
OwnWorstEnemy:	Hellooo!

Outside cyberspace my iPhone rings. I check the display. The number is not listed. This is strange.

I press 'answer', say, 'O'Neill.'

My mother's voice says, 'Hello, can I – can I speak to Connell, please?'

Mam often gets confused about time differences when I am travelling. But it is one-thirty a.m. in Ireland, i.e., this is something else.

I say, 'Mam, it's me. Is something wr-wrong?'

She says, 'Oh, Connell.' Her voice fluctuates. The silence that follows makes me feel cold, even though the room's air conditioning is set to twenty-three degrees for normal body temperature. It sounds like she is crying, although this is implausible.

I have to concentrate to keep my voice level. I say, 'Mam, it's OK, I am here. It's OK, it's OK.' I do not know why I say this, because it is inaccurate, i.e., I know it is not OK. 'What's wrong? Mam, tell me.'

'It's . . . Paddy. Your father.'

'What? Mam, *what*?'

'He . . . he had a stroke.'

'Oh God. When?' I don't know why I posited that question, because it is not what I want to know. 'Mam, is he all r-r-right?'

There is a long silence. When she answers, Mam is weeping openly.

'No. He's in the hospital. He's – he's in a coma. The doctors . . . they . . . they say they don't know. He might not wake up, or when he does—'

'He might have neurological damage,' I say, although I am not aware of consciously forming the thought.

'Yes. Or paralysis.'

'I am coming home. I will c-c-catch the first plane,' I say, throwing my suitcase on to the bed & unzipping it.

'Where – where are you?'

'Amman. Mam, are you all right?'

'I'm fine, pet.' Her voice grows stronger. 'Harriet's here with me. At the hospital.'

I do not recognise the name temporarily. Then I remember, Harriet is Mark's mother. I have always known her as Mrs Kinsella.

'Good. OK. Good. W-w-wait – which h-h-hospital are you in?' It takes me some time to pronounce the word 'hospital'.

'The Regional.'

'I'll be there as soon as possible, Mam.' I want to say something to make her feel better, but often things I say have the opposite effect. 'I will see you soon.'

I hang up, throwing items randomly into my case. After I have packed three cushions and the remote control, I force myself to slow down. My brain flickers in a manner similar to a broken projector. Think. *Think*.

My first objective is to get home. The second is . . .

There is no second objective.

I call AirMe, cancel my original ticket & book a seat on the earliest flight from Amman to Heathrow. While on hold, I go online & book a connecting flight to Limerick.

Then I call Mark.

He says, 'Conn,' as if I spoke to him yesterday instead of seven years ago.

'M-M-Mark.' Suddenly, I can't remember why I called him. It is as if my mind has been expunged.

'I'm at the hospital with your mam. What can I do?'

The sound of his voice prompts me. I say, 'I'm coming home. I need a hire c-car—'

'I'll collect you. What are your flight details?'

After I tell him, I am reluctant to hang up the phone.

He says, 'Conn, hang in there, pal. See you soon, all right?'

Before the recent interval, Mark had been my friend since his father found us putting onions up the exhaust pipe of his Datsun Sunny. It was probably longer, but I have limited recollection before the age of four.

I have never been able to work out what happened. Something must have, but there was no argument or anything like that. At least, if we argued, I didn't notice (i.e., no shouting, insulting each others mothers, knife wounds, etc.).

I didn't hear from Mark after I moved to London, but there was nothing unusual in that. We often went months without speaking and/or writing. I knew Mark would call me when he had something to say. But he didn't.

Ten months later, he sent me an email. He & Lara wanted me to be best man at their wedding.

Of course, I agreed. But whenever I thought about Lara with Mark, I felt so bad I wondered whether I had a terminal disease affecting blood flow to the heart and other major organs, e.g., Wegener's granulomatosis. I thought Mark would communicate location/date details, but he never did & I never asked.

When Mam told me Mark & Lara didn't marry after all, I was relieved.

Nine hours ago, Mark & I spoke for the first time since.

Mark waits outside the arrivals gate in Shannon Airport. He waves, says, 'Android! Over here!'

He is chunkier, has less hair. Otherwise he looks the same.

I am not sure what the protocol is for people who used to be friends. I consider shaking his hand. Before I have the opportunity, Mark hugs me.

'How was the flight?'

'Uncomfortable.'

He says, 'You look like shit.'

I recognise the familiar template & grin. 'You look like shit squared.'

'Yeah, but I've got brawn and brains and an abundance of natural charm.'

'You can carry a bag if you want to be useful.'

'That's a bit ambitious after a lifetime of general uselessness.' Mark takes the largest bag, puts it on a stray trolley.

I say, 'Good to see you.'

He nudges me with a shoulder & says, 'You too, Droid. It's been too long.'

'Yes.'

I wonder whether he wishes to discuss why. I am grateful when instead he says, 'Sorry about the circumstances, though.'

My stomach cramps. It has been doing that a lot over the past few hours. Maybe I have indigestion, although I have not eaten. 'Is there any news about Da?'

'There was no change when I left. The doctors say he's stable.'

Stable. The word implies steadiness, security, endurance. In this context, it means my father's condition is not getting worse – or better.

Nothing about this situation feels stable.

The automatic doors open on to a chill, grey afternoon. 'Agh!' I say involuntarily. Goosebumps stand out on my forearms. My short-sleeved shirt & lightweight trousers are designed for a Middle East summer, not Ireland.

In the car, I say, 'I want to go straight to the hospital.'

'Sure. You OK?'

'Yes. Well, no.' I clench my eyes shut, pinch the bridge of my nose. 'This all feels . . .'

'Surreal? Like you're inside a big, psychedelic bubble that kind of warps stuff?'

'No, it is as if I am removed from the situation. Like – like I'm watching it happen to someone else.' As we pass Bunratty Castle, I say, 'My job – there is so much travel. I only see my parents once or twice a year. Every time they are perceptively slower, measurably more forgetful. But I always thought – I thought I had more time . . .'

'Hold that thought, pal. Your father's not dead yet.'

The implication of this hits me like opposing particle beams in a Supercollider. Mark is right. I had been thinking of Da as dead or dying. Even this thought process results in a sorrow that feels as if it might rupture my chest cavity in a freak physical manifestation.

The last time I was in a hospital (note: apart from my birth) was after the accident. Nobody knew whether Lara would live. Certainly, her doctors were negative about her ongoing survival, and/or the consequences thereof.

She proved them wrong.

Obviously, this has no bearing on Da's situation. Just because Lara recovered, it does not follow he will, too. However, in this circumstance it is useful to remember that the hopelessness I felt then was unfounded.

I ask, 'Have you spoken to Lara recently?' I have to shout over a truck honking behind us.

Mark says, 'No. I heard she's going to America.' He makes a v-sign at the driver as the truck overtakes. 'Feckin' eejit.'

'On – on holiday?' Even as I ask it, I know the answer.

'To live.'

'When?'

Mark shrugs. 'I'm not sure. Soon, I think. Why don't you give her a call?'

I nod, but I know I won't. I think maybe Mark knows that too.

Mark pulls up in the hospital car park, switches off the ignition. Without looking at me, he says, 'By the way, Droid, I'm sorry.'

'For what?'

He shakes his head, exits the car via the driver's door.

To: OwnWorstEnemy

From: A:42

Re: Regret

Dear OwnWorstEnemy,

The reason I went offline earlier was because my mother rang. My father experienced an ischaemic stroke caused by venous thrombosis, i.e., a blockage of blood to the brain. The results of an MRI scan indicate extensive tissue damage. Da has not regained consciousness.

I'm at the Midwestern Regional Hospital. I have been here for two days. Da is in the intensive care unit on floor two. In the bed, Da looks smaller than I remember. Tubes extend up his nose & a large one is taped over his mouth. The machine next to his bed reports that he is alive, but the rise & fall of his chest is almost indiscernible.

All the doctors will say is that Da had a stroke. Even I could do that, without eight years (minimum) of medical training. Dr Patel says it is impossible to determine the likelihood of Da regaining consciousness, or the extent of neurological damage.

Irrationally, whenever I look at Da, I expect him to be awake, looking back at me. Maybe reading a newspaper, looking down through his spectacles with his mouth open. Or smoking his pipe: chewing the mouthpiece & tamping the bowl with his biro.

Of course, he never is. The likelihood of those scenarios is negligible (e.g., smoking is not allowed in the hospital).

Dr Patel said it might help if I talk to Da. However, even when Da is conscious, we rarely talk. He likes reading, so I read the newspaper to him. It takes approximately four hours if I include the television listings.

Although it is late now, I can't sleep. Mrs Kinsella took Mam home at nine twenty-three. I hope she gets some rest. The flesh around her eyes is dark, indicating that she is tired. I don't know when she ate last.

The ward is still & silent. It seems unnaturally dark. The only sources of light are the green glow from Da's life support monitor & my laptop screen.

I've been thinking a lot since arriving at this place. Not relatively, because I think a lot on a daily basis. I mean: I've been thinking about different things. E.g., death. Under normal circumstances, I do not think about death. Obviously, people have to die. Otherwise, the population would increase to unsustainable proportions. But I have never thought about death in the same context as my parents.

Da used to tell me I could do anything & I always operated on this principle. But he was wrong. Many things fall within my field of influence, but not everything. E.g., I can't make Da better, & I cannot miss him less. In summary: there is nothing I can do.

I always thought things either happen or they don't: a logical outcome results from a sequence of plans/actions. Hope does not belong in this scenario.

Now, I wish I had hope. But what is the point? It is a flawed concept. Especially when there is a real probability Da will die or suffer severe neurological damage in the event he regains consciousness?

It is strange how things that seemed so important are now irrelevant. My existence seems to have contracted, focused within the confines of these hospital walls. I feel angry. It affects my ability to think. I have read this is a normal response to the prospect of bereavement. I'm not like normal people in many respects, so it surprises me to have something in common with them.

Why did this happen to Da? He is a nice person. He pays his taxes. He eats low-fat yoghurt & does yoga. (Note: Mam makes him, but the result is the same as if he chose to.)

I know these factors don't determine someone's fate. Illogically, I feel they should.

Someone I used to know (Lara, the girl I told you about earlier) believed in the concept of fate/kismet/ destiny. She believed that life is engineered and/or predesigned, that individuals have no effect over the course of their lives. Conversely, I thought people determine the course of their lives by the decisions & choices they make. Da's stroke does not conform to this theory. Da's life seemed small, he & Mam never had much. But he always seemed happy (note: obviously, I can only speculate about this). I wonder whether his life was all he wanted it to be. I wonder whether there are things he regrets. In the inconceivable event that he dies, I may never know.

I wonder whether Da is proud of me. I suppose I am what is commonly referred to as a 'success', but I wonder whether love & grandchildren ever featured in his plans for me. Although I have everything I thought I wanted, somewhere along the way I lost myself.

I have so many regrets.

One of them is Lara.

I n school, Lara wanted to be an actress or a rock star. (Note: although she did not become a rock star, she would have been good at that). Therefore, I was surprised to note her presence in UCCD.

I hadn't seen much of Lara after that night at Champers. Our school was the biggest in Limerick. There was never an opportunity to say much more than 'Hello, Lara', which I did, on the rare occasions I passed her in the corridor. The only time I knew we would meet was in Maths, but the following term I went into the honours class. I didn't see her much at all after that. Mark told me she repeated her fourth year.

She had changed, but I recognised her instantly. Her hair was blue at the ends & looked like she had cut it herself with a pair of callipers. It was difficult to see her eyes in the middle of lots of smudged, black eye paint.

She was always in the middle of a group of girls who giggled more than was necessary. They also squealed on a regular/frequent basis.

I saw her long before I spoke to her. Technically, she spoke to me. Professor Quealy had just finished a fascinating double lecture on thermodynamics & fluid mechanics. I stayed behind to take some extra notes.

A voice said, 'Hey, you!'

It was Lara.

She had on a chunky black sweater with holes in the elbows. The cuffs were ragged & came down past her knuckles. She looked nice.

I said, 'What? Ah, I mean, um, yeah, hi.'

She said, 'Whatever', & pushed a length of hair behind her left ear. 'Julie said you called her stupid.'

I said, 'Who's Julie?'

'The girl you were talking to this morning. Black docs, black top, black jeans, black hair, quite spotty.'

Most of Lara's friends fell under that descriptive category. However, there was only one I had communicated with.

'Oh, her.'

'Well?'

'I didn't call her stupid—'

'So she's *lying*, then?'

'Technically, yes. I didn't say, "Hey, Julie, has anyone ever told you you're stupid? Because you are".'

'But you think she's stupid?'

'Of course. Well, she is.'

'Hey! She's my friend!'

I frowned. 'Why? Are you only friends with stupid people?'

Lara giggled, even though I wasn't trying to be funny.

She sat in the chair beside mine. I'd never seen anyone sit like she did. She jumped off the ground, pivoted in mid-air, & crash-landed in it. The end result was the same as if she had lowered herself on to it, except that the chair momentarily reared back on its hind legs.

She said, 'Suppose Julie could do with a few more brain cells.'

'Or a hundred trillion synapses.'

I'd never heard anyone laugh like her. It sounded like

jelly going down a drain. It made me feel like laughing too.

She said, 'You're funny.'

I mumbled, 'No, I'm not.'

Folding her leg, she put a scuffed boot between my leg & the edge of the seat. It was uncomfortable because she was wearing a pair of Doctor Martens boots. Also, her foot wriggled around a lot.

I didn't mind, though.

She said, 'I'm Lara. Lara Callaghan.'

'I know. We w-were in school together.'

'Gorgonzola Comp? Oh yeah. I thought you looked familiar. What a coincidence!' Many of our classmates attended UCCD, so I didn't think it qualified as a coincidence. However, I didn't say that. 'What's your name again?'

'I'm Conn-Connell. You know – Brainman? You kissed me, once. At Champers—'

'Excuse me?' Her eye paint relocated higher up her face.

'What?'

'I did not!'

'Oh. Maybe I kissed you—'

'I think I would, like, remember something like that. And I don't.'

'You-you don't?'

'No.'

I recalled the incident clearly.

Lara stood up, then sat down again. She said nothing. I didn't mind, but I was afraid she might go away. Girls didn't make much sense to me. They were unpredictable and illogical.

'Would you like a Mars Bar?' I asked.

'What?'

'We could go to the canteen and get a Mars Bar. If-if you like.'

'Dunno. I have lots of stuff to do.'

'Oh. OK.'

'S'pose I could. For a while. Maybe.'

'OK,' I said.

I gathered up my papers, closed my books, put them & my scientific calculator in my satchel, buckled my satchel, counted the pens in my shirt pocket, & put on my jacket. Then we walked across the Quad to the canteen. Lara did not say much. She chewed on a fingernail, although there did not appear to be much left to chew.

In the canteen, a bun fight had broken out by one of the bushes in a tub. We queued by the shepherd's pie & sausage rolls in the plastic display. I said, 'You can go and sit down at a table, if you like. I'll buy your Mars Bar.'

'OK. Could you get me a sausage roll and a cup of tea as well?'

'Oh, OK,' I said. A Mars Bar, a sausage roll and a cup of tea cost forty-one pence. I had forty-four pence. I'd already eaten my lunch sandwiches, but I calculated there was a fair-to-good probability I would survive until dinner.

Lara was sitting at one of the tables by the window. As I put down the tray, Lara said, 'You not having anything?'

I ducked an airborne scone. 'No.'

Lara unwrapped the Mars Bar, asked, 'When did you get glasses?'

'After the Leaving Cert. I went to see an optician. Couldn't even read the first line of the chart. I thought the "M" was an omega.' That was a joke, but Lara didn't laugh, so I carried on quickly. 'The optician said I "wouldn't see an elephant charging from ten paces".'

'There aren't many elephants in Ireland, so you're probably safe enough.' Lara opened her mouth & stuffed in half the Mars Bar in one go. Even Mark could only manage a third.

She said, 'Wam weh wesh?' I understood her, even though the words were stuck in a mouthful of masticated nougat & caramel.

I said, 'Yes, please,' taking the remaining half she proffered across the table. Lara smiled, revealing two rows of brown teeth.

I asked, 'What are you studying?'

She said something that sounded like, 'Arse on Humaniwies.'

'What?'

She swallowed. 'Arts and Humanities.'

'Oh. I thought you didn't want to go to university.'

'I didn't. It was the quickest way of getting out of Limerick, but.' Licking her lips, Lara picked up the sausage roll. 'I wanted to go travelling for a year in Cambodia and Vietnam, but Mum wouldn't let me.' She rotated her eyeballs. 'She is *such* a killjoy.'

Lara finished half the sausage roll, pushed the rest across the table.

'The only other alternative was marrying a dairy farmer from Cavan and pushing out sprogs at the rate of one a year until I dropped down dead from exhaustion or fanny fatigue—'

'Were you going out with a dairy farmer?'

'Like, *no*? Anyway. I decided to go to uni. My dad says a degree opens doors.'

'Arts and Humanities is not a real degree.'

'What d'you mean?'

'It's not useful for anything.'

'You can wipe your arse with a Batchelor of Arts degree just as well as with a BSc.'

I said, 'I suppose', although I didn't know why anyone would want to wipe their arse with either.

'Look, I didn't want to study law, because lawyers have the worst halitosis of any profession—'

'Really?'

'Yeah, I think so. And I thought about doing medicine, but I can't stand intestines and warts make me spew. Then I thought about doing architecture but I didn't have enough points.' She wiped her mouth with a napkin someone had left behind. 'In the end I got a prospectus from the university furthest from Limerick – which was UCCD – and decided to do Arts so I didn't have to make any serious decisions. Because, according to my mother, the choices I make now will reverberate through the rest of my life, until I die.' She swivelled her eyeballs again. Then she extracted a biro from her hair (note: I hadn't previously perceived the presence of writing implements in her hair). I thought she wanted to write something, but instead she tapped it against the edge of the table. 'What I really want is to be a writer, but obviously that's ridiculous.'

'Why? All you need for that is to know how to spell.'

'There's a bit more to it than that. I mean, who would want to read what I write?'

'I don't know,' I said. 'Depends on what you write, I suppose. What modules are you studying?'

'English as my major credit, with Linguistics and Philosophy as minors and Psychology and Information Studies as electives.' She shrugged. 'In the end, I figured it doesn't really matter anyway.'

'Is it interesting?'

'Nah, sucks. So, did you get a scholarship?'

I said, 'Yeah.' Then, 'You remember.'

'What?'

'From the night we— four years ago.'

'No, I don't.'

'Then how did you know about the scholarship?'

'I – you – you said. Earlier, in the lecture theatre.'

'No, I didn't.'

'You did.'

'I didn't.'

Lara stood abruptly. 'Listen, I can't have – I can't stay. I've got – there's – something. I have to do. Stuff. Catch you around, maybe.'

Some of the things Lara said made me think she remembered the time we met at Champers, even though she claimed not to. It did not compute.

When in doubt, it is my policy to say nothing. People confuse me. Their response to stimuli is irrational and frequently illogical. The only way to understand people is to put them together. Group dynamics are more predictable.

But I wanted her to stay, so I said, 'Stop, wait. P-perhaps I did m-m-mention it inside.' (Note: even though I was sure that was not the case.) 'B-but I know I said it that time – that night – at Champers. It's all right if you don't remember. Please, I – it's just that I r-remember everything. You came out, you were crying—'

'I was *not*—'

'Your top kept falling down your shoulders. I shared my jacket with you. You smelled nice. I was really pleased you talked to me.'

Lara paused, sat down again, slowly.

She said, 'Why didn't you call me?' Her voice was small, I had to listen really hard to hear her. 'It's not like I care or anything. I'd just like to know, as a matter of interest. Did you forget my phone number? I waited—'

'No. I mean, no, I didn't forget your number. It's three four three, nine five nine. I-I really wanted to call you, b-but I k-kept thinking that it was a mistake. You know, maybe you'd g-g-given me your number by accident or something. I kept thinking, why would someone like you go out with s-someone like me?'

'What do you mean, "someone like me"?'

'You were so c-cool, and I – well, I wasn't. Then, two days later, you were going out with Growler Fitzgerald—'

'That was just a *rumour*.'

'Really? Oh. I thought – anyway.'

'OK,' said Lara. 'I've got to go. Hey, but – there's a party this Saturday. Hey, I know! You could come. If you want?'

'I-I can't. I go home every month to see my parents.'

'Oh. OK.'

'B-but if I were here, I would really like to. Can we – maybe we could do something else. Like – like – I know! I build electronic circuit boards. I c-could show you my collection sometime. If you like? Or we could meet at Murphy's. The abattoir. I work there five nights a week. The manager sometimes gives me bits of cow. It's dead, obviously.'

'Wow. You seriously have no idea how to chat up a girl, do you?'

I was relieved she didn't seem to be upset by that. I said, 'No. Well, I have no previous experience. Although even if I had, I would probably still' – I decided to trial a new word – 's-suck on it.'

'At it. Look, I'm in the student union most evenings. Why don't you come down sometime?'

'OK,' I said.

*

After our conversation, I thought that maybe Lara liked me. She had been pretty upset about Julie, but when I explained what had really happened, she seemed to understand. Then we had a nice conversation. She had laughed & said I was funny.

I thought it would be good if she liked me, because I liked her. But, the following day, I met her coming out of Doyle Hall. She ignored me (note: I'm pretty sure she noticed my presence, because I was right in front of her. Also, I accidentally stepped on her.)

I was unsure whether I had to go to the Student Union to talk to her again, but I was uncomfortable with the unspecific nature of the arrangement. I spent a lot of time considering whether it was an arrangement or only a suggestion.

I was confused. This was a new sensation for me, not an agreeable one. Also, it worried me how often I thought about Lara. I couldn't concentrate on the mechanics of solids.

I decided to discuss the problem with Mark. He was at UCCD too, studying Marketing. I'm not sure how he got in because, although he was clever, he was not academically inclined. He would have been more suited to an apprenticeship, e.g., in the forestry industry.

Mark & I shared accommodation, but we hardly ever saw each other. Often, Mark did not return to the flat for days. Sometimes I met him coming out of the bathroom or scratching his armpits in the kitchen.

One morning, before going to university, I hid his shoes. That evening, when I returned to the flat, he was lying on the sofa watching *Home and Away*.

He said, 'Man, d'you know where the fuck are my

fucking shoes, the fuck?' (Note: he swore a lot back then.)

I said, 'I hid them. In the laundry cupboard.'

'Why?'

'Because I knew you wouldn't look there.'

'Fucking *no*, I mean fucking *why*?'

'I wanted to talk to you.'

'Why the fuck couldn't you have fucking left a fucking note?'

'Oh. I did not consider that.'

'For a genius, you can be a right fucking idiot.'

Mark got off the sofa. He walked into the television, then the door on the way to the kitchen. I followed, picking up the beer cans he kicked out of the way.

I asked, 'What's that smell?'

'Probably me. Haven't showered for three days. We're out of fucking soap.'

'I just use Fairy Liquid.'

'That's fucking disgusting, man,' said Mark, picking two teabags out of the rubbish bin. He flicked ash off them. 'Fancy a cup of tea?'

'Yes, please.' I dumped the cans on the table, cleared the debris off the single chair & sat down.

'What the fuck do you want to fucking talk about? Don't fucking tell me: fucking women.'

'Yes,' I said. Mark knew all about these things. Girls liked him because he was 'profound' & played in a band called Hymen Raider and the Fucking Penetrators. (Note: he was a Fucking penetrator.)

'Women,' said Mark, bitterly. 'Fucking leeches. They suck the life out of you and then, when you're a broken husk, they discard you and put out their cigarettes in your rotting skull. And laugh while they're at it. They're like fucking vampires.'

'I thought they were like leeches?'

'Yeah, that too. Like a fucking Frankenleech vampire hybrid.'

I nodded, although I had difficulty imagining a leech vampire hybrid.

Mark said, 'Anyway, you've come to the right fucking man, Grasshopper. Tell the fucking Love Doctor.'

So I told the fucking Love Doctor about Lara, what she had said, how I couldn't concentrate on the mechanics of solids.

When I had finished, Mark advised, 'Fuck her.'

'What?'

'Man, she's fucking you up, right?'

'I th-think so.'

'And you're trying to make sense out of it – but that's where you're going wrong, man. You see? That's what she fucking *wants*! It's all a great big psychedelic mind-fuck. I mean, you're a fucking mess.'

'Am I?'

'Yes! Look at you! You can't fucking eat, you can't fucking sleep, you can't fucking concentrate – every time you butter a slice of toast, you think about taking the knife and stabbing yourself in the heart over and over and over again.'

'Really?'

Mark mimed stabbing himself in the heart. From the look on his face, it was unpleasant.

I hadn't thought about toast in relation to Lara, but now that I did, I realised Mark was right.

Mark said, 'Man, *heed* the Love Doctor. Women are nothing but pain and fucking sorrow. They'll use your fucking razor and leave it covered in fucking hair.'

'Er—'

'Who is this fucking goddess, anyway?'

'Her name is Lara—'

'Not Lara Fucking Callaghan? From school? What a fucking bitch.'

'No, she's not. She's nice.'

'Really?' Mark looked doubtful. 'What's so fucking special about her?'

'Well – well, everything.' I had to think a while to specify the detail. 'She makes me laugh, which is unusual. But I like it. I've never met anyone like her before. She makes me think differently—'

'Stop, you romantic bollix. I'm misting up. How the fuck do you fucking *feel* about her, man?' I did not know how to answer the question. 'You know, feelings? Fuck me, you're a fucking android, man. Like when you want to fucking eat something, you *feel* hungry.'

'I-I like her.'

He sighed. He was probably tired. Mark did not get much sleep. He said, 'Fuck's sake. Look, the Fucking Penetrators are jiving the U tonight. Why don't you come?'

'The U?'

'The Student Fucking Union.'

I said, 'Oh, OK. What time?'

'Man, you need to fucking chill.' I was not sure what he meant by that. I could take off my jumper, but then I would be too cold. 'Any fucking time. And wear my leather jacket.'

After that, I was even more confused than before (note: although I hadn't thought that possible). I was sure Mark administered sound advice; I just couldn't figure it out.

But I didn't want to make the same mistake with Lara as last time. I resolved to go to the Student Union, because she had asked me to.

Usually I paid no attention to my clothing, but that evening I considered it carefully. There wasn't much to choose from, but it took a disproportionate amount of time. In the end, I wore: 1) Mark's black leather jacket; 2) my best brown corduroys; 3) my trainers (note: I had no other shoes).

I looked all right.

I'd never been to the Student Union. It was full of students who vomited. (Note: even though the library was also full of students, they did not generally vomit without warning.)

As I approached the building, the pulse of music hit the soles of my feet before my eardrums. When I opened the door, smoke poured out. It made me cough. By squinting, I established limited vision.

I had formulated a plan of action: 1) find Lara.

The equation was deceptively simple. In fact, there were layers of complexity within the task. For a start, in order to find Lara, I had to *find* her. I wasn't sure how to accomplish this with all the people around. The space had exceeded maximum capacity.

I put my shoulder to the crowd & pushed. The dense mass of humanity gradually yielded. Momentarily, I wondered if I would ever get out again. People jostled, pressed up against me. Somebody stuck his shiny, red face in mine. He said something I did not hear. (Note: I got the spit.)

At the far end of the Student Union, I saw Hymen Raider and the Fucking Penetrators. They were on a raised platform. Hymen Raider appeared to be eating his microphone. I waved to Mark, but he didn't see me.

I visually identified Julie in a group of people. They were adjacent to a speaker, which emitted a noise similar in effect to a prolonged sonic boom (note: this statement is hypothesis with no proof or accurate quantification).

Julie was sitting on a bench, talking to a couple having sex underneath it. Behind her, I saw some bright blue hair. From the available facts, I extrapolated that it belonged to Lara.

When I got closer, I noticed that the person on Lara's other side had his left hand inserted up her T-shirt. She didn't seem to have noticed there was a hand stuck up her T-shirt. However, when he started nibbling her face, I thought it improbable Lara would not notice that.

I felt like ripping his heart out of his mouth before stapling it shut (note: certain logistical problems with this plan included, but were not limited to, not having a stapler and having to locate his heart organ without any working knowledge of physiology).

My hands were shaking, so I closed them into fists.

Julie saw me when she tipped her head back to drink out of a bottle. She nudged Lara, who pushed the person off her face. Lara raised her eyebrows at Julie, who nodded in my direction. When Lara saw me, she smiled in a way that brightened the immediate vicinity (note: also, the smoke cleared momentarily).

Lara walked along the bench to reach me. She was only wearing a pair of tights under her T-shirt. She must have forgotten to put on her skirt.

She shouted, 'Hi!' A student pushed his face into mine. He had two black eyes. I wondered what had happened to him. Lara shouted, 'He's OK, Foetus.'

I wasn't sure whether I had heard her correctly. I shouted, 'What's his name?'

She shouted, 'I don't know. We call him Foetus,

because he looks like a giant foetus. Also, he doesn't talk.'

'Is he dumb?'

'No, just fucked in the head. He smoked a joint and then tried to study. We think it blew up his brain.'

'Who-who is he?'

'He's one of my evil henchmen. The other one's Bosco. Over there.' She pointed to someone with bright orange hair. It was bushy, looked like fur instead of hair.

'Why do you have evil henchmen?'

'They're good for moving and lifting.'

'Oh.'

The speakers emitted a screech of audio feedback. Then Mark's voice, but deeper, with an acoustic timbre.

'HOLD IT, WAIT. CUT THE FUCKING BASS, MAN. FOLKS, MAY I HAVE YOUR FUCKING ATTENTION PLEASE?'

Everybody in the Student Union fell silent (note: except for someone in the corner, who carried on smashing a chair against the wall). Lara looked at Mark. He winked & put out his fist & pointed at a spot on the ceiling with his thumb. I looked up, but didn't see anything except a patch of what looked like vomit.

'I WOULD LIKE TO DEDICATE THE NEXT SONG TO MY GOOD BUDDY, CONNELL, WHO IS ON A NOBLE QUEST TO SHAG THE BEAUTIFUL GODDESS, LARA CALLAGHAN. Shut the fuck up, man. THAT'S LARA THERE, FOLKS.' Lara smiled, waggled her fingers. 'LADIES AND GENTLEMEN, FUCKING GIVE IT UP FOR MY FUCKING MAN, CONNELL!'

Scattered applause followed the announcement.

E verything was black. Gradually, pinpricks of white grew out of the darkness. I realised I was looking at the sky. That implied I was horizontal. I checked. Yes, I felt the ground under me, hard & cold. My head appeared to be propped on something softer.

I shifted. Pain seized & squeezed the back of my skull.

'What—'

A voice said, 'Careful. Don't move for a while.'

I said, 'Lara?' I couldn't see her.

I felt cool, soft hands on my forehead. 'Yeah. You OK?'

'I'm – I'm not sure. I think so, although my head . . . I hope my brain isn't broken. Can you ask me something?'

Lara said, 'Ah. Um, OK. What is the difference between truth and illusion?'

'I-I have no idea. Can it be stated in mathematical terms? Is it relevant? To what? I don't – I've never—'

'Let's try something a bit easier. What is Pythagoras's Theorem?'

'The square of the hypotenuse is equal to – no, too simple. Something else.'

'OK, how about the fundamental theorem of algebra?'

'States that every non-constant single variable polynomial with complex coefficients has at least one complex root. Right?'

'No idea. Sounds good, though.'

I had a terrible thought. 'What if I'm wrong?'

'Could be disastrous: you might have to use a calculator. Can you sit up?'

My arms felt heavy. I managed to push myself into a sitting position. 'What happened?'

'My boyfriend lamped you one. Then you tumbled over and head-butted the speaker. Then the bouncers kicked you out.'

'Do you have a boyfriend?' I asked. Although she had referred to one, I wanted to confirm this.

'Yeah.'

'Why did he hit me?'

'I don't think he dug Mark telling the patrons of the Student Union you were going to shag me.'

'But that was a hypothetical construct.'

She said, 'I think he felt threatened.'

I said, 'I'm getting up now.' When I stood, my legs felt rubbery & shook slightly.

Lara said, 'By the way, you're banned from the Student Union for, like, for ever. Or at least until next week. Let's make like a tree and get out of here.'

'How does our departure relate to a tree?'

'It doesn't. It's what Biff in *Back to the Future* says. He gets it wrong, because the correct phrase is "make like a tree and leave". You know, "leave"? Like leaf?' That didn't make sense either, since 'leaf' is a noun, not a verb. Lara said, 'Tell you what, how about this: let's go.'

I nodded my head. It felt like it might fall off, so I was pleased when it stayed where it was. 'OK.'

Lara jumped on to a wall. Although the vertical plane adjacent to the path was low, on the other side, it dropped approximately two point three metres to a concrete walkway.

I said, 'Wh-what are you doing?'

'I'm walking the wall.'

'Why?'

'Because it's fun. And it's, like, a test of skill and balance and daring and it's exciting. And intrepid.'

'You might fall.'

'That's what makes it exciting and intrepid. Anyway, if I fall, you can save me,' she said, using my head to balance herself.

I failed to see the point of the exercise. However, I stayed close in a state of full alertness to save her.

We were heading in the direction of the Science Faculty, the Quad, or the river.

I asked, 'Where are we going?'

Lara said, 'Stop asking questions.'

'I only asked one.'

Lara said, 'I'm pre-empting others.' She jumped off the wall. I wanted to ask her why she spun round twice, but she had told me not to ask questions, so I didn't. 'So, I was surprised when I saw you in the Student Union.'

'But you said I should come down sometime—'

'Yeah, but that was, like, two months ago.'

'Oh,' I said. 'I wasn't aware there was a time limit.' I should have asked her about a validity period when she mentioned it in the canteen.

'What do you think of Gavin?'

'Who?'

'My boyfriend.'

'Well, he hit me.'

'Yeah, but before that.'

'Oh. Ah . . .' I hadn't talked to him, but I'd seen enough to summarise him accurately. 'He sucks.'

'You think?'

'He's a complete waste of complex molecular structure.'

'Oh,' said Lara. 'So you think he's nice?'

'Not even infinitesimally.'

'I know, I was joking. I could always dump him?'

I wasn't sure how to respond to this. I said, 'OK. We should find him so you can tell him. Where is he?'

'He got thrown out of the SU for starting a fight, so he went into town with Julie and the gang.'

We reached the Quad in the centre of the university. It was deserted. Lara lay down under one of the oak trees by the statue of UCCD's founder, Daniel O'Donnell.

The grass was dry & scratchy. I removed Mark's leather jacket, spread it on the ground.

I said, 'You can sit on this, if you like.'

Lara said, ' 'K.' She rolled on to the jacket. She lay on her front with her knees bent, her feet jiggling in the air.

She said, 'Chewing gum?'

'No thanks.'

'Take it. I need it for a project I'm working on.'

'What?'

'Just chew until further notice. Here, have two.'

'Oh. OK.'

Lara folded the remaining sticks into her own mouth. A strand of hair fell across her face. I reached down & tucked it behind her ear. When my conscious function caught up with the action, I snatched back my hand.

'Do you like me?' asked Lara.

'Yes.'

'How much?'

'I-I d-don't think there's anyone who could feel th-the way I feel about you. Maybe ever.' (Note: since that turned out to be prophetic, it would have been preferable had it been more articulate.)

Lara stared at the ground. It seemed like she was about to look up, & I did not want her to see me looking at her in case she thought I was a pervert. Then I sensed her looking at me. But when I checked, she was analysing some grass. I stared back at my feet, thought she looked at me again. But her hair was all over her face when I glanced back at her.

She rolled on to her back with a soft sigh.

She said, 'Look at that.' Her voice was soft, but not sufficiently so to qualify as a whisper. I looked up, following her arm. The night was clear & cold, no cloud cover.

'You mean . . . just the stars? What about them?' They looked identical to the last time I checked.

'Aren't they beautiful?'

I said nothing. I didn't consider things in terms of 'beautiful' or 'ugly'. These are not useful concepts, having limited to negligible practical application.

Lara said, 'Look, they're twinkling at us.'

'It's called stellar scintillation. Atmospheric turbulence makes them appear to twinkle.'

'Doesn't it make you feel small and insignificant?'

'No. Did you know, even though you can see the light, some of those stars no longer exist?'

'What d'you mean?'

'Well, the nearest star to Earth – apart from the Sun – is four point three light years away. So the light from that star took four point three years to reach us. Some stars are so far away, it takes hundreds of years for the light to get here. Hundreds of years,' I emphasised. 'Many of those stars no longer exist, but we still see the light they once emitted.'

'Wow. So it's kind of like looking back in time?'

'Yeah, I guess.'

I had never thought of it in those terms. I realised

Lara was really smart. Not in the same way I was; different. She didn't know as much as me, but when we discussed things, she made connections that I didn't. My brain was logical and thorough, but it followed a given route at a slower speed.

Lara put her head on my stomach. I was afraid if I breathed too hard she might remove it, so I rationed my intake of oxygen.

She said, 'Do you ever wonder where you'll be in five years?'

'Not really. After I graduate, I'll get a job, earn lots of money.'

'Oh.' Lara's head jerked and she looked up at me sharply. 'You want to be rich.'

'Not especially. My parents, they never had much. I always had a school uniform, books, food; but my parents never went on holiday. Mam wears the same clothes she's had for years. Da worked double shifts so I could come here.' I shrugged. 'I don't want them to live like that any more – but it's more than that. I owe them.'

'Money isn't everything.'

I pulled on a blade of grass. 'Only when you don't have it.'

Lara didn't say anything for a while, then, 'Do you ever wonder whether things will work out the way you expect them to?'

'Not really. I decide what I want, then formulate a plan to get it.'

'You're so sure of yourself. All I really know is that I want to get out of this place.'

'What, the Quad?'

'No, out of Ireland. I want to go somewhere and learn about other people. If I stay here, I'm scared I'll get stuck and never leave. Except for Lanzarote once a year, and a weekend in Cork.'

'Would that be bad?'

'Yes.' After a short silence, she said, 'Nothing bothers you, does it? Don't you worry?'

'About what?'

'Anything? Everything?'

I said, 'Worrying has no measurable effect on an outcome. It serves no purpose, apart from making you feel bad.'

'I worry all the time. About what I want to do with my life, about making a difference, about not *mattering*. People say – usually uncles and aunts and my mother – they say these are the best years of my life. I am so terrified the rest of my life will be crap.'

I wasn't sure how to respond to that, so I said nothing.

She continued, 'I worry about dying. I mean, humans are so ... so vital. You know? I have all these thoughts and feelings. I can't imagine not *being*. Experiencing only darkness.'

'You wouldn't experience anything. You'd be dead.'

'But that's the thing. How can there be nothing?'

'Before you were born, there was nothing. Why is it so difficult to consider you return to nothing?'

Lara pulled the corners of her mouth down. 'I never thought about it like that.'

We had been there for so long, dew had settled on our exposed skin. Our faces & hands felt clammy. (note: I can't say whether Lara's face and hands felt clammy to her, but they looked shiny.)

Lara asked, 'Is this the usual way you attract women?'

I said, 'What do you mean?' I was still holding my breath & was starting to feel light in the head.

'Kind of topple into them sideways and hope they notice you?'

That struck me as funny & I laughed. 'I don't know. I've never tried to attract a woman before.'

'Well, you suck at it.'

'Sorry. Mark told me—'

'Your friend from the band, yeah?'

I nodded. 'Yes. He told me to be myself. But I didn't think you would like me as myself. I am quite intense and often say the wrong thing.'

'That is such a crap thing to tell someone: be yourself. I mean, who the hell is that?'

'Precisely. I disregarded the advice. It wasn't useful.'

'How's your chewing gum going?'

'What do you mean?'

'Give it here.' Lara sat up, held her hand under my nose.

I spat involuntarily. Lara picked the chewed wad out of her hand, put it in her mouth.

I said, 'Why didn't you take a fresh piece of chewing gum?'

'Well, because there's none left. But mainly because that wouldn't serve the higher purpose. Give me a leg up.'

'What?' It often seemed to me that Lara spoke another dialect of English, one for which I had no dictionary.

Lara said, 'I'm going to have a little chat with our glorious founder.' She seemed to be indicating the statue standing in the centre of the Quad. 'I need a lift.'

'I-I don't—'

'Link your fingers, like this—' Lara demonstrated. 'Hold them here. I'm going to put my foot on them, like a stirrup? Now, give me a boost. Cool. Is it OK if I stand on your head?'

'Oh, ah, all right.'

She was heavier than she looked (I had approximated her weight at fifty-seven kilograms according to height, body mass & average bone density, but, in fact, it was closer to fifty-nine kilograms. I nearly toppled over when she pushed off. When I looked up, she was sitting on the edge of the plinth. Daniel O'Donnell towered above her, frowning for posterity.

I said, 'What are you doing?'

She said, 'Shh! Keep a lookout', in a loud whisper. It sounded like a shout in the deserted quad. I'm not sure whether the echo around the square was real or my imagination (note: in the interests of full disclosure, please note that I do not possess much imagination).

Lara broke into giggles.

I said, 'Be careful!' I was laughing too. I had no idea why.

Lara spat out the chewing gum. She placed it halfway up the statue, smoothed it out with her thumb. When I looked closer at that spot, I saw something I hadn't noticed before.

'Get me down!' whispered Lara, still giggling. She slithered off the edge of the plinth into my arms. Her hair brushed against my jaw. It was soft & tickly. It smelled lovely, like coconut & petrol.

She said, 'What do you think of Danny's codpiece?'

I stared. 'You-you mean the light pink—'

'Yeah.'

'That-that's you?'

'Thirty-six packets of Juicy Fruit and counting.'

'But why?'

'Why not? Don't you think Danny deserves a costume change every now and then? Anyway, look at him.' I looked. 'Fine figure of a man, but shamefully misrepresented in the lunchbox department. I feel it my duty to redress the oversight.'

Lara asked me to walk her back to her lodgings. I accompanied her to the Students' Residence, because that's where she lived. At the doorstep, Lara swung out of a railing by one arm.

She said, 'You got Professor Quealy tomorrow, yeah? D'you want to pick me up?'

'You mean on my bicycle?'

'Well, OK. Or, maybe we can walk over together?'

'That would be nice.'

She kissed me lightly on the mouth, but she didn't invite me in. I thought that was strange. (Note: I asked Mark about it later. He said it was fucking rude & it was fucking obvious she was fucking me around.)

I was concerned about the logistics of transporting a fifty-nine-kilogram human on my bicycle. On the rare occasions I'd observed two people on a bicycle around campus, the passenger sat on the crossbar. However, the crossbar on my bicycle was at an acute angle, since it was my mam's, i.e., if Lara sat on it, she would slide down and become wedged in my pelvis, which was likely to impede propulsion.

I decided she could sit on the seat & I could pedal standing up. The following morning I got up early & lashed a bag of potatoes to the saddle to practise. The potatoes fell off twice. However, Lara was more animate than a bag of potatoes. If I instructed her to hold my waist in addition to lashing her to the saddle, theoretically she would be stable enough for conveyance.

When I arrived at the Students' Residence, Lara

invited me in for a cup of tea & some crisps. (The crisps were soft & a bit chewy.)

The flat Lara shared with Julie was warm & humid. It smelled of fresh, warm hair, not sweaty socks & burnt toast like mine. It was covered in bits of underwear, shoes & tiny pots of coloured powders. One wall was the same colour as egg yolk. It was my first experience of that colour reproduced in emulsion. It was nice.

Lara was dressed, but Julie came into the kitchen in a pair of underpants & a vest.

Julie said, 'What the fuck is *he* doing here?'

I said, 'Who, me? I came to collect Lara.'

She said, 'I wasn't asking *you*.'

I said, 'You didn't specifically address the question to anyone. In any case, the purpose of positing a question is to obtain an answer. It's irrelevant who supplies it.'

Julie's mouth dropped open. She said, 'What the fuck are you laughing at?'

Was I laughing? I thought it unlikely that I was. 'I'm not—'

'Not *you*, idiot!'

Lara giggled, said, 'We're gonna blow this joint. See you later, Jules.'

After that, I collected Lara every Wednesday morning. Then I started collecting her on other mornings. Sometimes we met at the canteen to eat lunch. After a while, we met there for snacks, too.

Lara was still going out with Gavin, I couldn't understand why. He said horrible things about her, without even waiting until she couldn't hear; he talked loudly for someone so profoundly uninteresting; & he had no discernible positive attributes.

(Note: the preceding statement is inherently biased. In the interests of full disclosure, & also objectivism/ fairness, I should state that Gavin could fart a range of tunes and had a Renault the colour of a rotten plum.)

I was pleased when Lara told me they'd split up, but not when she said she was going out with someone called Smiffy.

One bank holiday weekend, Lara & I went to Limerick together. There were no seats (note: because the train was full, not because of a lack of seats). We sat on our bags between two carriages. The train smelled of industrial hand soap & Tayto crisps. We shared a cup of tea from the buffet car. Lara fell asleep with her head on my shoulder. That was nice.

It was Lara's first trip home since term started.

I asked her why she didn't go home more often.

'Too much hassle,' she said, & shrugged.

That didn't seem like a valid rationale to me. It wasn't that hassle-centric to pack a bag & catch a train or bus. Also, the degree of hassle was offset against seeing your mam & getting your laundry done.

I knew if I pointed this out, Lara would say it wasn't as simple as that, or she would redefine the word 'hassle', or she would say I didn't understand. (Note: there were lots of things about Lara that I didn't understand.)

That weekend, Lara came to my house. I was upstairs in Mam's wardrobe. I was aware of muffled voices in the hall. However, I was adept at tuning out extraneous noise so it didn't register. Until I heard her voice outside the wardrobe door, saying: 'Conn?'

I didn't want her to know I was in Mam's wardrobe. However, since she was right outside, I didn't see how I could avoid it. I thought if I said nothing, she might go away. Then I could come out and pretend I had been somewhere else, e.g., under the bed or behind the curtain or something. Unfortunately, somebody must have told her where I was, because the door rattled & then opened. Lara's head appeared in the rectangle of light.

Lara grinned, said, 'What the fuck?'

When I stood up, I got tangled in one of Mam's dresses.

Lara poked her head in; said, 'You *study* in here?'

My face felt abnormally hot.

I said, 'Yeah. There's nowhere for me to— my nan lives with us, so I sleep in the laundry room. I had nowhere to study, so Da constructed a desk and shelves and installed them in here.'

'This is *way* cool!' Lara peered past me. The desk lamp illuminated the rows of textbooks, jars full of pens & rulers, my ancient furry pencil case & Mam's Sunday frock. I unwound a sleeve from around my neck.

'I sometimes have to rearrange Mam's shoes to fit in. W-would you – would you like to . . . go somewhere else? You could come downstairs. Mam probably has something to eat.'

I was relieved when she said, 'Cool!'

Our kitchen was where my family spent most time. The Aga in the corner heated the entire house.

Da was reading a newspaper spread across the kitchen table, mouthing the words silently. When I came in with Lara, he raised the paper & concealed himself behind it.

Mam was at the kitchen bench, her back to us. I said, 'Mam, is there anything to eat?'

Mam said in her soft voice, 'Don't you have an

unnatural instinct for food? There'll be some scones ready soon, if you can bear to wait.'

Nan spent most of the time dozing in her chair next to the Aga. Her head jerked at the sound of Mam's voice. My nan was nice. She had false teeth and whiskers.

She said, 'So ya finally brought home a girl!' She pronounced it 'gerril'.

Lara stopped tugging her sleeves, so she could use her arms to pull her hair all over her face.

Mam turned, said, 'Are you going to introduce your friend, Connell?' She had a smudge of flour on her forehead.

I said, 'Oh, OK. This is Lara.'

Mam smiled, wiped her hands on her apron, took one of Lara's. She said, 'I'm Maggie.'

'Hey, ah, good afternoon, Mrs – Mrs O'Neill.'

I said, 'That's Da. The man at the table.' Da lowered the paper, said, 'Now', & raised it again.

'And that's Nan.'

Nan continued, 'When I was your age, I was a holy terror with the lads. Priest used to go around thrashin' the ditches with a hurley, to roust courtin' couples. I was always last out, stuck onta some lad's face. He used to say, "Margaret Clark, you will roast in hell until you are crisp to the end of temerity."'

Mam said, 'Ma, leave off the poor child.' To Lara, 'Don't mind her—'

'Don't mind her? I'll thank ye to be keeping a civil tongue in your head. I'm not horse food yet.' She waved her hip flask at Lara. 'What was yer name again? Maura, did ye say?'

Lara said, 'No, Lara—'

'Speak up, girl.'

'Lara—'

Nan said, 'What class of a name is that?'

Lara explained, 'She was the tragic heroine in *Doctor Zhivago*.'

'Doctor who?'

'*Doctor Zhivago*. The movie.'

'Tragic heroine, ye say? What happened to her?'

'She died of a broken heart, I think.'

'I hear that's a pure terrible way to go.'

'Oh, I think so too! Lots of writhing around and vomiting.'

Nan threw back her head, emitted a cackle. I think she liked Lara.

Da gave the paper a rustle. 'See here, now. Dan Quayle tried to put an "e" at the end of potato. Fancy not knowing how to spell potato! It's pure shocking to think a feckin' eejit like that is the Vice-President of America.'

Mam said, 'Aye.' Nobody else was listening to him, really, & I was distracted by the smell of baking scones filling the kitchen, which made my mouth generate excessive volumes of saliva.

Nan said, 'Come here so I can I look at ye, girl.'

Lara approached slowly. When she was close enough, Nan gripped her wrist, pulled her close, studied her. She observed, 'Fine child-bearing hips.'

Lara said, 'They're useful for walking too.'

'What colour is that for a head of hair?'

'Blue.'

'D'ye think that colour would suit me?'

Mam said, 'Sure, wouldn't you be only gorgeous with blue hair?'

Da said, 'The lads would come flocking. We'd have to get the priest around to bate them off you again.' Then he hid behind the paper once more, which shook silently.

'Aren't you a right pair of smarty pantses? It's easy to make fun of a poor, defenceless widda—'

'Defenceless?' said Da, putting aside the paper again. 'The woman whose tongue – whose tongue should be – should be classified as a lethal weapon? If you're a poor, defenceless widow, I'm a – a Russian capitalist!'

Even I smiled thinking about Nan's description of herself as a poor, defenceless widow.

Nan said to me, 'What are you smirkin' about?' Then she said to Lara, 'Are ye a bit short?'

Lara said, 'For what?'

Mam pulled out a chair at the table. 'Paddy, will you ever put down that paper. Lara. What a beautiful name.' She cupped Lara's cheek in one hand. 'It suits you. Beautiful girl.' Lara stared at my mother. 'Come and sit over here, pet. Will you have a cup of tea and a scone?'

'That would be lovely, Mrs O'Neill. Thank you.'

Mam put her hands on her hips & said, 'Paddy, will you ever come out from behind that paper.'

Da lowered the paper, slowly rearranged & folded it, then placed it square with the table edge. Then he said, 'Well, now.'

He rapped his fingertips on the table; opened his mouth, took a breath, released it again; crossed his arms, looked at the ceiling. Eventually, he took another breath, leaned forward.

He said, 'Nice weather.'

Lara responded, 'Yes, Mr O'Neill.'

He started tapping his finger again. Mam brought over a tray full of tea & scones, making a detour by Nan.

'I think Conn takes after my Paddy. Full of chat, the pair of them.'

Da grunted, reached for the newspaper. Mam got it first, placed it on the mantelpiece beyond his reach.

Da said, 'I'm persecuted in me own home.'

Mam said, 'How are you getting on up in the college, Lara?'

I didn't listen much, because Lara had already told me most of what she said to Mam. Instead, I watched Lara play with her teacup. She fingered the chip in the rim, rubbed her thumb over the porcelain.

From the corner, Nan periodically roared, 'Speak up!'

Then Mam asked Lara how she met me. Of course, I already knew about that too. However, I did learn that when Lara met me, she thought I was handsome & clever (note: although she didn't actually say that; she was just agreeing with Mam).

Da rustled loudly, said, 'Will ya look at that.'

Mam said to Lara, 'Buried in the newspaper again.' She frowned momentarily, but then she laughed.

Da said, 'Woman here, thrown in the jail for drowning two of her children in a well.'

Mam shook her head. 'Can you imagine? I don't understand how . . . If anyone hurt my Conn, I would destroy them. I would fight to the death – and you can be sure I'd take them with me.'

Mam's voice didn't change, but I knew she meant it.

I said, 'Lara, your eyes have gone all watery.'

'She has something in her eye,' said Mam, stepping in front of her. 'I'll bring you to the bathroom, pet.' She put her arm round Lara.

As she led Lara from the room, I heard Mam say, 'Men. They don't understand a thing. Come here, now. Tell me what's ailing you, pet.'

They did not return for fourteen minutes. Da stayed

behind the paper, grunting now & then. Sometimes he rattled it. Nan snored beside the Aga.

When Lara returned with Mam, her face was splotched with red patches.

Lara said, 'I must go. I'm meeting some friends down in Minty Blake's.'

As Mam brought Lara's coat, she said, 'I'm so glad Connell knows you. He needs to get out more, have a bit of fun.'

Lara grinned, said, 'I'll see what I can do, Mrs O'Neill.'

Da said, 'I beg him to go out on the lash, but he won't. He's a good lad.'

I said, 'I have to study for a first.'

Mam said, 'We'd settle for a second honour degree, love.'

Da said, 'Can you not have a bit of fun *and* get a first?'

After that, whenever I went to Limerick, Lara came with me. I noticed she spent more time at my house than her own. I wondered why she never invited me to meet her parents.

Lara broke up with Smiffy & started seeing Niall.

My digital clock read twelve minutes past two. I was in bed, so I deduced it was a.m., not p.m. I wondered why I was awake. Mark might have woken me. Sometimes he smashed bottles in the living room.

I didn't feel hungry or thirsty, but since I was awake, I decided to get a snack.

When I went into the hallway I heard the hammering on the door.

It was Lara. She had watery black streaks under her eyes.

'It's Niall. He's – he's – he's –' I couldn't make out the rest because she was crying too hard, but it sounded like: 'Hee ung wuh wuh wuh bub.'

I hated her being so unhappy, but I didn't know what to say or do. Lara collapsed into the hall. My arms came round her as if pre-programmed.

I said, 'It's OK. It's OK. Why don't you come in, if you'd like? Or – or you can sit on the hall floor, if you prefer.'

She wanted to come in, so I half carried, half dragged her into the kitchen. She appeared to crumple into a chair. The kitchen bulb had exploded sixteen days earlier, so I opened the fridge for light.

Lara covered her face with her hands. She emitted noises like she was malfunctioning.

My nan believed all problems could be solved with tea: cut knees, broken utensils, global warfare, etc. Therefore, I put on the kettle to make some. As I put a cup in front of her, Lara smoothed back her hair, ran her fingers under her eyes.

I didn't want to ask her what was the matter in case it upset her again. Instead, I said: 'Did you know, no piece of paper can be folded in half more than seven times?'

She said, 'What?'

'The height and width of the paper required, along with the height of successive folds, grows exponentially. If it were possible to fold an average sheet of paper in half fifty times, it would be about a hundred million kilometres thick. That's two thirds of the distance between the sun and the earth.'

Lara stared at me for a couple of seconds, then started to laugh. This surprised me, but it was better than her crying. Then I realised she was crying again.

I mumbled, 'Sorry.' I rotated my cup of tea anticlockwise & back again.

'Niall and I broke up,' said Lara. 'He cheated on me.'

I said, 'Oh.'

Lara said sharply, 'Did you *know*?'

'Not really. I have no concrete proof or circumstantial evidence.' Lara sighed. 'So y-you dumped him?'

'Try not to sound so pleased about it. No. He dumped me.'

That didn't make any sense at all.

She whispered, 'Why?'

'Wh-why what?'

Tears tracked down her face, dripped off her chin. 'Why do my boyfriends always do this?'

'Because you choose them.'

'*Pardon?*'

I said, uncertainly, 'You choose that type of person', because although she had asked, she reacted in a manner indicating she didn't want to hear the answer.

'I don't – they choose me.'

'Yes. But by not telling them to get lost, you effectively choose them.'

'But that's . . . that's mad. Why would I – why would I choose guys who cheat on me?'

'I don't know, but you do. You're like a moth. They have antennae – you know?'.

Lara stared at me, shook her head.

'Antennae are insect feelers, to sense smell, noise, vibrations in the air.' I extended my arms by my head to demonstrate what antennae look like. 'Not as big as my arms, obviously; but some of them have antennae which are longer than their bodies. Pheromones released by the female Cecropia moth can be detected by a male over eleven kilometres away. It's extraordinary. Nobody knows quite how they do it, whether—'

'Wait, wait, wait, reverse back up the hill there. What have insects got to do with me?'

'Yes, well – it's like you have idiot antennae. If there were just one single, finely calibrated, elite idiot in the whole of Ireland, you would detect him.'

Lara stared at me for a moment with her mouth open. Then she emitted a long, quivering wail. It sent chills down my back. Generally, I didn't inspire such extreme responses.

'No, no, no!' I said. I kind of patted her head. 'I'm sorry, Lara. Lara, Lara, I'm – I'm sorry. Look, I know I say the wrong thing – most of the time, not just now. But – just – I just want you to know that I really like you & – & if I ever say anything that upsets you, you should just ignore it. Because I don't – I don't mean it.'

After a while she grew quiet again.

She said, 'You are right, you know.'

'I might be wrong,' I said doubtfully. 'Perhaps I was mistaken. It's rare, but it does occasionally happen.'

She moved her mouth as if she was smiling, but it didn't look like a real smile. 'Are *you* an idiot?'

'No,' I said. 'If I were going out with you, I would treat you like – like something special.'

Lara's eyes released another flow of tears down either cheek. She swallowed.

'Maybe you should have some sleep,' I said. 'Why don't you— you can stay over. I will lie on the floor and you can have my bed. I w-w-warmed it up for you.'

'Was that a joke, Conn O'Neill?'

'Maybe?'

She said, 'I liked it.' This time she really did smile.

'Do you have anything I can wear?'

'Ah – you mean, socks and trousers? Or—'

'Like a T-shirt?'

'Oh! Yes, yes of course. I'll – wait here a minute.'

There was no wardrobe in my bedroom, so I stored my clothes in a box. Mam had washed my three T-shirts the previous weekend & I'd only worn one since. I picked out the Spiderman T-shirt, because it was the one with the least holes.

Back in the kitchen, I said, 'Here.'

'Great T-shirt.'

'Thanks,' I said. Nobody had ever complimented my T-shirt before. It was faded & too small for me. 'You can use my toothbrush, if you like. It's the one with no bristles. In the bathroom. And – and there's no soap or shampoo, only Fairy Liquid.'

Then we had an argument about who would sleep on the floor, because we both wanted to. More accurately, we didn't want the other to have to sleep on the floor.

'Why don't we share your bed?' asked Lara.

I didn't want to take advantage of her, but thought it must be OK if Lara suggested it. The thought of being that close to her made me feel hot & cold at the same time. A whole five hours pressed up against Lara . . .

A whole five hours trying not to press up against Lara, I corrected myself.

'Oh,' said Lara, when she saw my bed. 'I didn't realise it was that . . . small.'

'Why don't I—'

'I'm not that fat. Are you?'

'Um—' I was not sure how fat she meant. But I thought the correct answer was, 'No.'

Lara went into the bathroom to change. I straightened

the bedclothes & restacked my Vector Mechanics textbooks. Lara was gone so long I fell asleep in the chair.

When she returned, Lara stood on one leg and asked, 'Which side do you sleep on?'

'Oh – ah – what? The bed? Any. Which do you prefer?'

She shrugged & climbed into the side nearest the door. (Note: if you stood at the bottom of the bed looking towards the head, it was the right-hand side.)

I got in the other side, under the duvet but on top of the sheet. That way, there was a barrier between us & I couldn't accidentally have sex with her during the night.

Then I had to get up again to turn off the light.

When I returned, I was careful not to touch Lara. I lay on my back with my arms crossed & tried not to make any noise. Instead, I listened to Lara breathing. She was very quiet. After a while, I got an itch in my throat. I didn't want to cough in case it disturbed her.

'Conn,' said Lara's voice. It sounded loud in the darkness.

'Oh, ah. Me?'

'Yes. Could you – would you mind putting your arm round me?'

I said, 'Oh, OK.' I wanted to accept the offer quickly because I thought Lara might change her mind. I moved carefully, though, so that I didn't hit her. I thought that was a possibility because I couldn't see anything (note: it was dark & I wasn't wearing my glasses).

I felt her head lift & settle on my shoulder. Her hair tickled my cheek.

She said, 'You're my best friend.'

Then she fell asleep.

I wanted to stay awake because it was nice lying there holding her. However, I must have fallen asleep, because

I woke at six twenty-nine hours. Parts of my arm felt numb & other parts prickly, but I didn't mind at all.

Carefully, so as not to disturb her, I looked down at Lara. All I could see was lots of blue hair, like a small, furry, blue animal. Possibly a tree sloth or a hairy, blue frog. Her eyelashes fanned out against the soft curve of her cheek.

Lara stirred & I froze. She stretched & moaned softly. Then she raised her head & when she saw me, she smiled.

She said, 'Good morning.'

I leaped out of bed. My arm was stuck under Lara, but when I pulled it came free so suddenly I stumbled into the bookcase. It loomed forward.

I steadied the bookcase, mumbled, 'Morning. I'm getting up. Well, technically I am up, I suppose. You can stay here, if you like. Or you don't have to, if you don't want to.'

Lara yawned. 'You have a terrific body. Seriously unexpected.'

I grabbed the Aran sweater my mam had knitted me off the chair & pulled it on as I went to the door. This was the primary (but not exclusive) reason I ran headfirst into the door.

Lara said, 'Where are you going?'

'I – I thought I'd put the kettle on because you might like a cup of tea or coffee or even just hot water. My nan drinks hot water in the mornings with a slice of lemon. We don't have any lemon though—'

'You could always just ask me if I wanted something.'

'Oh. Yes. OK. Do you want something?'

'Have you any pineapple juice?'

'No.'

'Shame. I like pineapple juice. How about toast?'

'No, b-but we have some bread. And a toaster. So I could make some.' I looked at her a moment before escaping to the kitchen.

I think she went to the bathroom, because I heard the shower. When she came into the kitchen, she looked different. Her eyes seemed bigger than normal. I think the effect was due to her washing off all the black stuff.

'I have a lecture,' I said. 'In a while. You can make tea for yourself. I'll put the kettle on. If you see a strange person, that's Mark. But he shouldn't be up for another two or three days.'

'OK.'

'I have to go.' I hovered in the kitchen doorway. 'I w-want to ask you something,' I said. 'You can say no. Or yes. It's not an open question, so you can respond yes or no, or it would be OK if you wanted to provide supple-mentary information. Obviously, I would prefer it if you said yes. Well, not obviously to you, because you don't know what the question is yet. But I won't be upset if you say no—'

'Conn!'

'Yes?'

'Ask me.'

'W-w-will you go out with me?' I asked. Even though I wanted to, I couldn't look at her. Instead, I peeled a strip of paint off the doorframe. 'I w-w-would r-really like to be your b-b-boyfriend. I've considered it in depth. I would have less time for study, but I think I can work that out. And you are distracting, but that's unlikely to change much—'

'There don't seem to be any advantages to going out with me.'

'Oh there are! I mean, I would be with you. That – that's only one advantage and mightn't seem like much measured against all the disadvantages. But it's a really big one.'

'I'm flattered – well, a little bit flattered. But Conn, you're not my type.'

I said, 'I don't mind.'

'I'm not really sure I should be with anyone at the moment.'

'That's OK, I'll wait. But, could you try not to go out with anyone else in the meantime?'

Lara smiled, then she moved close & looked up at me.

'Can I check something?' she asked.

'What?'

She put her hand on my neck. Her grip was similar to a stranglehold, so I kept an eye on my windpipe (note: not literally, obviously). Her touch was firm but gentle.

'What are you doing?'

'Shh.'

When she raised up on her toes, I lowered my head instinctively (note: this is the first record of instinctive action in my life).

Lara touched my mouth with hers. All my senses engaged at once, focused at that point. Lara's lips were soft & tasted like warm vanilla. When she pulled away, I felt dizzy.

She murmured, 'Thought I'd do a compatibility test.' She didn't step away. Her hand was on my chest. It felt hotter than the maximum internal temperature sustainable by the human body without passing out or spontaneously combusting. It also had the effect of making my heart beat painfully fast.

I didn't appear to have any breath, so when I spoke, it

came out in a whisper. 'You didn't take a large enough sample for a conclusive result.'

'Is that right? You think we should try again?'

'Well, in order to obtain an accurate representative sample, we should repeat the test randomly and frequently for an indefinite but extended period of time.'

'Maybe we should try it without the tongue?'

'OK.'

I hunched over because I didn't want Lara to notice that my boxer shorts were doing a poor job. But then Lara moved against me & I was not conscious of anything else.

I was much taller than her. Although I was doubled over, it was still possible to maintain full facial & upper-body contact. But as I reversed again, I felt the kitchen wall at my back & realised I had nowhere else to go.

When I straightened up, Lara pressed all of her body against me. I still had her head in one hand, but I ran my other down her back & held her against me. She moaned &, after that, I was not aware of my actions being prompted by conscious will.

I don't know why we broke apart, because – I'm not sure about Lara – I could have kissed her all day (note: possibly longer).

She gasped, 'Was that conclusive?'

I said, 'I think so.' My breath was also short & fast. 'I was satisfied with the outcome.'

'Me too.'

5

I was not certain whether we were going out or not. Lara hadn't amended her response to my formal request for boyfriend status three months previously. However, I thought we might be because: a) we kissed on a regular/frequent basis; b) she wasn't seeing anyone else; & c) I was happy.

'Happy' was another original concept for me. I've never been good at quantifying emotions. Previously, I hadn't been unhappy. But when I was with Lara & talking to her & kissing her, I was actively happy.

One night, I came awake suddenly.

I mumbled, 'Limit as x approaches infinity.'

It felt as if something heavy had struck me. It also felt like time for a midnight snack. I pushed back the bedclothes. The light clicked on, I screamed.

'Lara! How – how did you get in?'

In a loud whisper, she said, 'Bathroom window. It was open.' She crawled into bed beside me. Her breath contained a large trace of alcohol, most likely peach schnapps or Bacardi breezer. 'Conn, listen. *We need to talk.*'

Suddenly I was wide awake and fully alert. Lara wanted to talk? In the middle of the night? Those words in that specific combination had never been addressed to me before, but Mark had told me about The Relationship Talk. I sat upright.

The Relationship Talk inferred that we were technically 'going out', although evidently not for much longer. I wished I'd known we were going out. I might have valued the relationship more while it had lasted. Perhaps not being aware that we had been going out might make the break-up less painful.

I said, 'Lara, what's wrong? Are you OK?'

'Are you awake?'

'Yes. What is it? What do you want to talk about?'

'Oh, I don't know. You pick a subject!' she giggled drunkenly.

'Wh-what?'

'How about airplanes? Or – I know! We could talk about those rubbish bins made out of elephants' feet. I brought you a present.'

'Oh. Where is it? What is it?'

'Guess!'

'Er. A rubbish bin made out of an elephant's foot?'

'No. A traffic light. Had to leave it outside, though. Couldn't get it through the bathroom window. It's bigger than it looks.'

'How can it be bigger than it looks?'

'We don't have to talk. I know! We could sing instead? Express ourselves via the medium of song. I read that in . . . somewhere.' She performed a medley of the singer Bruce Springsteen's greatest hits, then segued into a challenging instrumental. 'So, what'll we do now?'

'How about sleep?'

'Cool!'

Eleven seconds later, Lara was snoring softly.

Lara had an exceptionally low boredom threshold (note: except where trivia related to popular culture was concerned). Her person was in constant motion, like a cartoon character, e.g., a rodent equipped with a jetpack. She was always tapping a pen, and/or ticking her fingernails, and/or winding her hair around a pencil, and/or making pellets out of tissue paper. Even when she sat, both legs jiggled as if charged with a thousand volts of electricity.

Regardless of the whim that inspired it, once Lara made a decision she was absolutely, wholly committed – & fearless. She had only one speed: full-throttle Mach 3.

Whenever there was a minor explosion on campus, or a dorm room and its contents wrapped in tin foil, or the disappearance of Professor Quealy's personal items, it was a safe bet that Lara was the instigator and/or master strategist.

When I wasn't in the library, or doing practicals, or working at Murphy's, Lara pressed me into reluctant service as a technical advisor and/or tactical consultant for her schemes. In a way, it was exciting because my life was quite boring, i.e., not much happened apart from lectures, study, eating, working & sleeping.

However, Lara moved on to bigger challenges involving greater levels of complexity and/or technical difficulty. It was a natural progression, in a manner similar to graduating from cigarettes to cocaine, culminating in our being arrested by the police.

I had postponed my Construction Theories project for the third night in a row to meet Lara at the Student Union. (Note: Lara had devised a disguise to get me past the bouncers: fake moustache & tinted glasses. She said I looked like a drug smuggler circa 1970.)

As we left, Lara's blood–alcohol ratio was elevated.

She whispered, 'Look!', & pointed to a bus parked at the stop outside the Student Union.

'The-the bus?' I whispered back. This was one of her tactics for sucking me into schemes, so I resolved to talk normally.

Without moving her mouth, Lara said, 'The door's open.'

'Come on, I'll walk you home.'

'Just a minute. I've never been in a bus without a driver. Have you?'

'What? Been in a bus without . . . but—'

I was perplexed. Lara lived in Flat four, Building eight of the Students' Residence, which was within walking distance. We wouldn't have taken the bus even if: a) the driver had been present; & b) the bus took the route via College Park Road.

So I didn't understand why it made any difference whether the driver was present or not. Apart from the fact that, without a driver, the bus was stationary – which seemed obvious rather than extraordinary.

Lara disappeared inside the bus. I waited, hoped nobody would come along & ask what we were doing and/or attempt to pull off my fake moustache.

'Conn!' Lara's head appeared out the door. 'Guess what? The keys are in the ignition!'

'So what?'

'You can drive me home?'

'Lara, I can't—'

'Of course you can. It's a bus, isn't it? Its purpose is to convey passengers? In this instance, me.'

'But—'

'Get into the driver's seat.'

'Who, *me*?'

'Yes! Who else? Quick!'

'B-but I can't drive—'

'It's easy. Even Mum can do it. Come on!'

'Why me?'

'Well, I'm half pickled. It would be irresponsible.'

In the years since, my incredulity at partaking in this conspiracy has increased exponentially. The gear stick made crunching noises when I tried to operate it, so I left it in first gear. We were halfway up College Park Road, when I noticed red and blue lights flashing alternately in the rear-view mirror.

A police car overtook us, slowed down.

We might have got away with a reprimand for relocating a bus. Unfortunately, I hadn't practised braking & drove into the back of the police car. (Note: I know it sounds bad to severe, but it wasn't really. The back of the car was a bit dented. The momentum carried it up over the wall of the McGuinness Fountain, but it didn't explode or anything like that.)

Lara fell out the door of the bus, said, 'Weevening, Sergeant Garda Major. What appearsh t'be the prob blem?'

'Sergeant will do fine, miss. You have more than one problem.'

The policemen & I pulled the police car out of the fountain. It started on the first go. The sergeant pushed Lara into the back. Then the fatter fat policeman grabbed my head & pushed me in beside her.

I'd never been in a police car before. I thought it might be different, but it was much like any other car (note: apart from being relatively soggy. Also, the engine emitted a knocking noise.)

Being arrested effected a sobering influence on Lara.

She sat forward on the back seat, attempted to discuss the situation.

She said, 'Where are you taking us?'

The fat policeman, who was driving, said, 'James Street Police Station.'

'Are you going to charge us?'

The fatter fat policeman said, 'Too feckin' right.'

'With what?'

The fat policeman said, 'We'll start with the unauthorised taking of a bus. Throw in vandalism and damage to public property and – if you don't shut up – disturbing the peace.'

He had to stop the car on Finnehy Street to kick off the rear brake-light cover, which was trailing along the ground.

When he got back into the drivers' seat, Lara explained, 'We didn't steal the bus. It was abandoned at the side of the road. We were just bringing it back – weren't we, Conn? You might call it a-a public service.'

'You can tell that to the judge, miss.'

'Don't you have better things to do than to go around arresting students? Aren't there murderers and rapists marauding around our streets? What are you doing about that?'

The fat policeman said to the fatter policeman, 'God, I feckin' hate students.'

Lara said, 'Really? Why?'

'You go around hangin' offa lamp-posts and throwing rocks through windows and writing "dick" all over my car. And would it kill you to brush your feckin' hair once in a while? If it weren't for students, Dublin would be a crime-free zone.'

Lara said, reasonably, 'But if Dublin were a crime-free zone, you wouldn't have a job, would you?'

I whispered, 'Lara, don't talk to them any more.'

'It's OK, Conn. I'm charming them.'

'Your method is erroneous.'

I didn't feel well. Being in trouble with the police was something that happened in movies to people who were: a) rapists; and/or b) serial killers with shaved heads; and/or c) people falsely accused of murder.

I'd never considered I would grow up to be a criminal. I knew my parents would be sad. When I thought about that, I felt sad, too. I hoped I wouldn't have to spend much time in jail. Would it invalidate my scholarship? Would I even be allowed to continue my degree in jail? Would I have to get a tattoo?

I supposed that, as the driver of the bus, I was in more trouble than Lara. But I still worried about her, especially at the police station when she was taken into custody.

I was brought to another room, where I had to tell the fat policeman what had happened. I told the truth (note: except I said it was my idea to steal the bus, which was false).

Then the fat policeman went away with my belt & my shoes. I wondered why he wanted the belt because it was obviously too small for him. I hoped he only wanted to borrow it for a while, because it was the only one I had. Without it, I had to hold my trousers up with one hand or more.

The fatter policeman put me in a cell with no windows. The door made a loud noise when it closed. The grey walls were scratched with words & numbers in date format, single mattress on the floor, fluorescent light. There was no switch to turn it off.

Wherever Lara was, I hoped she was all right. I lay

down on the mattress & mentally recited Pi for a while until I fell asleep at the twenty-fourth nine.

I had no idea what time it was when there came a noise like a gunshot. The door swung open & the fatter policeman entered.

'Come on.'

He took me to a grey room. It was similar to my jail cell except that it had a large window, a light switch & a wall with a grille in it. A normal-sized policeman sat behind the grille.

As I entered, Lara was standing in front of the grille with a man & a woman. At least, I think it was Lara. She had her back to me, but she was the same height as Lara, & she had black hair with blue ends.

The man talked in a low voice to the normal-sized policeman behind the grille. The woman looked like Lara, I deduced she must be Mrs Callaghan. She appeared to be cross. (Note: she said, 'I am very disappointed in you, Lara', and didn't sound happy.)

The man said, 'Oh leave off, Dotty. Why do you always have to turn everything into a melodrama?' As he turned away, he opened his jacket & put what looked like a wallet in his inner pocket.

Lara turned towards me. Her eye shadow & mascara were all over her face. I don't know whether she saw me, because she didn't say hello. Then she left with the man & woman.

After that, my parents arrived: Mam, in her Sunday frock, Da in a suit I had never seen before. Mam held her handbag in front of her like a weapon. Da rotated his flat cap in his hands.

Outside, Mam said, 'Connell, pet, what happened?'

I mumbled, 'I perpetrated the unauthorised taking of a

bus and crashed it into a police car. That was an accident – crashing, I mean. Taking the bus was largely intentional.'

Da said, 'A bus! Fancy that. Good man, yerself. I've always wanted to steal one a dem. Was it a double-decker?'

Mam said, 'Whisht, Paddy.'

I said, 'I didn't mean it. I won't do it again.'

Mam said, 'Well, now. You can count on that, young man.'

Lara had once told me she was an anti-establishmentarian anarchist.

She said, 'I wanted to set up an Anti-Establishmentarian Anarchy Soc, except the nature of societies defeats the principle.'

The arrest made me realise Lara and I were incompatible. She was a disruptive influence. Although I liked that Lara was passionate and ferocious, it also made me anxious. Were I given to extremes (note: generally speaking, I'm not), I would have said it terrified me. A small part of me wished I were capable of that level of spontaneity, but a proportionately larger part acknowledged it was contradictory to my nature.

Therefore, I decided not to go out with Lara any more. Although I knew this conclusion was rational & logical, I felt very sad. I knew I should notify her that we were not going out any more, in case she wanted to get another boyfriend.

Instead, I avoided her. When I saw her on the campus, I concealed myself behind a column, a library shelf & my satchel (note: on different occasions, not all at once). One day, I met her coming out of Doyle Hall. I said, 'Hi', then ran away.

I couldn't decide what to do. I missed Lara, but I was also relieved. I had more time to study. There was less probability of being arrested. But the more time that passed, the more I missed her.

That's what I dislike about emotion. It changes all the time, therefore making it difficult to impossible to measure/quantify.

Three weeks & two days after the incident, Lara came to my flat at eight twenty-four.

She said, 'Here', & handed me a packet of Taytos Cheese & Onion crisps, a tub of pot noodles & a litre of milk.

I said, 'Thanks', & tucked the milk under my left arm.

'You've been ignoring me.'

'No, avoiding you. Although it may have a similar effect, it is fundamentally different—'

'But why? I mean, I'm really sorry about, you know, getting you arrested. It was an accident.'

'It wasn't an accident,' I corrected her. 'We stole a bus. The only accident was getting caught—'

'We only borrowed it. Anyway, I promise we won't steal another bus.'

'But it will be something else. Like covering Foetus's room in tin foil, or vandalising the maths lab. Lara, I'm not like you! I don't want to do things like that. I'm not suited to a life of crime—'

'Oh, and I am?'

'No! Although you have character traits suitable to a career as a cat burglar—'

'OK, look, sorry I bothered. Give me back my Taytos.' She took them. 'And the pot noodles –'

She tried to take the tub of noodles, but I held on. Generally I don't believe in intuition. Therefore, it must have been prelearned/pre-programmed instinct that told me Lara would no longer be my girlfriend if I released the noodles.

I said, 'Wait – wait a minute. These are my favourite flavour.'

'I know. That's why I got them.'

I attempted to get a better grip on the noodles, said, 'Lara, I can't do things like steal buses and stuff. You-you treat life like it is a big joke. I can't do that. If I don't achieve an A average, I will lose my scholarship. My parents would be – I've worked really hard for it. I can't go to the Student Union every night.'

Lara let go of the tub. 'OK.'

'OK?'

'Yeah, OK. Can I come in now?'

'Yes, please.'

I swung the door wider, she came into the hallway.

She said, 'Do you like my dress?'

It was very short, showed most of her legs. It had a swirly pattern. She was also wearing thick-soled shiny orange boots up to the tops of her legs. She looked like an alien enforcer I saw in a TV show once, called *Revenge of the Zombie Space Invaders*. Lara looked just like the heroine before she gets covered in liquefied yellow alien brain. (Note: the heroine didn't look much different after getting covered in liquefied yellow alien brain.)

'I like the geometric shapes,' I said. 'I suppose the overall effect is pleasing. It looks warm, which is the main thing.'

For several seconds, it seemed as if the world around us paused (note: more plausibly, this effect was due to a disruption in my perception of the time continuum).

Similarly, I can't describe the sequence of events that followed in their entirety. Somehow Lara was in my arms & I kissed her as long as I feasibly could without being equipped with gills.

'Woah!' said Mark's voice. 'That's fucking indecent.'

Lara pushed me away, wound her hair round her finger. She looked at me, then Mark.

Mark said, 'You Lara? Girl, you're a fucking fox. I'm Mark.' He shook her hand.

Lara said, 'Um yeah, we – we know each other. Well. We've, ah, we've met.'

Mark said, 'Really? Well, fucking A to meet you again. My man here's been like some fucking black, diseased cloud hanging over the fucking land. Has he told you he's fucking useless without you?'

'Er, no—'

'Well, he is, although if you held your breath you'd die of suffocation. Also, without you his fucking life isn't worth fucking living, and he's fucking mad about you. Jaffa Cake?'

Lara took my hand & pulled me towards my bedroom, said, 'No thanks. Maybe next time, yeah? Nice to meet you. Bye.'

She closed the door behind her, flung herself on my bed & said, 'Does Mark always wander around in the nip?'

'Not always. It depends on the ambient temperature, which, of course, is influenced by the season. Now that it's summer, he takes off his clothes a lot.'

'I see.' She peeled off her boots. 'Maybe we should follow his example?'

Suddenly it felt like my brain experienced a major malfunction. 'Wh-what are you doing?'

'Getting naked.' She unzipped her dress. Her skin was unfeasibly smooth.

'Did you – are you going to have a shower?'

'No.'

She crossed her arms, pulled her dress over her head. Her bra consisted of some sort of lacy substance. I wasn't sure why she wore one, because it didn't look like it supported her chest. She slid one strap down her arm, then the other.

Suddenly there seemed to be an oxygen deficiency in the room.

I said, 'Aren't you going to be cold?', although I was as hot as a polycrystalline silicon in a fluidised bed reactor microwave heating system.

'You're going to keep me warm. Here, take off your jumper.'

'Oh! You – you want to wear it?'

'No.' Lara slid her hands down my bare stomach.

'Hey!'

'Relax. It helps if both of us are undressed for this bit.' She undid my corduroys as she kissed me. Then she slipped her fingers down the front of my boxer shorts. 'How does that feel?'

'Quite – quite nice.'

'Not very nice?'

'Even b-better. Wh-what do I do?'

'Well, why don't you do whatever you want to?'

'What if I – if it's not right?'

'I'll tell you if you do something wrong, OK?'

I was doubtful. I wasn't sure what I wanted to do. But since Lara said it was OK, I picked her up & threw her on the bed. Lara seemed to like that a bit, so I tried some other things.

Lara said, 'Ow!'

'Sorry! Did I – did I hurt you?'

'Come back here at once! All right, try here. Oh yeah, that's right. Now, move like this.'

'Oh wow! Holy cow!'

'If it's – oh! – OK with you, would you – ooh! – mind not saying holy cow?'

'All right. This is really nice! Is – is that too fast?'

'No, not now. In fact, you could go faster.'

I was pleased about that, because I wasn't sure whether I could slow down even if she wanted me to.

After that, Lara & I studied instead of going to the Student Union, had sex instead of sleeping. It was great, although I was tired all the time.

Lara didn't hang out with her friends any more. This didn't surprise me, because her friends did not appear to like each other much. In many ways, they were like a collective parasite, or a mutating virus (note: except Foetus. He was nice, even though he didn't talk). They were largely comprised of losers, alcoholics, and/or computer studies students. They wore clothes that didn't fit & smelled strange. It appeared to be an organic group, because none of them stayed around very long (note: with the exception of Julie).

Then Lara stopped spending time with Julie, too. I was surprised, but I didn't mind. Julie was sulky & she touched me a lot, which made me uncomfortable. Once, Julie asked me if I wanted to go to Minty Blake's. When I said I'd check with Lara, her mouth touched my ear when she said, 'Lara doesn't need to know.'

I said no.

*

I was working an extra shift at the abattoir. That was good, because I could buy things for Lara. I got her caramel sundaes in BigBurger once I bought her a ticket to see *Groundhog Day* at the cinema.

I was also saving up to buy her a birthday present. The previous year, I got her a nice vase (note: Mark said girls like flowers, so I thought that was a good present). She was really happy when I gave it to her but unfortunately she lost it the next day.

This year, I wanted to give her something really special. When I consulted Mark, he suggested chocolate manufactured in the shape of a heart and/or stuffed animals, e.g., teddy bears. I couldn't understand why anyone would want those things. Additionally, Lara was scared of stuffed animals. I carefully considered the options, but I couldn't think of anything else.

One evening, on the way to Murphy's, I saw a charm bracelet in the window of Carmodys the jewellery shop. I noticed it because the silver links were in the shape of infinity symbols.

It was thirty pounds. With my salary from the abattoir (note: less, living expenses & an estimate for unforeseen expenses according to normal distribution), I calculated it would take me four months to earn enough money to pay for it. However, Lara's birthday was in July. I asked the supervisor for two more shifts. That way, I could afford it in two months.

When I gave the bracelet to Lara, she burst into tears. I thought she disliked it, but instead she said, 'No, no, I'm happy! It's so beautiful.'

I wanted to communicate the terms & conditions of the bracelet, so I said, 'I could only afford one charm, but you can add more. See? I can buy you a charm for birthdays and maybe Christmases. Although, it only fits six charms, so I'll have to think of another present in two and a half years.'

'Why did you get this?' She rubbed the charm repeatedly. It was a tiny ladybird, silver with red & black enamel.

I said, 'The first time we met, a ladybird landed on your hand. Remember?'

Instead of answering, she said, 'What if a cockroach had landed on my hand?'

I frowned. 'Well, I'm not certain. Carmodys didn't have any cockroach charms. But ladybirds are generally considered a portent of good fortune. Some people believe in that sort of stuff. Also, I liked it. Look: its legs move.'

She said, 'This is the best birthday present I've ever been given. I will never take it off.'

Sometimes I compared/contrasted how I felt now to a randomly recollected time in my past. My current reality was always better.

When I was with Lara, I was happy. People were often upset because of things I said, but Lara seemed to understand I didn't mean it. Sometimes I even said things that made her happy, which made me feel even happier.

Normally, the more you know about something, the more obvious it gets. However, it seemed Lara was more mysterious the more I knew her. That didn't make sense. However, I liked the things I did know about her. For example: the way she smelled, how she liked penguins, how she sang along to songs & made up the words she didn't know. I liked how, with her, I could just exist without her expecting me to be something else.

Most of all, I liked the way she looked at me. When she smiled, it made me feel warm inside, like I'd just drunk a cup of tea all at once.

Sometimes I stayed awake at night, lying with my arms round Lara, just listening to her breathe. That was pointless & illogical, since Lara's respiratory pattern was largely typical: in & out, as per normal. But everything about her seemed special, even that.

One weekend in Limerick, Lara invited me to her parents' house for dinner.

It was eleven point four kilometres from my parents' house to Castletroy. I calculated it would take thirty-four minutes to cycle that distance. I added twenty-two minutes to account for the light headwind, & another half an hour in case of a flat tyre or flash flood.

I arrived early, so I waited outside the gate. The Callaghan house was big. It was constructed of dark grey stone, with diamond-patterned glass & ivy covering the north wall. It stood in the centre of a huge garden surrounded by rose bushes. The grass was short, with lines on it.

I experienced a strange feeling. I realised it must be nerves. While I waited, I considered why I felt nervous. I was on the pavement, so I was not worried about being run over by a moving vehicle. I didn't think I was anxious about being attacked, because there are no man-eating creatures roaming around Ireland. In any case, I had never worried about that before.

Eventually, I thought the most likely cause of my nervousness was because I really really wanted Lara's family to like me.

Unfortunately, I had no idea how to achieve this

objective. When I thought about it, I felt like vomiting.

I'd never tried to make anyone like me before. Generally, people did. At least, they didn't scream & attack me. Sometimes they offered me tea & a slice of cake. (Note: on the whole, I thought that was a favourable response.)

After twenty minutes, the front door opened & Lara ran down the garden path.

She said, 'What are you doing?'

'Standing by your gate.'

'I can see that, but *why*?'

'You said six o'clock. I arrived early.'

'How long have you been here?'

'Forty-two minutes.'

'Baby cheeses! Come in, for the love of God. Here –' she swung the gate open. I wheeled my bicycle on to the garden path.

I said, 'Why have you got a newspaper on your head?' (Note: there was no way she could have read it at that angle or proximity.)

'I don't know if you've noticed, but it's raining.'

'Oh, yes. See?' I pointed at my feet.

'What?'

'I covered my shoes with plastic bags. To keep the water out.'

She said, 'You didn't think of covering your *head* with a *hat*?'

'Oh. No. My head dries out quickly.'

The hall was panelled in mahogany. The effect was sombre. The silence was like a black hole, sucking up all sound except that emitting from the grandfather clock opposite the stairs. Although I knew it was unlikely, its tick-tock sounded slower than a second's duration.

Lara said, 'I'll get a towel. Here, let me take your coat first.' Her voice sounded unnaturally loud.

After she took my coat, she said, 'What are you wearing?' Then she giggled & put her hand over her mouth.

'I –' I looked down at myself. 'I didn't have a shirt, so I borrowed one from Mark. The skull glows in the dark.' I looked at her face. 'Is it wrong?'

'No.' She put her hands on my face, kissed me. 'It's perfect. You're perfect.'

A woman's voice called her name. Lara pulled a face, ignored it.

Taking my hand, she said, 'Come and meet Daddy.'

She led me to a door, knocked.

'Come!' called a deep voice.

The room we entered was lined with books along two of the walls. The third wall had degrees & certificates & photos of Mr Callaghan holding other men by the shoulder. I deduced it was Mr Callaghan's office.

The deep voice said, 'How's my princess? How about a kiss for your old man?'

As Lara stepped up to him, Mr Callaghan looked at me over her head. His face was pink & white. He towered over his daughter. Atypically, he was even taller than I was.

The same woman called Lara's name again, faint but audible through the padded door.

Mr Callaghan said, 'Have you come to help me with the finances? You're a good girl. This is the profit & loss sheet from—'

Lara said, 'You're such a lamebrain!'

Mr Callaghan said, 'There's no thanks for being the world's best father these days—'

'Who said you were the world's best father?'

'It was on my last Father's Day card, so I have it in writing.'

Lara took my hand, tugged it. 'I want you to meet someone. This is Conn.'

I said, 'Hello, Mr Callaghan,' held out my hand.

As Mr Callaghan walked towards me, he adjusted his belt as if it were too large, though it looked too small.

He took so long that I was about to put my hand away. Then he took it & shook it. His eyes were strange, although I couldn't figure out why. They weren't abnormally large or small or deep-set or protruding or too close together or too wide apart. They were arranged in customary formation: a pupil set in a green iris, on a light-pink eyeball.

'Are you the young man who got our Lara in trouble?'

Lara giggled & said, 'No, no, I'm the one who got him in trouble. Conn's the good influence.'

I said, 'You mean the bus?'

'Yes. You owe me three hundred & forty pounds, young man.'

'I – what?'

'Cost of damages plus generous incentive to Superintendent Mahoney to drop all charges.'

Lara said, 'Oh, Daddy.'

'Oh!' I hadn't realised there was a cost related to the accident, although it was obvious now that I considered it. 'I could – I could pay you back—'

Lara said, 'Oh, he's just joking. Aren't you, Daddy?'

The study door opened & a woman's head appeared around it. I recognised the head as belonging to Mrs Callaghan, from the time I saw her in the police station.

She said, 'Did you not hear me calling? Dinner's

ready.' When she saw me, her face changed. It was like she put on a mask, her expression smooth & preset.

She entered the room & said, 'You're Conn, are you? Lara's friend? Welcome.'

She drew near, kissed me on the left side of my face, then the right. Nobody else kissed in 1994. The only time my mam ever touched me was when she licked her fingers & pushed my hair around.

Mrs Callaghan smelled like some deadly type of flower. Her scent irritated my nose, but not in a bad way.

'Dinner's ready,' she repeated.

Mr Callaghan said, 'What's the rush, Dotty?'

Instead of answering him, Mrs Callaghan said, 'Come into the next room, Conn.' She appeared to float rather than walk. I followed her & Lara followed me. I assumed Mr Callaghan was following her, but he must have run some errands on the way because it took him much longer.

The dining room was as dark as the hallway, with the same absence of noise. The table was big & very shiny. Mrs Callaghan showed me where to sit. I thought at first she had accidentally given me all the knives & forks, but then I checked and everyone else had four knives & forks as well. I wondered why we needed so many.

A plate slid noiselessly on to my placemat, I jumped. I fingered the tines of the fork next to the plate, looked at Mrs Callaghan. She slowly picked up the smallest one on the outside, & blinked one eye. I was ninety-nine per cent certain it was a wink.

'C-c-could you p-pass the –' I paused to mentally rehearse the word 'salt'.

Mr Callaghan said, 'Spit it out, young man.'

Mrs Callaghan said, 'Shut up, Robert. Conn, would

you like salt with that? There's also ketchup by Lara.'

Mr Callaghan said, 'I have never understood your incessant need to drench everything in that revolting goo, Dotty.'

Lara looked like she would have agreed with her father, except that she would have contradicted herself. She had just drenched her food in revolting goo.

Mrs Callaghan said, 'Contrary to your inflated opinion of yourself, there are many things you don't understand, Robert.'

I thought that was a joke, so I laughed. I stopped when I realised nobody else was laughing.

Mr Callaghan addressed me. 'Collum, is it?'

Lara said, 'It's Conn, Daddy.'

'I beg your pardon. I suppose this must be something of a change for you, my boy.'

'Excuse me, sir?'

'I imagine this is a bit different to what you're used to.'

I was confused. However, I attempted to clarify by saying, 'No, sir. I eat dinner, too.'

I put down the silver saltcellar. It skated across the table, whizzed by Lara's plate, fell off the other side. Lara disappeared under the table to retrieve it. Mr Callaghan frowned, but his wife giggled. She sounded a lot like Lara.

Lara replaced the salt on the table. 'It's so cool Daddy's here. He travels a lot. He has a very important job.'

Mr Callaghan said, 'Manager of Associated Irish Bank. The big one, in O'Connell Street. What does your father do, young man?'

'He works for the County Council.'

Mr Callaghan said, 'A civil servant?' (Note: his lip curled up to his nose as he said it.) 'Well, don't keep us in suspense. What is he? A tax collector? A ticket inspector?'

'He's a fire officer.'

'Well, well. Firemen fulfil an invaluable role in the community. How else would we get cats down from trees?'

I wondered whether Mr Callaghan was stupid. I hoped not, because he was Lara's father. I said, 'That's not all firemen do, Mr Callaghan. There was a fire in a building in Docklands last week. The department got there in time to put it out without any other unit being affected. If it hadn't, the whole row would have burned down.'

Lara said, 'Conn's father rescued a family trapped on the third floor. Didn't he, Conn?'

Mr Callaghan said, 'What a hero.'

Lara said, 'Conn's dad's way cool.'

'Society would break down without civil servants. People like firemen, bin collectors & sewerage workers provide invaluable public services. Don't let anyone tell you different.'

I said politely, 'Nobody does, usually.'

'No such thing as a menial job, long as it's an honest day's work. That's what I always say,' Mr Callaghan said.

Since I was unsure what he meant, I didn't respond. Another plate of food arrived & for a while the only sounds were cutlery scraping against plates & the clang of incisors on glass.

It was very different from mealtimes at my house.

I noticed that Lara only ate approximately one eighth of her food. This was unusual, but Lara was different with her parents. In her family home, Lara seemed diminished, like a slightly substandard replica of herself. Even her voice sounded insubstantial, like an echo.

I could understand why she didn't go home more often.

At the end of dinner, I was still hungry. A large bowl of fruit stood in the centre of the table. When I reached for a banana, Mr Callaghan barked, 'Don't touch the fruit!'

Lara said, 'Listen to you, Daddy. "Don't touch the fruit!" ' she mimicked.

Mr Callaghan said, 'That's enough out of you, young lady.'

Lara seemed to melt back into her chair.

Mrs Callaghan said, 'Robert, don't be ridiculous. Conn, please help yourself. The fruit is there to be eaten—'

'Conn and I are going to go and have a wee chat in my study, aren't we, my boy?'

'I – we are?'

Mr Callaghan stood & threw his napkin on to the table.

'Come along, young man.' He arranged his mouth & teeth in the format of a smile & put one arm round me. His fingers dug into my shoulder.

In his study, Mr Callaghan poured a brown drink into a cut-crystal glass & sat in his chair.

He said, 'Well, now. I thought it would be grand if you and me had a little man-to-man chat.'

'OK.'

I was uncertain whether I was supposed to sit or stand, but I felt like sitting down. So I did.

Mr Callaghan said, 'I suppose my daughter and you are an item now, hmm?'

'An item?'

'Don't play stupid with me, son. Frankly, I'm surprised you're still on the scene.'

I said, 'Sir?'

'It cannot have escaped your attention that Lara gets through boyfriends quickly. You've lasted longer than I expected.'

'She – she likes me.'

'A grand passion, eh? Hmm. Where exactly do you see this going, my boy?'

'I do not understand—'

'You and Lara. You must realise you have no future.'

'No, sir.'

'Oh come on, son. Lara is from a completely different background and class to you. She has different cultural references, prospects.'

I waited a few seconds in case he wanted to finish the sentence, but that seemed to be it.

I said, 'We went to the same school. We're in the same university—'

'That's not the point. Can I give you some advice?'

In my experience, people who said that gave advice that was either a) irrelevant or b) useless, so I said, 'No, thank you.'

'Don't get smart with me, my boy. I guarantee I am smarter than you.' I doubted that. However, since he was bigger than me, I said nothing. 'Look. All I'm saying is: have your fun – although for God's sake make sure you use protection. Lara seems fond of you, and I want my daughter to be happy. However, don't make the mistake of thinking this is a long-term thing. After college, you go your way and Lara goes hers. Do you understand?' Mr Callaghan appeared to mistake my silence for acquiescence. 'Don't take it hard. My daughter deserves the sort of future someone like you can never give her. A girl like Lara will end up with someone like – someone like—'

'Someone like you.'

Mr Callaghan said, 'Exactly.' He looked pleased. 'Son, I'm just saving you heartache in the long run.'

I sincerely hoped Lara would not end up with someone like her father. I didn't think he was very nice.

As I left Mr Callaghan's office, I realised what was unusual about his eyes. Once, I saw a programme about sharks on television. There was footage of a great white shark swimming towards a seal. Mr Callaghan's eyes looked the same as the shark's.

Two point five months later, Mark & I were eating pot noodles at the kitchen table one evening. Lara walked into the kitchen.

She said, 'Hi, guys.'

Mark said, 'Hey, Lars!'

I wished Mark wouldn't call her Lars, & that I had a special name for her instead. Now all I could think of was 'Lars', which Mark had thought of first.

Mark said, 'How did you get in?'

Lara said, 'Your bathroom window is still poked. You should really fix it.'

Mark said, 'Why? You worried someone might sneak in and steal a sink, or some Fairy Liquid? Want the rest of my noodles?'

'Ooh, yes please.'

I wished I had offered her my noodles.

Mark stood, pushed his tub across the table. 'I've gotta fucking blow this fucking joint. I have a gig. Catch you later, grasshoppers.'

Lara said, 'Bye, clownface.'

Mark left with a bag of shredded newspaper.

Mark & Lara got on really well. Sometimes this

bothered me, which made no sense. Mark was my best friend & Lara the most important person in the world. It was illogical that I wouldn't want them to get on. Of course I did. Just not quite so well, maybe.

Lara dipped her fingers into the pot noodles, extracted a mouthful with her fingers, said, 'Guess what I did this afternoon?'

'You devised a plan to make the McGuinness Fountain produce bubbles?'

'No. Terrific idea, though. Shampoo?'

'Let me think . . . The McGuinness Fountain contains approximately sixty-seven thousand, three hundred & thirty-two gallons of water. I would recommend a combination of shampoo and Fairy Liquid. Twenty bottles of each.'

'Brilliant! Thanks. No but, anyway, I saw a fortune-teller this afternoon. Julie went to him last year, and he told her pink was her favourite colour – which it totally is – and that she would wear a hat this year – which she totally does. He was in the Sisters of Mercy Convent this afternoon, so he told my fortune.'

'You believe in that?'

' 'Course. He was really good. Apparently I'm going to have a dreadfully miserable life.'

I snorted involuntarily. 'That's crap.'

Lara said cheerfully, 'No, no, I'm going to have a terrible time of it. Apparently, I'm going to live in a balloon for a while next year, and I should avoid eggs and vegetables that begin with "w". The good news is that I'm going to meet the one great love of my life on the tenth of June, 2009.'

Despite myself, I felt annoyed. Although it had no basis in scientific fact, Lara's believing it implied she did not consider me the one great love of her life.

I said, 'I think that's improbable.'

'Oh no, he was very specific about it. I'll meet him – or her – on—'

'*Her?*'

'Well, he didn't specify the gender, and I didn't ask. But I'm keeping an open mind until I try lesbianism. Anyway – are you listening? – I'm going to meet them on the tenth of June 2009 at Shannon Airport. Sucks that I have to wait so long. Isn't that romantic, but? He's probably some gorgeous pilot. I hope he has a peaked cap. It's going to be tremendously romantic.'

'I doubt it.'

'Why?'

'Well, if your life's going to be miserable, he'll probably crash his plane into the side of the terminal.'

'I'll realise he's the one great love of my life as he croaks in my arms?' Lara had tears in her eyes when she whispered, 'That's terrible.'

'It might be terrible, if it actually happened. Which it won't.'

'You can't cheat fate.'

'Lara, you don't know what your fate is going to be; and some random stranger certainly doesn't. Anyway, the theory that your fate or – or destiny is all premapped is erroneous—'

'Plenty of people believe in destiny.'

'They're mistaken. Your life does not conform to some mysterious, mystical force. It's defined by the choices and decisions you make—'

'What if you don't make choices?'

'Refusing to choose is still a choice.'

'Well, OK. What about things that happen which are

outside of your control? Like getting run over by a bus.'

'If you take adequate care when crossing the road – and I'm not driving the bus – you can minimise the likelihood of that happening—'

'Yes, *minimise*! Not guarantee! What if the bus's brake cables fail and the driver mounts the pavement?'

'Whether you get hit by a bus is immaterial in the scheme of things. It might make your life shorter, but what you do in the meantime is largely within your control—'

Lara said, 'Well, I don't agree.'

I said, 'I would prefer it if you did—'

'But I don't. We'll have to agree to disagree.'

I said, 'I don't like that.'

'You should probably get used to it.'

'Are we arguing?'

'No, I don't think so. Wait – are you arguing with me?'

'Yes.'

'Oh, please don't!' said Lara. She looked sad. 'I hate arguing. Can we have sex instead?'

I didn't have to think about that very long. 'Yes.'

'Great.'

Mark had awarded Lara 'one' on the Tequila Scale (a measure he formulated to accurately reflect the relative attractiveness of a woman. The subject's Tequila Rating was the hypothetical number of tequila shots one would theoretically have to consume before being compelled to sleep with the subject. Although it only went up to fifteen – i.e., hurt the eyes to look at her – the scale could be further calibrated by whether the subject would be required to 'go Dutch').

As I studied in my bedroom one night, I heard Lara giggling with Mark in the kitchen.

When she came in, she said, 'Mark's great, isn't he?'

I didn't like her saying and/or thinking this. I mean, I agreed with her: Mark was great & lots of other good things, too. But I would have preferred that Lara didn't notice.

However, I said, 'Yes. Why are you only wearing one sock?'

'That foot's cold. There are no teabags left, so I made you a cup of Bovril.' She put it on the desk, then jumped on the bed & extracted a book from under her bottom. It was called *Forbidden Desire* & had a picture of a man & a woman in dirty, ripped clothes on the front. It looked like the man had just stabbed the woman or something, because she looked unwell. Lara read many of these books.

The radio played a song I had never heard before. Lara said, 'This band's totally awesome.' (Note: it sounded like a cat being swung around by the whiskers.) (Note: this is supposition, since I've never heard a cat being swung around by the whiskers.) She said, 'I love them.'

I said, 'No, you only like them because everyone else likes them.'

'No, I don't!' After a while, Lara said, 'How's the study?'

'Great. I was trying to work out how X relates to Y in a vacuum and it was making no sense but then suddenly it did. I don't know why I didn't see it before—'

'Wait – I think my brain just melted.'

I said, 'Ha, ha.'

'I wish you got as excited about me as engineering.'

I said, 'B-but I do! You are much more exciting.'

'Really? How much?'

I thought about it. 'I can't say, because it's impossible to quantify. But definitely more.'

Lara didn't comment on that, but I saw her smile. Then she looked at me over the top of her book. 'You finished studying? We could do something.'

I pushed away from the desk, stood, stretched. 'Like what? We could go and throw stones in the river, or – it's too late to do much else.'

'Not necessarily. I could read you some of my book.'

'Why?'

'Maybe you'd like it.'

That was improbable, but I said, 'OK.'

'OK. *Forbidden Desire*, page one hundred and twenty, paragraph three.' Lara read in a soft voice. ' "Face flushed with desire Amber's fingers fumbled desperately with his zipper. Freed of its denim cage, Wolf's throbbing manhood reared up like a stag in the forest, untouched by time or space. He quivered at her touch like a virgin fawn. Dropping to her knees, she grasped it in her hand and bent—" '

My throbbing manhood winced. 'Stop! She doesn't –' I swallowed – '*break* it, does she?'

Lara giggled. ' 'Course not. It's a romance, not a horror story.'

'What –' I had to clear my throat – 'What happens next?'

'Let me see . . . "She grasped it in her hand and bent her lips to its velvety head. Wolf's fingers tangled in the cascading waves of soft, silky hair. His throat released a low, guttural moan as she kissed his splendid shaft . . ." '

For some reason, I imagined Lara doing that to me & felt like releasing a low, guttural moan too. I didn't understand how hearing about two fictional characters could make me feel this way (note: overheated).

Lara threw the book face down on her stomach, casually said, 'Hey, I know! We could try some of this.'

'What?'

'Well, I could read *Forbidden Desire*, and we could – you know.'

I thought I knew what she meant, but I wanted to be unreservedly clear about it. 'Do you mean I should listen to you read more?'

Lara rotated her eyeballs. 'No! We could do some of this stuff. You know – the same things as Wolf and Amber.'

I wondered how she could be so cool when I was hotter than plasma in a space continuum. But I said, 'I suppose so. OK.'

'All right. Is it OK if I fumble desperately with your zipper?'

'Yes.'

So she did that & everything else up to 'splendid shaft'.

By this stage I was having problems speaking, but managed to say, 'Wait! Read more.'

'OK.' Lara picked up the book, ran her finger down the page. ' " 'Wait!' Wolf commanded." – You got that bit right. Hmm, OK – "Amber raised bruised, questioning eyes to him. He gasped, deep in his throat." '

I obliged involuntarily.

' " 'My darling,' Wolf muttered, his voice husky with longing. 'I can't hold on much longer.' Drawing her into his strong arms, he savagely ravished her swollen, coral lips. 'My turn,' he rasped harshly. Wolf laid her on the sand with infinite tenderness and drew a line of fiery kisses down the column of her alabaster throat. She felt his lips on the very core of her being and an electric shock coursed through her. Waves of pleasure lapped the shores of her innermost self." '

Lara stopped, looked at me.

'Oh, right!' I picked her up. 'There's no sand . . .'

'On the bed.'

'I suppose Wolf must have removed Amber's clothes already, or maybe she didn't have any on to start with—'

'Let's not get too caught up in the technicalities,' said Lara, removing her top. 'Take off my jeans.'

'OK. Just to clarify, is this the very core of your being?' I touched her.

'Ow! Bit more gentle with the core of my being, please.'

'So do I put my lips on the very core of your being?'

'OK. Ouch. One minute, let me see what happens next – um, he kissed the core of her being like, er, in a very similar way to how he would have kissed a flower. In other words, gently and with his lips only for the moment.'

'Why would he kiss a flower?'

'I don't know!'

I tried it out for a bit, then checked with her, 'Is that OK?'

'Oh, yes! Ooh! Left a bit, and harder.'

'It says that?'

I didn't hear her response, because she wrapped her legs around my head & tried to smother me. That was strange but also strangely exciting. For a while, Lara lay on the bed & gasped.

Then she picked up *Forbidden Desire* again, said, 'Would you like to know what happens next?'

'Yes, please.'

'OK ... "Poised to thrust deep into her fiery depths, Wolf paused to gaze deep into the deep blue wellpools of her eyes. 'I'm so glad you understand what happened was a misunderstanding,' he husked. 'What misunderstanding?' she murmured, eyes glazed with a hopeless passion. Wolf murmured, 'You know I will never forgive myself for sleeping with your mother.'"'

Poised to thrust deep into Lara's fiery depths, I said, 'What?'

'Hmm, that was unexpected. About fourteen pages ago, Wolf – the hound dog – slept with Amber's mother. I didn't think he'd be stupid enough to bring it up in the middle of sex, but. What a dork.'

'So what, that's it?'

'Hang on, maybe she forgives him – " 'You did what?' spat Amber, angrily. My darling, my precious, my one true love. It was a mistake. It meant nothing.'" Yeah, that's what they all say. "Amber thrust him aside. 'If I had known,' she hissed, 'I would never have let you plunder my golden temple.' 'I see,' snapped Wolf, his eyes growing hard and cold as a stone. His face showed none of the traces of tenderness it had moments earlier." Um. Hold on a moment.'

Lara riffled through the pages, muttering random words under her breath.

'On page a hundred & thirty-four, Amber throws a pineapple at Wolf, and he storms off on page a hundred & thirty-five. Let me just see if he comes back. Um ... no. Oh, dear. Wolf accidentally sleeps with Amber's sister on page a hundred & forty-eight. Tell you what.' Lara reached up and pulled me down to her. 'Why don't we just make up our own story?'

*

Over the years, most of my memories have faded. Although I remember the detail, I can no longer recall the sensation these things evoked. E.g., although I remember how Lara's smile used to make me feel happy & special, I can no longer evoke that feeling.

These are now only vague impressions/recollections: the strand of hair that always fell across her face immediately after she tucked it behind her ear; the warm smell of her in the morning; the way her nose crinkled when she laughed; the wide, generous smile that always made me feel like smiling too.

Of the few memories that survive intact, many date from the summer before my final year. Before everything changed. When I think back, it seems as if every day was hazy & humid. Since it was Limerick, Ireland, this must be a distortion of time and/or memory.

That summer, I used to collect Lara after work on my bicycle & we would go to the Ardnacrusha Canal, Lara balanced on my crossbar, her skin brown & shiny, dress fluttering around her legs.

I can still see Lara poised on the bridge in her swimsuit, arms outstretched, shouting 'Conn! Watch this!' My heart always beat harder when she launched herself into nothing, arms flailing, legs running nowhere. The way she drew them together at the last moment so that the dark water admitted her with barely a sound or splash, & emerged on to the bank of the canal, arms raised to smooth her hair back from her face.

Lara was teaching me to swim. I was not sure her putting her hands down my shorts facilitated the learning process, but I didn't mind.

One evening, she sat on her towel beside me, her hair pulled back in a bunch. She stopped writing in her journal, wrapped her arms round her legs & said, 'Do you love me?'

I said, 'I don't know', looking at the wet strands of hair curling at the nape of her neck. 'Surely it depends on your definition of love?'

She turned to look at me, her face glowed in the evening sun. After a minute, I realised she was waiting for me to say more.

This seemed to be important to Lara, so I thought carefully how to respond.

I said, 'Well, I-I want to be with you all the time. And I miss you when I'm not with you. Except when I'm studying. I probably do then as well, but I just don't think about it. I only want good things to happen to you. I mean, obviously that is a hypothetical construct, but i-if you were involved in some theoretical circumstance, I would want it to be good. I certainly don't want anything bad to happen to you. And you're very nice—'

'Woah, don't get carried away there.'

'No, it's more than that. You are – you are . . .' It took a while to identify the right word. 'You are beautiful. Not just your head and knees and the rest of you. I mean, everything about you. And the longer I know you, the more beautiful you are.'

She smiled in that way that made biologically inexplicable things happen to my chest. 'You know, evidence suggests you might love me.'

'If you agree with my definition of love, then I suppose I must.'

'Do you think you'll love me for ever?'

'I do,' I said, because – despite the emotional and therefore intangible nature of the question – I knew I would. At least, it was inconceivable that I would not.

I pulled her down next to me, kissed her until I ran out of breath.

Lara said, 'Don't you want to know if I love you?'

'Not particularly.'

'Really? Why not?'

'It's not important. I'm just happy being with you.'

I'd been going out with Lara for three years & twenty-two days. We hadn't discussed what would happen after my finals. I can make no accurate assertions as to why this was the case. Theories include but are not limited to: a) since we didn't know what would happen in the future, there was no point discussing it; b) everything was so good, I didn't want to consider what happened next; c) I was worried what Lara might say.

Then I got the letter. It was in a brown envelope with a clear window bearing my name & address. It didn't look like something that would change everything.

I didn't discuss it with Lara, because even though theories a & b above no longer applied, theory c was more valid.

When something upset and/or worried me, I sometimes asked myself what Batman would think of the situation, & the problem went away. Otherwise, I applied logic & reason, considering possible outcomes, alternative scenarios, until either: 1) I identified a solution; 2) it didn't upset and/or worry me any more; or 3) it was supplanted by bigger problems.

None of these scenarios applied to this problem, & it didn't go away.

Superficially, it was a straightforward decision: I had to make a choice.

Realistically, it was more complex. For the first time in my life, I didn't know what to do. I tried not to think about it, but that was difficult to impossible. It was anomalous that, although I wanted to tell Lara about it, at the same time I didn't. Up to then, I used to discuss everything with Lara. Well, obviously not everything, because that's impossible, but important things & anything she wanted to talk about. I didn't feel good about not telling her.

Then something happened.

Lara had asked me to her parents' house. I said yes because I knew Lara wanted me to go (note: because she had asked me). I didn't really want to, because I disliked Mr Callaghan. Luckily, I hadn't been invited to the Callaghan house since the first time.

When Lara brought me into the sitting room, Mr Callaghan said, 'What's he doing here?'

I looked around to see if he was referring to someone else, but it was definitely me. Lara's mother sat on the edge of a high-backed chair. I noticed she gripped her hands together tightly, like Lara did when she was upset.

Mr Callaghan said, 'Lara, your mother and I need to discuss a family matter. We wanted to see you alone.'

Lara said, 'I'm going to tell Conn later, so you might as well discuss it with him too.' Mr Callaghan leaned back in his leather armchair, pressed his fingertips together. He looked at me over them, said, 'Very well. Dotty—'

Mrs Callaghan said, 'Don't call me "Dotty", you despicable shit.'

The word 'shit' sounded much louder than the small, quiet voice in which she had said it. Lara made a noise like a laugh, but it didn't sound like her normal laugh.

Mr Callaghan said, 'I think "Dotty" is marginally better than "despicable shit".'

'Not when accumulated over twenty-two years. Why don't you just get on with it?'

Mr Callaghan said, 'Very well.' He addressed Lara. 'Your mother has asked me to move out.'

Lara said, 'What?'

'Your mother—'

Lara rounded on her mother. 'Is this true? But – but why? Mum . . . she can just ask you to stay, right? Mum—'

Mrs Callaghan said quietly, 'No.'

'No? Don't I get a say in this?'

Neither of her parents said anything.

Veins stood out on Lara's forehead, her lips curled back from her teeth. She turned to Mrs Callaghan, screamed, 'Why are you doing this? You always ruin everything! You are so *selfish*!'

'There are things you – you don't understand,' said Mrs Callaghan. Her eyes were squeezed shut. When she opened them, tears ran down her face.

'So tell me! Go on!'

'Robert and I have discussed this and it's for the best—'

'For whom? Do you *want* to leave?' Lara demanded of her father.

Mr Callaghan spread his fingers wide, sighed loudly, said, 'No—'

'So it's all *her*!'

I said, 'Lara.' Put my hand on her arm. I didn't understand the reasons either, but I didn't think anything Lara said would change things.

Lara shook off my hand, turned to her father. Her lips

had turned an unusual shade of white. 'Why do you have to move out? Why doesn't *she*?'

Mr Callaghan said, 'It's easier this way.'

Mrs Callaghan said, 'Things have been broken for a long time. For goodness' sake, Lara, you couldn't fail to notice that—'

'I'm not green so much as cabbage-like, Mother; I noticed. You stayed together, but—'

Mrs Callaghan said, 'For you and Rose. I – we didn't think it fair to – to—'

'So – wait, wait, wait, reverse back up the hill. Let me get this straight. You stayed in this stinking carcass of a fucking marriage, because of *me*? Oh, that's great. Thank you. Thank you very much.'

Mrs Callaghan said, 'No, it wasn't just for you and Rose—'

'Does Rosie know?'

Mrs Callaghan said, 'She – she was supposed to come down this weekend, but she had to attend a seminar—'

Lara interrupted her. 'Does Rosie *know*?'

Mrs Callaghan spoke so quietly it was difficult to hear her. 'No. But I don't think this will come as any surprise.'

'What's so wrong with Dad? You fucking married him, didn't you? Did he drag you down the aisle by the hair? Lash you to the altar with your veil? He must have been all right then! What's wrong with him now? Did he beat you? Is he a compulsive gambler?'

Mr Callaghan said, 'Sometimes things don't work out. God knows, I've tried. I mean, of course, we have tried.' He emphasised the word 'we'.

Lara said, 'Can't you try *harder*?' It sounded like a reasonable question to me.

Mrs Callaghan said, 'I know how difficult this must be for you, Lara—'

'Oh, you do, do you?'

'I'm sorry.'

'Big, fat, hairy-arse deal!'

Mr Callaghan said, 'This is still the family home, Lara. You are welcome here whenever you want.'

Lara's mouth changed from wide open to a small, pinched thing. She looked at them both a long moment. She said, 'I will never come back here again.'

As far as I know, she never did (note: although since she forgot her rucksack under the hall table, the statement technically took effect after she returned to collect it).

When I turned five, I got a yellow balloon for my birthday. I really liked it. After a few weeks, the balloon sagged & puckered. Still, I carried it around everywhere until one day it was flaccid & slimy.

At the time, Mam said that change was necessary & good. However, I was not sure whether/how this applied to Lara's circumstance.

Lara changed. She cried a lot. She stayed in bed instead of going to lectures. Since this behaviour started when her parents told Lara they were separating, I inferred she must be upset and/or confused about that.

I thought Lara might want to talk about it, because usually she wanted to discuss everything. However, Lara didn't talk much any more, about anything. I missed our midnight conversations, which surprised me because they were about fundamentally inconsequential topics. I had always thought I would prefer to sleep.

In any case, there was no rationale for discussion in this scenario. Lara's parents had made a decision. There was nothing Lara could do about it. Talking served no purpose, because it would not affect the outcome. In some ways, Lara's parents' separation was bad, e.g., when Lara visited her parents it would take twice as long. But in another way, it was good. Mrs Callaghan could be with someone nicer than Mr Callaghan. I hoped Lara would realise this soon & be happy again.

I decided to give Lara some time alone to get over it. However, I missed her. I also worried about her, despite that being ineffective & essentially unproductive.

One day, Lara & I were in the kitchen of my flat when Lara started crying again.

I looked around but failed to determine the source of her distress. I presumed she must be thinking about her parents. However, to be absolutely certain, I asked, 'What's wrong now?'

Lara said, 'You don't have to speak to me like that.'

I was confused. 'L-l-like what?'

Lara said, 'If you must kn-kn-know, I can't find the coconut creams. That fuh-fuh-fucker Mark. Next time I bring around a pack of coconut creams. I'm going to d-d-dip the last one in arsenic.'

I was relieved that she was only upset about biscuits, since the problem was relatively minor & there was an obvious solution. I said, 'I'll go and buy some more—'

She said, 'No! I d-d-don't feel like one now.'

But she was still crying ten minutes later, so I said, 'I can see you are upset & I want to – I don't know what to do about it.'

'You could give me a hug.'

I was pleased I could do something. However, although I held her for a long time, and patted her hair like I saw in a movie about some singer & her bodyguard, she was still sniffing.

Eventually, she wiped her nose with a piece of orange peel & said, 'I'm sorry. I don't know what's wrong with me at the moment.'

'You said you wanted a coconut cream and—'

'Yes, but don't you think it's strange I got that upset over a coconut cream?'

'It is a tasty biscuit—'

'They're OK. Mikados are better, but.'

Although I knew she was correct, I was not sure what relevance this had, so I said nothing.

Lara said, 'Everything is falling apart.'

I looked around, but nothing appeared to be disintegrating or crumbling. I said, 'I don't understand.'

'Dad called last night. He's moved in with – with someone.'

'Who?'

'His secretary. We can call her "bitch" for the purposes of this conversation. When I asked Dad whether he was looking for another place, he said he's living with Bitch now. I don't think my parents are getting back together.'

'Well, of course they aren't. Otherwise, they wouldn't have separated, would they?'

'Conn, you don't have to say anything. I just need you to listen.'

'OK.'

For a long time, I was not sure what I was supposed to be listening to, because Lara was silent. She was busy picking the paint off her fingernails. I always wondered why she wore it, because she started chipping away at it as soon as it was on. Also, there was not much room for painting because her nails were bitten down to the finger.

As I watched, I realised Lara's hands were thinner. Her dolphin ring had slid round so that I could only see the back of it. The bones in the back of her hands were more pronounced.

Finally, Lara said, 'You know, when I was a kid, I never invited friends back to my house.'

I attempted to communicate the fact that I had registered her question via the art of body language, i.e., I nodded.

'My parents, they never stopped fighting. Rose and I used to pray they'd stop shouting at each other – well, it was usually Mother shouting at Dad. When they ignored each other it was almost worse, but. I always thought it was my *fault*, somehow. I always had this sense of . . . dread lingering in the pit of my stomach. But do you know what really kills me?' She did not appear to want a response, because she went on. 'It's that I was the reason they stayed together. Can you imagine being the cause of all that misery?'

I said, 'Can I – can I say something now?'

'Yes.'

'Your argument is fundamentally flawed.' Lara dropped her head, ran her fingers through her hair (note: it was nearly all black now, blue only at the ends).

I said, 'Wait! Wait! One: you were not the cause of your parents' misery. They were. Two: your parents decided to stay together. Their reasons for doing so are irrelevant for the purposes of this discussion. In summary: it was their choice and you had no input. Therefore you cannot hold yourself responsible.'

Lara looked at me, raised her eyebrows. 'You know what? That is actually quite helpful.'

'Really?' I felt pleased.

Even though Lara was smiling, somehow she still looked sad. She said, 'Parents. They fuck you up.'

'My parents haven't.'

'Perhaps not yet. But they will.'

'Maybe.' Even though I didn't believe that, I decided to consider the hypothetical (note: mainly because Lara was familiar with the concept). I said, 'Overlooking the fact that the term "fuck you up" is not clearly defined, if my parents did fuck me up, it wouldn't be on purpose. I mean, they wouldn't mean to.'

'Am I supposed to feel better that my parents weren't engaged in a master conspiracy to fuck me up all those years?'

'Well, yes. I think so.'

'Whatever.'

I held Lara's hand, because I thought she would like that.

She said, 'You are my family now.' Then, so softly I could barely hear her, 'I don't know what I would do without you.'

After a while, in the same tone of voice she used to suggest going to the Student Union, Lara said, 'Hey, I've got an idea. Why don't we move in together?'

I said, 'I – we – I don't . . .' Then I used the words 'er', 'um' & 'ah', but I can't recall the order of frequency. I was clearing a blockage in my throat when Lara removed her hand from mine, said, 'Forget it. You obviously don't want to.'

'No! No, it's not – I-I just haven't had t-t-time to think about it—'

'What's there to think about? You don't have to think about it; you either want to live with me or you don't. And you don't. No big deal. Fancy a takeaway?'

'N-n-no – I mean, I wouldn't mind a pizza. But it's not that I don't want to live with you—'

Lara said loudly, 'Well, what is it, then?'

I said, 'I-I-I've b-b-been offered a job. With Babco.'

'But that's great! Oh Conn, I'm so, so, so thrilled for you!' Lara had pushed back her chair; now she came around the table, sat on top of me. 'Oh, it's exactly what you wanted! Isn't it?'

'Yes, yes!' I really wanted to get up & pace around, but I didn't want Lara to fall on to the floor. 'Lara, if I spend three years with Babco, I can do – well, anything! Within reason – I mean I can work for any company in the world! Except those that conduct business in Italian. I'm not sure I could learn Italian, the grammatical constructs are illogical—'

'But any company that's not Italian—'

'Precisely! And apart from being the biggest construction company in the world, Babco's graduate training programme is the best in the industry. They – they train you while you work!'

Lara laughed, patted my cheek with her fingers. 'You're gas. Oh, I love you!'

She seemed so pleased, I momentarily wondered what I had been so worried about. Then I recalled what I hadn't yet told her.

With a feeling I later categorised as certain doom, I said, 'It's in Azerbaijan.'

Lara's fingers stopped wandering around my face. 'Where?'

'Azerbaijan.'

'I've never – is it even on this planet?'

'Yes, in south Russia. Beside Armenia.'

'Never mind, I'll figure out where it is.' Lara bounced

on my legs, clapped her hands. 'When are we going?'

I did not answer, because I was confused by her use of the word 'we'. It had never occurred to me that Lara would want to go to Azerbaijan. There was nothing there except oil & gas (note: I hadn't been there myself, but I'd read about it).

Then Lara said, 'Conn?'

'Ah, yes?'

She looked at me intently, her face close to mine. She said, 'Wait, wait, wait, reverse back up the hill there. You – you don't mean me, do you?'

The kitchen seemed particularly quiet.

Her voice sounded flat & dull when she said, 'And you're going.'

I cleared my throat, which seemed abnormally dry. 'Not necessarily. B-but Lara, this job – it's perfect. They want me to—'

'How long have you known?'

'About the – the job? Four months.'

Lara laughed, which I though was an unusual response until I realised she was not really laughing. She removed herself from my legs. 'And you tell me *now*? It would have been nice if you had discussed it with me before. Maybe pretended my opinion mattered.'

'Lara, it-it does. Of course your opinion matters—'

'So are you going to take it?'

I swallowed. 'I-I don't know.'

'But you want to.'

'Of course. Lara, if I don't take this job, I will always wonder "what if?"'

'I see. And what about us? If you leave me, won't you wonder "what if?"'

I was silent because I hadn't considered this. Lara began to sob.

I said, 'Oh please. Please, don't cry.' I hated when she cried, hated even more that I had made her. She said something I didn't hear. 'Lara, you know I love you—'

'R-r-right at this moment, I'm n-not sure about that at a-a-all. Please-please—'

'Lara,' I said desperately, 'suppose I don't accept this position—'

'There are others, you know—'

I said, 'Wait, let me finish. Suppose I do something else and – and – I don't know, I'm not good at considering the hypothetical. Say it doesn't work out and I end up being a rubbish collector or-or a dentist—'

'I think the probability of either is pretty slim—'

'Wait – this is my hypothesis. If it doesn't work out, and we're still together, I might blame you.'

'I get it. Although what I don't understand is why you don't like operating on the hypothetical level, because you are so very good at it. Tell me, Conn, did you never think of asking whether I wanted to go with you?'

It took me a moment to process what she said. When I did, I felt very excited. I wanted to be with Lara; yet I also wanted to be a Grade 8 Engineer for Babco. Whether the two were compatible had not previously occurred to me.

At the time, my world comprised of absolutes. Right/wrong. Success/failure. Black/white. I was unaware there are many shades of grey in many different dimensions. I failed to understand that compromise was a valid option.

But before I could respond, Lara said, 'Forget it.'

'Wh-what? But I thought you said—'

'If you wanted me to go with you, you would have asked me—'

'No, Lara, you're wrong! I-I don't know why I didn't think of it before! It's a great idea—'

'You're the one with great ideas. It mustn't be that great if you didn't think of it to begin with.' Lara picked up her jacket. 'Anyway, you should do this on your own.'

I said, 'Why?'

Lara put on her jacket, wound on her scarf. Tears still ran down her face, but otherwise she appeared very calm.

At the door, she said, 'At least this way, when it all goes wrong, you only have yourself to blame.'

'Lara, d-don't go. Please, come with me.'

She said, 'No.'

She left.

The following day, I looked for Lara on campus. I looked for the next week, then the next, and the one after that.

It was as if her personal gravity field had failed & she had levitated off the face of the earth.

I started going to her flat after lectures, but nobody answered when I knocked. So I stayed there one night until Julie came back at three-seventeen. When she saw me, she said, 'Fuck off, Dipshit.'

I said, 'I'm not fucking off until you talk to me.'

I don't think she believed me at first. She did after I shouted through the letterbox for a while. Eventually the flap opened, Julie's voice said, 'What?'

'Where is Lara?'

'If I tell you, will you fuck off?'

'Yes.'

'I don't know where she is. She packed her bags and left.'

'When?'

'About two weeks ago. Did you have a fight or something?'

I had finished talking to her, so I left.

In the days, weeks, months and years that followed, I thought about Lara all the time. Even when I was not actively thinking about her, she was always there.

Rewriting History

An overstuffed woman stares at me as I slalom through the restaurant.

Perhaps my throbbing, neon-red eyes are putting her off her pavlova. Or my Spiderman T-shirt, which I still wear since the fucking 'relocation specialists and consultants' packed the rest of my tops. Or the shiny plastic orange platform boots circa late crustacean seventies, which I inherited from my mother. At least the emerald-green raw silk Monsoon skirt conceals the fact that they extend to the thigh – although the skirt is more appropriate for a black-tie occasion and, furthermore, does not really match the T-shirt.

Perhaps it is a combination of all the above.

'Sorry I'm late,' I gasp, slinging my washbag on to the chair opposite my sister. (It serves as a purse since the packers made off with all my handbags.)

'Let me guess,' says Rose. 'Cat ate your homework?'

'A classic excuse that never goes stale, but no. I was delayed due to a freak accident involving an oil tanker and an exploding walrus.'

'Wow, that's a new one. Sounds serious.'

'It was, but the medics said there were no fatalities.

Don't get up.' I bend and kiss her. 'When are you due –
ten minutes?'

'Don't even joke about it,' says Rose. She runs a hand
gingerly over her bump, as if afraid it might pop at any
moment. 'You might have to do double duty as
godmother, still.'

'No way. I only signed up for one.' I fall into the chair,
pausing to raise a buttock and extract the washbag. I put
it on the table and breathe for the first time in approximately a week.

The overstuffed woman in the corner is still watching
me. What's her problem?

'I ordered an appetiser for you,' says Rose, 'but when
you didn't arrive, I ate it.'

'Aw, Rosie Posie!'

'Lara, I am eight months' pregnant. My constitution is
a terrifying thing to behold; nothing even vaguely edible
is safe.'

'What did I miss out on?'

'Thai fishcakes with lime and coriander dressing.'

It doesn't take much to move me to tears these days
and fishcakes are as good a reason as any. Especially
when I think about how hungry I am, allied with how
delicious fishcakes are, especially when accompanied by
a side order of sweet chilli sauce.

'Hey,' says Rose, shaking my hand gently. 'We can
order more.'

'That's OK,' I sniff. 'It's not the fishcakes.'

'I know. Mum said you were a bit fragile.'

'Yeah. I am suffering from excessive moistness,' I say.
Even talking about it makes me feel excessively moist, so
I am glad when Rose says, 'Are the packers gone?'

'Yeah. Can't you tell?' I pluck at the Spiderman T-shirt.

'I thought it was your usual anarchic sense of fashion, but.'

'That's good coming from someone who dresses like the secret love child of Cliff Richard and a geography teacher.'

It's hard to believe that Rose and I have any genes in common – or even chromosomes, for that matter. I wouldn't be surprised to find out Rose had been conceived by the milkman (although I *would* be surprised to discover our mother had shagged someone with such a financially unpromising career path).

Rose is four years older than me, but it might as well be sixty. She was born grown-up. There is no record of her ever being less than entirely responsible. While other girls dreamed of Maverick and Ferris Bueller, Rose fantasised about getting a pension scheme. She washed up without having to be asked; always pulled her socks up to the knee; went to university; became a doctor; married her first boyfriend and produced the first grandchild on schedule.

If I sound bitter, I'm not. For one thing, Rose being perfect takes a lot of pressure off me. For another – and this is the real truth – I adore my sister. Rose is a thousand shades of awesome. I would trust her with my life – or at least my purse.

She used to cover for me whenever I was in trouble with our mother. When I set fire to her Malibu Barbie once and melted its head off, Rose told Mother it was because she was ironing Barbie's hair. When there was nuclear fallout from the warfare at home, she used to take me to the secret hiding place in the centre of the rhododendron bush in the back garden – the one Dad always wanted to cut down – and read to me for hours.

We would pretend we were princesses in a secret kingdom (albeit dank and twig-infested).

We spent a lot of time there.

The only time we ever really fell out was at Rose's wedding. I was going through a hippy phase and insisted on fulfilling maid-of-honour duties in a hideous kaftan-yashmak featuring a faintly hairy quality. Even now, Rose still gets choked up when she looks at her wedding photos (to be honest, so do I).

I did consider falling out with her when she left home when I was seventeen. I didn't because, firstly, I couldn't really blame her. Secondly, she wasn't around to be sulked at, which would have made the whole exercise rather pointless.

'Is it OK with you if we order main courses?' says Rose, slavering slightly.

I order the fishcakes and a side order of potato wedges. While Rose grills the waiter over taste, texture and quantity (emphasis on quantity), I finger the Pi symbol on my charm bracelet and look around.

The overstuffed woman is still staring stealthily. I think she looks vaguely familiar. Do I know her? If so, I can't tell from where. Her face looks crumbly from a surfeit of powder, her lipstick is three shades too pink and her hair is arranged in a style about three decades too young for her. She shows four inches of hideous cleavage in a terrifying pink-and-black blouse with gold buttons. It probably cost a lot at a boutique store.

She looks away when she notices my squinty glare.

'Rose, do you know— oh, wait a sec.' My mobile is ringing. It's probably Leonard. Another portent: if it *is* Leonard, moving to New York is the Right Decision. I scrabble through the washbag's squalid depths and locate the phone by touch.

'Leo,' I mouth at Rose as I press the 'Answer' button.

'Hey, Babe,' says Leonard's voice through the handset.

The sound of his voice vaporises all my doubts. When I speak to Leonard, everything seems better. I miss him so much. I can't wait to see him again – and I will soon – in fact, this time tomorrow, yay!

I wish I could feel more like this when I am alone.

'Hey, you,' I say into the handset.

'Hey, yourself.' I hear him smile, and picture his craggy face. 'How's my babelicious?'

'OK. How about you?'

'Sorry I didn't call yesterday. Something cropped up at work and I didn't finish until after ten—'

'I would have been awake.'

'I know, but I wanted to wait until we could have – let's say – a *decent* talk—'

'Well, I'm out with Rosie at the moment—'

'Rosie! How's the pregnancy going?'

'Yeah, she's still pregnant.'

'Thought she had the sprog last month?'

'No, it's still a foetus,' I say, fingering the serrated edge of my knife. 'Leo, listen, I can't really chat. I'm in a restaurant –' Rose flaps her hand at me, I suspect to indicate I should carry on.

'How's the diet going?' asks Leonard.

'It's not, really. I ate a Mars Bar yesterday in a moment of weakness.'

'A Mars Bar won't make much difference—'

'And a packet of Ginger Nuts, half a box of chocolates and three packets of Snax.'

'Well, you're under a lot of – let's say – *pressure* at the moment. You can start again when you get here.' He drops his voice. 'What are you wearing?'

'Er –' I look at Rosie. She is preoccupied with a bread roll that somehow managed to escape previously. 'That long, green skirt I wore to the company dinner last year.'

'You know I don't like that skirt,' says Leonard in a different voice.

I had forgotten that. 'Um, I left it out to go in the rubbish,' I lied, 'but the shippers packed everything else, so I didn't have much choice.'

'Babelicious, I can't wait to see you again.'

'Yeah, me too.' I hear a noise across the telephone line, like a door shutting, then someone's voice. 'What's that?' I say.

'What?'

'That noise?'

'I don't hear anything. Oh, it's probably the radio. I have it on in the background.'

'Oh, OK –'

'Listen, I've got to go—'

'Wait! Leo—'

'See you tomorrow. Love ya.'

'I love you too,' I say, before I realise I'm talking to an empty telephone line.

Although I was keen to get Leonard off the phone, it all seems a bit abrupt. The familiar anxiety rushes over me.

'How is he?' says Rose.

'OK,' I say, frowning. I replace the phone in my washbag. 'He worked late last night, he's listening to the radio and he's looking forward to seeing me, apparently.'

'Of course he is,' says Rose with her easy smile. 'He

must really miss you. Listen, Lara, I'm so sorry Jack and I couldn't have you to stay. We really wanted to—'

'Oh God, Rosie, stop,' I say, squeezing her hand. 'I know that!' Rose's guest room is being reincarnated as a nursery. Rose still finds time to hand-stencil perfectly coordinated anatomically correct fairies on the walls in addition to working full-time shifts at the hospital, looking after my three-year-old nephew and crafting five-course meals for her family three times a day.

'Why didn't you stay with Mum and Bill?' she asks.

'Ugh,' I say, rolling my eyes. 'If Mum didn't drive me insane, Bill would.'

'What's wrong with Bill?' says Rose impatiently. I'm not sure why she bothers; we've had this conversation many times. It is an emotional landmine that we occasionally prod – although never too hard.

'He's a plonker—'

'Oh, Lara!' She has her disapproving voice on.

'He's so tedious, he should be declared a national treasure,' I say.

Rose's mouth twitches, and I know I have her.

'The man recycles glad-wrap,' I say, and Rose laughs.

'He makes Mum happy—'

'And we know how difficult *that* is.'

Fortuitously, the waiter chooses this moment to deliver food. I can almost hear Rose's internal struggle: torn between pursuing the line of conversation or tucking into her rack of lamb.

'Can you reach the table?' I ask to deflect her. Rose's bump is pressed right up against the edge.

'Aren't you a howl?'

'Yeah. Although I've been a bit off form recently.'

'How are you getting to the airport tomorrow?' she asks through a mouthful of spinach.

'Taxi—'

'Jack and I would love to take you—'

'No,' I say. 'No, thanks,' I say more gently. 'I'd prefer to get a taxi, really. I want to say goodbye here. Tonight. You know?'

Rose nods. She looks a bit moist herself.

'Excuse me,' says a deep, cultured voice. We look up. It is the overstuffed woman. She really shouldn't wear trousers. 'Aren't you the Callaghan sisters?' she asks.

'Yes,' says Rose. She smiles expectantly – in every sense of the word.

'I thought so! You know, I have a memory for faces. Not so much yours,' she says to Rose. 'But you, dear,' she addresses me, 'you look so like your mother.'

I nearly fracture an eyeball with the effort it takes not to roll my eyes.

'You probably don't remember me; you girls were very small last time I saw you, which must have been – oh my goodness – twenty, twenty-five years ago. Doesn't the time fly? My, but you have grown!'

'Thank goodness for that,' I say. 'I was about three feet tall as a teenager.'

I wish she would go away.

'My goodness, I'm forgetting my manners. It's Theresa. Theresa Mannion? Boomer?' she says when Rose and I look at her blankly. 'I used to be a member of the Lawn Tennis Club. Your father was such a wonderful player. My goodness, he could serve a ball. He was so handsome in his sweatbands. We all thought he was like Bjorn Borg.' She laughs, rather like a startled horse. 'And how are your parents?'

'Fine,' says Rose. 'Thank you.'

'Are they still living out in Castletroy?'

'I'm afraid they separated,' says Rose.

'Really? Oh, what a shame – although hardly a surprise, I expect.'

Rose's fingers idly twirl her glass.

'Why? Did you fuck my father as well?' she says conversationally.

'Rosemary!' I whisper. The shock of the words in this muted environment is doubled by the fact that Rose uttered them. My sister has never sworn in living memory – unless you count the time she found Malibu Barbie's melted head all over her stamp collection. The Hungarian stamps were ruined beyond retrieval but even then, all she said was 'blast it'.

'Ex. Cuse. ME?' gasps the woman, her hand pressing down her bosom as if she fears it is about to take flight.

'That is what you were implying, I take it?' says Rose, never taking her eyes off the woman. 'That's why Mum kicked him out. My father screwed anything that wasn't nailed down. If you didn't fuck him, you were in the minority.'

'I-you-oh! Oh! Oh! I have NEVER been so insulted –'

'I very much doubt that,' says Rose.

'*Rosemary!*'

The woman turns and stalks off. Three steps away she pauses, but presumably can't think of something suitably savage to say, so she carries on.

'Rose!' I gasp. 'How could you . . . how could you say those things?'

'What things?' Rose is pale and it is only now, as she releases her white-knuckled hold on the table, I realise she has been gripping it.

'About . . . Dad.'

'Lara, you have never been particularly fond of the truth—'

'What's that supposed to mean?'

'Dad shagged half of Limerick—'

'What are you talking about?' I say, bewildered.

'Lara, were you brought up in the same house as I was? Dad was a philandering prick—'

'That's a-a lie!' Then again, Rose is genetically incapable of lying. She would have to consult a dictionary for the meaning of the word. 'Why are you saying this? It's – it's Mum – you've always been on her side, buying into her propaganda.'

'Oh please, Lara!' At that moment, Rose sounds exactly like our mother. She looks at me closely. 'You don't remember, do you? Or you don't want to. Either way, it amounts to the same thing, I suppose. Don't you remember all the times Dad was supposed to collect us from school and never showed up? Or when he left us in the library and told us to wait for him, and the library shut and we had to wait outside on the steps? Or what about him working late at the office?' She bit this out.

'He had a job—'

'All right, how about the dinner? The one for Dad's clients and "business associates"?' Rose clearly enunciates the quotation marks. 'Mum cooked for three days, and Dad brought that whore home. Remember?' But the last word is less a question than a directive.

'Oh Jesus,' I whispered. The dinner. Dad had invited someone he introduced as his secretary. I was twelve, maybe thirteen. I thought Fiona was elegant. She was young, slim and attractive. I yearned for a perm and a miniskirt like hers.

Dad spent more time talking to Fiona than his clients. He touched her hair and laughed loudly at things she said. I thought Fiona must have been very funny. She looked up at him through her eyelashes. All the time they stood exclusively, unnecessarily close. Mum burned the roast and wept for an hour.

I was sent to my room after I ate the ice cream reserved for the baked Alaska. (I also cut off Dad's partner's shoelaces with a pair of scissors, but this was only discovered later. It made a change to be in trouble with Dad rather than Mother.)

Not only do I *know*, but also, subconsciously, I have always known. Although the evidence was there, the knowledge never made the journey to conscious – or else I ignored it. I'm good at that. I've had plenty of practice.

'Why didn't you say anything before?'

'Oh please, Lara. I *have*! You never heard, but you always made excuses for him – and I understand that. He's my father, too. I love him. Mainly because I have to, but. The fact is, Dad has never been loyal to anyone. He serially betrayed everyone that mattered. Especially those who loved him – like Mum. And you and me.'

The truth of this instils a sense of loss and grief so intense, it is like a blow. I swallow, but can't hold it back. Suddenly I am sobbing: huge, raw sobs that suck all the air out of my lungs. People glance towards our table, then avert their eyes.

'Oh God, Lara, I'm sorry,' says Rose, tears springing to her eyes. 'I shouldn't have – I'm so sorry. I didn't mean to – this isn't how I wanted to – the last time I see you for who knows how long. That woman, she upset me, and I'm hormonal and have had too many fishcakes—'

'No,' is all I can manage to say past the gulping. I

shake my head and reach for her hand, squeeze it in an effort to communicate that she should wait. 'It's not what you said,' I say when I can substitute words for gasps. 'Well, it *is* what you said, obviously. But I'm g-glad you said it. I just – I feel – I always blamed Mum for what happened—'

'I know.'

'It must have been awful for her.'

'Well, you of all people should know about that.' I ignore this because I haven't the emotional reserves for another Oprah moment, so Rose carries on. 'But Mum, she had no career, no prospects, nowhere to go – and she had us to worry about, too. She put up with it for years. It took guts to leave him, till. While I'm handing out hard knocks, you could consider giving her a break. It was awful for her, you know.'

'And all I've ever done is to blame her. Oh, Rosie! I just – I feel – I feel so ashamed of myself.'

'Don't give yourself too hard a time. It's Dad's fault, not yours—'

'How I treated Mum is my fault. I backed the wrong side, didn't I?'

'Lara, it wasn't a *game*. We all lost. Except for Dad, of course.'

'Men like him don't lose,' I say bitterly.

I am not necessarily referring to my father.

Rose shrugs. 'Perhaps they do in the long run.'

Rose's eyes flicker towards my half-eaten fishcakes as I push them away. I release her hand in case she rips my arm off when she goes for her fork.

'You know, I wish I had a better relationship with Mum,' I say. 'But it's as if we're doomed to follow the same tired old B-movie script over and over again. I wind her up, she disapproves, roll credits. Coming soon: *Mother's Wrath Part Four Six Oh Two.*'

'Lara, Mum's not about to change,' says Rose through a mouthful of fishcake. 'If you want a relationship with her, it's up to you. A first step might be acknowledging that she did the best she could under the circumstances. Stop blaming her for everything that's wrong with your life and take some responsibility.'

'You're very lippy today—'

'Sorry, sorry. Hormones.'

'Suppose you might as well get the most out of the excuse while you still can.' After a pause, I say, 'Mum doesn't like me as much as you.'

'Lara, forgive me if I sound exasperated, but it's hardly *surprising*! You're not very nice to her. For some reason, she loves you, but. We all do.'

'OK, now you're just *trying* to make me cry,' I say, sniffing. 'Rosie, how come I'm so fucked up and you're not?'

'We're just different, is all.' I notice she doesn't even attempt to deny that I'm fucked up.

'Yeah.' Suddenly, I feel exhausted. 'Is it OK if we get the bill?' I say. Rose nods, and when a waiter looks our way I endorse the air beside my head. 'My treat, I'll shout.'

'No, this is on me. Although you'll have to hand me up my bag.'

'Well, I suppose you did eat most of my food – and you're very insistent. Thanks, Rosie. Surprised you agreed to pass up dessert.'

Rose looks momentarily panicked, then relaxes. 'That's OK. If I eat any more, I'll explode.'

'How about I get the tip? I'm sure I have some change

in here.' I pick up my washbag, give it a shake and hold it up by one end. The contents spill on to the table: my phone, keys, some dirham coins, receipts, three scrunchies, topless lipsticks, a bottle of Tippex, an egg timer, a pair of headphones, a dictionary, my beloved kingfisher-blue notebook. And a passport photo, which twirls lazily mid-air before settling on the table.

I make a grab for it, but Rose gets there first.

'What's this?' she says, picking it up.

'No idea,' I lie, trying to snatch it out of her hand. Rose jerks it towards her, just out of reach.

'God! This was taken a while ago! How old were you?'

'Twenty,' I say, resigned.

'Look at that hair. Black with blue ends, wasn't it?'

'Yeah.'

'You look beautiful. And happy,' she says, sounding surprised. I suppose she's thinking of the grim horror zone of my teenage years: the festering zits, the savage hormones, the sulk attacks that showed no mercy. 'I'm impressed you were able to get your foot into the frame.'

'I was pretty limber back then.'

'Who's that you're suckered on to?'

'Conn O'Neill.' I strive for a casual tone. 'He was my – actually, he was my first boyfriend. We were a hot item for three years,' I say, slightly mockingly.

'Oh, right. I never met him, did I?' she asks, drawing the photo closer to study his face. 'Wow, he's cute.'

'Yeah,' I say. Rose hands back the photo and I can't help glancing quickly at it. I run my thumb gently across it, before reinstating the memory behind a stack of café loyalty cards.

Rose looks at me sharply. 'Weren't you just fooling around with him?'

'Er, no. No, I wasn't fooling.'

'You didn't think it was for ever, though? At that age?'

When she puts it like that, I feel silly admitting, 'Actually, I did.'

Rosemary says, 'Wasn't he a bit intense, though?'

'Yeah.' I smile reminiscently. 'Still is.'

'What do you mean, "still is"?' asks Rosemary.

I smile awkwardly. 'Er, well. Um, I'm kind of still sort of in touch with him.' Rosemary raises her eyebrows and waits. 'OK, look. About three years ago, I was researching extreme sports for an article, so I joined an online forum – you know, like a discussion board? – about triathlon running. And this member – A42 – started chatting to me—'

'A42?' says Rosemary.

'It's the answer to the ultimate question of life, the universe, and everything. It's from *The Hitchhiker's Guide to the Galaxy*?' Rosie shook her head. 'Anyway,' I carry on hurriedly, 'we got friendly, started emailing, and then one day, I realised it was Conn—'

'Wait, wait, wait. What was he doing on a discussion forum on triathlon running?'

'Oh, he runs ironmans, apparently. Took it up four years ago—'

'And did you know this when—'

'No, no, I hadn't a clue. I mean, Conn was always into sport. He cycled everywhere in college, and in Dubai he went jogging and swimming. But meeting him online was really . . . completely random,' I say, truthfully.

'So is he still gorgeous? I suppose he must be if he's a triathlete – although he'll probably have horrendous arthritis in a few years,' says Dr Jeffries.

'Yes, well, er. I don't know what he looks like. You see,

he doesn't know my true identity. That I'm me.'

'What?' Rosemary looks understandably confused. 'Who does he think you are?'

'Um, my online alias is "OwnWorstEnemy".'

'Appropriate. Are you going to *tell* him?'

I shrug. 'I've been meaning to – but it's so wonderful getting to know him again without having to unpack all the emotional baggage. You know?'

'I have no idea, but I'll take your word for it.'

I pour salt in a neat pile on the tablecloth, then brush it away with the back of my hand. I swallow before saying, 'If this is all I can have of him, it's better than nothing at all. Oh, *fantastic*! Here's the bill.' The only thing better than the bill's arrival would have been a minor explosion in a corner of the restaurant (as long as there were no casualties). 'I'll get this—'

'Thought I was getting it?'

'Oh, yes. Thanks.'

On the way back to the hotel after dinner, the taxi driver is keen to practise his English. He is grimly insistent about what grand weather we're having. Normally I would be the first to agree at length, before discussing the weekly forecast, the Prime Minister's hairdo and the annual arable yield of the Fields of Athenry.

Not tonight. I respond in noncommittal monosyllables and once – contradicting my Irish nature – ignore a direct question. To my relief, he lapses into sullen silence just before Ball's Bridge.

In the space of half an hour, the history of my life has been rewritten. I pick out the memories and examine them from a different angle. For so long, I have cast my mother as the evil villain, arch-nemesis supreme. It may be too early to stop automatically disliking her for the mere fact that the unfortunate woman is my mother.

I consider asking the taxi driver to make a detour by Mum's place. Not only is it eleven-thirty p.m., however, but I have also not yet figured out how to repair decades of damage. 'Sorry' might cover some of it. I suspect the remainder might take more than ten minutes and a cup of tea.

I occasionally considered how the separation must have been for Mum, but never from her perspective. I have no excuse for that because, in addition to the other – let's call them 'attributes' – I also inherited Mum's catastrophic taste in men. When it comes to the opposite sex, I am a disaster area complete with police tape, fingerprint specialists and a chalk outline of my body on a concrete floor.

I know what living with betrayal feels like.

I know about ignoring the pulsating ulcer, the churning bile in the gut telling you it's all wrong, wrong, *wrong*; denying the essence of what you know to be true, because you love someone.

I know about questioning your sanity when he swears he's never seen the knickers you brandish under his nose. When you find him shagging some slapper against the kitchen sink, and he sounds so *plausible* when he says she ripped off her clothes and he was actually trying to push her away. With his dick.

And I know all about making excuses. Lipstick on his collar? Quite likely that some woman fell on him entirely by accident (not even necessarily a woman). Lipstick on his penis? Could be permanent marker; or trace lines for an 'I love Lara' tattoo down his penis which he planned specially for my birthday.

See? Any number of possibilities. Because, however implausible, excuses are preferable to the truth. Which is: that I am worthless and do not deserve better.

I am familiar with desperately thinking I can change him. That maybe, if I wore sexier underwear, or washed up more, or talked dirty, or kept the fridge stocked with Corona, then he would be faithful.

And even though logically I know it is *them* and not me (apart from actually choosing the fuckers in the first place), it is no easier reconciling this knowledge with how I feel.

Which brings us to self-loathing. I am particularly adept at that. I know how it is to be terrified he will leave, because I might never find anyone else and am doomed to be forever known as the spinster aunt who smells strange and grunts when she sits down.

You hear about men being wired differently, how sex is nothing to do with love, what the little lady doesn't know won't hurt her, blah blah blah yawn.

It is bullshit.

Of course men know it's wrong, because they don't tell.

Is it the worst treachery one person can commit against another? What makes it so heinous is that the crime is perpetrated by someone who claims to love you.

I have evidently been subscribing to a pretty poor brand of love.

But you know what? The only man who was ever faithful betrayed me worse than any of them.

Conn's weapons were not deceit and lies. He wielded the truth with more devastating effect. You could call it extreme combat honesty.

Of course, betrayal is measured by the depth of hurt,

which is directly correlated to your feelings for someone. And I loved Conn with the ferocious, fervent, all-consuming passion of youth. No holds barred, no emotion untapped.

So, Conn. He was my first real boyfriend if you don't count Peter Hayes – which I don't. (I mean, Peter asked me out, said, 'I suppose you want me to kiss you now?' and I replied, 'Not really, but thanks for the offer', then broke up with him the following day because it was moving too fast.)

Conn was the first guy I ever kissed. I expected it to be a magical, transporting experience. The reality was more like a deep-conditioning tonsil enema. But Conn was a quick study.

His love validated me, made me special. Not many boyfriends withstood the nuclear force of my need longer than a week or two (the more cockroach-like, maybe a month). I was so violently codependent, I could barely stand to go to the bathroom. I surrounded myself with hangers-on, most of whom ... well, let's just say there was never a queue for the bathroom.

Naïvely, I thought love was enough. I was plugged into the mainframe of popular culture and believed the propaganda pushed by pop songs and movies. Yes, I am sorry to say I believed love was The Answer. There was no problem it could not overcome – apart from maybe running out of toilet paper.

I thought since Conn and I were In Love™ that would be enough. Conn and I, we wouldn't stumble into the same pitfalls other couples did. Any potential obstacles would be blown away by the force of our passion.

What I didn't understand (amongst other things) is that relationships have set-backs – all of them – even those with an excess of love and public face-nuzzling. The ones that last – the couples that prevail – are the ones that fight for it, the ones who don't just stand by and watch it all disappear.

Conn didn't fight.

I open my wallet and coax the passport photo out with my thumb. It is, in fact, two photos, folded along a worn join at the bottom of the first photo and the top of the second. I straighten it out and our faces flash orange in the streetlights.

In the top photo, Conn stares earnestly at the camera, weighed down with all that self-imposed expectation – or possibly the surfeit of brain matter. A lock of hair flops forward on his forehead like an inverted question mark. I smile, remembering how he used to alternately tug it forward (when reading or solving equations) or push it back (when stuck on a problem or eating noodles). In black and white the lean planes of his face are stark, and his ice-blue eyes almost colourless.

I know it is ridiculous, but it seems as if Conn actually *sees* me through the photo. I've never been able to look at it while picking my teeth.

I am sitting on Conn's knee, my arm slung across his shoulder, hand curled around his neck. I am in profile as I face him, tongue extended and poised to deliver an electric eardrum.

In the second photo, Conn is snapped at the moment he bolts towards the camera. He is blurred and his eyes are crinkled from laughing, but that gorgeous, great smile he so rarely aired is clearly visible. And me: I am looking at him as if he is the best thing in the world, possibly the universe, if not the entire galaxy (even the unexplored parts).

Which, at the time, he was.

I don't often look at the photos, mainly because, every time I see them, I feel a real echo of the pain of losing him.

Conn was possibly the most driven person I've ever known. He had a phenomenal work ethic, and was absolutely focused. He had his whole future planned out, and nothing was about to deflect him. Not even me.

He had been offered a job in Azerbaijan. I bite my lip, involuntarily remembering the day he told me. My heart was breaking and it wasn't just a stress fracture; it was cracking violently like an earthquake tears up ground. I couldn't stop sobbing.

I suggested going with him. I can still see the look on his face, like he was *trapped*; the relief in his eyes when I withdrew the offer.

'Please,' I had said. It was supposed to be a quiet, dignified request – for what, I'm not sure. Please don't do this, I think. Maybe: please don't leave me. Or just: please don't.

Please.

Unfortunately, the word surfed out of my mouth on a wave of pain, with the result that I sounded more like a drowning mammal.

Technically, I broke up with him but only because I got in there first. Yes, indeed, I salvaged some pride. I keep it in a jar on my mantelpiece.

For weeks, my entire body had been in pain. My heart burned like it had a cardiovascular case of cystitis. Every thought hurt; every emotion ached; every action seemed like a bleak, pointless drain of energy. I wrote things in my journal like: 'I am an oyster whose precious pearl has been plundered', and 'I ache like a pupa being eaten alive from the inside by wasp larvae', which – apart from being up its own arse, was a relatively accurate reflection of how I felt.

I made deals with destiny. You know, like: if I can have Conn, I'll give up drinking and smoking and being nasty about people behind their back.

Well, definitely the smoking.

And I ran away. Of course.

That's one of the few things I excel at.

I reverted to relationships based on mind games and power struggles. They were safer.

I built my life around avoiding Conn. It was my reason for existence. I rarely returned to my hometown. When I heard Conn was in Singapore, I made sure not to go there. In fact, I took every reasonable precaution to ensure that the next time we met Conn O'Neill would be busking before the gates of Hell.

So you will understand my surprise when I met him nowhere near Hell six years later.

Heat Recovery System Generators

I nearly fell off my chair when Conn walked into the conference room in the Dubai Branch of Voltech Ltd. I mean, what were the odds?

(Pretty slim. See previous page.)

Nine years before, when I went to UCCD, a hard bookie would have given you favourable odds that our paths would cross. After all, Conn was at the same university. I chose a mathematics stream, because I knew he was studying maths too. Also, I kind of stalked him. So when I contrived a ridiculous excuse to engineer a meeting, it fell less under the category of 'chance' and strayed more into the territory of probability.

But this; *this* was unexpected.

I'd been an Account Manager for Voltech Ltd for eighteen months. It was the latest in a wide range of work experiences: waitress, trainee plumber, Ms Whippy, receptionist for the porn production company Big Cocks Media Ltd, council worker specialising in traffic cone placement, dog groomer, and dental assistant.

I had no experience selling gas turbine generators, but answered Voltech's advert because I thought I might get a free holiday in Dubai. I invented 'a degree in Civil

Engineering or similar', although my only qualification for the job was fluency in English. The interviewer was also impressed by the size of my norks (although I wasn't sure of their efficacy in a Muslim country, I needn't have worried; it appears men are men, regardless of religion).

In fact, the job wasn't challenging. Gas turbines are much simpler than, say, mixing filling cement. They transform combustion fuel to electricity; once you've seen one, you've seen them all. As long as you can get the word 'megawatts' into any given sentence, you're grand.

I had just conducted eight interviews in succession. The last applicant had high-fived my manager and me, and addressed us interchangeably as 'dude'. As my manager, Philip, opened the door to evict the surfie with the career crisis, I was distracted by a compelling impulse to bang my head off the table. Instead, I closed my eyes and pinched the bridge of my nose, so I did not see the next applicant enter. Even when Phil said, 'Connell?', I ignored him (I thought he was offering me a nut).

It was only when that low, authoritative, unmistakable voice said, 'Hello', that it registered. When I say 'registered', my central nervous system distributed a seismic shock to all my nerve endings.

Thereupon I was guilty of perpetrating a number of terrible clichés. I froze in my seat; my pen dropped from my trembling fingers; and my eyes filled with tears. Thankfully I had replaced my glass on the table, or it would have shattered all over the floor to illustrate with unnecessary symbolism what Conn had done to my heart. Although to accurately demonstrate that, you would really have to vaporise the glass as well.

I had almost managed to convince myself that I would

see Conn after all these years and wonder: '*What was I thinking?*'

But no, I could see *exactly* what I had been thinking, because my head was currently staging an updated version of a sort of erotic porn fairytale.

Unlike other ex-boyfriends, I had never wondered What He Was Doing Now. You know: where he was, what he looked like, whether he was happy or, more relevantly, unhappy.

No. In Conn's case, I had *obsessed* about it.

I had imagined meeting him again. It involved me looking gorgeous and unattainable, wrapped in a cocoon of fame after winning the eight hundred metres gold at the most recent Olympics, or an Oscar for my heart-breaking portrayal of a lesbian cripple triumphing against insurmountable odds.

Certainly not like this, sweating lightly in a Middle East-appropriate suit and a blouse I had hand-sewn brass washers on to.

The fucker looked as good as ever. Better, if anything. Considering how little he noticed or cared, Conn had always been unnecessarily handsome, but in college he had sometimes looked a bit like a starving dog (his nan once described him as 'all ribs and balls').

Over the years, he had obviously grown into his own skin. I was infuriated how well it suited him. He had the same intent, mildly grim and unsettlingly sexy look. Even from three metres away, I could clearly see the fine black lines circumscribing his irises. His hair was still slightly too long and I thought he could have brushed it for the interview; but instead of the wave of irritation I anticipated, the effect was more rueful affection. I would have to watch out for that.

My legs straightened of their own accord. They felt insubstantially wobbly, so I leaned a hand on the conference table.

'Well, well, well,' I said, my voice unnaturally high in my ears. 'If it isn't Conn O'Neill.'

Conn looked over. 'Lara!' He looked genuinely thrilled to see me. Or as thrilled as Conn was capable of – which, calibrated to most peoples' standard emotional spectrum, was around the level of 'quite pleased'. He shook off Philip's hand and covered the distance between us in two strides.

Then he embraced me. I was totally unprepared for it. I closed my eyes briefly as I smelled his signature scent: a mixture of pheromones, shampoo and lightly sautéed brain cells. I experienced a wrench of longing, regret and pure rage. Breaking free, I took a step back and a firmer grip on the conference table.

'What are you doing here?' asked Conn.

Stealing my question too, I fumed. The *cheek* of the fucker.

'You know each other?' said Philip.

I considered denying it and claiming Conn was some weapon-concealing psycho. Unfortunately, before this thought process had a chance to fully mature, Conn said, 'Yes.'

'Oh yeah, we know each other,' I said. Even though there was nothing funny or even vaguely humorous about the statement, I laughed. It was too loud and featured a jagged edge. Philip glanced at me with his eyebrows raised and I stopped abruptly.

'We attended university at the same time,' said Conn, 'and we—'

'We were also at school together,' I said quickly.

'And we—'

'We were both members of the Drama Soc.'

'No, we weren't,' said Conn, frowning. 'We—'

'Conn, I was *there*. You don't have to remind me.'

'Imagine meeting here like this,' said Philip, looking from Conn to me and back again. 'What a coincidence!'

'What a coincidence!' I repeated, and laughed again. It sounded so bitter that I resolved not to repeat the exercise in the immediate future. 'So, tell me,' I said to Conn, 'what are *you* doing here?'

Conn frowned. 'Is this the interview for Product Support Manager for Voltech Limited?'

'Yes. But I thought you were a civil engineer,' I said.

'I am. I also have a higher degree in electrical engineering.'

'*Why?*'

'I was bored, thought it would be interesting.'

'Allrighty,' said Philip, 'would you like to take a seat?'

Conn nodded and folded himself into the chair. He propped the ankle of one leg on the knee of the other and sat back, waiting, with the stillness that had been his trademark when I had known him.

What I wanted to know was: why the hell was Conn crashing my interview and impersonating a genuine job applicant? But then I reached for the pile of CVs Phil had shortlisted, shuffled the first one to the back and there, at the top of the next, it said 'Connell O'Neill'.

I had thumbed through the list of résumés Phil had shortlisted – of course. I had given them a good thirty seconds of full, undivided attention before the first applicant arrived. Conn's name had failed to register. Generally speaking, I've never understood why people put their names in the most prominent position on a CV.

When faced with a stack of applications from people describing themselves as 'concsientous with exemplary attention to detail', the only things you want to know – apart from whether they can spell – are their qualifications, relevant job experience and whether they list 'hiding' as a hobby/interest.

Now that I saw Conn's name, the letters sizzled off the page and branded themselves across my corneas. There in black and white was Conn's attendance at Gonzaga Comprehensive, Limerick; his first class BSc in Civil Engineering from the same university I had attended, the year before I was supposed to graduate.

His CV had evidently piqued Phil's interest. He had highlighted sections and annotated it with questions. I saw he was particularly interested in Conn's two years' experience in the Far East installing gas turbines with heat recovery system generators, auxiliary boilers and back pressure steam turbines. Not only because Phil had no life to speak of, but also because Voltech was contracted to supply the same type of turbines to my major client, Abu Dhabi Electricity Board.

With a shock, I realised that if Conn got this job, I would have to *work* with him. Oh my God! Nine hours a day, six days a week, with business trips and the occasional lunch.

No, no, no, no, no.

That could not happen.

'So, Conn,' Philip was saying. 'Tell us a bit about yourself.'

'Oh, this should be fun,' I said, and snorted. Although I didn't actually see it, I wouldn't have been at all surprised had it produced flame, smoke and whirling sparks.

Conn stared at Philip blankly. 'What do you want to know?'

'Er, well. Just. Generally,' said Philip, rotating his hand as if stroking an imaginary cat. 'Let's try something more, er . . . for example, where did you go to school? What did you study?'

'That is covered in detail in my résumé.'

'Sure. Ah – OK. Do you have any interests?'

'Mr O'Neill builds circuit boards,' I said, sketching a cartoon depicting Conn being decapitated by an airborne squid.

'Er,' said Philip, 'I see. That sounds . . .' He decided even 'interesting' did not cover it.

'I used to,' corrected Conn. 'I donated my collection to Dr Barnardo's.'

Philip laughed nervously. 'No, seriously.'

'You see, Philip,' I said, adding another splatter of blood with a satisfying slash of my pencil, 'telling you about himself would serve no purpose because that would be Mr O'Neill's *opinion* and, as such, largely subjective—'

'Excuse me,' interrupted Conn, 'wholly subjective.'

'What?' I snapped.

'My opinion is not largely subjective, it is wholly subjective. Therefore, it has little to no relevance to your assessment of my suitability for the position.'

Philip's mouth had dropped open. 'Mr O'Neill, these are standard interview questions, designed to give some indication as to the applicant's aptitude—'

'They are designed to gauge the applicant's perception of themselves,' said Conn. 'In some instances, it may provide a measure of the applicant's social skills and/or their ability to fabricate lies. Since this is a technical position, my response would be immaterial.'

'Well, then. How are we expected to assess your suitability for the position, Mr O'Neill?' said Philip.

'Excuse me,' said Conn. 'I do not understand, due to the obtuse nature of the question. Do you want me to advise you how to conduct an interview?'

'No. No, no,' said Philip, shaking his head slightly as he looked at Conn. He looked like he was questioning his will to live. I fully sympathised. I had first-hand experience of how Conn could have that effect on people. It looked like I didn't have to worry about Conn getting the job. 'How about . . . OK, what would you say are your strengths?'

'In relation to the job?'

'Yes, in relation to the job,' barked Philip. Great: he was rattled. None of the other applicants had achieved that, not even the one who had tried to hug him at the conclusion of the interview.

'I am a brilliant engineer,' said Conn. There was no bravado behind this statement; he presented it as fact, in much the same way he might have said, 'I have two legs ending in foot appendages.'

'According to what criteria?' I said starchily. His composure annoyed the crap out of me. When I was making such a genuine effort to be obnoxious, the least he could do was to get even a little bit disgruntled. On the contrary, he was positively brimming with gruntledness.

'I have a first class BSc in Civil Engineering, and a masters in Electrical Engineering,' said Conn, leaning forward. 'The technology I developed as part of my thesis on reducing gas and thermal emissions is now widely accepted as standard in the industry.'

Conn grew animated as he talked, using his hands to

draw transformers in the air, writing equations on the palm of his right hand, once leaping up to scribble lines of symbols on the whiteboard. Conn was still as passionate as ever – about some things.

On my right, Phil looked a little shaken by Conn's unbridled enthusiasm for power generation.

'Well, it certainly sounds as if you are qualified for the job, Mr O'Neill,' said Philip.

'I think you will find I am overqualified.'

'Er—'

'Philip, I should say Mr O'Neill would be over-qualified for most positions – although let's not be overly positive about that. Mr O'Neill, why are you interested in this job? Since it is so clearly beneath you.'

'Beneath me?' said Conn, frowning slightly. 'That is inaccurate. There are aspects that interest me—'

'For example?'

'In First World countries, power schemes have to be integrated with legacy systems, but here – this region – in the Middle East everything is less than four decades old. This country's infrastructure is built on the latest technology. The United Arab Emirates is at the cutting edge of power generation,' he said, practically drooling with the wild excitement of it all.

'Allrighty,' said Philip, nodding with increasing vigour. 'May I ask, Mr O'Neill, what are your weaknesses?'

Conn thought about this for a while. 'Some people think I'm strange,' he said. I snorted again.

'I er, noticed that,' said Philip. 'That may be an issue. Although this is primarily a technical position, you would be required to visit client sites.'

'Previous employers stipulated I was permitted to say "hello", "nice to meet you", and "maybe". I was also limited to answering direct questions. It was generally effective.'

I picked up Conn's résumé and riffled through it, turning each page with a loud *crack!*

'Great,' said Philip. He slapped his hand down on Conn's CV, crumpling a page in mid-flip.

'Any other weaknesses?' I snapped. 'What about, for example, betrayal and abandonment?'

'No,' said Conn firmly.

'Nothing?'

'I'm not good at cutting out circles.'

'What?!' Beside me, I could practically hear Philip trying to decide whether Conn was hilarious or obtuse to the extent of having much the same effect. Whatever the final decision, he gave a sharp burst of laughter.

Uh-oh.

That was a bad sign.

'OK,' said Philip, stretching the vowels to breaking point. 'If Lara has no other questions?' He raised an eyebrow at me, and I shook my head in response.

Crack! blah blah school, blah qualifications blah, *crack!*, blah blah work experience – wait!

'Well, I think that about covers it,' Philip was saying.

'Actually, not quite,' I said. 'Mr O'Neill, I note from your résumé that from September 1995 to 1998, you were employed by Quantam Electronics in Dublin.'

'That is correct—'

'Now, this surprises me, Mr O'Neill. Because as far as I was aware, you were offered a placement in Azerbaijan.'

'Yes—'

'But – surprisingly – in fact, astonishingly – well, I don't know if anyone else here is astonished – but I, for one, am *amazed* – to find that you actually remained in

Dublin. Not even a day – not even half a fucking hour – forgive my language – in Azerbaifuckingjan.'

'Lara!' gasped Phil. According to his frightfully English code of public school manners, I had just committed the verbal equivalent of climbing on the desk and firing a ping pong ball out of my vagina.

'I turned down Babco because I was offered a position with Quantam. I was attracted by their extensive training programme. The company funded my masters degree in energy con—'

'How deliciously lovely.' My voice wobbled precariously.

'Lara, I never said I worked in Azerbaijan. I did not think rejected job offers were relevant. If you like, I can list them. It might take some time—'

'That will not be necessary. I am only interested in this particular one.'

'The circums-stances changed—'

'Evidently.'

'Lara. I t-tried to—'

'It was just an excuse, wasn't it? You couldn't think of any other way to tell me – it was the easiest, the most convenient way to—'

'No! Lara, no, that's n-n-not what it was at all.'

Philip stood abruptly, sliding his fingers round my upper arm. 'Excuse us one sec, will you?' he addressed Conn, tugging me to my feet. 'I need a quick word with my colleague here.'

Philip hustled me out the door and into the corridor, where he shook me free. A jackhammer from the road-works outside provided a fitting soundtrack.

'Christ, Lara!' he hissed. 'What is *wrong* with you? I'm surprised he hasn't walked out—'

'So am I. He's pretty stubborn, but give me another five minutes—'

'What do you think you're doing?'

'He's not suitable—'

'What are you talking about?' said Philip, hitching his belt agitatedly. 'He has the best qualifications of anyone so far, along with overseas experience—'

'He is socially inept—'

'I know he's not exactly a people person—'

'Oh, *you think*?!' I snapped.

'Well, that's what you're employed for—'

'What about when we're at a client site – what do you want me to do? Duct tape his mouth shut?'

'Our clients are all wallawallas; they won't understand a word he says. Hell, *I* don't understand half of what he says. Lara, he is the best candidate by far—'

'I liked the guy with the Hitler moustache—'

'The one whose email address is *sexmachine@ geturfreakon.com*? He took out a sandwich in the middle of the interview!'

'He was hungry – I can understand that! And he offered it around—'

'Lara, he forgot the word for "turbine".' That might not sound like much of a big deal, but it is in the energy supply business.

He had me there.

'How about the one before him—'

'The one you hypnotised with your breasts? I don't entirely blame him, but I'm concerned how it might affect his productivity.'

'Look, Phil, I have to work with whoever we hire. You said,' I sternly disciplined the tremor in my voice, 'you said I would have executive decision –'

'Within *reason*, Lara! I have a duty to the company too. You can't deny that technically, Mr O'Neill is extremely competent. And you need a Product Support Manager for the AEB upgrade.'

We spent a few minutes glaring at each other, then Philip sighed.

'What did the guy ever do to you?' he asked, leaning a shoulder against the wall and crossing his arms.

'He – he attacked me! All right? Six years ago, when we – he – he tried to stab me with a with a sawn-off toothbrush.'

Philip gasped. 'Lara! That's terrible. Did he really?'

I hesitated, but I knew Philip's Google search on 'Connell O'Neill' and 'sawn-off toothbrush' would yield no results. 'No, not really—'

'Dammit, Lara!' He slammed the flat of his hand into the wall. Thankfully he missed my head.

Only by half an inch.

'Philip,' I raised my chin. 'I'm not working with Conn O'Neill.'

'I see. That might be awkward when he's your Product Support Manager.'

'No, no, no. No *way*. It's – it's him or me,' I said.

'Allrighty. Well, I suppose Voltech can pay you thirty days severance and work out your gratuity later—'

'You're *firing* me? Sacrificing a loyal staff member for that verbally constipated—'

'Lara, you are biting my balls off!' (I would like to point out the metaphorical nature of that statement; I was by no means on my knees snapping at Philip's groin.) 'I don't respond well to ultimatums.'

'At least I know how much Voltech values me, which is not very much—'

'You are extremely valuable to Voltech.'

'I will reflect on that comforting thought while I clear my desk.'

'I don't suppose there's any way I could make you change your mind,' said Philip, sidling closer.

'No,' I said, reversing into the wall.

'I would be sorry to lose you,' he whispered, sliding his hand up my arm. 'Mr O'Neill is not half as hot as you.'

I rolled my eyes.

'Look,' said Philip. His fingers caressed my breast through my blouse. A passer-by would not notice he was tickling my nipple unless they performed a forensic examination, but I glanced nervously down the corridor regardless. 'Give O'Neill six months – to the end of his probation. If he doesn't work out, we'll fire him.' He smelled my hesitation. 'You can do it personally.'

'Could I have Security throw him out?'

'Yes, I don't see why not.'

'Through a window?'

'I don't think Voltech's insurance covers that, but the heavies could probably rough him up a bit in the back alley.'

Someone rounded the corner. It was Voltech's receptionist, Vino, stumbling against the wall as she figured out how to operate a pair Dolce and Gabbana heels.

Phil backed away from me. We were not 'official' yet – and even if we were, there were professional standards to be maintained. In fact, Vino knew about Phil and me, since she was the closest I had to a friend in Dubai. 'Well, I'm glad we have that sorted out,' he said formally.

He opened the conference-room door, squeezing my waist as he propelled me through.

'Sorry about that,' Philip addressed Conn, hitching his trousers as he returned to his seat, 'Have you any further questions, Mr O'Neill?'

'No.'

'You realise Voltech follows a six-day working week from Saturday to Thursday?' I asked. The question was motivated by pure altruism. Philip had overlooked that minor detail at my interview, so I was concerned that full disclosure took place.

'Five and a half,' said Philip sharply.

'Thursdays are seven a.m. to two p.m. with no lunch break. Voltech's PR Department never successfully convinced me that seven hours constitutes a half-day.'

'That is acceptable,' said Conn.

'Also,' I directed another pointed look at Philip, 'as per UAE labour law, your thirty days leave include weekends, which works out as just over four weeks, not six weeks as you might think—'

'Mr O'Neill, thank you for your time,' said Philip, rising to his feet. 'We'll be in touch. By the way, Voltech is also looking for a marketing manager. You wouldn't know of anyone, would you?'

'Actually,' said Conn, 'I know someone with a marketing qualification, but he's a petrol attendant now.'

When I returned from work that day, Philip had let himself into my flat. He was sprawled across my sofa wearing a fat-hugging leather outfit accessorised with metal studs.

'Philip's been a naughty boy,' he said.

Oh, for the love of – I had no idea where he got the impression I was into that sort of stuff; I had certainly never said anything. (I mean, how do you even bring it up? 'If I squeeze into a rubber costume, would you be on for a bit of spanky panky?')

I sent him to bed without any dinner while I changed into a rubber bustier with matching suspenders. Then I tied his testicles in a reef knot and belted the crap out of him with a hairbrush.

Side Effects: Temporary

I mentally prepared for Conn's arrival by pretending not to think about him, snapping at Phil and pickling myself in alcohol.

Three weeks later, when Conn walked into my office, I realised my preparations had been insufficient. I wondered whether seeing him would always feel like my spleen had spontaneously imploded.

'Hello,' said Conn. He smiled at me. It plucked my stomach lining.

I raised my eyebrow (I had practised in a mirror until this looked edgy and ambiguous, and occasionally dangerous in the right context). 'I would appreciate it if you knocked.'

'Why?'

'I don't need a reason,' I snapped. 'It's my office.'

'OK. Can I come in anyway?'

'I'm really very busy,' I said, pecking industriously at my keyboard. Salk frog wadger boik tyffer, I wrote.

'I can wait,' he said, taking the chair before my desk.

'Might take a while.' Alsk eur; powi ahg hopper9.

'That's OK.'

'Probably the rest of the day.' Boknads, fk7 ask dij. Kiqweur polyps.

'All right.'

I shrugged. 'Suit yourself.'

'Thank you,' said Conn with no apparent sense of irony.

While I pouted at my screen, hitting random keys in carefully considered flourishes, I marvelled at Conn's enduring appeal.

He was not the best-looking man I had ever dated. That would be Erik Kvist, the Norwegian whaler with cheekbones you could hang towels on. He was a stunning piece of craftsmanship. Unfortunately, the fact that he used to daydream about himself and actively seek out reflective surfaces detracted from the overall effect. (He also smelled a bit like burned fish curry.) (Looked great in photos, though.)

Also, there had been things about Conn that had made me seriously consider aggravated assault with a loaded coffee mug. Like, for example . . . OK, the way he used to describe Gary Larson cartoons. 'You know the one with the bear in a cave telling bedtime stories to his cubs, and the caption says, "Gee, I wonder what's in this cave . . . I dunno . . . Let's take a look". HAHAHA! Oh, you see, the bear has human skulls on either paw – like puppets. I suppose I should have mentioned that earlier.'

And the way, when he bought a new cassette tape, he used to play it over and over and over again, and then play it some more, until the fifth Ice Age thawed on Judgement Day and God sent him straight to purgatory for aggravated noise pollution.

Not forgetting his complete lack of a social censor.

However, over time my anti-self-preservation instinct

had malfunctioned. Sometimes these flaws seemed more like endearing eccentricities, especially when offset against his attributes. Such as his self-assurance and quiet intensity. The way he always knew what to do. The integrity that informed all his decisions.

And, of course, his complete lack of a social censor. If truth hurt, Conn would always be *agony*. He had no hidden (or even partially concealed) agenda. Conn could always be relied on to deliver the raw, unseasoned truth, however unsavoury.

I had never been sure what Conn had seen in me. Didn't matter; whatever it was had obviously not been a permanent effect.

Half an hour of gibberish later, it was clear Conn had more capacity for waiting patiently than I had for pretending to write a non-existent proposal.

'Mr O'Neill,' I said primly.

'Lara,' he said quietly. 'Please call me Conn.'

I sighed. 'Conn,' I said, hating the way it sounded so familiar. I pressed my thumb and forefinger against the bridge of my nose, closing my eyes.

A headache stirred in my frontal lobe. It was not wholly attributable to Conn's presence (although that in no way abdicates his responsibility in the matter). To be fair, it probably had more to do with the clamour of the building site outside. From the din, it sounded like the six-lane highway under construction was being routed right through my office.

'What are you doing here?' I said, over a concentrated flurry of drilling.

'Voltech hired me—'

'I *mean*: what are you doing in my office?'

'Our office.'

'Excuse me?'

'Mr Jacobs said there was a spare desk here.'

As if summoned, Philip's head appeared around the door.

'*Ciao, ciao,*' he said.

'Does nobody fucking knock around here?' I snarled.

Philip looked surprised. 'Um, not usually—'

'Conn says you told him he could share my office—'

'Well,' he said, spreading his fingers, 'it makes sense, with the two of you working so closely together.'

'Thanks for discussing it with me.'

'Did I not? Sorry about that.' I have to say, Philip looked less remorseful than overfed.

'How was your flight?' he said, addressing Conn. 'Settled into the hotel OK?'

'Yes—'

'Allrighty. Now, since Lara is the Account Manager on the Abu Dhabi Electricity Board project, you will be reporting to her on a temporary basis and for the duration of the project.'

'OK,' said Conn.

'Do you have a problem with that?' I said.

'Not at all.'

'Because if that will be a problem—'

'The arrangement is acceptable.'

'Great,' said Phil. 'Just to fill you in, the AEB project involves installing a fifth turbine to generate an additional capacity of a hundred megawatts—'

'That makes no sense,' said Conn. 'Why doesn't AEB upgrade their four existing turbines? It is more cost effective and would ultimately generate more power.'

I said, 'That's crap' at the same moment Philip said,

'That's what Lara thinks.' If my glare was even half effective, it temporarily paralysed Philip's sphincter. 'Er – Lara will fill you in on the specifics. I will leave you in her inflatable hands, haHA! Oh I say, if you don't have plans for Friday night, why don't you come over to Lara's place? We – she's having a Mexican party, so bring your sombrero. Hahaha haha HA.'

'Fantabulous,' I said, glaring at Phil.

'Next Friday?' said Conn. 'That's your birthday, isn't it? Twenty-third of July?'

I tried not to be touched that Conn remembered. After all, he remembered everything.

I nodded. 'It's kind of a birthday party,' I said. 'Do come. More the merrier. Bring the cat, and your tax consultant if he's at a loose end.'

'I don't have a cat. Or a tax consultant,' said Conn.

'Haha, good one, mate,' said Phil. He patted the doorjamb twice and disappeared.

'Is there something I can help with?' asked Conn.

'Thank you, but I have done this job quite well without your assistance for the last eighteen months,' I said, primly.

'I am sure you have. I thought I would offer—'

'No, thank you.'

'Ask me a question,' he said, smiling at me again.

I really wished he wouldn't.

'What's the difference between truth and illusion?' I asked, regretting it even as the words broke free and wreaked havoc in the world.

'Nietzsche claimed that truth is an error arising from attempting to make what are inherently particular human perceptions universally valid; in other words, truth is merely a human perspective and therefore illusory.

Interesting analysis, despite having little to no relevant application in the real world.'

'When did you look that up?'

'The day after your ex-boyfriend hit me at the Student Union.'

'Christ, I remember that. What was his name again?'

'Gavin the Human Amoeba.'

I nodded, and decided against smiling reminiscently. I couldn't afford to share nostalgia with Conn. Similarly, I would have to watch out for any in-jokes, inadvertent endearments, cute little catch-phrases, or impromptu foot rubs.

'Oh, hey,' said a smoky voice.

It seemed my office was command central that morning. 'Hey, Vino,' I said. She wore a pair of trousers that gave her one of the most outstanding examples of camel toe ever recorded. 'What's up?'

'Oh, I just came to say hi-ee,' she purred, flapping her stick-on eyelashes at Conn and extending a hand.

'Hi.' Conn rose unhurriedly.

'LOVELY to meet you. Mm, I like your SHIRT. Is it cotton?' she ran her French manicure up his arm.

'Ninety-eight per cent cotton, two per cent rayon,' said Conn.

'Mm.' Her hand was now in the region of Conn's pecs and she pretended to brush off some lint. 'Do you need someone to show you around? I can show you the SIGHTS.'

'Well, if that's all,' I said, clearing my throat pointedly.

Vino widened her eyes at me and whispered, 'Oh my GOD, he's so HOT!', before sidling out of my office.

Conn stared after her in bemusement, then turned back to me.

'It's good to see you again,' he said, so quietly I could barely hear him over the beep!beep!beep! of a reversing vehicle outside.

'All right, so.'

'After you left, I thought about you – a-all the time. I missed you.'

'Yes, well, that's a side effect of breaking up with someone, Conn,' I snapped. 'I'm surprised you didn't figure that out with that industrial-sized brain of yours.'

'Did you miss me?' he asked.

'Don't flatter yourself!' I scoffed, even though there was no vanity in Conn's question. 'Not at all. I couldn't have cared less,' I said, frenziedly stapling everything in sight. 'I mean, look, relationships break up. Happens all the time. I suppose at that age, you think you'll never get over it, but then you're off shagging someone else the following week. It was no big deal. I mean, I was a bit upset – for a while – few days – not even that long, probably. And, you know, everything works out for the best. I have a great boyfriend, a terrific career, two goldfish – and a car – it's a Jeep Wrangler – doesn't matter – the point is: I am unbelievably happy. Happier than I ever dreamed possible.' Although the wobble in my voice belied this. 'Shite.' I had stapled my credit card to my shirt.

Conn would have made a great interrogator: he could apply the silent treatment to devastating effect. After performing some laser surgery on my nerves with his eyes, he said, 'I am pleased we will be working together—'

'Oh please,' I sighed wearily, trying to pry open a staple with my fingers. 'Spare me. Conn, I didn't want Voltech to employ you. I recommended we employ the guy with a degree in philology. Although your qualifications were superior, I felt he had more strength of character. Just so we're absolutely clear – because I know how important that is to you – I lobbied Philip not to hire you.'

'Why?'

Now that was a fair question. To which there were any numbers of answers, including: because you shattered my heart into little pieces. And: even after all these years, it has never fully regenerated. Or how about: because you look so whole and *undamaged*. Or mainly: because I cannot afford to let you get too close.

As a compromise, I said, 'Because I don't want you in my life.'

Conn's face went blank. That used to indicate that he had rerouted all available processing capacity to his brain.

'Lara—'

'I don't wish to discuss this further. Look. We have to work together, so let's keep our relationship strictly professional. I don't want to talk about anything outside the job. Not the past; not you and me and the glory days; not how nice the weather is; not how was your weekend? Nothing that could be construed as personal in any capacity. We will discuss generators and turbines and volts per square inch.'

'Volts are not measured per square inch—'

'Exactly! If we have to talk at all, this is the sort of conversation I want to have.'

'You want to reduce the verbal interaction between us—'

'That's correct.'

'By what factor?'

'Let's start with three and work up from there.

Realistically, I don't see any reason we should have to talk to each other at all.'

There was silence for a while, but for the noise from the construction site outside: drilling, chipping, banging, revving and the rolling drum of cascading rubble.

Then Conn said, 'If that is what you want.'

'It is.'

'OK.'

'OK.'

For the rest of the week, whenever Conn looked like trespassing into personal territory, I distracted him with a set of technical documentation or AEB correspondence files, or asked him to compare and contrast the challenges of nuclear power generation.

The afternoon of my Mexican-themed birthday party, I tried to convince myself I always took this much time getting ready. I took pride in my appearance, I told myself as I carefully stuck on false eyelashes, then removed them for being too sixties flower power.

After swiping on eyeliner, I considered myself in the mirror and groaned. Utter crapness! I looked like an ancient Egyptian vampire.

Ideally, the look I was going for was devastating, irresistible, testosterone-taunting, pheromone-annihilating sex goddess with the ability to make men cry on demand.

It was proving time-consuming.

Since I had already used up the remainder of my cotton balls, I wiped my face clean with a handful of tissues dipped in cold cream. Another coat of foundation and powder over my stinging face, then a light blush, pink eyeshadow and a light sprinkle of glitter.

There were many things I resented, amongst them

in no particular order: being born with straight hair, anything else I could blame on my mother, working a six-day week, and Rick Astley. I *particularly* resented the sick, churning excitement that made my hands shake and stab myself in the eye with the mascara wand. Yet, every time I thought about Conn being there – in my apartment – my heart made a break for the border.

It was ridiculous, of course. What did I think was going to happen? That Conn would stride into the party in a black vest and mullet and growl, 'Nobody puts Lara in a corner', then tickle my armpit and twirl me around his head? That seemed unlikely. For one thing, Conn's wardrobe did not stretch to black vests. For another, his idea of dancing was a kind of one-step shuffle. Furthermore, it was a policy of mine never to fancy men with mullets, after Niall. (Shame it hadn't been a policy before I met Niall. Anyway.)

And of course, Phil would be there, along with a small, intimate gathering of close friends (no more than fifty people, maybe a hundred).

Speaking of which, '*Ciao, ciao!*' Phil called from the hall.

I used a damp tissue to rub a clear hole in the bathroom mirror and grimaced at my cloudy reflection.

I supposed I might be able to make men cry with the size of my pores.

'Sorry I'm late, babe,' said Phil as I walked into the kitchen. He leaned against the sink. Sweat patched his T-shirt. I wished he wouldn't wear his sunglasses on his forehead.

'That's OK,' I said.

'Fuck me, it's like the devil farted out there,' he said,

wiping his shiny face with his arm. 'I can't remember it ever being this hot—'

'You said that last summer,' I pointed out. 'How did the booze run go? Took longer than I thought.'

'Traffic was pants coming out of Sharjah. Interesting look you have going there. Psychedelic fairy, is it?'

I moaned and bolted back to the bathroom. He was right. In fact, I looked like a psychedelic fairy with a chronic case of acne. However, I was afraid that if I wiped off my make-up again, my face might go with it. Grimly, I plastered a smile across my gob.

'You OK?' said Philip, as I came into the kitchen where he was enthusing over his first beer. 'I didn't mean to upset you. You look gorgeous as a psychedelic fairy. Maybe later you can show me your magic wand. Hahaha haha HA!'

I experienced an uncharacteristic surge of irritation, although I successfully ignored it for the time being.

'I've been squeezing limes all afternoon,' I said, relocating a crate of beer so I could sit on the kitchen bench. 'My fingers are killing me – I can't straighten them. Where's the tequila?'

No answer. When I glanced across at him, Phil had that look he got when clients asked him to include a clause guaranteeing product uptime in a contract. 'Philip? You didn't forget the tequila,' I said on a rising note. 'I told you – how many bloody times – how could you have forgotten?'

'Do you need tequila for margaritas? Can't you use something else?'

'You mean, like, *beer*? No, Philip,' I said, pressing the heel of my palm to my forehead before I considered what it was doing to my make-up. Then again, it was probably an improvement. 'That's like making omelette with *bananas* instead of eggs. Aw, wanky wanky shit bollocks!'

'Babe, take it easy—'

'Don't call me babe, Sonny Boy Jim Bob Billy Ray Cyrus III!'

'Lara,' said Phil in his calm, soothing, reasonable, placatory voice that made me feel like setting his face on fire. 'What are you getting so worked up about?'

'How about the fact that I spent half of the only scummy day of my precious weekend squeezing three hundred fucking limes, and you forget the tequila? It's not like I asked you to procure three ounces of premium-grade plutonium! Yet instead, you turn up with a crate of beer and a bad case of stubble. Tell me – what the fuck am I supposed to do with three gallons of lime juice?'

'Lara, take a chill pill. We have plenty of beer—'

'Fuck *beer*! You can't have a fucking Mexican party without margaritas. It's like having St Patrick's Day without *green*!'

Just then, the first group of people arrived and Philip escaped to socialise with more reasonable, less high-pitched people.

I turned and pressed my burning forehead against the kitchen window. At some level, I knew my response was disproportionate. But first the psychedelic fairy look, and now the notable absence of tequila: they were bad omens.

After taking some deep, cleansing breaths to discipline my yang, I turned my attention to the drinks situation. A quick overview of the booze cupboard revealed seven bottles of Bacardi and a dusty bottle half full of bright green liqueur that smelled like apricots. I poured everything into a large bucket, along with the lime juice and several litres of pineapple juice. I could call it molotov margarita.

Ideally, when Conn arrived, I would have liked Philip to be by my side, preferably gazing adoringly at me and hanging on my every word instead of pointedly ignoring me from the far side of the room.

All the above probably accounts for why I drank too much – although that could also be attributed to my pouring copious amounts of booze down my gullet. This in turn went a long way towards explaining how I ended up assaulting a police officer.

But in the meantime, I circulated. In Fujairah, the neighbouring emirate, a woman had just been condemned to death by stoning for having relations with a married man. Everyone was talking about it: that, and the beach party the following weekend.

Keeping constant surveillance on the door, I handed out mini enchiladas and tortillas, and flicked my hair around and laughed too loudly.

I was doing my fêted Speedy Gonzales impression when Conn arrived. Although the light was behind him, I knew it was Conn by the way he stood immobile in the doorway, surveying the room. With a sensation similar to digesting a brick, I registered the fact that he was not alone.

I had always carefully avoided thinking about Conn in the context of other women. I had convinced myself he was living a hermetic, monk-like existence, abstaining from sex. Evidently, I had a remarkable capacity for self-delusion.

'Conn,' I said, hoping I hit the right note of rampant sexuality and seductive gorgeousness with equal measures of regretful unavailability. I was not certain how effective this was in a yellow and maroon poncho. 'And . . . um, Vino. Come in.'

'DARLING!' exclaimed Vino, kissing me three times as I precariously balanced a tray of nachos on one hand.

'Where's your Mexican costume?' I asked sourly. Her bikini wax didn't count; it was a different region of America. She was wearing a stunning Dolce and Gabbana minidress that provided basic coverage, although it was so tight that the only thing left to the imagination was the colour of her thong (and that only because she was not bending over).

'You were *serious* about that? Oh Lara, you *are* fun-*nee*. Nice CAPE—'

'It's a poncho,' I snapped.

'CHIC.' She crinkled up her nose. I think the effect was intended to be unbearably cute, but it was mainly just unbearable. 'Conn,' she said, sounding like she was savouring an after-dinner mint. 'Would you like a DRINK?' She gave his arm a quick hand-job.

'OK.'

Vino minced away gingerly in the direction of the kitchen.

I hadn't thought Conn was Vino's type. Not rich enough. In fact, I had always suspected Vino of having one or more private benefactors. She was surprisingly coy about it, considering she regularly divulged disturbingly graphic details of her sex life. Conn didn't drive a high performance car (I didn't think his Mongoose mountain bike counted) and was more likely to gift her a set of screwdrivers than a designer handbag.

Vino and I were friends of sorts. Our relationship was based on Vino teaching me Arabic swear words, so far limited to terminology describing women of lenient moral standards – much like herself. It was as solid a basis for a friendship as any, although I was presently reassessing it.

'What are those?' asked Conn, interrupting my frenzied reflections.

'Tortillas. And nachos,' I said, realising that the loaded tray probably did nothing for my seductive gorgeousness. Also that, by this stage, I was more lopsided than strictly upright.

'May I have one?'

'Help yourself.'

'Is my sombrero all right?' he asked, taking a handful of tortillas. 'I had to buy it, because I didn't have one.'

'Well, I'm sure it would be fine,' I said, 'except it's a Stetson, not a sombrero.'

'A what?'

'A cowboy hat.'

'Really? The man in Karama Souk said it was a sombrero.'

'There's a surprise,' I said. 'You know, Phil was only joking when he said to bring a sombrero.'

'Really? It wasn't funny.'

'Yeah, well, that's Phil's jokes for you.'

'I brought you a present,' he said, handing me a package wrapped in pewter-coloured paper. It would have been minimally tasteful bordering on elegant but for the fact that it was secured with masking tape.

'Oh! I – thank you,' I said. 'But why?' Nobody else had brought a gift, preferring to focus instead on other birthday benefits like free alcohol.

'Why not?' said Conn.

'Fair enough. Should I open it now?'

'I think so. Or – unless you can think of a valid reason not to.'

'Not a one,' I said, grinning. 'Here, can you hold these?' I said, awkwardly handing over the tray.

I tore the wrapper off and threw it on the floor. Inside was a book, covered in beautiful kingfisher-blue Thai silk, which changed colour to navy then green as I tilted it.

'It's a notebook,' said Conn unnecessarily. 'I noticed you didn't have one. I read an article in the *Irish Times* last week, which said a writer should carry a notebook around. To write things in. It said you never know when a really good idea will hit, but it's often when you don't expect it. Like, for example, when you're at the petrol station or buying lamb shanks. You should always be prepared.'

Gently, I ran my fingers over the cover. A butterfly embroidered on the corner looked vibrant enough to unfold itself and flutter off to socialise at any moment.

Many years before, I had dreamed of being a writer. It was the only thing I was any good at – apart from drinking vast quantities of alcohol without toppling over backwards (which was more the result of diligence than genuine talent).

It was all I could imagine doing (again, if that was the extent of my imagination, hardly a solid basis for a career in literature). I used to envision myself at an antique desk in a book-lined study, before French windows which opened on to a lushly beautiful landscape – the ocean perhaps, or a garden of wildflowers with the scent of honeysuckle wafting in on a warm breeze, dust motes twirling lazily in rays of sunlight – where I would craft a masterpiece with words like 'ficus' and 'shinsplints'.

Instead, I became an account manager for an energy products vendor.

'It is a good size – see?' said Conn, helping himself to a stack of nachos. 'It can fit in your pocket. As long as the pocket measures a minimum of thirteen centimetres by ten. And I know you like aesthetically pleasing things, so I thought – I thought you would like this.'

'I do,' I said past the lump in my throat. 'It's beautiful. Thank you. I – I haven't written in years, though. I don't really – I don't do that any more.'

'Why not?' said Conn. I shrug. 'You should. What will I do with this?' he asked, indicating the tray.

'Oh! Sorry. Here, I'll take it. Only twenty-one more nachos to offload. So, are you with Vino?' I asked, successfully making her name sound like I was choking on an ice cube.

'No. Well, she gave me a lift here.' I felt an inappropriate wave of relief, which was chased off by an equally inappropriate wave of revulsion when Philip came up and slung a heavy arm around my shoulders. I successfully dealt with both feelings by slugging my molotov margarita too fast.

'Lara! How's my favourite employee?' Philip moved in for a full-frontal snog. I couldn't make a run for it because the tray hampered my agility. Instead, I turned my head and got slobbered down the cheek.

I wished Philip wouldn't broadcast these public displays of affection to my colleagues. I had asked him not to often enough.

Phil addressed Conn. 'O'Neill! Prize-fighter!' He put up his fists (one of them still clutching a bottle of Corona), lurched to the left, then pretended to punch Conn in the ribs. He must have been insanely drunk – at least, I hoped that was his excuse.

'Stop, I surrender,' said Phil, hitching up his trousers. For some reason, everything Phil did annoyed me right now, but the trouser hitching in particular. It made him seem so middle-aged.

'How was your first week?' Philip asked Conn.

'Fine.'

'Great! Did Lara fill you in on the AEB project?'

'Yes.'

'Allrighty! I'm sure you'll get the hang of it soon.'

'I have the hang of it,' said Conn politely. 'It is straightforward.'

'Um, right. Good. Oh hey – I'll have one of those.' He grabbed a nacho and patted my bottom. 'Good job, babe. You make a great waitress. Must be nice to know you'll have something to fall back on if the power industry doesn't work out for you. Hahaha haha HA!'

Then he tried to bond with Conn by slapping him between the shoulder blades. Conn merely looked at him as if Phil had just posited the theory that electromagnetic fields were produced by the effect of gravity on sound waves.

'Excuse me, I see a drink with my name on it. Catch you later, chuckles,' said Phil. Then he weaved off to laugh at his own jokes.

Conn looked after Phil, who was in the process of hitching his trousers right up his crack. 'What a cock,' he said.

I looked at him, startled. It was so unexpected, I started giggling and found I couldn't stop.

Through the throng, I saw Vino fluctuating back towards us. 'Here, take these will you?' I handed the tray of nachos to a girl passing by in shorts and a bikini top. Then I took Conn's arm with my drink-free hand. 'Would you like to go outside?'

Outside, we walked into a solid wall of clammy heat. My skin crawled. In Dubai during summer, the temperature at night would still roast you medium rare.

In the centre of my apartment complex, the communal pool glowed turquoise neon. Stars jostled one another in the Middle Eastern sky. It reminded me of the time Conn and I had gone to the Quad at UCCD and lay out on the grass and talked about what at the time seemed deep, existential, philosophical stuff. In retrospect, it was largely a pile of pretentious crap.

It seemed like an awful long time ago.

I sat on the dusty tiles by the edge of the pool and dangled my feet in the water. Conn crouched beside me, elbows on his knees. I barely even noticed the lean, solid length of his thigh within touching distance.

'Where did you go?' asked Conn after a while. 'After you left UCCD.'

I narrated an abbreviated version of the intervening years. Although I described my erratic career path around the globe, I applied heavy censorship to the rest. Like how I dropped out of life for a couple of years to process a lot of dope. Similarly, I deleted all the one-night stands, in particular the time I woke up to find my date had left a hundred dollars on the dresser (cheap fucker). I might also have forgotten to mention the abortion.

'I tried to find you,' said Conn. 'But you – you disappeared. I talked to your mother. She didn't know where you were. She was really worried.' I snorted. 'She was. I called your father. He didn't know either. Or Foetus, or Bosco—'

'I didn't really stay in touch with anyone,' I said, shrugging.

'Why not?'

'Oh come on, Conn. How many people do you still see from university?'

'Nobody. But I didn't have any friends in college. Apart from Mark. I still see him. If more people had liked me, I would have stayed in contact with them too—'

'People lose touch. You don't mean to; it just happens. You know, you lose someone's address. Or you don't write for a while and then find it's been five years. Or people die.'

'Who died?'

'Nobody. I'm just saying there are lots of reasons you lose track of people.'

'I thought you would stay in contact with Julie—'

I snorted. 'Why would you think that?'

Conn looked surprised. 'She was your best friend—'

'*Was*,' I said, emphasising the past tense. I recalled the last time I had seen Julie. Ugly scene. I had called her a 'slagheap'. Turned out Julie did not appreciate honesty. She threw an ashtray at me. It missed. My aim was better, but not my choice of projectile. Even now, I still regretted lobbing an empty Fanta can at her instead of, for example, the television or a large landmass. 'You remember Niall?' I asked.

Conn frowned as he searched his databanks. 'You – the only Niall I know of was your boyfriend. Before me.'

'That's right. Remember we broke up because he was getting the leg over some slapper?'

'Yes.' I waited for Conn to figure it out, but the problem was evidently not complex enough for him.

'Julie was the slapper.'

'That – the one that Niall w-was—'

'Yeah. I found out later.'

'Oh,' said Conn. 'Now I understand why you didn't like her.'

The babble of conversation from the party increased momentarily in tempo, then subsided again. Must have been a fresh round of molotov margarita.

'Are you going out with Philip Jacobs?' asked Conn.

Leaving my feet in the pool, I flopped back against the tiles, still warm from the day's heat. 'I thought I asked you not to get personal?'

'You didn't ask. It was more a directive. I thought it only applied to the workplace.'

'It doesn't,' I said, but my curiosity got the better of me. 'How did you know?'

'I'm not sure. I suspected at the interview. Then again when Philip invited me to your party. Mainly because he belongs to the same subset of moron you used to go out with in college – just older.'

I giggled. 'Gee, thanks. You know, Conn, you never cease to amaze me. How can you know these things, yet be such a – an emotional wanker?'

'I don't know. I've a number of theories, but they are largely conjecture.' After a pause, he asked, 'How long have you been seeing him?'

'Seven months.'

'Did you sleep with him to get your job?' asked Conn.

I rose up on my elbows, choking on an air molecule. 'What?' I said.

'In the office, I overheard Phil talking to – I think his name is Martin, although I didn't hear it properly—'

'Conn!'

'Martin said, "Go on, Phil, spill. Did Lara shag you to get ahead?"'

'And?'

'Phil responded that he couldn't call into question a lady's virtue, but that you weren't the only one getting head.'

I shouldn't have been so upset. It's not as if I didn't know the context my colleagues used when talking about me – but *Phil*. That stung. Perhaps it had been funnier when Phil had said it. Conn never could tell a joke.

Then again, neither could Phil.

I think I managed a fair impression of a laugh. I said, 'Anyone with half a brain knows I was employed because of the size of my norks – which, if I say so myself, are well worth the salary. That was a joke, O'Neill.' I flicked water across the pool with my toes. Then, 'What do you think?' I asked.

'I don't know.'

'Conn, I asked what you *think*,' I said. 'I am interested in your opinion. You know me fairly well – or at least, you used to. Do *you* think I would sleep with someone to get a job?'

Conn gave the question inconsiderate consideration. 'Probably not.'

'*Probably?*'

'Well, you treat sex like currency. As if it is a commodity—'

'What?!'

'You use it to achieve something. Generally to make people – men – like you. But I don't think you would use sex to get a job, because your career is not that important to you. Or because you don't attach that much value to yourself. I am not certain which—'

'What are you talking about? I value myself!' I protested.

'Not enough. Otherwise you wouldn't simply accept what Phil said—'

'OK, look, I don't *accept it*, but what do you want me to do about it?'

Conn shrugged. 'You don't have to be with someone like that.'

I wondered how Conn could see right inside me – or maybe he just said what others didn't. I took a moment to decide whether to laugh or cry. Since I was too drunk for the latter, I laughed.

I stopped abruptly when Conn reached across and stroked my cheek. Then he ran his fingertips down my neck and along my throat. His fingertips were cool against my burning skin. I shut my eyes.

Once, Conn had said he loved the hollow just behind my collarbone. With an unprecedented romantic flourish, he said it was as if that spot was made for his fingers, they rested so perfectly in the groove. Then he ruined it all by saying it was probably a sensory illusion.

I looked up when I felt Conn move away suddenly.

'I'm sorry,' he said in a low voice. He looked away. 'I shouldn't – I should go. Sorry.' He pushed off the tiles and walked quickly across the landscaped gardens to my flat, where the crowd swallowed him.

My neck tingled from his fingerprints.

Unfortunately, my recall is a little hazy from here on in.

My default position is at the eye of the party, so it seems logical to deduce that this is where I made my re-entry.

At some point, Phil trespassed into my vicinity. 'You're drunk,' he said, superfluously.

'Well, I won't hold it against you,' I said magnanimously, trying and failing to smother a giggle. 'You're a *cock*, but I won't hold that against you, either.'

From my disjointed recollection, third-party accounts and circumstantial evidence, it appears that shortly after this exchange, a policeman arrived. There is a fair likelihood he said something like, 'Who is owner of this residential establishment?'

Whether some helpful guest or I volunteered this information is immaterial. In light of what happened next, however, it is important to relate that, rumour has it, I allegedly stepped up to him and said something along the lines of: 'Well, hel-LO Officer Sergeant Major.'

Afterwards, I was left to assume that because I was drunk, it did not occur to me to question the availability of a strippergram service in a Muslim country. I do remember thinking, however, that his UAE police force uniform was admirably realistic and that he was really in character and wondering which of my friends had hired him.

Eyewitnesses testified that the policeman said, 'Madam, there is complaint making. Very loud music. Too much noises.'

Since Philip was at least half as drunk as I was – i.e., absolutely plastered – he unreliably reported that I shouted: 'Oh yeah, *right*! Very loud music – good one! Get your kit off!' and seized the policeman by the front of his trousers.

Whereupon, according to Philip, there is a fair likelihood the policeman backed out the door, dragging me by the belt buckle, plaintively repeating, 'Madam, please not to touch.'

Other accounts then reported that I roared, 'Come on! Don't be coy! Show us your leopard print g-string!'

Then – and I myself have a vague, horrible recollection of this – I attempted to rip his trousers off at the ankles, which I know from experience is the most effective way of removing garments with Velcro seams – as I was convinced they were.

Turned out they weren't.

Shortly after I am rumoured to have said, 'My, what a big gun you have', whilst blinking lasciviously. The policeman drew the aforementioned weapon and blew a hole in my Sanyo stereo system.

Shortly after *that*, all remaining eyewitnesses including my feckless boyfriend fled the scene.

Since I sobered up you might say *spontaneously*, I have a first-hand recollection of subsequent events. In fact, Officer Ahmed turned out to be a lovely man when I was not attempting to divest him of his pants. I mean, he could have asked to see my liquor permit and then I would have been in *real* trouble.

Instead, in exchange for the remains of the molotov margarita mix, a pineapple, and fifty dirhams to repair the rip in his trousers, Officer Ahmed agreed not to file a report.

After he left, I flopped on to the sofa and surveyed the debris: plastic cups collecting in companionable groups, nachos in various degrees of entirety strewn across the floor, along with a jewelled flip-flop and two limp bodies I hoped were not carcasses. In the corner, the only visible damage to my stereo was a hole where the volume button used to be, but it emitted staccato bursts of fizzle – or it could have been one of Aerosmith's early hits.

The mess could wait until tomorrow. Hard to believe it would look twice as bad in the morning, although from previous post-party experience, I knew it would.

Philip walked in the door. 'What did the policeman say?' he said.

' "I am thanking you for pineapple",' I said.

'He didn't ask for your booze licence?'

'Did you see him escort me to his police car in handcuffs? No! Where the fuck did you disappear to?'

'I was outside waiting for a taxi and saw the policeman leave.' He probably thought he could get a bone in. Too bad I didn't have the energy to even look at him – although that was not a mandatory requirement for the sexual positions Phil favoured. 'You made a right tit of yourself, didn't you?' he said, leaning against the far wall with his arms crossed.

'Really? I hadn't noticed, but thank you for your support, Phil.'

'You spent the entire evening flirting with Connell O'Neill—'

'Wait, wait, wait, reverse back up the hill there. I ask a policeman to show me his g-string and then *assault* him, and you want to make an issue out of my talking to Conn?' I rolled my eyes.

'It was embarrassing,' said Phil, cocking an index finger at me like a gunslinger. 'You were all over him like ugly on a gorilla.'

Whenever he had a few drinks or several, Phil got jealous and possessive and unpleasantly shiny.

'Phil. I talked to him for half an hour—'

'About what?'

'I can't remember! I offered him a nacho. I thanked him for his present—'

'Present?' said Phil as if he had uncovered a decomposing corpse with its entrails crawling with maggots. (Admittedly, we hadn't checked the bodies on the floor.)

'Yes, a *present*! It is traditional to give someone a gift on the occasion of their birthday, Phil; not a cosmic cup of skank. Look, I'm going to bed—'

'What was it?'

'What – the present? A notebook! All right?'

'What kind of notebook?'

'Unlined pages bound with a cover. Standard formation.' I couldn't hide a smile as I used the expression.

'What the fuck are you gurning about? Pass me that beer, will you.'

I picked up the unopened can of Heineken and surreptitiously shook it. Resisting the urge to aim at his nose and hurl, I lobbed it across the room underarm. Phil juggled the can a while before catching it. When he popped the pull, lukewarm beer sprayed all over the place. He swore, flicking the fingers on his free hand.

'I take it what the fuck I am gurning about is a rhetorical question,' I said, pushing off the sofa. 'I'm off to bed. Oh, by the way, you forgot to say "Happy birthday, Lara, I'll just wipe the beer off the paintwork and show myself out".'

Now, I'm sure you can recognise that as a natural scene break: Phil's cue to throw his beer can at the wall and slam the door on his way out. I would have collapsed into bed and staged disturbing dreams about insect swarms and that time I touched Bruce Springsteen's sunglasses, and woken the following morning with a hangover and furry tongue. Phil might have called around midday to apologise and, after an obligatory sulk and complimentary bunch of flowers, our relationship would have reeled along for another couple of months.

Instead, some perverse urge made me pause in the bedroom door and wonder what I was saying even as I said it. Which was: 'You know, Phil, you have some nerve. You have made no commitment to me whatsoever, apart from storing a bottle of mouthwash in my bathroom. This relationship – I'm being generous with the expression – is entirely on your terms. Everyone at work thinks my job is conditional on you screwing me—'

'That is ridiculous—'

'To be honest, I'm starting to wonder myself. As soon as we are officially going out, you can accuse me of chatting up other guys. Until then – let me put this delicately – you can blow it out of your arse.'

Phil snorted. 'Oh come on, Lara, we've been over this time and time and time again.' Every time he said 'time', Phil slapped the back of one hand against the other palm. 'We can't move in together. Quite apart from the fact that it's illegal in the UAE for—'

'Philip, that's crap. I mean yeah, yeah, yeah; I know it's illegal for unmarried couples to cohabit, but everyone does it. You've had seven months to think up a plausible excuse – come on, tell me. Is your wife likely to drop in? Is—'

'You know I'm not married—'

'Is your porn collection too large? Do you have an artificial torso? Come on, Phil. What's the real reason? Is it insanely, perversely unreasonable to expect just a little bit – maybe half an iota – of commitment?'

'All right,' said Phil.

'All right, what?'

'If that's what you want,' said Phil with a pained expression.

'Wh-what?' I said, stalling in the face of this unexpected outcome.

'Let's live together. I suppose you can move in to my place. Your flat isn't big enough.'

It was probably an inappropriate time to mention that I couldn't stand Phil's sterile, shiny apartment full of hard, cold surfaces: glass, brushed steel and shiny black tiles. I had always thought the place looked like a giant bathroom.

Instead, I said, 'Really?'

'Yeah, really.'

'OK,' I said. I felt as if I should throw myself into Phil's arms or something, but I wasn't sure whether he would catch me. Instead, after a pause, I said, 'Right so. I suppose we should go to bed.'

This had been one of the big pressure points of our relationship, but now that it was resolved it all somehow felt like an anticlimax.

At least it proved one thing: I couldn't still be in love with Conn O'Neill.

But later, as Phil detonated beer and nacho-scented snores, his arm draped heavily across my chest, I stared into the darkness and wondered why I felt like I had just buried myself alive.

Commitment

Now that I was committed to Phil, I fortified my resolve to keep Conn at arm's length. However, it was increasingly difficult. My arms weren't that long to start off with.

Every now and then, my mind messed with me. Sometimes I looked at Conn and forgot six years had elapsed; and it was as if we were back in college and I still felt that way about him. Then the current time dimension would catch up and I would remember that he had dumped me, and we were now merely colleagues.

The following week, Conn and I waited on the first floor of Dubai Airport to greet Voltech's New Potential Marketing Manager. Because Conn had referred him, the company considered the interview a formality; they had already applied for his residency visa. All he needed to do was turn up semi-conscious to the interview – which was not necessarily a given unless the candidate had had a personality transplant since university.

We watched disembarking passengers from the balcony overlooking passport control.

I blurted out: 'I'm moving in with Phil.'

I had rehearsed a variety of ways to tell Conn. None

of them had been quite so blunt – or, for that matter, squeaky.

Conn glanced at me, then looked away. He shook his head.

'Aren't you going to *say* something?' I asked archly.

'What? Is there some social etiquette regarding you moving in with your boyfriend?'

'You could say you're happy for me.'

'I'm not happy,' he said. I experienced a brief swell of hope, until Conn murdered it, tied the bloody carcass to a concrete block and tossed Hope's mangled remains off the end of a desolate wharf, by saying: 'Why would I be happy about something that will make you miserable?'

'Baby *cheeses*. Do you go up to people and wish them a hideous birthday?'

'Of course not.'

I sulked with him for a while, but eventually decided I was more bored than annoyed (we had been at the airport for over two hours).

'So, is he still a Fucking Penetrator?' I asked, hanging over the balcony.

'Don't do that.'

'Let go of me – I'm not going to plunge to certain death. At least, not right now.'

'No. After college, he joined The Unstoppable Maggots. He was kicked out of the band so he gave up playing—'

'Really? Why?'

'He said the music industry was not equipped to cater for someone of his genius fucking talent –'

'No, I mean: why was he kicked out of the band?'

'Oh, OK. He threw an amplifier at the manager.'

'Good old Mark,' I said, watching a bottle-blonde on

white heels wave her arms at the man on passport control. He shook his head imperturbably. 'I can't wait to see him again. Do you know he is the only person who has ever beaten me at tequila shots?' Conn shook his head and grinned. 'Where the fuck is he?' I asked. 'The flight from the UK arrived ages ago.' I checked my watch again. 'Is this thing broken?' I shook my wrist.

'No. At least, it was functional less than three minutes ago. So although not entirely improbable, it is unlikely—'

'I think it's you. Perhaps your presence affects the nature of time, because it definitely went slower just then.' Conn smiled and returned his attention to the arrival area. 'Conn, he should have come through ages ago.'

'I know. Something's wrong. I don't know what could be—'

'Maybe he missed his flight? But what I don't understand is why he hasn't called.' I plucked Conn's mobile out of his shirt pocket. 'Phone on, no missed calls,' I said, puzzled. 'What's coverage like? Four bars. And the battery's charged. Let me just check.' I dialled Conn's mobile from mine, and the Nokia tune jangled around the arrivals hall. An Indian businessman frowned at me. I frowned back. As I rejected the call, something struck me. 'Does Mark know your number?'

'What?'

'Your phone number. Does Mark know what it is?'

'Er, p-possibly not,' said Conn, rumpling his hair like he used to when trying to solve a particularly technical equation, or identify his feelings.

'Co-onn!' I groaned.

'I didn't think he would need it—'

'OK, look. Wait here in case he just fell into an open suitcase or got thrown off the baggage carousel. I'll try to find out something.'

It took me some time to corner Airport Security, and more to find one who spoke rudimentary English (my Arabic had not progressed beyond '*asalaamu alaikum*', '*shukran*', '*inshallah*' and Vino's lexicon of swear words).

It is well known throughout the expat community that any communication barrier can be overcome by simply shouting louder. Despite employing a combination of high-decibel nouns supported by vigorous gesticulation, the policeman resolutely refused to understand me.

Eventually, he produced the passenger list for flight EK001. I ran my finger swiftly down the 'K' section. 'Mark Kinsella' was circled in pencil and highlighted by a thicket of greasy fingerprints: not a positive sign.

'Where is he?' I asked the policeman.

'Perhap he go shopping,' he shouted, shrugging.

I returned to Conn. 'Any sign of him?' I asked, even though I could see that, unless Conn had concealed him under a floor tile, Mark was not in the vicinity.

'No. Did you find out anything?'

I shook my head and stared at the exit doors, willing Mark to appear.

He didn't.

'Hold on a moment,' I said. 'I know someone who might be able to help.'

I dialled the number on my mobile. It rang so long I was about to hang up.

'Who—?'

I held up my finger at Conn. '*Asalaamu alaikum!* It's Lara here. Girl from party? You shoot my radio? I give you pineapple? Yes, that's me. Could you do me a favour?'

*

Phil was unconcerned about Mark's whereabouts. 'Lara, he probably missed the flight—'

'But the passenger list—'

'Look, Lara, he's a grown man. He's probably lying under a table at Cyclone or The Irish Village—'

'I *told* you: he didn't come out of the airport.'

'He'll turn up. Don't worry about him.'

But I was worried. People had been known to disappear in Dubai (mainly Eastern European prostitutes – but still). The government's promotional material presented the crime-free nature of the place in much the same way as a tourist attraction, like the world's fastest Ferris wheel. But I had always suspected Dubai was more media suppressed than crime free.

Anyway, while it might have been true of the small stuff – purse snatching, vandalism involving graffiti, misappropriation of plastic fruit – when it came to organised crime, perhaps involving a spot of large-scale prostitution, gunrunning, money laundering, high-level corruption, and domestic abuse on a phenomenal scale, the UAE was a criminal haven.

Three days later, Conn and I were scheduled to drive to Abu Dhabi to finalise the contract with AEB. Officer Ahmed had still not located Mark. He was no doubt distracted by the furious negotiations surrounding the value of information in litres of Jack Daniel's. Every time we agreed a quantity, Officer Ahmed raised the stakes in a kind of kamikaze haggle jihad.

Phil refused to let me postpone the meeting. 'This meeting has been scheduled for weeks,' he said. 'You know how important it is.'

'As important as a man's life hanging in the balance?' I declaimed.

'No,' said Phil, unperturbed, 'but at the moment, it's only his whereabouts hanging in the balance.'

As I drove us to site, the air conditioning in my Jeep belched out sweltering heat – I would have to take it in for a service.

'You still listen to this artist?' said Conn as I drove us to site.

'Bruce?' I asked, turning down 'Born to Run'. 'Of course. He has been the one great constant in my life. Aren't you worried?'

'About what? Oh, that your taste in music is outdated?'

'NO!'

'What, then?'

'Oh, I don't know, let me think,' I said, slightly hysterically. 'How about your mysteriously disappearing friend?'

'I suppose so,' said Conn.

'How can you be so unconcerned?' I said, slaloming past the speed cameras on Sheikh Zayed Road.

Conn frowned. 'Lara, we are doing everything we can to determine his whereabouts. Worrying is counter-productive—'

'Oh, I'll just stop then, will I?' I rolled my eyes.

'Do you have to drive so fast?' asked Conn mildly.

'Yes, I think better at higher velocities. You know, my life was deliciously lovely before you turned up to complicate things.'

'Was it?' said Conn, but the look he gave me implied he knew better.

'Don't look at me like that,' I hissed.

'Like what?'

'With those fucking eyes of yours.' Like a pair of searchlights sweeping across the surface of my soul. I could do without that. My soul preferred dark, humid conditions.

'I can't look at you any other way—'

'So just *don't*!' I was so irrationally incensed I snorted half a bottle of Masafi water down my windpipe, which effectively shut down the conversation – along with my oesophagus.

Temporarily, I ignored the fuming to concentrate on the meeting. After weeks of negotiation, AEB had finally agreed the specifications and terms of the contract. If all went according to plan, I would get mildly spaced on Arabic coffee and leave Abu Dhabi with a bag of complementary AEB promotional material and – most importantly – an autographed contract.

I was wearing my kick-ass client outfit which curiously compelled clients to agree with me: red and purple paisley pencil skirt barely grazing a pair of shiny, knee-high black boots, topped off with a white blouse hinting at lace underwear. Just within the bounds of decency as defined by the Middle East.

There was just one reason proceedings might deviate from plan.

Conn.

His presence was a bit like introducing a bull into a china shop after equipping him with an Uzi submachine gun. Conn was liable to say anything. I remember – back in college – he had told a friend of mine she was stupid.

About a hundred and fifty kilometres and ninety minutes later, I pulled into AEB's carpark. It was like a pop star's landscaped garden: outsized palm trees and meticulously pruned hibiscus, bronze flamingos regurgitating water. I took off with my laptop case, locking the car over my shoulder.

'Don't we need hard hats?' asked Conn.

The quickest way to access the AEB office area was through the Turbine Room, a restricted-area hard-hat zone. In fairness, it was more of a guideline; AEB did not enforce their rule with any great enthusiasm. Anyway, it was hardly likely a turbine would fall on me – and if it did, I would have more to worry about than a lump on the head.

I unlocked the car, however, and Conn reached into the boot and picked out my hard hat. 'I like it,' he said, grinning. I think he was referring to the bull's-eye I had painted on the crown; although he might have liked the tasteful shade of dildo pink.

The vast scale of the Turbine Room always awed me. Its cavernous reaches were dominated by four turbines, each roughly the size of a nuclear submarine. They emitted a deep, mechanical thrum that gently vibrated everything in the vicinity.

We reached the offices and were shown into a conference room by a silent woman swathed in black.

'All right,' I whispered, raising the lid of my laptop. 'Remember what we discussed.'

'Don't worry. I can be diplomatic. It's not that difficult. Social intercourse is a set of rules. As long as you follow the rules, people don't get upset—'

'Seriously, have you compiled a list of these rules?'

'No. I am not familiar with all of them, only the generic ones.'

'What about your Voltech interview?'

Conn raised his eyebrows. 'I knew Voltech would hire me. The company required my expertise for this project. Tact was not requisite.'

I still hadn't got to grips with Conn's brand of diplomacy when our AEB clients arrived, Mr O'Hara leading the parade.

'Lara!' he boomed, surfing into the room on a wave of aftershave. He always acted as if the sheer force of his personality blew women away – or at the very least, their knickers.

Mr O'Hara was AEB's Financial Director. His title was more impressive than the reality. In the Middle East, everyone was a director: Commercial Director, Director of Catering, Director of Directors. Chances were Mr O'Hara had been fired from some executive position in Europe and moved to the Middle East to avoid prosecution or extradition or worse.

Mr O'Hara featured slicked-back black hair with a distinguished white badger streak up the centre, a burnished leather tan, and gold crucifix nestling amongst the thickets of virile chest hair spilling out his open collar. He looked rather like an Italian lounge-crooner, except he was Irish. In many ways, Mr O'Hara was the type I normally went for: extremely married, trappings of success, rich, brimming with excessive flirtatious charm.

In this case however, my knickers were in no danger of being blown away – or even mildly exposed. I didn't know how desperate I would have had to be to go out with him. Let's just say, it would probably coincide with a frosty Christmas in Hell.

Still, I was rather fond of my client and his effusive bonhomie. 'Mr O'Hara,' I said, putting my hand in both of his.

He kissed me on either cheek, in accordance with Middle East expat custom.

'When are you going to run away with me and be my lover?' he enquired.

'When you're not married,' I responded. I might have added: also, when you grow ten years younger.

'You look beautiful, as always,' he breathed. 'Do you grow more lovely every day?'

'No, only my knees.'

'Really? You must show me sometime,' said Mr O'Hara with a glance down that stopped about a foot and a half above my knees. 'Of course, I would not be – let's say – *averse* if there was anything else you wanted to show me at the same time.'

'Right, then,' I said, side-stepping sharply to escape his hand's friendly exploration of my right buttock. To his credit, Conn accepted Mr O'Hara groping his bottom without comment.

'Mr O'Hara, I'd like to introduce you to our Product Support Manager, Connell O'Neill,' I said.

While Conn and Mr O'Hara sniffed each others bums (clarification: that was a metaphor), I greeted the rest of my clients. Mr O'Hara's lush greeting contrasted starkly with that of the other AEB employees, most of whom, due to religious constraints, didn't even shake my hand. AEB always fielded a team for these meetings. The company was covered in the event of an impromptu soccer match or a last-minute order to invade a small country. Otherwise I had no idea what half of them did, apart from take notes and text their friends.

'Let's get down to business,' said Mr O'Hara, tiring of pissing around the perimeter of the room (clarification: another metaphor). He took a seat at the head of the table and switched smoothly into Business Mode.

I sat on his left and leaned down to remove the

contract from my case. Mr O'Hara gave a pretty good impression of not looking down my blouse.

'Right,' I said, laying the contract on the table as if it were made of fine-spun glass. 'Mr O'Hara, I emailed you the amended contract version two point four one last week and you indicated it was acceptable, with the exception—'

'As I responded to *you*, Miss Callaghan, the timeframe Voltech proposes is – let's say – unreasonable. AEB requires the additional turbine to be operational within three months.'

'That should not be a problem, *as long as*,' I delicately underlined the condition, 'the contract is finalised today, and initial payment issued before the end of the week. I have updated the contract version two point four two accordingly.' I flipped open the contract and pointed to item one point five point four two subsection iv, clause a.

Mr O'Hara placed a stubby finger on the contract and drew it slowly across the conference table towards him.

'Do you need a pen?' I asked.

Mr O'Hara held up a hand for silence, then read the entire contract yet again. Clients in the Middle East – especially government agencies – were notoriously shy of committing to anything.

Well, it is a male-oriented society.

It was a tense moment (assuming forty minutes counts as a moment). I spent the time minutely examining Mr O'Hara's gold-and-black enamel cufflinks.

'Yes, please,' said Mr O'Hara eventually.

'Excuse me?'

'The pen.' He extended his thumb and index finger towards me without looking up. I burrowed around my laptop case, but despite some frenzied rummaging, the only vague equivalent I could locate was an eyeliner pencil stub in sparkly emerald green.

'Conn!' I hissed across the table. It took a moment for Conn to return from theoretical space. 'Pen!'

Conn felt around his jacket pocket and produced a blue and red KFC pen, the end of which featured a hysterical-looking chicken wearing a Kentucky Fried uniform and a peaked cap backwards. Conn reluctantly handed it to Mr O'Hara.

'If you would like to sign here, and here,' I jabbered, hoping to distract Mr O'Hara. Despite my best efforts, he pressed the button halfway down the pen, which activated a kinetic dynamo that made the chicken's head peck frenziedly. 'Where the x's are, and if you could date and initial all pages.'

Mr O'Hara steadied the last page with his fingertips. He adjusted the pen, then brought it down to the signature line, paused a moment to work on his flourish . . .

Which is when Conn decided to make an invaluable contribution to proceedings.

'Do you understand that the solution outlined in this contract is not optimally feasible?' he enquired.

The decision to kick him under the table was more an involuntary response than a rational, carefully considered plan. Unfortunately, I underestimated the distance from me to Conn, while simultaneously misjudging Mr O'Hara's proximity. The impact of my foot against Mr O'Hara's shin reverberated all the way up my spine; it actually hurt my teeth.

Thankfully, Mr O'Hara had a hide like a rhinoceros; or mistook my violence for spirited footsie; or was so focused on events at the table that he decided to overlook it for the time being.

'Excuse me?' said Mr O'Hara to Conn with a short laugh.

'What Mr O'Neill is referring to is what I suggested when AEB first approached Voltech for a solution,' I said quickly. 'We discussed upgrading AEB's existing turbines to address increased capacity requirements, but AEB said—'

'Mr – O'Neill, is it?' interrupted Mr O'Hara and Conn nodded. 'What do you mean?'

'Lara is correct,' said Conn. 'Installing another turbine works in the short-term, but it is not an efficient long-term solution. It makes more sense to upgrade AEB's existing Units one to four. It costs less,' Mr O'Hara frowned when my leg ricocheted off his again, 'but provides more capacity. If you proceed with Unit five, you should at least consider upgrading Units one to four in parallel.'

Then Conn repeated exactly what I had said, but Mr O'Hara had failed to hear due to the magnetism of my personality – or the size of my tits.

I could have been grateful that Conn didn't suggest generating electricity out of exploding sand or something. But I wasn't.

Mr O'Hara had sharply hit reverse, and bolted backwards out of the conference room, clutching the unsigned contract and muttering about how he had to 'think about it'. The car windows were at risk from stress fractures from the force of my rage.

I flashed my lights and honked at a Mercedes with blacked-out windows. 'Get out of the fucking way!'

'Lara—'

'Don't fucking talk to me!' I snarled at Conn.

'You said that an hour ago—'

'Just assume the directive applies until further notice.'

'How long will that be?'

'Until the end of fucking time, then a bit longer,' I said, undertaking the Mercedes and simultaneously unleashing my middle digit (a highly illegal manoeuvre in Dubai). While I had it out, I showed it to Conn too.

'Lara—'

'OK, I tell you what, Fatbrain – and by the way, I don't want to hear the words "optimal solution" come out of your face in the next five minutes – in fact, make that *any* words. Here's the thing: do you know how long I worked on that contract? Do you? DO YOU?'

'I—'

'Rhetorical question, O'Neill, because I'm going to tell you. I could have started with the answer, but posing the question first added more gravitas, I felt. Months. That's the answer: *months!*' I screeched around a cement lorry doing forty kilometres per hour in the fast lane.

Then I took a moment to balance my fucking chi.

When I was sure I had the volume under control, I said to Conn, 'I have worked on the AEB contract for nearly a year. Then, just as Mr O'Hara is about to sign contract revision number eight-nine,' my voice trembled as I recalled Mr Chicken twitching over the contract, 'you commit a random act of sabotage—'

'Lara—'

'I'm not finished. Conn, I have worked so hard – you have no idea – this job – it was the first time in my life I have ever been taken seriously.' I coughed, hoping to jump-start my voice again. 'At least, I thought so – but suddenly, you, O'Neill, you turn around and reiterate exactly precisely what I told the client at the outset, and it's the best fucking idea since – since—'

'Twisted pair cable,' suggested Conn.

'No! No, not twisted pair cable. Toast. I'm going with toast, since it has had a more critical impact on my life than fucking twisted fucking pair cable.'

'I doubt that. Twisted pair cable is—'

'I don't care! I don't care what twisted pair cable is! OK?'

'What Voltech proposed was not—'

'You'd better not say "optimal solution", or I will rearrange your testicles with Mr Chicken.' I gritted, snatching the pen out of his shirt pocket, gripping it in both hands and waving it threateningly at him.

'Watch out—' Conn grabbed the steering wheel.

'Conn, your suggestion is hardly revolutionary or ground-breaking. Everybody knows upgrading the existing turbines is the better option – me better than anyone. But AEB expects a solution within two months, which is already ridiculously unrealistic. How do you propose to do that, if it takes – at a conservative estimate – another month to finalise the contract?'

'That timeframe is not feasible—'

'Well, you forgot to explain that to AEB. If they sign the contract, they will put huge pressure on Voltech to finish the job before October, which means higher risk. People cut corners, overlook things.'

'I will ensure—'

'You'd fucking better. Our health and safety officer has the keen mind of a pterodactyl. Martin Charge wouldn't notice an exploding gas turbine.'

At that hour of the day, the only available parking was on the far side of the building site. The construction company had erected a metal catwalk over the highway.

'Lara, I'm sorry—'

'Gosh, well, that's OK, then,' I said, picking my way through the rusty nails and rubble strewn on the catwalk. It was hazardous going, even in kick-ass boots. 'You should also know, however, that I am graciously overlooking the fact that you just fucked my sales target for the next two quarters. Also that Head Office is threatening to shut down Voltech's Middle East branch if we don't achieve our target, because that's just speculation, albeit documented in the form of various emails and memos.'

'I didn't know—'

'Conn, it's *my job* to know those things. All you have to know about is Voltech's products.'

'My comments were limited to Voltech's products and their application in AEB's environment.'

I looked at him and seriously considered throttling him with a length of scaffolding and dumping his mutilated body in a skip down a dark alleyway overrun with rats and stinking of urine. I only rejected the proposal because – realistically – the likelihood of smuggling his body out of the construction site without anyone noticing was slim.

I took a deep breath and enunciated clearly, 'Conn, you do not operate in a bubble. Your actions have consequences. Repercussions. You might want to study causality. It's another philosophical concept: cause and effect. You might find it useful.'

I was conflicted how to present the AEB fiasco to Phil. On the one hand, if I reported that Conn had gone off like a faulty Duracell bunny, my resistance to hiring him would be vindicated. Too late, Phil would realise his mistake in employing Conn. I would be proved right. I like being right, so that would be nice. Most compellingly, I could spend the foreseeable future reminding Phil of his error.

But something held me back. Disregarding recent events, I thought maybe I would prefer if Conn stuck around. Just for a while. Honestly, I really wasn't pushed one way or the other, but.

In the end, I presented a modified version of events, wherein Mr O'Hara had threatened to sign with another vendor. I recast myself as the heroine of the piece by boldly thinking outside the box to snatch victory from the jaws of defeat.

'That fucker!' snarled Phil. He was referring to Mr O'Hara, since I had made no mention of Conn's best efforts to force-feed defeat to the jaws of victory. 'What the fuck is he playing at?'

'I think he's concerned about the quality of Voltech's products,' I said, cunningly.

In fact, this was my concern. Voltech adopted a fairly carefree approach to health and safety, as personified by our health and safety officer, Martin Charge. Basically, he occasionally kicked a turbine and declared it sound if it didn't break.

This attitude had bothered me ever since I joined Voltech. If one of our products malfunctioned, people got fired – in the most literal sense of the word. First degree burns, melted eyeballs, decades of skin grafts; that sort of thing.

Voltech's actions – or inactions – contradicted their frequently issued memos about the value they placed on health and safety. Realistically, as long as there were no costly court cases or adverse publicity, Voltech considered product malfunctions a side-effect of business (insert the word 'regrettable' for any printable quotes).

Phil said, 'Why don't you have Martin do a—'

'Phil, you know Martin Charge wouldn't spit at me if I was on fire. In fact, he'd throw lighter fluid.'

'OK, I'll tell him to send a report. He can fucking make it up—'

'The client has requested on-site product quality assurance testing before the turbine goes live,' I said hastily.

'Fuck! Is that really necessary?' I raised my eyebrows at him. 'Fuck. OK.'

Distracted with how to spin the setback to Voltech's head office, Phil bugged me less for kinky sex. That, at least, was a positive result.

I'm not sure when it had started, but recently I had noticed more things about Phil irritated me, even when he wasn't trying. Like – OK, it's difficult to pick out anything in particular – but here's one example: the *tac tac* sound effect he made picking his nails. And there was his habit of picking food out of his back teeth with his finger; and the way he snorted when he laughed; and pretty much anything sex-related (although that didn't annoy me so much as make me feel vaguely nauseous); and the way he folded his underpants in thirds vertically across the pouch and then once across the middle; and the way he breathed: in and out with a kind of gusty sound effect – oh look, you'll have to take my word for how *completely* irritating it was.

In balance, my life seemed to have taken on all the characteristics of Wile E. Coyote piloting a tank of liquid nitrogen down a steep hill which ended, improbably but inevitably, at the top or bottom of a sheer cliff.

Just when I was expecting Road Runner to make an appearance, I got a phone call.

'Did you have anything to do with this?' I asked Conn, hanging up. It was the first time I had directly addressed him in three weeks.

'What?'

'That was Mr O'Hara. He said AEB is going to contract Voltech to install the fifth turbine, and upgrade Units one to four simultaneously.'

'I have spoken to Mr O'Hara and his operations staff on several occasions.' It was not in Conn's nature to look smug, but his face definitely hosted the ghost of a smile.

That didn't mean I forgave him.

Extended Vacation At The Government Hilton

Officer Ahmed called to tell me I owed him the balance of sixteen bottles of Jack Daniel's. In an inspired initiative of detective work that involved him checking a police database, he had located Mark.

According to the Police, customs had discovered a quantity of hashish or heroin ('same same,' said Officer Ahmed) on Mark's person. Officer Ahmed could not ascertain the exact quantity of hashish and/or heroin, where it had been concealed, whether Mark would be charged and/or when.

The only thing we knew for sure (and even that wasn't definite) was that Mark was being detained in the Government Hilton aka Dubai Central Prison.

One Sunday, I drove us to the prison complex at Al Aweer. The air conditioning in the car was on maximum volume, coldest setting, but neither that nor the atmosphere between Conn and me made any difference to the temperature in the Jeep.

'What's going to happen to him?' asked Conn.

'I don't know,' I said tersely.

'I suppose he will be tried—'

'Conn, how the fuck would I know?' I snapped. 'It's not as if I have inside knowledge of Al Slammer, or experience springing perps out of jail.' I wiped the sweat off my forehead with the heel of my hand. 'Sorry,' I said more gently. 'I am far too middle-class for this sort of thing. I'm just – I'm worried.'

With good cause, I felt. When it came to its legal and penitentiary systems, Dubai was bandit country. If it ever came down to it (and assuming I had any choice in the matter), I would choose the Law of the Jungle over Sharia Law any day. Sentences often appeared to be whimsical and/or based on the state of the judge's haemorrhoids – or who the defendant was. Members of the royal family were above the law, but Allah help you if you were a low-income expat – or a woman.

With a jolt, I recalled Penny, Voltech's pre-Vino receptionist. She had been raped and made the mistake of going to the police. The accused – a UAE national – claimed it was consensual. Penny was found guilty of adultery and defaming the character of an upstanding citizen, and spent six months in jail before being deported to the UK.

In fact, most of the expat community were one degree of separation or less from someone who had been booted into Al Slammer for cohabiting with someone who was not their spouse, or kissing in public, or having consumed alcohol without a licence, or possessing anti-inflammatory drugs legally prescribed elsewhere.

The prison shimmered in the heat. I parked on a sand dune and peeled myself off the seat.

In accordance with most companies, Voltech's HR Department held their employees' passports (according to the Policies and Procedures handbook, this was for their 'safekeeping'). Like many UAE institutions, the prison insisted on passports for identification. Conn had forgotten his, so he was not allowed past Reception.

By pure chance, I had mine, having recently returned from a trip to Jordan.

I emerged into an expanse of desert enclosed by tall walls topped with coils of barbed wire. I blinked behind my sunglasses, adjusting to the glare of the sun after the dingy prison reception. UV rays shimmered off the sand. It burned my feet. I wished I had worn more substantial shoes.

I lurched slowly across the yielding sand towards a fence at the far end of the enclosure. Three metres away, another fence ran parallel to this, beyond which milled the inmates of the Dubai Hilton. Visitors and prisoners shouted across the gap.

I scanned the crowd six-deep beyond the far fence. Most of them were Indian and Pakistani, so Mark was easy enough to spot. In any case, he hadn't changed much. He still looked like a water buffalo.

'Mark!' I shouted, waving when I established eye contact.

'Hey!' Mark called. He pointed to a spot further along, where the crowd was marginally thinner.

'Hi, Mark,' I said, threading my fingers through the fence. His orange jumpsuit was grimy and accessorised with sweat rings around the neck and armpits. He looked tired, but that had been Mark's default state in college – when he wasn't comatose, that is. Otherwise, he looked remarkably positive.

'What's with the weather in this fucking country? It's

like living in a fucking volcano,' said Mark, leaning a shoulder against his side of the fence.

'Welcome to summer in the Middle East.'

'Cool,' said Mark, inaccurately. 'How the fuck are you?'

Tributaries of sweat met at my spine and formed a gushing torrent down the back of my knickers, but I said, 'I'm fucking – er, great. Great. How about you?'

'Sure, can't fucking complain.'

'Glad to see you're in good spirits. Are you OK?'

'Yeah. Can I ask you a personal fucking question?'

'You can ask,' I said.

'I hope you don't think I'm rude, but who the fuck are you?'

'Lara. Lara Callaghan?' I hoped the penny would drop of its own accord, since I didn't have any cash to throw at him.

'Fuck me!' said Mark. 'Is that Lars?'

I grinned. 'Yeah.'

'What the fuck you doing here?'

'Er, I work with Conn. At Voltech.'

'No shit?'

'Not a skid mark.'

'Speaking of Droid, where the fuck is the dude?'

'He wasn't allowed past reception—'

'Did they discover his cunning plan to break me out of here?'

'Er, no. He forgot his passport. Oh, while I think about it, so um, hey! By the way, Voltech fired you. I suppose – technically – they didn't actually hire you. Although I'm pretty sure they would, had you turned up for the interview and not been arrested for possession of drugs.'

Mark was outraged. 'What the fuck happened to fucking innocent until proven guilty?'

'I'm afraid it's the other way round here. Guilty until proven innocent.'

'What a suckfest.'

'Pretty much. Speaking of which, have they – the police – told you how long you're going to be here? Detained. In prison, I mean. I suppose – is there going to be a court case?'

'Yeah.'

'When is it due?'

'No fucking idea.'

'OK. Well, I'll try to find out. Do you want me to get you a lawyer?'

'Nah.'

'Mark—'

'I'm a fucking innocent man, Lars. Justice will prevail.'

'So you weren't smuggling drugs into the UAE?' I said, relieved.

'Fuck me, no.'

'Oh, thank goodness. I didn't believe even you would be possessed of enough pure, distilled stupidity to bring drugs into the UAE.'

'Right on! It was just a bit of skunk stuffed down my sock.'

'*What?*'

'It was for fucking medicinal use! I suffer from nerves.'

'Baby cheeses, Mark! Most people grow out of dope, you know—'

'I thought it about fucking time I consolidated my bad-boy image.'

'Only ten years too late. Mark,' I said, after a pause, 'you need a lawyer. The UAE has a zero tolerance policy

on drugs. Smuggling is considered a serious offence
here—'

'Right on,' said Mark, nodding vigorously. 'Drugs are
a major problem, should be dealt with severely.'

'Yes, Mark,' I said, exasperated. 'So you need a *lawyer*.
You don't know what you're dealing with. You signed a
police statement in Arabic, right? So you have no idea
what you will be tried for. There's not much in the way of
legal precedent. Proceedings are conducted in Arabic, so
if you defend yourself, you're dependent on an Arabic
speaker accurately interpreting what you say.' (Although
I couldn't help thinking if they censored the swear words,
that might be a good thing.)

'Oh, lighten up, Lars! It was just a bit of grass—'

'That defence kind of blows, if you don't mind
me saying so. There's no such thing as "a bit" in this
scenario. Furthermore,' I raised my voice over Mark's
protests, 'grass is the same as coke or heroin in an
Arabic court of law. Do you get that? No difference! Same
same!'

'Look,' said Mark, 'I shagged someone studying law in
UCCD. It didn't sound that hard. There's not much to it.
I'll lay out the facts objectively. Do a bit of tai chi. "I
object, your honour! This man – me – has been falsely
accused of a heinous crime! Can you handle the truth?
Can you HANDLE the fucking TRUTH?"'

I winced, imagining the carnage. 'Mark, you have
obviously been watching too much TV, while smoking too
much dope—'

'I didn't do it, Lars! I swear: I didn't do it!'

'But you *did* do it!' I bawled. A guard glanced at me
and fingered the holster of his gun. I lowered my voice.
'Mark, you don't know what you're doing. The justice

system here is not like at home. If you are found guilty of possession, the minimum sentence is four years.'

None of this appeared to have any effect on Mark's determination to pervert the course of justice by defending himself. I said, 'You know they still stone people in Fujairah?'

'Where?'

'Neighbouring emirate. About a hundred kilometres east. Don't worry; it's pretty rare the death sentence is carried out in Dubai. They only lash people here.'

'So I'm fucking grand, then.'

Wading back through the sand, I reflected that at least in prison Mark was protected from the grievous bodily harm I felt like perpetrating on his person.

At Reception, Conn was fixing a telephone for a friendly policeman.

'Can we go?' I asked. I felt filthy and exhausted.

'How's Mark?' asked Conn as we left the squat, dust-coloured building behind.

'Oh, he's deliciously lovely,' I said, wedging my sunglasses on my nose. 'Never been better.'

The following week, the court was closed on the date set for Mark's first court appearance – 'the Accusing' – because the UAE police force hadn't noticed it coincided with a public holiday. The second time, a sheikh died and the UAE shut down for two days.

Conn and I went to the Accusing to provide moral support. As I sat in the women's section of the court, I wondered whether Conn felt as helpless as I did. I was worried about what I felt was the very real possibility that Mark might be sentenced to death for being criminally irritating. It's not as if anyone could testify that Mark wasn't as annoying as alleged by the prosecution. After all, the incriminating evidence would be standing right there in the dock.

In the event, Mark objected to the lawyer Conn had retained on his behalf and moved to strike. Thankfully, the judge appeared to ignore him. On balance, I felt it went pretty well.

Mark's sentencing was three weeks later. The Dubai Court of Criminal Justice had gone easy on him.

He was given a three-month sentence.

I had engineered it so that Conn and I had little to do with each other, which was no small feat when we shared an office the size of your average parking space.

I was contemplating considering thinking about re-establishing lines of communication with Conn. It was getting awkward pretending not to hear him, especially during meetings and conference calls. I had moved in with Phil and was blissfully ... well, agreeable, at the very least.

One scorching Friday, Phil and I were on the beach as usual. Phil was sprawled out on a towel, an open *FHM* magazine on his face, the rest of him positioned for maximum UV exposure.

When a BMW four by four pulled up beside us, regrettably, I was in the process of manually inflating a rubber camel. Pushing back a limp hank of hair, I squinted irritably at it. Enough was enough. I mean, thirty kilometres of empty beach, and the fucker had to park *right there*? Come *on*! This time, I would definitely say something.

I was mentally summarising that very sentiment ('Um, hi, would you like to borrow my inflatable camel?') when the driver's door opened and two Prada wedge sandals appeared beneath it.

Vino. I could have done without the competition. She made even my ankles look fat. And who puts on make-up and false eyelashes to go to the *beach*?

Inopportunely, I discovered it was difficult projecting poise and grace when covered in sand with a throbbing, shiny red face. It was *impossible* dressed in a Mexican poncho serving duty as a skirt, and a suede-effect one-piece with a cowgirl fringe. It had looked funky on a hanger in the shop, but was several shades of naff squaring up against Vino's plain white bikini with matching sarong knotted casually about her hips.

At least the huge, floppy hat she wore was plain silly; she had to tilt her head back ninety degrees to see. Even though my hair was scraped into a squeegee and covered in suntan lotion, I felt I had the edge there.

'*Ciao, ciao!*' said Vino, cocking her head. I'm sure the effect was supposed to be coquettish, but I was reminded of a budgie.

Vino sashayed across to our camp. I have no idea how she achieved it (it is notoriously difficult on sand).

'Hi, Vino,' I said, tugging up the top of my togs.

'Darling,' said Vino, removing her hat to give my aura a good snog.

'The lovely Vino,' said Phil, squinting up at her. 'Hello, there.' Nudging his sunglasses over his nose, he repositioned the *FHM* magazine across his groin.

'Is it OK if we join you guy-ees?' said Vino.

Phil's *FHM* magazine twitched. 'Pull up a pew. If you can't find a pew, a towel should do the trick. Hahaha haha HA!'

He really laughed far too hard at his own jokes.

About the same time I registered Vino's use of the word 'we', Conn emerged from the other side of the BMW.

'Darling!' said Vino. Although 'darling' was her standard form of address for pretty much everyone, it sounded like she meant it more when applied to Conn. 'Over here! Bring my BAG. Where's the umbrella? I can't sit in this sun without an umbrella. I have VERY sensitive SKIN.'

I could have pointed out that her hat cast a shadow all the way to Abu Dhabi, but didn't. Yet another opportunity squandered.

'Hi,' said Conn, unclipping the umbrella. He wedged it in the sand, after assessing relative wind speed and optimum angle for maximum shade.

'Darling, can you bring the mat, and my TOWEL? It's the Louis Vuitton,' she addressed Conn, then turned back to me. 'I LOVE your – is it a swimsuit? WHERE did you GET it? You have such ECCENTRIC "taste",' said Vino, clearly enunciating the quotation marks.

'Thank you,' I said. 'It's from Fungi Shiitake's latest collection.'

'Fungi who?'

'Shiitake. Hot new Italian designer. From Armenia. All the celebs are wearing him. There's a waiting list.'

At least that shut her up while she mentally referenced her back editions of *Elle*, *Vogue*, *InStyle* and *Marie Claire*.

Conn returned from the car and handed Vino her towel. She breached the first cardinal rule of beach etiquette by flapping it out next to Phil. (Not that I was worried about it or anything. I'm just saying, is all.)

As she settled on to her towel, I noticed Vino's arse

was too small to be raddled with cellulite. I was pleased to remark, however, that mine was perkier and a much nicer shape.

'Here, darling,' she said to Conn, patting the patch of sand beside her.

Behind my sunglasses, I watched for signs of intimacy. At least Conn wasn't calling her Angel Ears or Snoopy Snoop Mamma. In fact, there was little interaction between them, apart from the transfer of provisions. But was that just wishful thinking on my part?

'I didn't think the beach was your gig, Vino,' I said.

'Oh, Conn wanted to come,' said Vino, applying suntan lotion with two fingers. 'He said you guy-ees come here. Conn, darling, could you put some lotion on my back?'

I got to my feet abruptly. 'Anyone for a dip?'

'You go ahead, babe,' said Phil, although I was already striding down to the waterline. 'Like a fish, that one,' I heard him inform Vino.

Terrific. He could have likened me to a panther, or a gazelle, or Princess Grace of Monaco, but no. A *fish*. I wondered what type he had in mind. Shrimp? Lobster? Blowfish?

'Not me. My hair is so DRY,' said Vino, her voice growing fainter.

'Looks fine to me,' I thought I heard Phil say.

Although the Gulf looked refreshing and sparkly and blue, at this time of year it was the temperature of a warm bath. When it was deep enough, I dove down to the bottom and stayed there until I ran out of breath.

When I surfaced, I saw Conn had joined me.

His eyes were the same colour as the sea.

'What if Vino has a suntan lotion crisis?' I asked cattily.

Conn looked doubtfully towards the shore, where Vino was discussing tanning technique with Phil.

'She can reach most bits of her own self,' he said mildly. 'If necessary, she can temporarily lie on her back.'

I was cheered that Conn did not appear seriously concerned about Vino's potential third-degree burns.

'So: you and Vino.' Then, 'You and Vino, HUH?' I said aggressively, when Conn made no response.

'What about – about me and Vino?' said Conn, pushing his hair back with both hands.

'Nothing,' I muttered. A moment later, I tried again: 'You make a lovely couple, but.'

'Oh,' said Conn. Typically unhelpful.

'I didn't think you were Vino's type.'

'No?'

'No.'

Conn frowned. 'I don't know what her type is.'

'Mainly rich. You see a lot of each other?'

'Not really. Of course, I see her at work. We went to the cinema last night.'

'Really? What did you see?'

'Vino wanted to see *Pearl Harbour*.'

'Did you have fun?'

'Not really.'

I crouched and pushed off backwards. For a while, I floated in the warm embrace of the water. Conn was still there when I resurfaced, having apparently survived the whirlpool effect created by my poor, churning head. I felt marginally better.

'Do you like living here?' asked Conn.

'What, Dubai? It's great, I suppose,' I said, tipping my head back to dip my hair in the water. 'I don't much like the six-day working week. That's a cosmic cup of skank. I wouldn't have got a job like this back home, but. You know: no qualifications, no skills apart from speaking fluent English. The salary's generous. Tax-free, too. It's crime-free; nice being able to walk around without being raped or mugged. Terrific weather – well, six months of the year. You can spend weekends on the beach, have barbecues in the evenings. There are palm trees.'

'But?'

'But what?'

'Well, after you said "palm trees", you sighed. But I know you like palm trees, so that implies there is something you don't like.'

I shook my head. Living in the Middle East, I had learned not to think about certain things. Conn waited while I struggled to find words. 'You . . . you have to ignore so much here.'

He nodded.

'I mean, the UAE – it's a dictatorship. A benign dictatorship, but still. And a lot of it is the . . . the cost of living in an alien culture. You mightn't like certain things, but you can put them down to . . . a different way of doing things.'

'For example?'

'For example . . . the status of women. The way domestic violence is not only tolerated, it's almost expected. Media censorship – have you noticed that films are edited so that all traces of human affection are removed, but any amount of gore and violence is acceptable? And pages ripped out of magazines.'

I paused, balancing on my toes and moving my hands slowly through the water.

'But . . . there are other things. You don't have to scratch hard to discover . . . horrific . . . unthinkable *grinding* poverty, coexisting with excess that is somehow . . .'

'Immoral.'

'Yes. You know, on the surface, everything looks great. And if you are a Western expat, it is. But not if you are a Pakistani or Indian labourer working the building sites, or a housemaid paid next to nothing by us expats to be on call seven days a week in case of a dusting emergency. Phil says they're getting a better deal here than they would in their own country, but . . .' I shrugged helplessly as I ran out of words.

Conn frowned. 'But being *less* exploited doesn't make it right. It's degrees of wrongness: some things are more wrong than others. But they are still wrong.'

'Exactly! Exactly.' Although I had been aware of this fundamental flaw in Phil's argument, I had never managed to fully express it. 'People say: if you don't like it, leave; but that doesn't change the fact that these things happen. And you ignore these atrocities, the abuse of . . . basic human rights, since there's nothing you can do about it. But . . .'

'It's a compromise.'

'Yes. I don't know why more people don't understand that – although it appears to be a bigger compromise for some than others. I mean, Phil's been here for seven years and he goes on about how great Dubai is and how much money he earns. I just feel . . . there has to be a better definition of accomplishment.'

Conn nodded. For a long time we floated companionably in the impossible turquoise blue of the Gulf, sparkles of sunlight twinkling in the water.

I gathered my hair and secured it with the elastic band from around my wrist. 'Speaking of accomplishment, how's your swimming coming along?' I asked him.

'Well, I haven't drowned yet,' said Conn with his slow smile.

'Race you to the crow's nest,' I said, pointing to the lookout off the breakwater about a kilometre away. Without waiting for a response, I started swimming.

That evening, Phil and I had a huge argument. He accused me of abandoning him on the beach, and I said he didn't look like he minded much at the time, and he confided his embarrassment that a girlfriend of his would carry on like that, and I asked him to clarify 'that' whilst remarking that on the scale of shame it was hardly in league with developing a boner that looked like it would burst out of his swimming trunks and inflict injury on innocent bystanders, although I conceded there weren't many innocent bystanders.

I'm not sure which part Phil took offence at, but he definitely started it. At least it made a change from quarrelling about Phil's wallpaper. It may have been designer wallpaper, but it was printed with what looked like giant penises in bas-relief.

I didn't know how much longer I could live with it.

12

Zombie Llamas Strike Again

I came gradually out of a state of sleep where it seemed entirely probable that I was about to be savaged by a herd of zombie llamas. For a moment, I panicked wondering where the llamas had gone (were they lying in wait?) and where I was. Then I remembered: I was in a hotel room in Abu Dhabi.

Conn and I had spent the afternoon reviewing the provisional acceptance test results with AEB. Unit five was installed and ready for operation, but AEB had concerns about the valve operator which had stuck on two of the tests. However, since it didn't affect the system functionality, we eventually persuaded Mr O'Hara to sign PAC – result.

Phil had been surprisingly understanding when I had called him at eleven-thirty p.m. from the AEB office, and asked if he would authorise hotel rooms for Conn and me. I explained that the meeting had gone on longer than anticipated, and went into some detail about how exhausted I felt (never felt the like of it before) and the size of the bags (burgeoning) under my eyes (heavy and itchy).

However, I had expected to have to get graphic about

how the Jeep's air conditioning had crapped out completely and how, although summer was almost over, the desert was still sweltering even in the middle of the night. But before I even suggested there hardly seemed any point driving back to Dubai when we had to be back on site for the safety check the following morning, Phil said, 'No worries, babe. When will you be back?'

'Well, I'm meeting Charge first thing tomorrow morning to do the quality assurance check. Review scenarios and tolerance levels. It will probably take up the rest of the day. Seven, seven-thirty?'

'No problemo.'

Phil wasn't so bad. Like when he did something like this. Or when he was unconscious.

Lying in the hotel bed, I looked forward to being asleep at six a.m. instead of having to bury my head under my pillow while listening to the mosque fifteen feet from Phil's bedroom window. In fact, I was looking forward to it so much I could hardly *wait* to go back to sleep.

I thought I was aslumber when I dreamed I needed to go to the bathroom, but then I realised that was real. I groaned aloud. I had achieved the perfect position, I was snug and warm. How much did I *really* need to go?

Hmm. Quite a lot, it seemed, the more I considered it.

I slipped out from under the bedclothes and padded across the room. I fumbled for the bathroom door. I remembered the layout. No need to go to the effort of opening my eyes. Consequently, no need to turn on the light.

Crouching, I turned and backed over to where the toilet was, directly opposite the door. Funny, I didn't remember it being as far away as this. It also seemed surprisingly bright. I could see the inside of my eyelids.

Putting out a hand to steady myself against the wall, I promptly toppled over.

What the fuck?

Opening my eyes, I realised I was sprawled in the corridor outside my room. Shite! I must have opened the wrong— I dived for the door of room 508 as it swung closed and grabbed the handle. It clacked uselessly in my hand. I threw my weight against the door, but it would not give.

Now that I was wide awake without a trace of zombie llamas, it did not take long to deduce that I was locked out of my room. In the nip. But for my watch and favourite pair of earrings – which didn't provide much in the way of coverage – I was absolutely naked, at maximum exposure, pretty much 110 per cent clothes-free.

I bitterly regretted heeding the questionnaire in *Vanity Fair* that suggested sleeping naked was daring and sexy. Now, it felt entirely foolhardy, and only sexy if you got an erotic charge from goosebumps.

I visually rifled the corridor for something to camouflage my extensive expanses of flesh (although now I was technically covered in a cold sweat, it was still quite revealing). There were no windows, hence no curtains – no laundry trolleys, not even a napkin to cover my crème brûlée: nothing. At that moment I would have even welcomed a stray zombie llama.

Shite, shite, shite! Of all the places to be locked out of your hotel room in the nip, Abu Dhabi was the worst. Except for Ras Al Khaimah, or Sharjah, or Fujairah. I suppose they would have been worse. In fact, as Emirates went, Abu Dhabi wasn't the worst after all; and as countries went, it certainly wasn't as bad as Saudi Arabia or Afghanistan.

Strange I didn't take more comfort in that.

Well, I could either stand around trying to batter the door down with the force of my nakedness – which was admittedly strong – or do something. I could get another keycard – yes, that was a good idea – reception was only five floors down – the elevator was right there – but I would have to walk about three kilometres through the expansive, marble-tiled lobby. Maybe if I crouched by the wall and impersonated a pot plant nobody would notice me.

That seemed unlikely.

Mortification seemed to have seized my brain, but regardless, a solution presented itself – possibly because, with the limited options available, it was the *only* solution. Conn's room was right next to mine. What if he were asleep? I would have to wake him – although he used to exist on less than four hours sleep a day – either way, it was a minor concern compared to being arrested for indecent exposure.

I felt he'd understand.

Hands clamped strategically, I backed swiftly over to Conn's door, swivelling my head right and left. When I knocked, the door seemed to absorb the sound – I pounded it with my fist. Nothing. Turning, I kicked the door with my heel.

Inside Conn's room, I heard a dull thud. Oh, thank God thank God thank God!

'Yes?' came Conn's voice from inside. I imagined him placing his eye to the viewfinder, and swiftly put my finger over the lens.

'Conn, Conn! It's Lara,' I hissed. 'Quick! Let me in!' I heard the rattle of the security chain. '*Wait!*'

'What? I thought you wanted to come in?'

'Yes – but you've got to promise not to look.'

'At what?' Conn sounded bemused, as well he might.

'At me.' My skin prickled from a blast from the air conditioning.

'Why?'

'I have no clothes on. Hurry up!'

'I'll let you in, but I can't promise not to look.'

'Can't you just hand me something through the door?'

'Like – like what? I have the remote control for the television, or – or—'

'Baby cheeses, *no*! A towel or something.'

There was silence while Conn contemplated this.

'Just let me *in*!' I bawled, hammering both hands on the door. When at last it blessedly opened, I shot past Conn into the bathroom. Inside, I grabbed a standard-issue terrycloth robe and wrapped it around me with luxurious relief.

I paused a moment to gather my dignity. Unfortunately, I couldn't find any. Chances are it had deserted me in favour of a sordid life of crime.

I exited the bathroom cautiously. Conn was sprawled on the bed, one leg bent. I don't suppose he set out to look sexier than Bruce Springsteen (the 'Lucky Town' era) dipped in chocolate, but that was the overall effect. Belatedly, I noticed he was also more or less naked, but for the crucial detail of a pair of running shorts. I looked away hurriedly when I realised I was trying to stare up the leg.

I flicked my hair outside the neck of the robe and sank into the single armchair in the corner of the suite. When I glanced at him again, Conn had shifted so that he sat on the edge of the bed, elbows propped on his knees.

I had to clear my throat before I could speak. 'Did you see anything?'

'What do you mean?'

'When I . . . earlier – well, five minutes ago . . . when I came in.'

'I don't understand.'

'Did you see my lady bits?' I asked, clutching the neck of the robe.

'Oh,' said Conn, running his fingers up his jaw. 'Well, of course. You had no clothes on.'

I was annoyed he looked so blatantly amused. Suddenly, his lips twitched. He smiled broadly, then he laughed.

I scowled at him, but then I was laughing too, the sort that bubbles out of some deep spring and appropriates your bodily functions and feeds off itself like some animal-related flu virus. Every time I thought I was done, Conn set me off again.

The mood gradually gave way to a comfortable silence. I brushed tears away with my fingertips, feeling spent and deeply relaxed. I looked across at Conn: at his eyes, alert as always, now fixed steadily on me; the unkempt curls, one loosely falling across the broad expanse of forehead; the hollows below his cheekbones; the sinewy breadth of his shoulders.

'Conn.' When I spoke his name, my voice sounded deeper and richer to my ears. I cleared my throat, but instead of what I wanted to say, I asked, 'Could you call reception and ask them to let me into my room?'

'Of course.'

As with everything he undertook, Conn gave his full attention to the short discussion. Afterwards, he replaced the receiver and stared at it intently.

'Lara,' he said softly. 'What happened to us?'

I realised that, ever since Conn had walked into the interview, I had anticipated this conversation. Still, I had the sensation of being tipped over the crest of a roller coaster, and seeing the rails stop at the edge of a cliff that plunged down to a huge sea foaming around jagged rocks and full of sharks. And jellyfish.

'What do you mean, what happened?' I said, fidgeting with the hem of the terrycloth robe. 'You know what happened. You were there. I'm sure your recollection of the facts is better than mine.'

Conn said, 'Of course, I remember what *happened*. But I do not understand—'

'You left me—'

'No. No,' said Conn, rumpling his hair. 'Technically, you left me. Since I remained in the same location, therefore—'

'Conn, *you* broke up with *me*. I merely speeded up the process.' I wound a stray thread around my finger.

'You don't know that. You can't—'

'You accepted a job in Azerbaijan—'

'That is inaccurate—'

'Conn, perhaps you are forgetting that *I* was there too,' I said tightly.

'Of course not. But I didn't accept the job. I never accepted it.'

'That's just a technicality,' I said dismissively.

'Babco only offered me the job—'

'Four months before you told me, still.'

'Would it have been different if I had told you earlier?'

'Who knows? Probably not, but.'

'Why?'

'Conn,' I said, pressing my fingers against my forehead. 'You made a *choice*.'

'I didn't – I can see how you might have th-thought that. But you – you don't understand. I wanted that job—'

'Oh, I understood *that* all right.'

'But I wanted you, too. I didn't know I could have both.' Conn unfolded himself from the bed, came over and hunkered down beside me. He put his long fingers round my left knee. I had not realised my legs were cold until I felt the warmth radiating from his hands. The effect was entirely unnerving, although I left my knee in his grip. 'When you said you would go with me, I was really pleased. I didn't understand the concept of compromise. Of course, I knew the theory, b-but I was not sure how it worked—'

'OK, we're going to take a little detour into hypothetical conjecture here. Conn, what if I had said: you must choose between me or your career?'

'I d-don't understand the hypothesis,' said Conn, tightening his hold on my knee.

'Bear with me. If I had said: you can have one *or* the other.' The silence that stretched between us seemed to crackle.

'B-but I didn't have to. You said—'

'Conn. You chose your career over me.'

'Yes. At that point in time—'

'That's the time frame we're working with, Conn. You see. It was never about whether or *when* you told me. It was about what was important to you. And it wasn't me.'

'You *were* important—'

'Just not enough.'

'But I-I loved you—'

'Perhaps you did, Conn. But *not enough*.' I felt my heart might explode with grief. I thought I had dealt with all that rage and pain and stored it in boxes cross-referenced with neat labels.

Obviously not.

'Lara, I didn't – I never meant to upset you—'

'Let me put this in terms you will understand: your intent had no bearing on the outcome.'

Conn said, 'I don't know what you want—'

'Well, I'll tell you,' I said, springing to my feet and pacing over to the television. 'I want someone who thinks I am the most important thing in the world. Someone who puts me first – or at least considers my needs. Someone who dares everything for *love* – not a job in Azerbaijan. I want a man who will slay dragons for me, not someone who completely discards me and my hopes and dreams to follow his own.'

'That is an unrealistic ideal—'

'Well, it's *my* ideal and I LIKE IT!'

'Why are you shouting?'

'I JUST WANT TO MAKE SURE YOU HEAR ME!'

'You would still be audible if you dropped your voice by up to forty-five decibels –'

'FUCK YOU!' I roared. Conn rose and closed the gap between us in two strides. He put his hands on my shoulders. I pushed him away, hard.

'Lara. How can I fix it?' he said. His face was paler than normal. 'How can I make it right?'

'You *can't*,' I said. 'Get away from me. Get AWAY!' I drummed his chest with my fists. I was winding up to delivering a good, old-fashioned slap around the chops, but Conn seized both my wrists in a grip that hurt.

'Lara. Lara, wait, stop—'

I writhed futilely against him, while I assessed escape strategies (at that point I was seriously considering a quick head butt).

'Let go,' I gasped. Instead, Conn pinned my arms against the wall behind me.

Then I made the mistake of looking up at him, and the world stood still. If you noticed that – it occurred at three forty-eight hours GMT plus four on 5 October 2001 – now you know: it was due to a massive chemical reaction in the Middle East. NASA has it filed under 'unexplained phenomena' (the information is classified in the event it induces mass hysteria).

Conn was so close I could smell him: toothpaste and fresh shampoo and pheromones. My whole body was washed with a tidal wave of memories and distilled lust.

I'm not sure who made the first move. When it happened, the kiss was savage, ferocious, fuelled by three months of latent want. I pressed against him; I could not get close enough.

Conn's grip on my wrists relaxed and he slid his hands up to mine. I clasped his fingers as hard as I could. When we stumbled, Conn put out a hand for balance; swinging me round, he braced himself against the wall and pulled me into him. He smoothed back my hair, gripped it at the nape. I heard him groan and my legs gave way.

The kiss had changed into something softer, gentle and regretful, when I became aware of the knocking. Conn evidently heard it too, because he pulled away from me. He pressed his forehead briefly against mine.

The knocking grew more insistent. When I took a step back, the world jolted back into action.

'Shit,' I said with feeling. I was gasping. My mouth tingled.

'Infinite shit to the eighth power,' said Conn. He tugged gently at a strand of my hair.

It was the concierge with a spare card for my room.

My fingers trembled as I rifled Conn's wallet for five dirhams to tip him. Conn closed the door.

'Lara—'

'It doesn't change anything.' I did not look at him.

Clutching the card in one hand and the neck of the bathrobe in the other, I left.

The following morning, there was nothing I wanted to do less than meet Martin Charge, except maybe hack off my lower limbs with a blunt axe. Even then, it would depend on how blunt the axe was, and whether I had ready access to tequila.

Martin Charge: possibly my least favourite person in the world. Although this changed on a minute-by-minute basis, Charge sometimes spent whole weeks in the position.

I had specifically requested this meeting, since I was still concerned about the system safety – specifically, the sticking valve operator.

'If you don't highlight this, I'm going to report it to Philip,' I said through gritted teeth.

Martin looked down his nose at me (not that he was particularly tall; in relation to me, most people had a height advantage).

'Yeah, you go running off to your boyfriend, Callaghan,' he sneered. He pronounced my surname with a hard 'g' and somehow managed to insert a 'b' at the end as well. 'See how far it gets you.'

'Obviously further than talking to you,' I snapped. 'Look, are you going to do your job or what?'

'Don't tell me what my job is, Callaghan—'

'Well then, I'll tell you what your job isn't. It's not giving management an anal enema with your nose—'

'That's rich, coming from someone who got her job sleeping with the boss—'

'That's not true. I only gave him a handjob at the interview, but it was the blowjob I gave the HR Director that swung it for me. At least I'm good at my job; I don't know what your excuse is. Look, these turbine faults are potentially dangerous – particularly the integrity of the valve operator. If you don't tell Phil, I will—'

'Nobody *cares*, Callaghan!' said Martin, looming over me threateningly. I resisted the urge to step backwards, even though his halitosis blistered my skin. 'Let me put this in terms your teeny, tiny brain can process, Callaghan. Do you really think your boyfriend wants to know? He doesn't give a shit! It might affect the bottom line—'

'Phil's not like that,' I said staunchly.

'Oh, no?' Martin smiled like a raptor. 'Give him a whirl, Callaghan – but then I'm sure you will. Smell ya later.'

Groin first, he swaggered out of the Turbine Room.

I slammed my hand against Unit five, but stopped, fearing it might irreparably damage the structural integrity. I was furiously angry. That fucker, Charge! I would show him. I would – I would—

OK, the plan to wreak my horrible revenge needed some fine-tuning. Charge was right, in that I didn't think Voltech's upper management would care about the fundamental flaws in their product. The previous week, a Voltech substation in Russia had blown up, resulting in three critical injuries, but 'no fatalities!' gloated Voltech's PR Department. They seemed to consider this a major achievement.

I wondered how they would like to have 70 per cent of their skin melted off.

At least I had tried. It wasn't my job to ensure the turbines were safe to operate – but that was a shabby excuse and I knew it. If someone did end up with 70 per cent of their skin melted off, I would be responsible. I resolved to tackle Charge again tomorrow.

In the meantime, at least we could leave site early. I was exhausted. That was not a good excuse for not speaking to Conn on the way home, but it was the best I could do at short notice.

I couldn't face the thought of returning to the office for half an hour, so after dropping Conn back at his place, I drove straight back to Phil's.

What a crappy day. At least it couldn't get any worse. It was the anniversary of when Phil and I met each other, so it was bound to get better, I thought.

As it happened, I was wrong.

According to past experience, sooner or later – and in most cases sooner – I almost *expected* to turn up early at my current boyfriend's apartment to find him shagging some slapper.

Perversely, it was kind of comforting. I mean, if I were ever to stumble across proof that men weren't total shits, it would have rocked the foundations of my very existence.

So when I found Phil shagging some slapper doggy style across the kitchen sink, there was an air of inevitability about it. Not the sexual position, so much. I mean, it could just as well have been the missionary position. Similarly, the kitchen sink was interchangeable with the dining table or the laundry chute.

I felt the difference when I entered his flat. Oh, nothing obvious like the stench of airborne sperm particles, or the sound of the headboard banging rhythmically against the wall, or a woman shrieking, 'OH MY GOD YES YES YES YES YES!' (because much as they liked to believe otherwise, none of my boyfriends were ever *that* good – or that rich).

If anything, it was the charged silence of the place.

'Phil?' I called cautiously.

Since I was holding my breath, I'm pretty sure I would have heard a response.

I checked the bedroom first, sidling up to the door and pushing it open with the tips of my fingers. Next I headed for the kitchen, because I wasn't sure whether I heard or imagined a noise from that vicinity and also, I felt a bit peckish.

My relationship with Phil had persisted for nearly a year and there had been few of the usual signs, so my guard was down – although not as far as Vino's knickers.

At least I had the common decency to pull my guard straight back up again.

Philip did not notice me because I was outside his line of sight and he was concentrating on trying to stick it up Vino's arse without her noticing – a move with which I was well acquainted.

I felt detached, as if it were someone else witnessing the carnal carnage. I remembered thinking, however, that Philip looked a bit like a rutting slug in the harsh sunlight of late afternoon.

I also noted bitterly that Vino wasn't dressed up like some ex-schoolgirl nun with ambitions for world domination. Philip had adopted a fairly pedestrian, vanilla doggy style. Nothing kinky about it at all (unless you counted Vino texting on her mobile). Must only be me Phil liked dressing up in hot, restrictive, rubber clothing.

'Excuse me,' I said. Phil leaped off Vino like her cervix had suddenly grown fangs.

'Lara!' he gasped. Vino wriggled out from between Philip and the sink.

'Yes, we've met,' I said conversationally. 'We are colleagues, and up until pretty recently we were also going out together. I have to say, Phil, your taste in women is almost as bad as your décor. Mind you, I am either criminally stupid, or my taste in men is even *worse* than your décor.'

Philip looked around frantically for something to cover himself with. He seized a slice of bread and slapped it over his wilting penis. 'Oh please, don't mind me,' I said. Vino paused in the act of scuttling around the kitchen picking up pieces of clothing. She looked as if she were about to take me literally, so I snapped, 'I was being sarcastic, babycakes. This is your cue to make like a tree and fuck off.'

'Come ON, Lara,' said Vino reasonably. 'It was only SEX.'

'Oh, is that all? That's all right, then. Silly me, I thought it was something else entirely.'

Vino shook her head pityingly. 'You take this sort of thing so *seriously*.'

' "This sort of thing"? You mean loyalty and decency? If you can't take that seriously, what else is there? I'll tell you one thing I find hard to take seriously: someone showing so much pubic hair. Can I offer you a slice of bread?'

'Fuck YOU!' said Vino, tossing her hair (the normal variety, not the pubic variety).

'That appears to be more your department. Indeed, if

you text Philip in half an hour, I'm sure you will find him available and willing to do just that – at least until he finds some other slag.'

'Phil's wanted to break up with you for AGES,' said Vino. 'He didn't want to while your mother was so sick—'

'Wait – my mother's *sick*? Phil, why didn't you tell me?'

Vino glanced uncertainly at Philip, who seemed to have no better place to look than at his penis sandwich. 'I suppose he also said I don't understand him and I'm no good in bed. Oh look, I'm not in the mood to chat about man problems and bikini waxing. Just get out.' Vino opened her mouth and I screamed, 'GET OUT!'

Vino flounced out, moulting hair all over the espresso machine as she left – my last birthday present to Philip. I would have to remember to take it when I left.

When I put up a hand to wipe my mouth, it was trembling.

'You – you're back early,' said Philip.

'What are you going to do about it? Shag another woman? Oh wait, you've already done that. I can't believe – I can't – I came home early because I thought you had something special planned for our anniversary.'

'What anniversary?' sputtered Phil.

'Our one-year anniversary! Of the first time we kissed. I expected flowers, maybe some chocolates – not a naked woman on the end of your penis.'

'Babe, I'm so sorry—'

'Tell you what, let's get the post-mortem small talk out of the way. So, how many times have you shagged Vino?'

'It was just the once,' said Philip, a fraction too quickly. 'I swear. This was the first time—'

'Is that so? For the moment I'll disregard the fact that I don't believe you. Let's focus on how you seem to feel this is more acceptable than shagging her multiple times. Will you ever put on a pair of underpants?'

'It will never happen again,' said Philip, moving in for an embrace.

'Get back,' I said. 'I don't care whether it happens again or not. In fact, I really think you should get it on with Vino. You two are ideally, if not uniquely, suited.'

Philip decided on an offensive strategy – an audacious move, given that he was armed only with a slice of sperm-encrusted bread.

'Is this about Connell?' said Philip accusingly.

'Who – Conn? No, Philip. This is about you being a horn dog—'

'Don't change the subject! Are you having it off with Connell O'Neill?'

'Not at the moment, no. I think you would have noticed him, unless he engaged his invisible cloak shield.'

'You're sweet on him—'

'So what if I am? In this instance, it doesn't matter how I *feel* about him. Since your definition of fidelity appears to be the exchange of bodily fluids, I haven't had sex with him – or not for at least six years.'

'Oh come on Lara, it meant—'

'Yeah, yeah, it meant nothing. Wait – I feel another coming on – don't tell me. Your inability to keep your trousers on is actually *my* fault. Maybe for dyeing your favourite underpants pink, or putting the cheese on the wrong shelf of the fridge, or not wearing corsets often enough or any one of a number of spurious reasons that – let's face it – you would have mentioned before if they had any basis in fact, reality or validity—'

'Well, now you mention it, it would be nice if you initiated sex more often—'

'Philip, we have sex – wait. We *had*, in very much the past tense if not the *historic* tense, sex every night. Sometimes several times. So forgive me if I did not initiate sex more. Evidently, I was too busy being SCREWED AT THE TIME!'

'Lara.' Philip put his hand on my arm and I smacked it away.

'Stop. Quite apart from knowing *exactly* where your hand has been, I don't want to catch any diseases. Back away.'

'Lara, I—'

'Let me save you the trouble. You're so sorry. Now that you might lose me you clearly see the error of your ways. Vino meant nothing to you. God, my life is one big, fat, high-cholesterol cliché. Philip, I've heard it all before. You're not the first asshole who's fooled around on me. Quite frankly, I'm sick of it. Get out.'

'What?'

'Get out of my sight. Take your things and leave—'

'It's my apartment.'

'Oh,' I said. 'Right. Well. Excuse me while I pick up my things.'

'Oh, come on, Lara! It doesn't have to be like this—'

'Like what? Like you shagging someone else? I agree, but unfortunately it *is* like this, to the extent of being practically indistinguishable.'

'Lara,' said Phil soothingly, moving towards me. 'You know how I feel about you. Don't let something like this ruin what we have together. Hmm?'

Did he really think I had that little self-respect?

But I didn't move away because I had just had an idea.

A rather brilliant idea. Although I hadn't had time to completely formulate it, and it might need a bit of tweaking. It was also dependent on Phil being arrogant enough to fall for it – but I wasn't concerned about that aspect.

Phil put a finger under my chin and lifted my face to his. I arrested the shudder just before it manifested itself physically. Unfortunately, I couldn't suppress it when he kissed me, but luckily Phil misinterpreted it as an expression of hopeless desire.

'You've been a naughty boy,' I said slowly. Phil's eyes lit up, and even more when I gripped his windpipe and squeezed it hard.

'I have!' he gasped. 'A *very* naughty boy.'

'What happens to naughty boys, Philip?' I said witheringly, although it appeared to have had the opposite effect on at least one part of Phil's anatomy, judging by the prodding sensation against my lower stomach.

'Mistress punishes naughty boys.'

'Indeed. Go to your room immediately!' I barked.

Philip practically galloped into the bedroom – although he was helped on his way by the kick up the arse I administered.

Once inside, I distracted him with a nipple clamp and an elaborate description of coming attractions as I tied him to the bed with a selection of his own ties. I picked out his favourite to stuff in his mouth, and secured that with another.

'Too tight?' I said. Phil nodded, so I pulled harder.

'Wait right here,' I said, when I was sure he was securely lashed.

I collected all my stuff and stuffed it into a couple of bin liners. It was just my books, clothes, some cosmetics and a wooden giraffe. The espresso machine was heavy, so I stood it on a towel to drag it to the front door.

Then I went to find Phil's mobile phone. It wasn't in its usual place on the hall table. I checked the living room and the kitchen. Eventually I found it on the kitchen floor, in Philip's trouser pocket.

'Right,' I said, re-entering the bedroom. Philip sported an erection that could have drilled holes in concrete. 'Philip, it occurs to me there is little incentive for you to behave when you relish punishment so much. I thought maybe we should try a different approach.' I held up his mobile phone.

'Wumph wum muff muff,' said Philip, his eyes darting from my face to the phone. Suddenly his abominable penis didn't look quite as perky, although it flexed as I flipped open his phone.

He probably thought I was going to stuff it up his urethra.

'Just a moment, I'm concentrating. Now, how do you compose a text message on this thing? OK, here we go. Right. Let me see.' I leaned my shoulder against the doorjamb and read aloud as I tapped the keys. ' "Must talk. Somethings come up meet me at my apartment its three one two al ghurair building sh zayed rd. Battery dead ciao ciao." Let me just send this to The Don . . . what's our boss's real name again?'

'Mmf muff.'

'It doesn't appear to be stored under that. Isn't it Antoine Something? Let me see . . . Abdul . . . Alan . . . Ali . . . Aniket . . . Antoine, here he is.' I pressed 'Send'. 'Right, that's on its way. You can expect rescue within half an hour.'

Phil lashed his head against the pillow, and strained uselessly against the bed.

'See you in the office, Phil,' I said, tossing his mobile on the bed between his splayed legs.

I doubted he'd be able to operate it with his knees.

I left his door open as I left, dragging my things behind me on the towel.

Outside Al Ghurair Building, I flagged down a taxi. When the driver asked where to go, I realised I hadn't thought that far ahead.

Although I knew loads of people, these relationships tended to be limited to shopping, parties, nightclubs and margharitas. There was no shortage of acquaintances with whom I could debate the merits of kitten heels versus wedges, but I could think of none who would welcome me and a hijacked espresso machine into their home for an extended visit.

Briefly, I considered Conn. I had landed on his doorstep once before, however, and it had brought me nothing but trouble. Well – three years of incandescent happiness, and *then* nothing but trouble.

I asked the driver to take me to the Crowne Plaza Hotel off the Trade Centre Roundabout, where I booked into the cheapest room. I curled up on the bed with a mini bottle of Baileys and stared unseeingly at an Arabic soap opera, which involved lots of spitting.

I was upset, undoubtedly – although not about breaking up with Phil. (Actually, I felt mildly relieved).

No; I felt like such a *failure*. It appeared that the only thing I had learned after years of making the same mistakes, was that I had the fortitude, resilience and pure stupidity not only to make them again, but to reproduce them *exactly*.

At least I knew the agenda for the immediate future.

Change my hair; sporadically wail into my pillow; eat a year's supply of Oreo cookies.

I decided it was about time I swore off men for a while. It occurred to me that it had been years since I had been single. I had never spent more than a week without a boyfriend.

It was time to change that. Spend a while revelling in my self-sufficient independent womanhood. I rather fancied the romance of solitude: a lone love warrior.

It appeared the cosmos had other plans for me, however.

The rest of the week was better than expected. I bypassed much of the wailing, and managed not to overdose on refined sugar. Even working with Philip was not as bad as anticipated. Instead of a revenge strategy based on sabotage and GBH, Philip opted for a variation on the silent treatment.

That worked for me.

I was more concerned about the situation with Conn. On the surface, our relationship hadn't changed, but now I felt a sense of dull resignation. All things considered, it might be time to find another job. Apart from everything else, I had been with Voltech six months longer than my preferred average.

The following week, Mark was released.

Outside Central Prison, Mark embraced Conn. I was touched how Conn patted Mark awkwardly on the back.

Mark gave me a shorter clinch, but I didn't mind because he was covered in sand (he had insisted on throwing himself to his knees outside the prison gate and snogging the ground). 'You the *man*,' said Mark emotionally, gripping my shoulders for extra emphasis. Then he hugged Conn again.

Mark had emerged from prison a changed man. At least, he said he was. He was certainly a *lesser* man, and his conversation had acquired a philosophical flavour.

'You should value your freedom,' announced Mark, spraying the dashboard with sand. He turned his head to spray me, 'You never know when it's going to be snatched away by the fickle hand of fucking fate.'

I smiled instead of suggesting that one could minimise the likelihood of being fingered by the fickle hand of fucking fate, e.g., by either smoking them, or flushing the drugs down the toilet *before* arriving at Immigration.

I braked sharply to avoid a yellow Ferrari zipping in front of me on Sheikh Zayed Road.

'Dude, mind the hair,' said Mark, rootling around the glove box. He put on my spare sunglasses, a fetching purple pair with diamanté stems. 'You know, it's a terrible thing to have your liberty sodomised by the System. By the way, you fuckers were useless fucking accomplices. Why didn't you fucking tunnel into my cell with a dessert spoon and break me out? Or you could have baked me a fucking cake with a file in it.'

'Sorry,' I said.

'We'll remember that for next time,' said Conn. He smiled at me in the rear-view mirror. I was annoyed to realise I had been looking at him.

'You'd fucking better,' said Mark.

'Have you somewhere to bunk?' I asked.

'Nah.'

'You can stay with me,' said Conn. 'You can have the bedroom. I can sleep on the sofa.'

'I wouldn't dream of imposing upon your hospitality any more than I already fucking have,' declaimed Mark.

'But since there's nowhere else, I graciously accept. Thanks, dude.'

'I would offer a spare bed, except I'm currently homeless myself,' I said.

'Don't you live with Philip?' asked Conn.

'I *did*,' I said brightly. 'Until recently.'

'Are you and Philip—'

'Yes,' I said sharply. Did Conn need everything spelled out in Braille 152 point font? 'Listen,' I addressed Mark when I pulled up outside Conn's building. 'The AEB Unit five launch dinner is this evening at the JW Marriott—'

'What the fuck is an AEB Unit five launch dinner?' said Mark.

'All you need to know is there's free food.' I grinned. 'See you there.'

'I had a dream about you last night,' said Mr O'Hara, looking down my top.

'Really? Did you wake up crying?'

'I wish I had never woken up,' he growled. 'You were doing all manner of filthy things to me. I loved every minute of it.'

I wondered where the fuck Con was. He could help distract Mr O'Hara by boring him about the project, or how many times you can fold paper in half. Someone entered the JW Marriott restaurant, and I periscoped my head over Mr O'Hara's shoulder to see if it was Conn.

It was Phil – with Vino. I had no idea why Vino was at the dinner, since she had nothing to do with the AEB project. She was swarming over Phil like a case of gonorrhoea, when he wasn't all over her like an outbreak of herpes simplex.

Phil caught my eye and glared at me coldly.

I wondered whether I should tell him it made him look like he was constipated.

Conn and Mark had still not arrived when we sat down for dinner. Mr O'Hara took the seat next to mine.

'Lara,' he said, 'have I thanked you?'

'For what?' I said wearily.

'For being born.' He was so cheesy, I was concerned about overdosing on calcium.

'Right,' I said. 'I didn't have much to do with that, Mr O'Hara.'

'Lara,' he said, with a pained look. 'Don't you think we could move our relationship on to a – let's say – less formal footing? Why don't you call me Leonard.'

'Listen,' I said. It was a spur-of-the-moment decision, even though I had thought about it all week. 'About Unit five—'

'Let's not talk about work,' said Mr O'Hara. 'Why don't we—'

'I'll only say this once,' I said hurriedly, before he could get on to what he wanted us to 'don't'. 'If I were you, I would have an independent consultant do a quality assurance check on Unit five.'

'What?' said Mr O'Hara. He was much more attractive in Business Mode.

'Won't you excuse me?' I said. My chair toppled over with the force of my backdraft.

As soon as I was in the hotel lobby beyond visibility range, I commando-rolled under a giant cheese plant. Peering around a leaf, I saw that although Mr O'Hara was headbutting one of his employees, he kept glancing in the direction I had come.

I looked around. The lifts were not only too exposed, but

they were also positioned directly in Mr O'Hara's line of vision. Just beyond them, a low partition adjoined a ramp down to the fire escape. I made a dash to the partition, then scooched down and crawled to the fire escape.

When I emerged into the hotel's landscaped gardens, they spun around for a moment. I had drunk far too much in a futile effort to make Mr O'Hara appear more attractive. I lurched around until I found a patch of grass to fall backwards on to.

Despite the prickly salt-resistant grass scratching the back of my knees, and the ants launching sorties across my face, I tucked my hands behind my head. The desert sky was stuffed full of stars.

Conn had once told me that, because the light takes so long to reach earth, some of the stars you see no longer exist. Whenever I look up at the night sky I think of that. Also, Conn ravishing me on a tropical beach.

The fire escape door rebounding off the wall made me jump.

'Lars?'

'Hey, Mark,' I said. 'What took you guys so long? Is Conn with you?'

Mark walked over and crouched, balancing on his haunches. 'Conn had to go to some client place—'

'The AEB site?' I said, propping myself up on my elbows. 'Really? Why? What happened? Is there a problem?'

'Um. OK. I think those were all the same question, were they? From what I understood, one of the engineers called and said the thingy on the thingy was stuck—'

'The turbine valve operator?'

'That's the one.'

'Did Conn fix it?'

'Yeah. He hit it with a fucking hammer and it's fine now—'

'He did what?!' I said, catapulating off the ground.

'Lars, I was only messin'. Conn sorted it.'

'Oh,' I said. I sat back down on a stone lion's head. 'Sorry. It's just that if the valve operator malfunctions when the turbine's operating, it's pretty serious. Exploding gas, fireballs, burning people running around screaming—'

'I know. Well, Conn said it was critical, but he didn't go into the graphic description. You know Conn.' I did not respond to that, so after a pause, Mark said, 'What are you doing out here?'

'I needed some fresh air. My client was trying to drown me in testosterone. Also, Vino was getting off with my recently boyfriend, who is now an ex-boyfriend thanks to her. I just felt trapped, you know?'

'I have an idea,' said Mark. Although he smiled, I felt awful.

'Shite, Mark, I'm sorry—'

'You're grand, don't worry about it.'

'Are you OK?' I asked after a pause. Mark seemed more subdued than normal.

'Yeah, I'm cool,' he said, tugging at a tuft of grass. 'Well. This probably sounds fucking stupid, but all those people – I'm not used to it any more. I couldn't handle it. It was kinda – kinda – *overwhelming*, you know?'

I nodded. Mark had always been so flip about his incarceration, talking of it in the same terms as a free vacation.

'Was it terrible?' I asked.

'It wasn't all bad,' said Mark. 'I got really bored inside, so I started composing again.'

'Really? You mean, songs?'

'Yeah. Would you – if you would like to see, I have one here. In my pocket. I wrote it on a piece of toilet paper. Just the first verse. It was all that would fit.'

'I'd love to,' I said, carefully taking the tissue Mark had eased from his back pocket and reading it aloud:

> *'I am forever scarred*
> *'By the stripes*
> *Branded on my skin*
> *Bars grip me*
> *In their steely embrace*
> *I chafe against*
> *The ties that bind*
> *Railing always, always, always*
> *Against the cruelty of fellow man*
> *Miserable bunch of fuckers.'*

'It's really good,' I said, folding the tissue paper and handing it back to him. 'I never realised you were so creative.'

'Yeah? You got the bit about the stripes? Like, from the sun coming through the fucking prison bars?'

'Yes; although the sun wouldn't burn stripes into your skin, would they? Surely the bars would block the sun? Unless they were made of glass.'

'Glass bars? I hadn't thought of that. It adds a whole new layer of fucking complexity.'

'What will you do now?' I asked.

'Think I'll stick around for a while. I like this place,' said Mark.

It was impossible not to laugh. 'You know what, Mark? You are madder than a crate of kung-fu frogs, but I admire your irrepressible spirit.'

Mark turned and gave me a grin of surprising sweetness. It was not in keeping with his image. The last time I recalled him smiling was on stage in the Student Union. In fairness, that had really been more of a ferocious grimace.

'So, what about you and Conn?' asked Mark. 'Have you two put it together yet?'

'No,' I said shortly.

I was surprised when he took the hint. Perhaps he had acquired some subtlety in prison.

'How come we never got it on in university?' asked Mark.

'What, you and me? Um. Actually, we did,' I said.

'No shit! Really? When?'

'Before I went out with Conn. You used to play in the Student Union with your band—'

'You were a groupie?'

I snorted. 'Oh, that's good. Hymen Raider and the Fucking Penetrators barely managed an audience, never mind *groupies*.'

'Man, that's cold.'

'Not as cold as you not remembering who I was afterwards.'

'Aw man, that *is* cold. Did I really? I was an awful fucking waster. I can't believe I didn't ask you out. What the fuck was I thinking?'

'Probably that you could murder another beer.'

'Shit, I knew fucking nothing back then,' said Mark.

'And you know so much more now,' I said, grinning.

Then, and I'm not sure how this happened, Mark was kissing me. It was all wrong.

I would normally have gone along with it because it was just too much effort to pull away and make up some light-hearted comment to save face. And of course, I had not forgotten my resolution to revel in my self-sufficient independent womanhood.

I pulled back and opened my eyes, arresting Mark mid-pucker. I placed my fingers against his lips.

'Sorry,' I mumbled, wincing. 'I can't ... It's just ... this is too complicated. You being Conn's best friend and ... everything. You know?'

'Hey, no worries,' said Mark, but even in the dim light I could see he blushed bright red.

'Hey, you must be hungry,' I said brightly, although I felt suddenly cold.

'I'm fucking ravenous.'

Mark stood and reached out to help me to my feet. 'Listen,' he said, 'we go back a long way and I just want to say, you really are a top-class bird. I really appreciate you coming to see me in prison.'

He wrapped his arms round me. After a moment, I sank into him. It felt warm and comforting and not the least bit erotic.

I wasn't sure whether I heard the clack of the fire escape door, but when Mark released me and stepped back, I realised someone else was there.

'What are you doing?' asked Conn. There was no inflection in his voice.

'It's not what you think,' said Mark quickly. 'Nothing happened, dude. There was no fucking tongue action, nothing like that.'

'OK,' said Conn.

He was so impassive.

'Would you be bothered?' I said, my voice slicing through the heavy night. 'If I went out with Mark? It seems to me you don't give much of a shit – not even a skid mark – but I'm curious. Would it matter to you?'

Conn was silent a long moment, then said, 'If that is what both of you want.'

He couldn't have done more damage had he lowered me head first into a giant blender.

'Right,' I said. 'Well, that's tremendous. Catch you later, then.'

He walked away, blatantly defying my heart which was willing him to stop, turn back and say he was gutted, that he *did* give a shit, that it really mattered to him, that he wasn't OK with it at all, and that he couldn't stand to see me with anyone else, even Mark.

But he didn't.

Something ran across my hand and I slapped it, hard. Fucking cockroaches.

But closer inspection revealed that it was not a cockroach.

'Oh, no!' I moaned, cradling the insect in my palm. 'No, no, no! Come on, breathe, dammit! You're OK, you're fine, you're not dead—'

Unfortunately, the ladybird did appear to be largely deceased in nature. Frantically, I contemplated mouth-to-mouth resuscitation, but that carried a high risk of inhaling it. When I tried to massage its crinkly little legs back to life, I only succeeded in pulling one off.

Restricted Area: Hard Hats

The following morning, I collected Conn and we drove to Abu Dhabi in a silence so chilly it would have frozen the flame on a lit match.

If I had known this would be the last time I would see Conn, I suppose I would have been a bit nicer to him. Maybe asked him to solve the Fibonacci Sequence, or told him that he was the most incredible person I had ever met and that my idea of a perfect life was sharing it with him.

But of course, I had no inkling that in less than three hours, all that would stand between the afterlife and my current incarnation was a life-support machine.

I pulled into the AEB visitor car park with a jerk and bolted out of the car.

'Aren't you forgetting something?' called Conn after me.

'Conn, we both know rhetorical questions aren't your freaky little thing,' I snapped, spinning around. 'Why don't you just tell me?'

'Your hard hat,' he said coldly.

'I'll be fine. I have a hard head,' I said, tossing it.

He swung open the boot of my Jeep and rummaged

amongst the water bottles, beach mats, damp towels, a boogie board and the inflatable camel, until he located my hard hat.

As he walked towards me, I quailed at the look on his face. Although I always had a unique talent for infuriating people, it had never been that effective on Conn. Since his natural disposition was easygoing to the point of being stretched out in a yogic trance, it made quite an impression.

'If you don't wear this hat,' he said conversationally, 'I will personally weld it to your cranium.'

His eyes were glassy and remote, his mouth set in a grim line, the muscles in his jaw quilted.

He had never looked sexier.

'Fine!' I snapped. 'Are you going to give me the hat, or stand around holding it all day?'

Conn shoved the hard hat into my chest, then turned and strode away.

'What the fuck is wrong with you?' I said, trotting to keep up with him. I was completely wrong-footed. Feeling stoically wounded was my role.

I was also not accustomed to trotting.

'Lara,' he said in a gravelly voice, 'I don't understand you. When I joined Voltech, I was so pleased to see you. I realised you were going out with Phil, but I knew that wouldn't last—'

'Hey!'

'Well, it didn't, did it? The fact that you dated him in the first place implies your boredom threshold is at a critically low level, but even you couldn't sustain such a degree of tedium for long. Then less than a week after you break up with him, you are with Mark. At least he is better than your normal calibre of idiot—'

'Nothing happened with Mark,' I said heatedly. Nothing much, I amended silently.

'You can't stand to be alone, can you?'

'Conn, you might find this hard to understand, being a – an emotionally-challenged machine. I *like* being in a relationship. It's not unusual. Nobody wants to be alone—'

'But you are so desperate to avoid that fate you go with whatever loser chooses you—'

'Hey! They might *choose* me, but it's on my terms. I break up with them—'

'Only because they leave you no alternative. What about Philip Jacobs? What did he do?'

I swallowed. 'Nothing! Nothing, OK? I got tired of him.'

Conn shook his head, but instead of taking me up on that, he said, 'Why don't you choose someone you like?'

'It's not that simple, Conn. I'm coming to the end of my expiry date—'

'What do you mean?'

'It's not the same for women as men. You know?' Conn shook his head. 'You, you get better, like a fine wine. Me, I'm like shrimp in a curtain rail. You know, all wrinkled and mouldy and smelling rotten.'

'There are other reasons someone would want to be with you, not just your appearance. You're clever. And funny—'

'Yeah, well, those attributes don't appeal to the average guy, Conn.'

'Why do you want an average guy? You should be with someone different, someone who knows how special you are, but people like you—'

'What's that supposed to mean?' I snapped. ' "People like me"?'

'Needy, obsessive—'

'Ooh!' Conn must actually believe that; he wouldn't have said it otherwise. The fact that he wasn't even trying to be malicious made it worse. 'You know, all you do is cover my life-force in cess,' I snarled. 'It may simply be an unfortunate side-effect of your presence, but as you yourself would say: the result is much the same. Why don't you just get out of my life?'

'That can be arranged,' he said flatly.

Conn supervised the AEB operations staff as they increased Unit 5 to 90 per cent capacity. For once, I was grateful to be present in a purely decorative capacity. The Control Room, panelled with buttons, knobs, levers, gauges and blinking lights, always made me feel like fiddling with them, but not today. For once, I was grateful to be present in a purely decorative capacity. I stood at the window overlooking the Turbine Room and stared unseeing over the vast vault.

My stomach squirmed nauseously as I replayed the argument with Conn. What did he mean by 'that could be arranged'? I could ask him – before or after I apologised – although he had said horrible things to me – FUCKING BASTARD! – but then he thought Mark and I were – but he could hardly complain about that – although I supposed he could – oh GOD! – my one great love! We should talk, but what was the point? – maybe it would be better if Conn did get lost – I was wasting my life wistfully yearning for him from afar – I mean, if he left, I would still wistfully yearn for him from afarther – but maybe not with the same piercing intensity . . .

The thoughts churned around my head. I was grateful for the hard hat, because my head might have exploded without it. I glanced across at Conn. He was explaining something to one of the operations staff. He shoved that stray lock of hair back impatiently. He was so sure of himself in this environment, in full control. It was a total turn on – although he could have picked his nose with a gasket wrench and I would probably still have been turned on.

We had to talk. Thrash this out once and for all.

And I suppose there would have been plenty of time to say something when we descended to the Turbine Room floor to inspect Unit five's valve operator, but I couldn't decide whether I wanted to stab him or shag him which was an important distinction in determining the direction of the discussion.

Then, when we returned to the Control Room to report a strange noise coming from Unit three to the operations staff, I could have talked to him, but I was still mentally rehearsing.

I nearly opened talks on the drive back to Dubai, but I kept hoping Conn would say something first.

He didn't.

I drove around for ages looking for a spare car park, but the nearest I could find was on the far side of the construction site.

As we mounted the metal catwalk suspended above the site, a vicious chunk of rubble attacked me. Conn grabbed my upper arm to steady me. 'Thanks,' I muttered. 'I hate this place. It's a fucking death trap.'

Far below us, the semi-completed highway curved then stopped in a mess of steel reinforcing mesh and scaffolding.

Conn released me and I realised it was now or never, sink or swim, do or die. I swallowed and said, 'Conn. Can we – can we talk?'

'Of course,' said Conn.

You know how, in movies, explosions unfold in slow motion with a burgeoning cloud of smoke and roiling flame? Well, the reality is nothing like that. It all happened at once. There was a noise that sounded like a prolonged CRUMP! and a flash that bleached the world momentarily. It was all underscored by an extended roar, the sort of noise that assaults all five of your senses and a few that are as yet undiscovered. It sounded like vast quantities of gas escaping into the atmosphere – mainly because, I found out later, that's what it was – together with a bass of shattering concrete and an uneven percussion of shards of metal meeting inanimate objects at high speed.

In an instant, I was engulfed in thick, black smoke. I had no idea whether I was up or down, straight or bent or inside out. All I knew was that my throat was on fire, and that I must be dead because this was exactly what I had always imagined Hell to be like. Well, my version had featured more damned souls screaming in agony, whereas this had only one; and, in fairness, I was coughing more than screaming. But if Satan had appeared and said, 'Welcome, please make yourself at home', I would not have asked him to crack out the leopard-print g-string.

In addition to being totally, utterly terrified, I was really rather pissed about ending up in Hell. How could I have missed the tunnel – and the light? Everyone said it was pretty bright; virtually unmissable, in fact. And I had always strived not to do anything bad – at least, not intentionally. I suppose some of the pranks I played in college might qualify as 'bad', but I preferred to think of them as more mischievously playful.

I felt pressure along the length of my body, and deduced that I must be horizontal. Yes, I could feel the metal of the grille against my palms and left cheek.

Up to this moment – probably only milliseconds after the explosion – my state of being would best be described as a confused discomfort. That shifted to utter terror when I felt the grille burning my face.

Something grabbed my hand, and I thought it was another Damned Soul come to give me a guided tour. I would have screamed, except that my spleen was trying to escape via my oesophagus.

'Lara!' shouted Conn's voice. 'Lara! Are you all right? It's OK. Come towards me. Follow the sound of my voice.'

The grip on my arm increased. Smoke still clogged my vision; my eyes stung. I kicked my legs, but that appeared to have no effect. OK. I needed to get into a crawling position.

I pushed up with my arms, but when I shifted my weight, the catwalk segment I was on gave way. Somehow – because have no recollection of it – I grabbed a metal rail by one hand. I swung wildly – legs desperately scrabbling for a foothold that wasn't there – as my hand – slick with sweat – slipped inexorably off the rail.

There seemed to be no getting around the fact that I was largely screwed. The clammy hand of doom clenched my heart. I had never been goosed by the clammy hand of doom before, but I presumed that was what it was (due to the clammy sensation).

The smoke thinned enough for me to let forth a good, blood-curdling scream.

Then it cleared further, and Conn's head appeared,

framed against the incredible, vibrant blue of the Middle Eastern sky. I realised he still had his fingers locked round my wrist, which was probably the only reason I retained my tenuous grip on the catwalk rail.

That particular situation was feeling more and more temporary.

'Lara!' shouted Conn. 'Lara, grab on.'

It was only when I tried that I realised my other hand was already desperately clawing for a hold.

'I can't – I can't reach—'

'You *can*,' said Conn, blatantly disregarding all the laws of physics. He leaned out further – precariously far – but our fingertips barely brushed. Conn switched his attention to the arm he already remanded in custody, but gravity is a harsh mistress.

'I'm going to die,' I sobbed.

'You're not going to die,' said Conn, but I looked into his eyes and knew he was lying. Just terrific. My truth monitor was finally calibrated properly a split second before I died.

That sucked.

Conn leaned out even further and managed to grab my fingers, but I knew it was a fragile grip – if it even qualified as a grip – and the rail steadily increased its resistance to my hold.

'Conn, I can't – I'm going to fall.'

'No! Lara, hold on—'

My hand slipped off the rail – I managed to wrap my fingers around Conn's wrist – for a moment, Conn held me, but then he lurched forward and – I made a split decision – perhaps it was instinct – I let him go. For a moment it seemed as if I was suspended by the force of my desperation. Then I fell.

It was twenty metres to the ground, which – you might be surprised to learn – is plenty of time even at terminal velocity to think, 'This is going to fucking hurt.'

(Later, much later, I regretted that, as last thoughts went, it hadn't included a little more grace, peace and love.)

I stared into the glare of the Middle Eastern sun, and wondered whether *this* was 'The Light'. I would have run towards it, but my legs refused to move.

Apart from a general lack of cooperation on the part of my body, I felt *great* – kind of floaty, insubstantial. It made me think maybe I was in heaven.

But no; there was Conn's head. The left side of his face was covered in blood and he looked a bit weird, so I tried to ask him if he was all right, but the words came out all garbled.

'Lara!' he gasped, but it sounded as if I had wool stuffed in my ears. Maybe it was a critical build-up of wax. No, I cleaned my ears with cotton buds, a lot. A vision of an enormous cotton bud swam into view and I giggled.

'Lara! Lara!' said Conn's voice. The cotton bud turned into Conn but he refused to come into focus. I wondered whether he was doing it on purpose.

Conn's face contorted and the tendons in his neck stood out.

He he turned his head and screamed, 'GET AN AMBULANCE! SOMEBODY GET A FUCKING AMBULANCE!'

Conn never swore. Wow, I thought; someone must be really hurt. I wondered who it was, and whether I could help. I tried to get up. When that was unsuccessful, I tried to look around.

'Don't move,' said Conn. He sounded like he was being strangled. He put his hand on my forehead, brushed his thumb across my cheek. 'Don't move. It's going to be OK. Everything's going to be OK. My love, my love, don't – don't go to sleep. Look at me, Lara, look at me.'

And I tried – I really, really did – but my eyes were disobeying direct orders from mission control; and, speaking of which, mission control seemed to be malfunctioning too.

I heard him say something like, 'Oh Jesus, oh Jesus, Lara, no, no, no, no, no.'

Conn hated repeating himself, so I knew it must be serious.

I opened my eyes just long enough to see his face sort of crumple and collapse in on itself. He said, 'Lara, Lara, Lara.' It sounded like a moan, like he was in pain. I wanted to tell him it was OK, I was fine, but this time, when I tried to speak, nothing came out at all.

Lights flashed by, like the end credits rolling up a screen. Bright. They hurt my brain. Squeak of rubber soles on ceramic. Men wearing face guards, light-blue pyjamas.

I was vaguely aware of Conn's presence. He stroked my face. On one occasion, it seemed he held my hand and pressed his mouth against it – although when I recalled this later, it seemed pretty unlikely. I tried to say, 'Show us your leopard-print g-string.'

Unfortunately, I fell asleep instead.

I appeared to be lying down. It took some time to make out anything. It was a surprisingly energy-intensive effort. The result was hardly worth it: a plain room with seriously naff minty décor and, dead centre, a TV. The sound was muted, but the figure on the screen – if I was not mistaken and, in fairness, he was quite orange, but even so – I was pretty sure it was JR Ewing.

I wondered for a moment whether I had transmuted to a different dimension of time. The television was a wide-screen flat model with no walnut panelling, however.

I assumed it was a rerun of *Dallas*.

I rotated my head – baby cheeses, it hurt like an Afghan manicure – and saw I was lying in a bed. Tubes ran into the elbow creases of both arms. Like the desire to scratch an itch, I immediately wanted to bend my arm.

Something loomed over me. It took another three minutes to focus on the figure – I hoped that would come right.

'Mother,' I tried to say, but my mouth was drier than a bat's snatch. My tongue felt like it had quadrupled in size; I almost expected to see it extending out in front of me.

I noticed that the woman, who last cried circa 1995, was weeping.

'Thank God,' she said, 'Oh, thank God.' Then she bawled: 'Nurse! Nurse!' She examined me as if my mouth really *was* a bat's snatch. Then she said in a gentler voice, 'Hi, love. Good to have you back. You've been unconscious for days. You had us all worried.'

I thought: you've got to admire someone who can make a person feel guilty about being in a coma.

She reached out and smoothed my hair back. I tried to pull away, but I was caught between a rock and, well, a pillow – but a very unyielding, hospital standard-issue pillow.

It took me three goes, but eventually I managed to whisper, 'Where's Conn?'

'Ceylon?' she said, eyeing me warily. 'I am not sure. It's where tea comes from, I think.'

'No,' I rasped. '*Conn*. Where's Conn?'

'Conn?' she said. She flattened my cover sheet nervously. 'Do you mean the boy you were friendly with in UCCD?'

I nodded weakly.

'I don't know, dear,' said my mother in the sort of tone you might use to address an escaped convict armed with a four-slice toaster.

When a doctor entered the room, Mother tackled him to the floor. From their hushed conversation, I made out the phrases 'imagining things', 'a boy she used to know', 'over six years ago' and 'hallucinations'.

'I'm not hallucinating,' I said, blinking at the doctor who was inconsiderately shining a torch into my eyes.

'Mm-hmm,' he said. 'Follow my finger.'

'I work with him,' I said urgently.

'I see,' said the doctor, replacing the torch in his breast pocket.

Turning to my mother, I heard him say, 'We'll give her a mild sedative. She'll be fine, Mrs Hanley.'

Apparently I had landed on a prefab shed, hitting it dead centre. It was the only soft thing in the construction zone – 'soft', in this context, being a relative concept. While ideally, I would opt for landing in a large inflatable device, a prefab shed was infinitely preferable to concrete or scaffolding.

I was extraordinarily lucky, since the prefab shed was pretty small and I hadn't exactly been aiming for it. The shed had not only broken my fall, it had also shattered my right leg. While I was unconscious, it had been reset and pinned over the course of numerous operations. Unfortunately, the doctors hadn't given me a bionic leg, but it featured more steel than organic marrow.

More seriously, my spine had also been broken – only in one place – but, although it had been extensively operated on, I had no feeling in my lower body.

I tried to concentrate on how lucky I was not to be paralysed from the neck down. It was time-consuming, but there wasn't much else going on.

I had just fallen out with my physiotherapist (again) when Philip visited.

He didn't have flowers, so I assumed it was a business call.

'God, you look rough,' he said, holding the door open in case he needed to make a run for it.

'Why are you here?' I said weakly.

'I regret to tell you that Voltech has had to let you go.'

He didn't look as if he regretted it as much as, say, missing lunch or getting a parking ticket.

'On what grounds?' I said.

'Exceeding your annual sick leave,' said Philip, picking a shred of vegetation out of his teeth, before examining it and nibbling it daintily off his forefinger. 'You have been absent for over a month. According to UAE labour law, you're only entitled to a maximum of nine days in any twelve-month period.'

I wondered what I had ever seen in him. Certainly not the mange-infested bald spot on the crown of his head. In fact, I had actively missed that. Come to think of it, his entire head looked a bit like a scrotum.

'Whatever,' I said tiredly, shutting my eyes. 'Philip, this might come as a surprise to you, but I have bigger things to worry about at the moment.'

'No,' said Philip, holding up a hand. 'I would be remiss if I did not fully explain the situation. Since the company fired you, it is not obliged to pay your gratuity. Voltech also cancelled your medical health insurance, and you are no longer sponsored by the company. As such, you are now in the UAE illegally.'

I looked at him for a moment, then laughed. Granted, it had a hysterical edge, but I certainly wasn't going to give him the pleasure of seeing me cry.

'Philip, there's something you should know, and I would be remiss if I did not fully explain the situation. You, Philip, are a *cock*.'

Unfortunately, Dad was unable to visit because he had a lot on at work. He sent his love, though.

Apart from Mother, my only other visitor was Mark. He came to the hospital every day, read me the *Gulf News*, and wheeled me around the hospital grounds in the evenings. He brought me gifts: belay ropes, a pair of goggles. I assume he was trying to be encouraging, but it simply made me fear for what I might have lost for ever. The only sensation I had in my legs was a dull, throbbing ache, which came on in the dead of night.

I clung desperately to the hope that I would walk again, but the uncertainty was agonising. Hope is a fragile and elusive thing in anyone's life. I was unsure whether the faint glimmer I nurtured was merely a modified version of avoiding reality. My doctor would not confirm I was permanently paralysed, but there were days I wished he would. At least then I could get on with the rest of my life. In the meantime, I was stuck – literally – on the border between hope and despair.

I tried not to spend too much time in the wastelands of despair, but sometimes I wished I had missed the shed altogether.

Mother stayed around to argue with the medical staff, nag me to do my physio exercises, and top up my critical supply of *Vanity Fair* magazines. She collected my things from the Crowne Plaza Hotel, and settled my bill.

'Mother,' I said one day, more to distract her from trying to force-feed me yoghurt. 'I had a bag – the day of the accident. Do you know what happened to it? My things?'

'It's right here, dear,' said my mother, opening a bedside locker I hadn't really registered. She handed over my bag and I emptied the contents on to the bedspread. I picked out my silk notebook and put it carefully on the locker.

'They found this, too.' Mother held out her hand and I picked up the little heap of silver in the centre of her palm. 'Your bracelet. One of the links broke in the fall. I had it fixed for you.'

'Thanks,' I said. My hands shook so much I could not do up the catch.

'Here, I'll—'

'I can do it!'

'Darling, let me,' said Mum gently.

After she left, I cried for hours.

I remember the moment I felt a suggestion of feeling in my left leg, like the onset of pins and needles. I tried to temper the wild excitement with reality, because if it didn't mean what I hoped it did, the disappointment might do what the accident had stopped just short of.

As the nerves and muscles woke up after a long hibernation, my legs felt familiar yet alien. Feeling returned achingly slowly.

One day, I picked up the notebook and turned to the first page. For a long time I sat looking at the smooth, pristine surface of the paper. I remembered a time when writing had been as essential as breathing. I discovered myself when I wrote. It was the only time I was really me: no mask, no conforming to someone else's agenda.

I had stolen a biro from one of the doctors. When I finally started writing, the action felt unfamiliar at first. After a while, six years of thoughts, ideas, hopes and fears, memories, dreams, random phrases, different words for 'delicious' – rushed out faster than my fingers could move.

I thought about Conn all the time, and sometimes in between – so nothing much had changed. At least now I thought of him with gratitude and affection, rather than wanting to gouge his eyes out with a fork.

Mark told me Conn had not left my side for a week. Voltech fired him after he refused to return to the AEB site to address the ongoing operational problems. When I was moved out of intensive care, he left. In other words, he did exactly as I requested. Good old Conn: ever constant.

'Where did he go?' I said in a panic.

'Back to Ireland,' said Mark.

'Do you know how to get in touch with him?' I asked.

'Yeah, sure.'

Mark's visit visa expired and he called to see me at the hospital before he left. He took me on a victory lap around the hospital grounds.

'Thanks for everything, Mark,' I said, hugging him.

'No worries, Lars. Least I could do. Look after yourself, now.'

'I will. Can you do me a favour?'

'Yeah?'

'Can you give this to Conn? Please?' I handed him a letter.

I had thought for days about how to contact Conn. A letter was the only way to express exactly what I wanted to say – although for a while, I wasn't sure what that was. Thanking someone for risking their life for yours is trickier than you might expect. Turns out 'thanks a million' didn't quite cover it. I hoped twenty-four pages did.

I also struggled to convey how I felt about him without coming across like a Carpenters lyric. In the end, I decided you could do worse than The Carpenters. (Dr Hook, for example.)

'Sure,' said Mark, tucking it in his jeans pocket. 'Hey – look me up when you're home.

I did more than look Mark up. When I couldn't stand any more of Mother's cuisine (a solid foundation of slimy cabbage and boiled ox tongue) and Bill's incessant hoovering, I moved in with him.

And then he asked me to marry him.

For a long time – in the region of years – I wondered why Conn never answered my letter. Although I knew Mark fancied me, I don't doubt he delivered it. Not only was he Conn's best friend, but he also had his own freaky code of honour.

When Conn didn't respond, I considered asking Mark

about it. You know, how Conn had looked when Mark gave him the letter, what he'd said, whether he'd ripped it open on the spot, etc. But Mark and I were together at that stage and – I don't know – it felt a bit . . . disloyal.

In any case, Conn was under no obligation to respond. The purpose of writing was to thank him. The last thing I wanted to do was put pressure on him. After all, he had saved my life – or tried very hard, anyway.

Maybe I should have included an RSVP.

He never replied.

Dream Lagoon

Back in my current reality, the taxi deposits me at the Dream Lagoon Hotel near the airport. The décor might have been the definition of groovy chic in the early seventies, but now it just looks dingy, even with all the lights turned on. I'm not sure where the advertised lagoon is. Probably a tadpole-infested ditch in a field out back.

I make my way to my deluxe room with 'superb views of the Shannon'. Undoubtedly there are superb views of the five-storey car park next door, but the River Shannon is evidently conditional on superb, X-ray vision.

I wish I were staying somewhere marginally more plush (don't be misled by the de luxe room; the only available categories were de luxe, super-de-luxe and mind-blowing de luxe featuring two bath towels rather than one).

Leo would struggle to reconcile such expenditure for an overnight stay en-route to New York, however. That's OK. I don't require much more than the bare essentials: toilet paper, basic sanitation including hot water, ample reading light, minimal insect activity.

I throw my washbag on to the telly, sink on to the bed

and absentmindedly stroke the duvet. Hard to tell whether it is grime or polyester.

For days now, I have felt like an observer in my own life as it flashes past my eyes. Now, suddenly, it feels like tomorrow might never come. It is so late as to nearly qualify as the next day, but the nervous, twisty sensation in my gut renders me wide awake. Last-minute nerves, I'm sure. Plus too much information to process.

I turn on the telly. There is not much on at this hour, and a snowstorm has struck the only channel showing anything even vaguely bearable (an early episode of *Absolutely Fabulous*). I turn to BBC World, just for the background noise.

I take a shower, stretching the experience into a good half an hour, then manage to dispose of a few minutes rubbing in the hotel-issue body lotion that smells vaguely like a ferret's sex hormones.

In bed, I check the telly again and briefly consider watching a documentary on deep-sea jellyfish-spiders. I am heartened to find my life is not *that* bad.

It must be nearly time to get up, surely? I check my watch. No, surely that can't be right – but it is, according to BBC World, not even one o'clock in the morning.

I turn out the light and stare into the darkness. I am too hot, so I peel back the bedclothes; then I am too cold, so I return the covers and stick my feet out the side.

A tin can rattles across the car park, followed by the yowl of a tomcat. I am so exhausted my bones, my very *soul* feels weary, but my mind is still tossing and turning. It reviews the mental To Do list, screens random flashes from the past, frets at this decision I have made.

It momentarily touches on Leonard.

When I was in the Middle East, Leonard was one of

my clients. I met him again three years later, when his company sued my ex-employer for millions of dollars. I testified at the hearing in Dubai.

At first, I had no interest in Leonard. To be honest, I thought he was a bit of a sleaze weasel.

Around about the time Leonard moved to Ireland to take up a job in Dublin, Mark and I broke up. Leonard pursued me relentlessly. I was pretty raw. I was also undeniably flattered.

Eventually, it was easier to capitulate and copulate. At least, I thought, Leonard must have *really* wanted me (I often mistook the thrill of pursuit for genuine ardour. In fairness, I'm not sure I would have recognised genuine ardour if it ravished me up against a wall).

This is the usual format. I have no problem attracting men; like bees to a honey pot (or, more accurately, flies to shit).

Sorry if I've given the wrong impression of Leo. He isn't bad. I'm very fond of him.

Do I love him?

No, no, no – and that's not the answer to the question, just that I'm not going there. It's a bit belated to be airing that question.

OK, I need to focus on sleep. Repel wakefulness, drum up some drowsiness.

I close my eyes and try counting sheep for a while, but they wander around falling off cliffs and getting lost and stuck in quicksand and stuff. I eventually give up when the flock makes a break for New York, where I find two of them engaged in a kinky threesome with Leonard.

I try thinking about my father's job. That sends me to sleep under normal circumstances, but not this particular one. Then I roll my eyeballs back in my head, which sometimes makes me feel sleepy. I am not sure why; perhaps it is voodoo sleep.

No; I am more alert than a lertish lert from the royal lert family. Not the barest hint of a 'z'.

I turn the light back on.

Then the TV (*Home and Away*).

Since I have read the *RTÉ Guide* from cover to cover including the adverts and page numbers, I pick up the hotel services guide.

The information brochure informs me the Leisure Centre closed at five p.m. Never mind; according to the hotel's standards, the 'state-of-the-art gym and sauna' is probably a couple of running machines in a closet with rising damp.

What else is there? Room Service finished at eleven p.m. and Laundry is available only during normal working hours.

Then I see it: the Business Centre on the third floor, open round the clock.

I throw on the standard-issue bathrobe over a pair of acid-washed jeans. I haven't checked my email for two days. I feel a thrill of anticipation, knowing A:42 will probably be online.

A:42 isn't online, but my heart surges when I see the email from him.

But his message fills me with horror: his father has had a stroke.

His poor, poor father.

I read the panic, the despair between the lines. Conn's life was so measured. He believed there is no such thing as 'fate', that you make your own destiny. He never understood there are certain things outside your control.

This is a harsh introduction.

An image of Mr O'Neill flashes into my head. Conn is so like him: still and silent, utterly dependable. Unless Mr O'Neill dies, which would be pretty unreliable.

I used to spend a lot of time with Conn's family. His parents were different to mine. In my family, there was a rule that one person spoke at a time – usually Dad. Interrupting was improper and impolite. Despite that, my parents often talked over each other. They wielded words like weapons: darts, missiles, knives, flailing hatchets.

Conn's family argued all the time, but without that sense of impending doom. They all talked over each other, but nobody seemed to mind. In fact, they appeared to enjoy it. And Conn's parents – the way they looked at each other – it was almost indecent. People weren't supposed to look at each other like that – especially *parents* – especially not in nineties Ireland.

My heart squeezes as I think of Mrs O'Neill and how she must feel. All that fear and uncertainty.

Conn believes that life is defined by choices. A 'sequence of choices', I think that was it; that the decisions you make determine your path in life (according to that philosophy, I would be the one stumbling along tripping over my feet).

But Conn was wrong.

Sometimes life turns on a chance.

15

A voice, weak & hoarse, slightly slurred, says, 'Is that you, my boy?'

I start, look up. Da appears the same in the diluted early morning light – i.e., his eyes are still closed, he is still a shade of whitish grey – but I am sure I heard him speak.

I'm on my feet faster than spontaneous combustion. I catch my laptop a split second before it potentially falls to the floor, balance it on a water glass on the nightstand. Bending over the bed, I say, 'Da?'

I check the statistics on his life-support machine. His vital functions – heartbeat, breaths per minute, blood pressure – are within normal range. I look at his face again, this time I see his lips move when he says, 'Has the plumber called?'

I say, 'Probably not.'

Da's eyes open slowly. He says, 'Where am I?'

'The Stroke Unit on the second floor of the Midwestern Regional Hospital, Limerick.'

'What the feck am I doing here?'

'You had a stroke, Da.'

'Well, now. That explains why I feel a bit under the weather.' His eyes focus. 'The feckin' Stroke Unit? I always wanted to go out in a hail of bullets, or wearing concrete shoes or something like that.'

I doubt Da has a secret life as a criminal overlord, but all I say is, 'I'm pleased you're not going out yet, Da.'

'It's good to see you, son. Even if I had to half die to get you home.' He laughs but it turns into a cough.

I say, 'I'll get Dr Patel.'

Dr Patel's preliminary examination suggests that Da's cognitive functions are good. However, he has extensive paralysis down the left side of his body, which affects his speech & movement. Dr Patel says these symptoms might improve with therapy, but he cannot say for certain.

This frustrates me. I say, 'What *can* you say for certain?'

Da says, 'Whisht now, son.'

After Dr Patel leaves, I say, 'I'll call Mam.'

'Where is she, anyway? I give the best years of my life to her, not to mention a fine son. The woman could attend my deathbed. Thought she'd want to know about the life assurance at least.'

'Well, she's been here every day. I sent her home—'

'Ara, I know, I know, I know. When you're on to her, ask her to bring a pair of pyjamas – me arse is hangin' out of this gown. And – and my pipe and spectacles. And tell her to pick up the *Irish Mail*.'

'I can look up the *Irish Mail*'s website and—'

'Naw, I want ta read Aunt Agony.'

'Aunt who?'

'Aunt Agony. She tells gerrils what to do when their fellas can't get stiffies, or accidentally have the sex with some other gerril. She's great. Ara an' tell your mam to bring yesterday's paper if it's lying around.'

'OK.'

'Jaysus, I feel half dead,' says Da, prodding his stubble.

I say, 'Well, relatively speaking, you are more alive than dead.'

Da says, 'Could you do something for me?'

'Of course.'

'Is there any chance of getting a hauld of an aul brush or a comb? I don't want your mam seeing me with me hair all sticking up like a thicket of thorn bushes.'

When I tell Mam about Da, there is a long silence.

I say, 'Mam? Are you still there?'

'Aye,' she says, 'So I won't be collecting the life assurance yet.'

Da's life assurance must be worth a lot.

After I hang up, I buy a comb, razor & shaving cream from the chemist in the lobby. A nurse called Dora gives me a towel, face towel & an enamel basin, which I fill with hot water in the bathroom.

Da says weakly, 'What's that you have there?'

I say, 'Thought you might like to have a shave', & place the basin on his nightstand. Steam curls over the rim. 'The nurse said you could, if I help you.'

'Is this what I've come ta? My definition of daring reduced to shaving without a nurse's permission?'

'That depends on how you define daring. Come on, Mam's on her way and it might take a long time to make you presentable.'

'You're awful bold. It's lucky you are I'm not at the peak of my strength, or I would take slices offa ya.'

'Let me help you sit up.'

I put my arms around Da, lift & hold him while I rearrange his pillow. Da is lighter than I thought he would be, he feels insubstantial in my arms. I lay him back gently against the pillow after I have rotated it ninety degrees.

I squirt shaving foam into my hand, dip the other in the basin, then rub them together. When the lather reaches optimal consistency, I reach over, place my fingers on Da's face. I spread the lather over his lower jaw & neck, smear some above his lip with my forefinger.

'Hand that here,' says Da as I pick up the razor.

Silently, I place it in his right hand. The razor shakes as he raises it to his face. It feels as if my heart expands – or perhaps my chest cavity contracts – although realistically, either scenario is implausible. (Note: I might be experiencing a heart attack, but that also seems unlikely.)

I close my hand over his & say, 'I'll do it.' Carefully, I remove the razor.

Da says, 'It's better you do it. I have no mirror.'

I think about offering to get a mirror. Then I just nod.

I position the razor for the first stroke. The practical elements of the exercise are relatively straightforward, but I'm nervous. Obviously, I've shaved myself numerous times, but rely on sensory feedback to gauge my progress.

Just before I start, I realise what the towel is for. I spread it across Da's front, tuck the edge into the neckband of his gown.

I say, 'Relax.'

'How am I supposed to relax when you're armed with a weapon?'

'The instruction was for me.'

'Is that supposed to inspire confidence?' says Da, closing his eyes. 'Janey mack.'

I remember being thirteen years old, standing with

Da before the mirror in the bathroom at home. Sunlight beat against the bobbled glass of the single window. Da had bought me a shaving set: a stainless-steel razor like his, a matching bowl, & a wooden-handled brush with real badger hair. I asked him how he could afford it and he told me to mind my own business.

He showed me how to work up a lather in the bowl with the brush, then how to use the razor. He tilted my head, stretched my skin taut with his fingers to facilitate the glide of the blade, taught me how to reach the awkward spots.

Now, I do this for him. I start at the top of his sideburns. Da's whiskers are white & softer than I anticipated. His skin is slack beneath the pads of my fingers.

Da says, 'She's a grand woman, your ma.'

'She's quite nice, all right.'

'You don't like to overstate things, do you?'

'Not really,' I say, wincing in case I nick him. This is obviously counterproductive. It is more likely I will cut him with this involuntary movement.

'How come you never settled down, my boy?'

I rinse the razor in the basin while I think how to respond. I say, 'I made a mistake.' Da folds his lips over his teeth as I reach his orbicularis oris. 'Anyway,' I shrug, 'I don't really have the time. Long hours. Lots of travel.'

'You woah my boy, you aw a good lad. You aw a ood son.'

I feel ashamed. 'I'm not really—'

'Sure 'n you are,' says Da, tilting his head back to expose his neck. 'Didn't you buy your mam an' me the house? Don't you send the money every month?'

'I don't see you enough—'

'Sure 'n you do. Your mam an' me don't want some nancy boy livin' on our doorstop. Do ya know, Molly Darcy's boy is still bunkin' at home, an' the man's fifty-seven!'

After a moment of shocked contemplative silence, Da says, 'My boy, you are everything a man could ask for in a son. I am proud of ya.'

Da does not usually talk to me like this. Conversational topics are strictly limited to world politics, technological advances & the weather. Although I know Da is proud of me (note: at least I have never thought otherwise), it feels different hearing him say it. I didn't think his words would affect me this way.

I want to acknowledge what he said somehow, but I'm not sure what constitutes an acceptable response.

Da clarifies, 'Ya don't have to say anything. I just want you to know tha' I am proud of ya. But my boy, all I ever wanted was for you to be happy.'

I pick up the face towel to remove the last traces of shaving foam. Da grips my arm with his right hand, shakes it gently. 'Ya understand? That's all I have ever wanted for ya.'

Suddenly I realise how exhausted I am. Da seems to feel a similar effect, because sometimes he gives a little snort & his head jerks. He regularly/frequently looks towards the door of the ward.

He seems to wake up when Mam enters. She's still wearing her dressing gown.

Da says, 'You took your blithering time, woman. Did you stop off to do a bit of shoppin' or play a round of golf?'

Drawing a chair to his bedside, Mam says, 'You're lucky I came at all, with the scare you gave me.'

Instead of sitting down, she slightly adjusts the neck of Da's hospital gown. I can't see that it makes any difference. She pulls Da's covers higher, tucks them around him, then pats them smooth, then again.

'Will ya ever stop fussin', woman?' says Da. 'Takin' advantage of me, when I'm too weak ta fight ya off.'

'At least there's someone wantin' to take advantage of you. You know, I think I preferred you in a coma.' (Note: I'm pretty sure she doesn't mean it).

'How are you feeling?' Mam peers at Da as if inspecting him through a microscope.

'Fine, fine. Never felt better. Go wan now, don't you be drippin' tears all over me.' Ma wipes her eyes with a scrunched-up tissue in several segments, replaces it in her cardigan sleeve. 'Did you bring the paper?'

'I did,' says Mam, sinking into the seat. 'An' your spectacles; how did you think you were going to read it, you old eejit?'

Da says, 'Sure an' I'm younger than you are.'

'I'm an old eejit as well, so. I have your pipe here, too. I don't think you can smoke it in the hospital, but you can put it in your gob and suck on it now and then and you won't know the difference. And' – Mam presents items from her bag like Santa Claus might if he weren't a fictional character – 'your favourite pair of pyjamas, a cap to keep your scrawny old skull warm, a baked potato, *The Gulag Archipelago* by Alex-Alexander Sausage-Schnitzel, a bottle of Lucozade, and fresh scones – they have jam in them.'

'What kind of jam?'

'Crabapple and blackberry.'

'Aren't you a great woman?' says Da, groping for her hand. When he locates it, he squeezes it.

Mam snorts, shakes him off, but she looks pleased as she pats Da's bedclothes again. She says, 'Oh, and here's your *Irish Mail*.'

As she lays it on the bed, the date catches my eye. 10 June 2009. At first I think something happened on this date, but of course that is illogical, because the date is current, i.e., it has not happened yet.

10 June ... the ballpoint pen was patented on 10 June, but that was in 1943.

'Here're Mark and Harriet,' says Mam. 'They were parking the car.'

Mrs Kinsella wears a fine net over those plastic cylinders women wind their hair around. She says, 'Now! Paddy, I've never seen you lookin' better. God, I'm withered with this weather! Stirs up the rheumatic arthritis in me joints. An' I have a ferocious migraine – I should really be flat on my back in the bed. But sure an' all, we each and every one of us have our burdens to bear as best we can.'

Da says, 'Good of you to come, Harriet.'

Mrs Kinsella cheers up when Mam suggests breaking out the bubbly.

She reverts to herself when the bubbly turns out to be Lucozade.

I sense Lara's presence before I see or hear her. It is a sort of prickly feeling, like an army of ants swarming down the back of my neck.

I can't explain this phenomenon; it has no basis in established scientific theory. If she emits a pheromone to which I am particularly attuned, I'm not consciously aware of it. Similarly, although it seems like the room brightens when she enters, I doubt a device installed to measure ambient light would register anything untoward.

I turn. Lara wears a coat similar in character to a bathrobe with 'Dream Lagoon' printed over the left breast pocket, a T-shirt that looks familiar, & a pair of jeans that look like she accidentally spilled perchloric acid down them. Her boots are shiny & orange, the soles about seven centimetres thick. I suppose they must be for traversing puddles.

I have not seen Lara for eight years. Although I was aware of missing her, seeing her again somehow concentrates that feeling. It is like a physical sensation, e.g., hunger or pain. It is curious that I feel her absence more now, when she is present.

'Hi,' she says, tugging down her T-shirt. 'I hope – I hope I'm not intruding. I got – I heard Mr O'Neill was – was ill.'

Da says, 'Is that Lara Callaghan? I didn't know you were still "on the scene".'

Lara says, 'Well, I-I'm not really.' She laughs but it seems a nervous response rather than an expression of mirth. Quickly, she goes to the bed, kisses Da on the cheek. 'Mrs O'Neill, Mrs Kinsella.' She nods at the women as she speaks their names.

Mam goes to Lara, smiles. She takes her hands and says, 'Well, isn't it so good of you to come, pet?'

Mrs Kinsella's lips tighten, she raises her head briefly. 'Well, now! If it isn't Lara Callaghan. Have you come to abandon my Mark at the altar again? The nerve of you. And those jeans are two sizes too small, missy.'

Mark says, 'Hush, Mum.'

Lara retrieves her hands to pull the hem of her T-shirt down again. Drawing the coat around her, she says, 'Hi, Mark.'

Mrs Kinsella says, 'Now! Don't you be battin' your eyes at him again, you brazen hussy.'

Mark steps towards Lara, says, 'Don't mind her. It's good to see you again.'

'You too.'

They smile at each other, then embrace. I experience an unfamiliar feeling, abnormally strong. I identify it as jealousy.

Lara looks at me for the first time. 'Conn,' she says. She puts her hand lightly on my shoulder, reaches up to kiss me. I don't think to dip my head in time, so she only reaches as far as my chin. Her hair smells nice: roses & bacon. 'I came as soon as I heard. I'm-I'm not really sure why I'm here, but. I thought maybe I could do something—'

Mrs Kinsella says, 'I'll tell you what you can do, is take your scrawny arse off away again.'

Lara smiles, says, 'I have to go, anyway. I'm-I'm on the way to the airport. Flight to catch. It was good to see you all again. I'm so glad you're feeling better, Mr O'Neill.'

Mrs Kinsella makes a noise like she is attempting to expel her oesophagus through her nose.

On the way to the lift, Lara tugs at her T-shirt, says, 'I hope you don't want this back. It's hiding a major case of camel toe. Baby cheeses, these jeans are *killing* me.'

Then I recognise it: the T-shirt is mine. Or it was, fourteen years ago.

I say, 'You-you can have the T-shirt. What's camel toe?'

Lara says, 'You don't want to know. It's a er, descriptive term for an unfortunate physical effect.'

In the second floor lobby, Lara presses the button to summon the lift. She says, 'You don't have to see me out.'

She presses the button again, even though it is already lit. 'You should go back to your family.'

I say, 'That's OK.' The lift doors slide open. I put my hand over the sensor on one of the doors, so they remain open. I stand aside (note: not because she is fat, but so Lara has better access to the lift).

Lara presses the 'close door' button, then 'G'. She looks at the ceiling, then runs her fingers over the buttons, presses the 'close door' button again (note: even though the doors are closed), looks at the floor. She jabs the 'G' button repeatedly with her thumb.

It is strange how, in such a small space, she avoids looking at the largest relative object, i.e., me. In contrast, I can't look away from her. I wonder when or if I will ever see her again.

Lara stares at the floor. A single strand of hair falls forward across her face. The rest reaches halfway down her back. The length, colour, movement are precisely the same as the first time I ever saw her, when she was a teenager.

Involuntarily, I reach out & tuck the strand behind her ear. Lara looks up at me. Her face somehow seems to be happy & sad at the same time. Then – I can't recall exactly how it happened – she is in my arms. Although she presses her body against mine, her hands against my forehead push me away.

I kiss her so hard my mouth hurts. Then I'm afraid of hurting her so I draw back, but she pulls my head down & kisses me the same way (note: it hurts).

I hear the lift doors open, tear away from her. A doctor & three nurses stand outside the door. As I walk her to the hospital lobby, I taste rust on my lower lip. I realise it's blood.

There are no taxis at the rank, so we wait.

I say, 'Don't go.'

'What do you mean, "don't go"? I have to go. My possessions are currently in some holding area in Hong Kong, Leonard is waiting for me—'

'Leonard O'Hara?'

'Yes.'

'He doesn't love you—'

'And you do, I suppose.'

'Yes!' I say desperately. 'Yes, I love you.'

After a long silence, Lara says, 'It's too late, Conn—'

'How can it be too late?'

'You know, you can't just come waltzing into my life like this.'

'Technically, you came waltzing into mine this time—'

A taxi pulls up. Lara says, 'I have to go. Goodbye.'

She gets into the taxi. It drives away.

She doesn't look back.

I return to the ward. Mam is talking to Harriet, whose mouth looks like a cat's arse (as my nan would have said). Mark stares out of the window. Da has his *Irish Mail* spread on the bed – which reminds me.

The date.

10 June.

In my memory, I see Lara sitting in the kitchen of the flat I used to share with Mark, reaching into a packet of coconut creams. She had just been to see some fortune-teller, who claimed he could see her future. He told her she would meet her one great love of her life.

Today.

10 June 2009.

I say, 'I have to go.' Everyone looks at me.

Mam smiles. 'You'd better run,' she says.

I am at the lift, when something holds my shoulder. It is Mark's hand. He says, 'My man.'

'What?'

He says, 'You'd better have this.' He hands me something that looks like a lump of blue cheese. When I take it, I realise the weight is not consistent with blue cheese. Upon closer inspection, it appears to be a clump of paper mashed together, white with streaks of blue running through it.

I ask, 'What is it?'

'It's a letter. Well, it was a letter. Lara gave it to me. To give to you. Er. Eight years ago. Just before I left Dubai. I, er. I forgot it,' he says. I can't determine what the look on Mark's face signifies. 'I left it in my jeans pocket. It's been through the wash a couple of times. When I – when I tried to dry it out, it all stuck together.'

'Oh.'

'I wanted to tell you before, Droid. I suppose it was easier not to. And then – well, Lara and I were spending a lot of time together and one thing led to another. I didn't want to lose her. But I never really *had* her.' He smiles, but the overall effect is more sad than happy.

'Why are you telling me now?'

'I thought you should know. Lara's, like, your walrus.'

'My what?'

'Your walrus. They mate for life.'

I frown. 'I don't think walruses fall into the three to ten per cent of socially monogamous animals. These include wolves, beavers, gorillas, gibbon apes, prairie voles, termites, French angel fish, and anglerfish. The praying mantis by default, but only because the female kills the male whilst mating. Certain species of penguins

– in fact, ninety per cent of birds engage in social monogamy, although—'

'Christ, Droid, it is a mystery why you are still single. What I am trying to say is, you belong with Lara.'

I ask, 'What did it say?'

'What?'

'The letter.'

'Not a fucking clue, Droid. Go and ask her.'

Camel Toe

What had I been thinking? Turning up at the hospital like that? I *hate* hospitals, with their urgent jangle of telephones, beeps, barked instructions, the fluorescent tube lighting that makes everything look sweaty. And the odours: the clinical smell of antiseptic masking the sour tang of stomach acid and the metallic hint of blood.

I had felt quite panicky.

And *camel toe*? Groan! Just the mental image I wanted to leave with The Love of My Life or That Prick – who, at this particular moment, is more the former than the latter. Conn hadn't known what camel toe was – but that was a temporary state of mind. He was probably conducting in-depth research into camel toe on his PDA right now.

Mind you, as far as mental images go, I suppose it's on a par with turning up in stonewashed fucking jeans and a decomposing Spiderman T-shirt.

I bang my head against the taxi window, and again.

'There's a handle if you want to roll down the window, love,' says the taxi driver.

A smart arse.

Just what I need.

What the hell had I been thinking? What did I expect? That I would turn up and comfort Conn in his hour of need?

Stupid stupid STUPID.

I consider how it had felt to see Conn again – I've never felt that way about anyone before or since – but am I deluded? You know, stuck in the past trying to relive old glories, like a female Rocky Balboa?

And that kiss. I should have walked away, except it was in a lift, so there was nowhere to walk except around in circles – which wouldn't have got me anywhere (apart from the far corner of the lift, which was of limited use apart from being another apt metaphor for my life).

'Don't go' Conn had said – what am I even thinking about this for? – I've questioned it enough over the last few days – weeks – months, even – but have never seriously considered not going. I mean, what else is there for me? And I'm on the way to the *airport*, for God's sake!

Anyway, all the omens – although I don't really believe in all that crap – but OK, just for the hell of it, one last sign to confirm once and for all that I am doing the right thing . . . I'll make it a hard one, just to prove my stars are in alignment and Jupiter is rising in the fourth quadrant or whatever.

Here goes: I will definitely move to America if . . . I see a . . . purple car . . . in the next . . . ten seconds. Just to leave no room for chance, not even a square millimetre, make that Conn in a purple car.

And a penguin.

I stare out the window.

On the other side of the dual carriageway, a red car

passes, then a silver car, silver again, a blue car, silver – what was that behind it? Green. Then a blue truck – do trucks count? No, the terms of the omen are limited to cars. A yellow bus, three more silver cars.

Something appears at the periphery of my vision and pulls level.

It is a purple taxi.

And – I start forward as the taxi eases ahead – in the back window is a stuffed penguin.

Mumble from *Happy Feet*, I think.

I press my face against the window. There is a passenger in the back seat, but I can't make him out – only the back of his head.

'Hey, mister!' I shout to my taxi driver, slapping him on the shoulder. 'See that taxi! Can you catch it?'

'Not a chance, love. He's going twenty over the speed limit.'

Just my luck to have the one law-abiding taxi driver in the country.

'How about if I give you this – this nice pair of furry dice for your rear-view mirror?' I say, producing them from my washbag. They were granted a reprieve due to my forgetting to throw them in the skip.

My driver doesn't bother to answer.

'How about if I tip you a hundred euros?' I say.

'Speed kills, love,' says my chauffeur primly, slowing down, if anything.

'Look, mister,' I say desperately. 'That taxi might feasibly contain the only man I have ever loved, and will ever love, and this could be the last time I ever see him before I catch an airplane to the far corner of the world.'

'Well, you should have thought of that, love, shouldn't you?' says my driver, braking for an imaginary dog.

It's not a rumour, then.

Romance really *is* dead.

I didn't tip the taxi driver. Furthermore, I left the furry dice on the back seat just to spite him.

I don't know whether it was Conn in the back of the taxi, but it's hard to disagree that two out of three ain't bad (even though I've never been a fan of Meat Loaf). What were the odds? A purple car, a stuffed penguin. It was an omen. A sign that I should go to New York.

And it's crap. All of it.

Mum is right: I have run away from things all my life. Sometimes I can fool myself into thinking that I'm seizing opportunities rather than running away. In this instance, the truth is that, hard as it has been to pack up my life, going to New York is the easy option.

It's time to make some changes. This is why I am standing at the end of my mother's driveway.

I pick up two of the suitcases and move them inside the gate. Then I take the third, tuck my washbag under my other arm, and walk up the path.

I ring the doorbell. And wait.

Suddenly, I really want to see my mum.

She swings open the door. 'Lara!' she says. Her hand fingers her pearls, the familiar nervous gesture.

'Hi,' I say.

'What are you doing here? Isn't your flight—'

'Taking off around about now, yeah,' I say. I try to smile, but instead find I am crying.

'I see,' she says. Just for a change, I give her the benefit of the doubt and think maybe she does. 'Come in, love. Bill!' she calls.

Her husband appears in the living-room door.

'Hello, Lara,' he says formally, then, seeing my face, 'Oh.'

'Darling, would you mind fetching Lara's bags from the end of the garden?' Mother puts her hand on his arm as he passes.

Then, in a particularly bold flanking manoeuvre, she moves to tuck my hair behind my ear. I freeze. Why, why, *why* is she always trying to groom me? And now, of all times?

'Mother.' I focus on controlling my voice. 'Why do you always do that? Can't you overlook a rogue tuft of hair just this once? Why are you always trying to . . . to . . . *fix* me?'

Mother's face has fallen during the course of my speech and has reached the bottom.

'I never – it's the only way I know how—'

'How to *what*?'

'How to touch you.' I stare at her, stunned. 'You always pull away.' Mum looks close to tears herself. She wouldn't recklessly risk her mascara like that, I think; but no, she sweeps her fingers under her eyes and—

'Mum,' I say in a state of mild shock, 'you smudged your mascara.'

'Feck the mascara,' says my mum, who was last heard swearing at my father thirteen years ago – and in light of recently uncovered evidence, he probably deserved it.

'I'm sorry,' I say shakily. 'Oh, Mum. I always thought – I always thought you were trying to improve me—'

'Why would I want to improve you? Except, I suppose, you could be less sarcastic.'

I look at my mum. If I am not mistaken, Dorothy Callaghan just cracked a joke.

'You know, Mum, I'd prefer if you hugged me.'

'Really?'

'Yes, please,' I say. And I'm not sure whether I go to her, or she to me. At first the embrace is unbearably awkward, but then it's not, not at all.

In my mother's arms, enveloped in her distinct aroma of L' Air du Temps and Mr Sheen and *safety*, I rewrite history. Eyes squeezed tightly shut, I remember it all. How, in the quicksand of my childhood, she was the only rock. How, after the accident, she came to the Middle East and stayed until I was well and negotiated a continuation of my medical insurance and brought me home. I even remember that terrible day I found out my parents were separating and only now understand that, even then, she tried to protect me.

When she has me installed at the kitchen table with a cup of tea, Mum says, 'Tell me what happened.'

I shrug. 'There's not much to tell that you haven't already guessed. I'm not going to New York. It's not – it's a bad choice. I have to tell Leonard. I'll call him later.' I pause. 'I admire you for not saying "I told you so".'

'I was only thinking how to phrase it,' says Mum. Another one! Baby cheeses, as the woman herself would say, after a stiff cup of tea.

'I had dinner with Rosie last night,' I say, turning my teacup round and round by the handle.

'She told me. Said you had a big talk. She was worried maybe she was a bit hard on you.'

'She wasn't that worried when she was bludgeoning me with the salt cellar,' I say tartly and Mum giggles. 'Mum, I'm really sorry—'

'You don't have to apologise.'

'I do. I've always – I've never—'

'Lara—'

'Please, Mum. I need to – to say this.' I swallow and

try to breathe. 'All these years, I've blamed you for Dad leaving. You know?' Mum nods. 'Not only that, I blamed you for everything.'

'Well, it was as much my fault as anyone else's. If you want to apportion blame, I am as good as any. Although, you know, what happened happened. Does it have to be anyone's *fault*?'

I think about that. 'No. But it was easy to blame you. I couldn't face the alternative, that – that Dad didn't only leave *you*. He left all of us.'

'It's all right.'

'It's not. Mum, I'm so sorry. It must have been awful for you – and I was horrid—'

'Lara,' said my mother. 'Hush. There's nothing to be sorry for. You are my astonishing, precious, beautiful daughter.'

I drop my head. 'My life is a mess,' I mumble into my hands. I feel Mum stroke my hair gently.

'It's not,' she says. 'Even though it might seem that way. It all works out eventually.'

'Thanks for the platitude,' I say.

'You're welcome,' says my mum. 'Would you like another scone with that?'

'Is it OK if I stay with you and Bill a while?' I hiccup.

'Of course,' says Mum serenely.

I distinctly get the impression I didn't have to ask.

I'm not sure what I will do now, but I feel strangely invigorated. Things will be different. I will be worthier, I decide. Maybe take up charitable works, exercise more, bake things with cream of tartar, do the laundry before it stages a coup. One way or another, I see a lot of fairy cakes in my future.

I'm also going to write another letter.

I think I'll deliver this one in person.

17

Lara got the last taxi; it is eleven minutes before another one pulls up at the taxi rank outside the hospital. It appears to be advertising some sort of fruit of the forest yoghurt drink.

I say, 'Shannon Airport, please.'

As the driver pulls away, something falls from the ledge behind my seat. Initially I think it is a large stuffed chicken, but upon closer inspection, I believe it is supposed to represent a puffin. Regardless how often I replace it, it keeps toppling over on to the seat.

At the airport, I monitor the Aer Lingus check-in desk. On a secondary basis, I also stake out other flights to New York, all airlines with routes to America, and other airlines that fly anywhere. I think I have most available options covered.

I stay until I am certain to within an acceptable tolerance that Lara is not present at the airport.

Her absence could be due to a number of reasons:

1) Lara lied about going to New York;
2) She was kidnapped on the way to the airport;
3) Or otherwise detained;
4) She got the Aer Lingus flight to New York, but I failed to see her (the possibility of this is negligible but not unfeasible, since Lara is relatively small, although I

attempted to minimise the likelihood of Lara being concealed behind a larger person by viewing the lounge from a variety of angles);

5) Lara decided not to go to New York after all.

There's not much I can do about possibilities one to four, but I can verify scenario number five. If Lara didn't leave, she might be staying with one of her parents.

I call Mark, ask him for Mrs Callaghan's number.

The Art of Skinny Dipping: Remove Clothes

Today, the Ardnacrusha Canal is grey beneath the waters' choppy surface.

In summer, Conn used to bring me here on his bicycle. His mum sometimes made us egg sandwiches, wrapped in tinfoil or greaseproof paper. If we were really organised, we had a plaid picnic blanket and a flask of iced tea wedged in the hinge of Conn's bike carrier.

More often, we came on a whim, armed only with our swimming togs – or not. I remember one evening, the sinking sun bathing the canal in a sepia glow. Everyone else had left with sunburn and damp towels.

'How about a swim?' I said.

'We don't have our togs—'

'Let's go skinny dipping.' I grinned at Conn in the dusk, kicking off my sandals.

'You mean swimming without any clothes on?'

I was already stripping off my clothes on the bank. 'Yeah,' I said. 'Come on – what are you waiting for?'

'Wh-what if someone sees us?'

'So what? You afraid they might be scandalised to

death? If they haven't seen wriggly bits before, it's about time they did; consider it a public service.' I draped my knickers over his head. 'Come *on!*'

After we swam, we made love in the water.

It kind of chafed.

We used to sit under this willow tree. It is where Conn first told me he loved me. Well, he didn't come right out and say so. As memory serves, he was agreeing with me.

Now, although it looks the same, it feels different. I feel different. Older – definitely older. I miss the potential, the *promise* of those days.

The sun momentarily bursts through the scudding clouds. I squint, looking out over the canal. Light glints and sparkles on its surface.

To my left, a movement catches my eye. Someone is coming towards me. I hope it's not a murderer or rapist or someone whose dog recently died tragically of a tumour.

There is a willow tree at the canal. Lara and I used to sit there because:

1) It was private;
2) It was a nice shade of green;
3) It was shady.

Although it is June, the day is windy, grey. It'll be cold under the tree. However, I know Lara will disregard practical considerations for sentimentality.

She is there, sitting cross-legged on the grass. She doesn't look surprised to see me.

I say, 'Hi.'

She smiles. It is not a big smile. However, she definitely looks more happy than sad.

She says, 'Fancy seeing you here. I was just thinking about you.'

'Really?'

'It must be fate.'

'No. Your mam told me where to find you.' I sit on the grass next to her & say, 'What are you doing?'

'Writing.' She puts the ribbon marker along the interior spine of the book.

'You haven't done much,' I observe.

'Actually, what I wanted to say only took a sentence. I

was trying to pad it out a bit. Being a writer, I can only condone the use of as many words as possible.' She closes her notebook. I recognise it because I gave it to her for her twenty-eighth birthday. It has a lepidoptera sewn on to the front cover, on the top left-hand side.

I say, 'I w-want to ask you something.'

'Fire away.'

I clear my throat. Suddenly, I feel exceedingly nervous. 'D-d-did you m-m-meet the one great love of your life yesterday?'

Instead of saying 'No', as I had hoped, she says, 'What?'

'Yesterday. The tenth of June 2009. At the airport.' Lara shakes her head. 'You told me once, when we were in college – you went to see a fortune-teller who—'

'Baby cheeses! That freakoid!'

'Yes, I concur. However, he predicted you would meet the one great love of your life yesterday.'

The One Great Love of My Life

It takes a while to recall what Conn is on about. After all, it was, at least fifteen years ago, maybe more. Julie's aunt's neighbour's hairdresser was also a mystical shaman who did some fortune-telling on the side. He had dreadlocks and a shiny cape with frayed yellow half-moons stapled on to it.

Conn looks so anxious, it is all I can do not to take his beloved face in my hands, smooth the frown lines with my fingers, touch the lock of hair falling forward in an inverted question mark, and snog the face off him.

'I can't believe you remember that,' I say. Then, thinking about it, 'Actually, I can.'

'I w-was at the appointed place at the appointed time,' says Conn. 'Where were you?'

'I thought – you said it was all rubbish!'

'Yes, of course. But you believed him.'

I manage to stop giggling long enough to say, 'I completely forgot about that, sorry. I never got to the airport. Did you bump into him – the one great love of my life? I expect he's swarthy and permanently perspires. Probably wears an eye patch, and loafers with no socks.'

Conn frowns again. 'There were a number of persons

matching that description at Shannon Airport. So maybe. But I don't think that's the one great love of your life.'

'I see,' I say. 'So who is?'

'Me.'

L ara sounds short of breath when she says, 'Listen,
there's something I want to ask you.' She rapidly
clicks the top of her pen with her thumb. 'So um . . . hey!
Does the word "OwnWorstEnemy" mean anything to you?'

'Of course. It's your online alias.'

'Wait, wait, wait, reverse back up the hill there. You
know?'

'Yes.'

'But *how*? I was very careful . . .'

'The first time I met you on ironman.com, we were
chatting and you typed, "baby cheeses, I never knew
Vaseline could be so handy". I have never met anyone
who says and/or writes "baby cheeses" apart from you.
Admittedly, I haven't met everyone in the world, but most
of the global population don't speak English, i.e., they
wouldn't say "baby cheeses".'

'Right.'

'What I've never been able to ascertain is why you
joined a discussion board about triathletes. Your definition
of exercise is changing the channel on television—'

'I was researching an article on extreme sports. For
the *Weekly Farmer*.'

Nodding, I say, 'Oh, I see. That makes sense.'

Lost in Transit

Well, I'm glad *he* thinks so. 'Why didn't you tell me you knew?' I ask.

'I just did,' he says. Conn's concept of time has always been fairly fluid; he seems to consider it as something he can apply with discretion to bend and shape to suit his will.

'Why not before?'

'Well, in Dubai, you told me to get out of your life. Then you were unconscious, so I thought you probably hadn't time to change your mind. You never formally amended your position on my presence in your life. Anyway, why didn't you tell me who you were?'

'Well, when you didn't respond to my letter . . .'

'Oh yes, thanks for that.'

So he got my letter. I swallow the lump of disappointment, but it lodges halfway down my throat. 'This is a delayed response, even for you.'

'Not really. Mark only gave it to me yesterday.'

'Yesterday? The letter I wrote eight years ago?' Lara raises her eyebrows when I nod. 'He's worse than the fecking post office.'

I extend my arm, open my hand with the streaky lump of pre-soaked paper on it. She giggles, says, 'What the fuck is *that*?'

'Your letter. Mark washed it. Unfortunately, it is illegible. What did it say?'

Lara shrugs. 'Not much. General stuff. You know: having a great time, lovely weather, wish you were here. Thanks for saving my life.'

'I didn't—'

'Depends on how you look at it,' says Lara.

All That Matters

I swallow. 'Don't you want to know what happened with Mark?' I say.

'No,' says Conn. 'It has no relevance.'

'But, Conn—'

'It doesn't matter. All that matters is that you're here, and I'm here.'

'Speaking of which, what are you doing here?'

'I came to find you,' says Conn.

'Why?'

'I can be who you want me to be,' he says. 'You once asked whether I would wonder "what if" in relation to us. I thought – well, that doesn't matter. But you were right. I never stopped wondering "what if" and I always preferred the hypothetical to my reality. Do you remember that night in Abu Dhabi, when I asked you what you wanted? It took me a while to work out what you were saying.'

'It took you eight years?' I ask, winding my hair round my fingers.

'No. Only a few months. Lara, I don't know if you are the most important thing in my life. That's impossible to quantify. But I've loved you since I first met you. I think about you all the time. I want to make you happy. Because that makes me happy.'

For a while, we are quiet.

'Why?' I ask again.

It is my policy to not speak until I have fully formed a thought. In this instance, the thought is fully developed and cohesive in my head, but I'm unsure how to verbalise it.

Also, I am distracted by Lara winding her hair round her index finger. She has done this as long as I have known her, when we were in school. Maybe I will remember this precise moment when I see her doing the same thing in twenty years.

'Because . . .' I frown. 'Well, you're lovely.' I think that's a positive start. 'You're kind.' Maybe I should give some examples. 'You rescue kittens and spiders stranded in the sink. You're brave and funny. You cross the "t" before you even write the letter. I like that. And – and people meet you and don't realise how amazing you are. *You* don't realise how amazing you are. But I do. I know this about you – although I know lots of things – and me knowing this about you is important, but it's not the main point, which is: the only time I ever feel normal – you know, like I'm not some alien sub-species – is when I'm with you. Things don't really make sense when you're not there. Not the facts, the proven theories; those make sense. I mean, I understand them. But it's as if, without you, something is missing. All the time. And I might spend the rest of my life looking, but I won't – I don't think I will ever find someone like you. I mean, obviously every person is unique, so I know I would never find someone *exactly* like you. But I want to be with you because you *are* exactly like you. That's why I love you, i.e., because you are you.'

Full Measures

On the surface of it, that might not seem like the most romantic thing ever uttered by another human being, but then this is Conn. I know he doesn't deal with half measures. His speech was peppered with non-specifics and emotion-related material that was completely alien to him; it was obviously a major concession.

Conn says, uncertainly, 'Does that answer your question?'

'Yes,' I say. I pick up my notebook. 'I was actually writing you another letter when you arrived.'

'Really?'

'Yes. Would you like to read it?'

He takes the notebook and his long fingers trace the ribbon to the page I was working on.

' "Dear Conn",' he reads, ' "will you spend the rest of your life with me?" '

I am quite pleased.

Amendment: this description is inadequate to describe how I feel. I think I am 'ecstatic'.

I say, 'Yes, please.'

Lara smiles. Her eyes are abnormally shiny. She says, 'Really?'

'Do you want it in writing?'

'No, that's OK.'

Something lands on my nose, Lara brushes it away with the backs of her fingers.

I say, 'What was—'

She says, 'A ladybird.'

Then she kisses me.